The Brides of Maracoor

The Brides
of Maracoor

A Novel

Gregory Maguire

HARPER LARGE PRINT
An Imprint of HarperCollinsPublishers

HarperCollins books may be purchased for educational, business, or sales promotional use. For information, please e-mail the Special Markets Department at SPsales@harpercollins.com.

FIRST HARPER LARGE PRINT EDITION

Illustrations by Scott McKowen

ISBN: 978-0-06-311773-0

Library of Congress Cataloging-in-Publication Data is available upon request.

21 22 23 24 25   LSC   10 9 8 7 6 5 4 3 2 1

For Katherine Kleitz and Iris Lee Marcus

. . . This rough magic
I here abjure. . . .

. . . I'll break my staff,
Bury it certain fathoms in the earth,
And deeper than did ever plummet sound
I'll drown my book.

—SHAKESPEARE, *THE TEMPEST*

An ending is no more than a point in sequence, a snip of the cutting shears. Benedick kissed Beatrice at last; but ten years later? And Elsinore, the following spring?

—JOHN FOWLES, *THE MAGUS*

Rain, Rain, go away.
Come again another day.

—TRAD.

Contents

PART·ONE

The Brides of Maracoor

1

Sing me, O Muse, the unheroic morning. When the bruised world begins to fracture for them all. Sing me the cloudless dawn that follows a downright shroud of a night.

A long night, one that had lasted for days.

Rain had run along the edge of it, playing for time.

Wind had sounded, then silence sounded—in that uncanny, hollow way that silence can sound. Then wind picked up again.

A world waiting to be made, or remade. As it does every night.

Waves slapped the harbor sand with soft, wet hands.

At sea level, strokes of lightning silently pricked the horizon.

The seagrass bent double from wind and wet. Bent double and did not break.

Above the clouds—but who could see above the clouds?

Build the world, O Muse, one apprehension at a time. It's all we can take.

With ritual dating from time out of mind, the brides on Maracoor Spot welcomed the first day after the storm. One by one they took up the whips of serrated seagrass from the basket in the portico. They wound the ends of the grass around their hands, using cloth mittens for protection. Each bride in her private nimbus of focus, they set to work etching their skin, laterally and crosswise. They flayed until the first drops of blood beaded up. Raw skin was better because it bled faster—the calluses from last week's mutilations took longer to dig through.

Then the brides bound their bruises with muslin already dyed maroon. It cut down on the frequency of bridal laundering if the linen was a deadblood color to begin with.

2

Then the brides—the seven of them—picked their way down the path along lengths of salt-scrubbed basalt. The ledge dropped in levels, finishing at a natural amphitheater shaped to the sandy harbor.

The world today, as they found it, as they preserved it:

A few thornbushes torn up and heaved on their sides, their leaves already going from green to corpse brown.

A smell of rot from fish that had been flung ashore in tidal surge and died three feet from safety.

The brides sat in a row on the lowest step. After chanting an introit, they began their work of twisting kelp with cord into lengths of loose netting. One by one each bride took a turn to wade into the calmed water up to her ankles, where the salt stung her daily wounds and cleansed them.

The oldest among them needed help getting up from a sitting position. She'd been a bride for seven decades or maybe eight, she'd lost count. She was chronically rheumy, and she panted like a fresh mackerel slapped on the gutting stone. Her stout thumbs were defter than those of her sister brides. She could finish her segment of the nets in half the time it took the youngest bride, who hadn't started yet this morning because her eyes were still glossed with tears.

Acaciana—Cossy, more familiarly—was the youngest bride. She wouldn't be menstrual for another year or two. Or three. So she cried at the sting of salt, so what?—she still had time to learn how to suffer. Some of the others thought her feeble, but perhaps they'd just forgotten how to be young.

Helia, Cossy, and the five others. Helia and Cossy, the oldest and youngest, wore white shifts that tended to show the dust. Only the oldest and youngest went bareheaded at tide weaving. Their hair, though pinned up close to the scalp, moistened in the insolent sun that came sauntering along without apology for its absence.

Beneath their sea-blue veils, the other brides kept their eyes on their work. Mirka. Tirr and Bray. Kliompte, Scyrilla. Their conversation wasn't as guarded as their faces. Mirka, the second oldest, muttered, "I don't think Helia is going to last another winter."

"Netting for drama already?" murmured Tirr, the bride to her right. "And it's just come summer."

The others grunted.

"No, I mean it," continued Mirka. "Look at the poor damaged old ox. She's forgotten how to stand by herself. Those waves are almost too much for her."

"Well, these storms," piped up Cossy, trying to air a voice unthrottled by tears. "A whole week of it! Did that ever happen before?"

The more seasoned brides didn't answer the novice. The oldest woman did seem unsteady as she walked in. She'd looped her garment in her forearms to keep the hems dry. Her mottled shanks trembled while the sea pulsed against her calves.

"What happens if Helia dies?" asked Cossy.

The youngest one always asked this question, always had to.

The second oldest, who was proud of the pale mustache that proved her status as deputy-in-readiness, snorted. "You remember the coracle that comes round the headland now and then. If it beaches and fewer than seven brides are here to greet the overseer, he goes back to procure a replacement bride."

"Goes back where?" asked Cossy. "Mirka? Where?"

This question went unanswered. Since each new bride always appeared in swaddles, arriving before her own memory could set in, the notion of anyone's specific origins was largely hypothetical.

Though they all knew where baby animals came from.

Cossy was at the obstinate age. "Goes back where? Someone must know. Does Helia know? I will ask her."

"Don't bother Helia," said the deputy-in-readiness. "Look at her. At that venerable age! She's about to move on ahead of us, she can't think backward."

"You're not the boss of me, not yet," Cossy replied. "And don't think you are, Mirka."

Helia had finished soaking her wounds. Using her staff for balance, she picked her way back to her place. Once she'd taken up her portion of netting, she muttered, "I'm not as deaf as you think, Mirka. Don't be getting airs. You're not going to be senior bride anytime soon. Cossy, I don't know much about the mainland but I know it exists, and it is where we come from. But listen: you can ask me anything you want. What little I know I share. That's my last job before I die. All in good time, so Mirka, don't go pushing me off a cliff."

But that night at the temple Helia suffered some contortion, and the next morning, while she took breakfast, she didn't speak at all. Cossy might ask all the questions she wanted, but to no avail. Helia was beyond answering.

3

But who could see above the clouds? Or from them? And descending through them, spy Maracoor Spot? Seeing, what, what—if you were to approach the place from above—say, as a traveler in a hot-air balloon, or a harpie out of the old stories? Looking upon this dollop of land in the midst of the great cold sea?

A spine, foremost. A spine to the island, heaving its rim-rock crenellations out of green wilderness. You might say: like a pivoting lizard with finned vertebrae on display.

On the east side, marine cliffs. Shellacked a glaring white, guano from cliff-dwelling rocs and gulls. At the base of this unapproachable break-front, rollers ate away at the ankles of the island, scooping them out. In a million years the ocean would snap the spine of the island at last, then pass over it to munch upon some farther shore.

Toward the west, the slopes were more relaxed. They tumbled upon one another like fresh, unfolded laundry. The climate here balmier, the winds less belligerent. Pine forests gave way to more relaxed orchard. And the colors here proved more various— olive leaves cupping tiny blossoms of pale yellow; fringe-headed grasses turning mint or amethyst over the hours; stony earth or sable, torn up by the single plow. Bees threaded the apple groves. A few fields of hay and grain, vegetable gardens, two donkeys in a paddock, goats on the loose, a chicken coop. Freshwater springs made Maracoor Spot habitable to humans, fowl, and wild boars, and a small inbred population of skittish, piebald gazelles.

The harbor was deep enough to drown a giant out of prehistory, as far as anyone knew, but the mouth of it had been silted up for aeons. Ships couldn't cross except once every few years, at a storm tide. This was access so unpredictable that no traders bothered. There was little to plunder, in any case, and nobody to trade with. Brides didn't count.

Was Maracoor Spot beautiful? The brides who lived there couldn't say. It was the only home they'd ever known. No one had ever left except in death. Standards of beauty—like those of truth, or justice—are arrived at by the practice of making comparisons.

Another word for poverty of choice is innocence.

By holy writ Maracoor Spot supported seven human citizens, no more, and no less, and made do with only one real building. The temple, or grange, was a boxy arrangement of pockmarked, smeary marble. It stood on a platform of large rectangular blocks and was flanked on three sides by ranks of grey-white stone columns, some of which had lost conviction and lain down. Inside, a single large chamber was divided by rattan screens. That was it, unless you counted the windowless, sacred space at the back of the building, which just about ran into the hillside.

At this stage in its unimaginable history, the columns supported triangular pediments front and rear. In their recesses lurked statues of writhing, blurred, and genderless humans. Their motivations remained vague and their lessons unknowable, the specifics thumbed away by wind and time. Above the sculptural drama, a roof made of logs and thatch. This fell or blew off every few years. The brides knew something about construction, but perhaps not enough. Their repairs were always temporary. But so were their lives.

Any scrutinizing eye aloft in the trade winds, looking down upon that whole world, would see the spine of Maracoor Spot hugging the island's single harbor, its entrance channel so narrow that from certain viewpoints the sides could seem to be touching.

And opposite the harbor mouth, that tablet of temple roof: the only stamp of rationality in the organic blot and curl of nature.

If you were climbing the highlands on a certain day, you might see a coracle coming around the headland. That day couldn't be predicted. It happened when it happened. Like the occasional ship with pale sails that, appearing and disappearing, proved the horizon had a future as well as a past. But little else.

4

Cossy claimed perhaps ten summers under her cincture. The adolescent bride nearest her in age had begun her menses a year ago. Oh, but Cossy's former friend had grown aloof! Scyrilla the Scourge. Pimply and moody. Scyrilla didn't like to talk about the secret wound. Old Helia had been brusque about the matter when Cossy asked. Herself was out the other side and a good thing too, Helia said. The other brides were opaque on the matter, or inept. Though Cossy tried not to show it, the mystery of that red flood terrified her.

The chores of the day were winding down. Cossy sat at the foot of Helia's cot, rubbing olive oil into the senior bride's wounds. Helia was sitting up so she could glance out the doorway. Not that there was much to look at—a scoop of sea, emerald green at this hour, and a peerless, watered-down sky without clouds. So welcome after those storms.

The aged woman cleared her throat. While words had fled today, her grunts and sighs, oh my. Opinions plenty. Cossy guessed they were riddled with bitterness and gratitude alike. And perhaps compassion—Helia didn't shut out Cossy as the other brides so often did.

In sailed Mirka, folding back her blue veil. Though her hair was clasped at the nape of her neck with string, the long grey coils below had come free, an animal pulling from a snare.

"You're dawdling here, Cossy." A statement, not a question.

"I just finished with Helia's salve."

"It's not suppertime yet. You're still wanted in the garden. Turnips ready to pull. The moles will get them if we let them sit another night. And bring a bucket of water to sprinkle on the redweed. It's looking peaky."

Cossy sighed and squeezed Helia's hand. The strong old thumbs pressed down in Cossy's palm.

"We're sorry to see you brought low, Helia," said Mirka with icy formality. She was getting the clean pails used for milking the goats. "You've been a great inspiration to all of us. I want you to know this if your time among us is coming to a close."

Behind Mirka's back, Helia made a rude gesture at her. Cossy, who now was truly dawdling, tried to swallow a giggle. Mirka ignored it.

"Where will we bury Helia?" asked Cossy. "With the goat bones?"

Helia clapped her hands once and raised them to the ceiling.

"All in good time, Cossy, don't be rude," said Mirka. "Run along now. I have some things to say to Helia before I get back to the goats."

"But she can't answer you."

"No concern of yours. Some statements require no reply. Go away."

So Cossy left for the turnips, but she dawdled along the outside wall, listening. A time-honored custom among the younger brides. A year ago it would have been Cossy and Scyrilla together. Part of their schooling, you might say.

Mirka was purring in a low voice, but full of urgency. "You need to let me know where the key is hidden. There's little time left, Helia. You could kick off this evening or tomorrow morning. It's forbidden to take your knowledge to the grave. Would you threaten all our lives? If the key isn't in the temple, point out which way it is, and I'll help you walk there. I'll bring a shovel if it's buried somewhere. This is your final obligation,

Helia. You are obliged to yield your authority. You may not deny me this."

No doubt Helia had flashed another obscene gesture, for Mirka remarked, "How dare you be so rude to me. I could suppress your dinner portion for that."

Though she couldn't have said why, Cossy was glad that Helia was still too obstinate to obey Mirka's commands. The youngest bride tiptoed away, skittered off the porch, and flew like a gull's shadow toward the garden.

5

Along the path she stopped to collect the bucket of rainwater. It was nearly full. She peered at it. A mouse was paddling away, three inches from the rim, unable to get purchase. She left the bucket there— the redweed could manage. She wanted to see what a drowned mouse would look like. Maybe it would be dead by the time she came back from the garden. She could tip it out and see if it came back to life, the way fish sometimes did if you threw them back.

When she was nearly done with the turnips, she glanced up to gauge the sun's position on the horizon. She saw a movement not unlike the flailing mouse, but larger, out there crossing the harbor mouth. It skirted on the safe side of the buoy, that bobbing knob of cork warning against the most treacherous of the submerged rocks.

A dolphin? But dolphins rarely came into the harbor, as if they were afraid they might beach themselves in the shallows.

On second glance, Cossy knew it was no dolphin. Nor was it the coracle of the overseer, though the other brides were saying, since the squash vines were in flower, that the time of his annual visit was nearing. Anyway, he always arrived in the morning.

Cossy didn't speak, didn't cry out. Even though two of the brides were working nearby beneath the stunted apple and sparrowleaf trees. In the bellies of their blue veils they were gathering wormy fruit for the donkeys.

The women were turned uphill, away from the harbor. "I've dug the last turnip," Cossy called. "I'm off to the keeping-stall." Her companions didn't swivel to verify. Cossy had no history of lying. (That they knew of.)

The girl scrabbled down the rocky path with such haste that a few turnips bounced from her bucket. Most of the brides were working at outdoor chores. And no doubt Mirka was ensconced in the goat shed by now. The brides usually spent early morning at their nets and midday at the gardens, while reserving late afternoon for animal husbandry. By then the wind had begun again to sweep in from the sea, keeping the flies down and pushing the odor of animals upland.

Helia would be alone at the temple.

Cossy tore through the doorway. She'd thought she might hiss the news at Helia, making her raise herself and glance out the doorway, but the oldest bride lay still, her white shawl pulled up to her chin. Her eyes were closed. She had the look of a squid that has exhausted itself in the nets. Cossy let her be.

Rolling the turnips out upon the unpainted tabletop, the youngest bride rushed back outside. Through the stripes of the pillars, she saw that the sun had begun its evening spectacle of shine upon the waters. The item she'd first thought a dolphin was more frantic than before. Forget the drowning mouse. Something about the panic in the harbor made Cossy hurtle herself toward a rescue.

A moment for her alone. A sign of fate, one way or the other. Any other day of the year, Helia would have been eagle-eyed on the stone porch, pithing apricots or sifting lentils.

Cossy the only witness vouchsafed for this instant of flex and fracture.

So down she flew, like a white bird among sawgrass. At the edge of the harbor she shielded her eyes to peer at the progress of the beleaguered creature.

So much water dashed about the entity in trouble that Cossy couldn't identify it at first. Then she saw. A large bird—roughly the size of a roc from the island's cliffs. But rocs didn't come into the harbor. And they were believed rarely to land on the sea. They dove for fish but lifted back up again at once.

Cossy whispered a basic magick, perhaps the most basic. Whether it was child's play or powerful, she was too young to guess.

Spill a spell
To make things well.

Something was trapping the creature's second wing, looping about it. The bird, rather like a goose, turned a desperate and intelligent eye toward the shore. It saw Cossy, and quawked as if giving instructions. The closer it came, the more it headed toward her, as if for help.

Cossy paid no mind to the white hems of her chiton or to her cross-hatched heels and soles. She plunged into the harbor up to her waist. She met the goose. She helped release the noose that was constricting the second wing. It was the arm of a human being locked around the bird. The salt water buoyed up the person's body enough for Cossy to drag it up on the sand. The goose sank its chinless chin in the soil, panting.

6

C ossy wasn't sure which she hoped more: that the
sodden human castaway was a male, or wasn't.
She backed off, waiting to find out. The figure was
more grown up than Cossy—perhaps closer to the age
of Scyrilla, the second youngest bride of Maracoor. The
one who had vied with Cossy for being most petted.
Scyrilla now a scheming, adolescent viper.

But female, yes, that much was now certain. And
alive. The goose, having rallied, was jostling upon the
girl's belly. Seawater gurgled from the human lungs
with a back-gulping sound, the kind that water makes
when poured too quickly from a narrow-necked flask.

The goose quawked again at Cossy, and again. Cossy
had only seen geese a few times, as they weren't native
to Maracoor. She didn't know their ways. Whenever

they preened about, looking belligerent, she'd always kept her distance. This one, more dark brown than grey, fairly seethed with outrage. Cossy felt upbraided. She decided that, as long as the drowned lump wasn't a man, there was no benefit in keeping the secret to herself any longer.

She hurried up the track, pivoting on the path once or twice to make sure she hadn't imagined the whole affair. The goose and the castaway weren't going anywhere. They'd fallen upon their own shadows, amidst spreading pools of seawater.

"Mirka," cried Cossy, then "Helia!"

Mirka the officious emerged from the goat-hold. She made an angry gesture that meant, *Silence befits you first, and everything follows from that,* but she set the milk pails down so she could hurry faster. When she drew near, she said, "Cossy, you must govern your spirit with greater restraint, or it shall have to be governed for you."

"It's important." Cossy wheezed and held her side against a stitch of pain there. "A person has arrived. On the sands."

Mirka grabbed Cossy's hand. They ran together to the nearest rise, where the harbor opened before them like a book.

When she could speak, Mirka said to Cossy, "Ring the bell, child; ring the bell at once."

"Do we need to tell everyone?"

"We don't know what danger this is to us. Do as I say."

Cossy regretted not having found a way to hide the castaway, keep her for herself, but now there was nothing left for her to do but obey Mirka's orders.

The other brides, all but old Helia, gathered in a knot and linked arms. Mirka muttered some sort of a prayer under her breath that Cossy couldn't make out and didn't try. Then, five women in blue veils and a girl in a white veil, they made their way with improvised ceremony to where the victims of sea still lay, nearly insensate, upon the sands. The sun was a gold brooch in pale orange netting. The air smelled faintly of herring. Herring, and distance.

"The goose has given up on the human. She's probably dead," said Cossy.

"Cossy, shut up," said Mirka.

7

The intruder's eyes were closed. The brides didn't want to hurt her. They didn't want to touch her.

But when Mirka gave the word, she and Bray, who was stout and strong, took the foreign girl by the shoulders and sat her up. Water drained out of her nostrils. Bray cradled the crown of her skull as one would an infant's, to protect the neck from snapping. The others removed their veils and lifted the person upon them. They hauled her up the slope to the temple. Cossy carried the waterlogged broom that had been dislodged, with some effort, from the castaway's clenched armpit.

The goose followed at a distance, settling on the portico. With that capacity for skewing that birds' eyes have, it trained its gaze at several points of the horizon at once. Before long, however, it tucked its head under the wing that had done all the work hauling the traveler to shore. It became a statue: *Sleeping Goose.*

Though Mirka had made a sign that they were to be quiet, Helia must have heard them. From her corner of the dormitory the senior bride banged her oakthorn staff against the wall.

"You go quiet the old maenad," said Mirka to Cossy. "She is soft on you."

"What'll I say?"

"Say nothing."

That was little help.

Cossy didn't want to leave. What if the visitor died while Cossy was gone? What a thrilling moment to have to miss. But with Helia bedridden and mute, Mirka was thumping around as senior bride, even if she wasn't yet sporting the white veil. So Cossy had little choice but to obey.

Helia rolled her fist forward in the air, a gesture that meant *Haul me up to a sitting position.* Cossy didn't think she was strong enough to do it by herself, but Helia leaned on her staff and pushed, too.

Then the old sack of bones was sitting up, sniffing the air like a cave dog. She grunted in the form of a question. Cossy replied as nonchalantly as she could manage: "Everyone's come in early today."

Helia wiggled one hand forward laterally, clearly meaning *Coracle spotted on its approach?*

Cossy raised her eyebrows. She didn't want to lie to Helia or disobey Mirka. "Do you want some water?"

Helia bit her lip, thinking. Then she nodded.

Cossy hurried to the water basin and dipped a clay cup. When she got back to the side of Helia's bed, she said, "Here."

Helia took it, smiled at Cossy a little, and dashed the water to the floor. Then she placed the cup upside down on the end of the staff and hurled the clay item over the screen. It shattered against the wall above the other brides.

At once, Mirka was at the screen-fold, a scold. Fists furled, old Helia pumped both her arms up and down. The message was clear. Wordy or wordless, Helia was still in charge. Tirr and Bray were called to her side. They hoisted the senior bride from the bed, and helped her get to the common room.

There the old woman put her hand on her breast, suddenly a delicate gesture. Behind her, Bray snorted. Helia gave her a backhand slap without even looking. Nothing wrong with the old bride's hearing.

She moved forward. Peering, peering, like a newborn chick at the very new world.

8

The floor was wet around the table, where seawater was still sluicing. The brides had been drying the visitor with towels of raw linen. Her breastbone rose and dropped, proving stubborn life; otherwise she was as much like a laid-out corpse as Cossy could imagine. How did the dead hold so still? How did they use the privy? It was such a mystery.

Under Mirka's instructions, the brides of Maracoor surrendered to the guest a small portion of their precious pale cordial, made from upslope flowers that bloomed only two weeks a year. Not all the brides were happy about this largesse. Each drop of liqueur was reward hard to come by.

But the medicine seemed to work. The damp thing

began to shiver. Old Helia made an upturned wave. *Strip her wet clothes off.*

No one could argue with Helia because she couldn't argue back. So Mirka knelt to work at a metal clasp that fixed to a strap around the woman's waist. A second strap slanted across a shoulder. The straps attached to a sort of saddlebag. With some effort, Mirka removed the bag and handed it to Cossy to put aside. There was nothing within—Cossy peeked—but a sodden onion with a bite taken out of it and an elegant whorled sea-shell, a nautilus. Water ran out of its alabaster sleeve.

Buttons were undone. Bodice ties gave way. If the castaway had had boots or shoes, they'd been lost in the sea. The plum-black skirt came off. The chemise and the knee-length pantaloons were in such sad repair there wasn't much point in trying to keep them intact. Helia scissored her fingers, and Cossy ran to fetch the utensil from the workbench.

Supported by her sister brides, Helia leaned over the table and snipped the strings at the clavicle and at the waist. They peeled the woman as they might a passion fruit.

Helia snapped her fingers. Kliompte lunged forward with a towel. Helia wiped the stranger from neck to ankles. When instructed, Bray rolled the naked tide-wrack over onto her stomach. Helia dried the woman from nape of neck down to shins and the raw, untrammeled skin of her bare feet. Is *this* like preparing a body for burial, wondered Cossy. It's not like plucking a hen to roast, or descaling a fish; there's nothing to pluck or scrape.

The brides avoided nudity among themselves, so Cossy's interest was as much clinical as morbid.

The sun now trained its evening spotlight into the temple. The sun only ever gilded the interior for a few moments before sinking into the sea, for the deep portico kept the rooms in shadow most of the day. But as if it had waited all day to see the castaway for itself, the lowered sun speared suddenly through parting clouds.

The water sluicing off the young woman onto the stone floor wasn't the green water of the sea, as Cossy had thought. That runoff was clear as salty tears. Now dried by the administrations of the brides of Maracoor, the traumatized naked form was all over green—except the untempered soles of her feet. Those proved a vulnerable and intimate pink.

9

Though it was a warm evening, the brides wrapped the visitor in blankets of goats' wool. Then they set her on the floor so that if she began to roll or twitch, she wouldn't fall off a bedstead and hurt herself.

So low that none could hear her, Cossy muttered a baby magick.

A spell to keep
You safe in sleep.

Outside, the goose had awakened from its long rest at last. It slammed its wings against the slatted door until Bray, perhaps the most kindhearted among them, opened it. The goose ambled in regally, approaching the green creature and glancing, as if to make sure she was still breathing, and settled down next to her left shoulder.

"I'm not sure it should be in here," murmured Scyrilla to Cossy. "It could well be a gander, you know."

"So what?"

"Well, this is a house of brides, stupid. Males aren't to be allowed."

Cossy rolled her eyes with disdain. Everyone knew some winds were male and others female, and no one closed the shutters against either if the humidity was high enough.

The brides settled to their evening meal: a pottage made of garden carrots and tree carrots, some apple halves, and a grip of hard bread. Helia took up her old place at the table, displacing Mirka back to where she belonged. Mirka, however, ran the discussion. Pale globules of soup stuck in the shadow upon her upper lip, but she was too agitated to wipe them away.

"We have no protocol for this situation," said Mirka. "Practice, custom, memory? The common code hasn't prepared us for anything like this. We have to think for ourselves what to do."

"Make her better," said Bray. She so rarely spoke up at table that they all started. They used to call her Donkey, for her brute strength, till the time she hawed her disapproval, renaming herself Bray.

"Why must we do anything, Mirka?" asked Tirr. "If the common code doesn't speak about hospitality, we can settle the matter for ourselves."

"Don't be a fool, Tirr. Of course the common code speaks against hospitality," replied Mirka. "By dint of the matter never being raised, don't you see. Were we expected to entertain guests, there'd be protocols in place. We are brides precisely to eliminate the need to be social. This is a crisis. Someone must take it in hand."

"She wants a good night's sleep, and some pearlfruit tea at dawn," declared Kliompte, mistress of domestic order. "Voices down, shall we? And let her sleep."

Keeping voices down sounded like secrecy. Cossy thought this part was fun. No one lives on an island with six other females without learning how to whisper.

"This is a sacred community of seven," Mirka stated, as if that fact was not as plain to them all as the tides that rose and fell. "We are not to be eight."

Helia cleared her throat and drew her finger across her neck. Whether she meant *Kill the guest* or *Don't worry, I'm dying soon enough* or *Shut up before I shut you up* was unclear. But Helia could be forceful even without her words.

"Stupid rule. What's the harm in our being eight

brides?" asked Scyrilla. "Who would even know?" Pouting. Cossy thought: Scyrilla doesn't care whether we're seven or eight, she just likes arguing with anyone in charge. Once again Cossy wished she could avoid turning that age herself, it was so ungainly. The anger, and the cramps. But a problem for another day.

"We don't expect you and Cossy to understand the significance of our traditions," began Mirka. Don't lump me in with Screechy Scyrilla, thought Cossy, but under her breath. I'm still human for another year or so.

Mirka tore her bread into pieces but didn't eat it. "The brides of Maracoor are seven. That's settled science. Annually the overseer counts us, and if one of us has died since last year, she's replaced by the next baby bride. That's how it works. Now listen. It's almost the time of the overseer's visit. What if he arrives in his coracle and we march out to be counted and he finds that we are one extra?"

"Who cares, not me," said Scryilla tauntingly. Enjoying the chance to be stroppy. "Anyway, Greenie can just stay in the temple. The overseer never comes into the temple. At least that's what you've told me *so far.*"

Mirka said, "And just how do we stop Greenie, as you call her, from standing up and walking out the door?"

"Well, we could just kill her. Then the problem

would be solved, wouldn't it." Scyrilla rolled her eyes and mock-yawned: *All this is too tedious.*

The goose jerked as if it could understand human speech. Its head went back on its supple neck like a serpent's head, considering.

"No killing nobody," growled Bray. Helia thumped the table in agreement, and the other brides dropped their eyes to their soup bowls.

"Then just let her be," said Scyrilla. "Don't jump all over me. I'm just saying who cares whether there are seven or eight of us?"

"Seven is the sacred number," insisted Mirka. "Furthermore, she's green, she'll stand out."

"So if the overseer comes she can just run into the orchard and she'll be invisible. Lost in the trees." Scyrilla began to laugh at her own high wit.

The goose quawked again, as if it couldn't bear keeping its opinions to itself. "Might we turn that creature out of the house?" requested spidery Kliompte. Just like her: always refolding linens to sit squarer, always sweeping the floor for invisible dust. Always improving the quarters. "The very noise of it, it fades the light."

But Helia stayed the conversation with a chop of her hand. The goose quawked again. With a lunging movement, Helia swept Mirka's uneaten clumps of bread onto the floor. This quietened the goose as it waddled to chase its skittering dinner. Kliompte sighed, probably thinking of goose droppings to wash down in the morning.

Cossy stifled a giggle. Somehow, Helia was still in charge. But Mirka looked as if she'd sat on a cushion stuffed with thorns and poison oak.

10

After the table was cleared, Kliompte flapped out the napkins and swept the floor. Rest time eddied in, a different sort of tide. When oil from beached narwhals grew scarce, the brides simply talked in the dark until the third or fourth yawn, and went to bed.

Tonight they were rich. Kliompte spilled a half-spoon of oil into the declivity of the flat stone set in the middle of the room. In it she stood a wax-stiffened coil of wick. Cossy was allowed to light the taper from an ember they kept warm in a thurible.

Some of the brides spun cord out of goat's wool while Cossy and Scyrilla played their games of stones and sticks on the floor. Helia prayed, fingering hollow seedpods strung on a looped cord. Usually the brides stayed mute as she mumbled her devotions. But tonight they gossiped quietly over the clicking of her beads.

"What are we going to do with the guest when it's time to sleep?" asked Tirr.

"'The guest?' Really? Well, perhaps it's premature to call her 'the threat,'" said Mirka. "We'll wait and see."

"Enemy or friend, we need someone to keep vigil, no?" replied Tirr. "In case she decides to thank us for our hospitality by slicing our throats in our sleep?"

"Who cares." Scyrilla pointed. "Look, Cossy, you missed a point there. That's not touching. Too late."

"You kicked it."

"Did not. I wouldn't bother to cheat."

"Maybe someone should stay awake and keep guard," said Mirka. "Are you volunteering, Tirr?"

"Me? I'd enjoy having my throat slit in my sleep. It would be a mercy."

"Well, the younger ones can't stay awake. Nor should they be asked to. Scyrilla and Cossy, look at them, they're nodding as we speak."

Tirr said, "Since you're posing as deputy elder, Mirka, I think you might do it."

"Frankly, I doubt any of us will sleep a *wink*," said Kliompte, pulling her shawl close over her narrow shoulder bones.

"Are you kidding? Look, Bray's asleep sitting up."

It was true. Bray was sloping in her wooden chair with her ear almost on Tirr's shoulder.

Helia paused at her beads. She grabbed for her staff and thumped it twice on the floor. The goose took its head out from under its wing and looked, too. Helia replaced the staff and thumbed to herself. She'd stay up.

"Well, that's settled," said Mirka, obscurely affirmed. "Are you satisfied, Tirr?"

"And we'll all hear Helia when she screams for help without a voice," said Tirr, but the oil was already guttering. Tirr was the first to stand, starting the sequence of visits to the privy that they all made before turning in.

"But where will I sleep?" Cossy asked Mirka.

Mirka considered. Usually Cossy rested on a pallet in Helia's nook so when something was needed in the middle of the night, the child could fetch it. But if Helia was sitting up the night, Cossy was unanchored. And Cossy had never before slept in the dormitory corridor with the rest of the brides. "You heard her. Who wants to make room for the little ferret?" asked Mirka of the room. "Go on, she won't bite."

No one volunteered.

"You can squeeze in with Scyrilla if she lets you," decided Mirka.

The guest, the goose, and Helia remained in the main salon. It was too warm to need a log in the hearth.

Helia settled herself as upright as she could in the one chair with arms. The others repaired to the dormitory behind its screens, a row of three single beds and the platform Bray and Tirr had rigged up to share. They murmured good nights in the dark.

"If you fart in your sleep I'm going to kick you onto the floor," said Scyrilla.

"Likewise, thank you," said Cossy, inching onto Scyrilla's cot.

All night the sea made a lullaby, a petting sort of hush. Cossy didn't know if everyone else felt the way she did, that the scars in her feet pulsed more painfully at night. She lay there awkwardly, resenting that Scyrilla's body relaxed so quickly. When Scyrilla gassed away in Cossy's direction Cossy rolled over. She could guess by the softly rising hills of blanket, serried in silhouette down the chamber, that most of the brides were asleep.

11

In the middle of the night, perhaps having had enough of the warm damp of Scyrilla, Cossy woke up. This was the only time that her feet felt at peace. She padded to the edge of the dormitory screen. The temple shutters were drawn but their vertical slats remained opened. Thin stripes of moonlight pin-lined the floor, the table, and the heap of guest. Helia was slumped in the great chair, her hands capping the oak-thorn staff.

Cossy—but was she still Cossy in the middle of the night, a question she'd always been too timid to ask out loud—Cossy was afraid that Helia might have chosen this hour to die, and no one to witness it.

But oh, Cossy wanted to see it, if it had to happen. She loved Helia, but she sheltered in her young breast a hunger for things to break and fall into a startling new arrangement. Change, blessed, damned change: the only promise given to the young that is always honored.

The susurrus of Helia's breathing kept time with the tide in the harbor. The goose didn't hear Cossy's footfall on the pale pitted flooring.

The guest turned her head, though. It was the first movement she had made on her own. Her eyes opened. Whether she saw Cossy or not, the youngest bride couldn't say. Unveiled, uncertain, Cossy stood as still as she could.

This wasn't death, not half as good, just watching someone come to life.

Still, one other small victory over Scyrilla. Something Cossy had to herself that her nearest rival didn't.

12

Came the morning in its casual scrutinizing way, light poking over the hip of hill behind the temple.

The brides made their morning ablutions in silence.

At their own whim they broke bread at the broad table.

They sawed the soles of their feet with rough grass until the first bloody beads appeared. Cossy, Scyrilla, Tirr, and Kliompte still wept regularly at the process. Bray, Mirka, and Helia were more vicious with themselves, more efficient. Stone-faced.

They were all done except Cossy, who found it hard to manage on her own. Sometimes she had to ask someone to finish for her, while she gripped a forearm for support. The brides didn't descend to their salty foot-bath and their morning of working the nets until they were united again in blood.

"You're taking your time today," observed Mirka. "No holidays, Cossy."

Cossy replied through her morning tears, "I don't know how to go faster."

"Keep go," huffed Bray. Having finished, she was doing exercises with a length of heavy charred timber. She said it took her mind off the pain. The practice had grown her forearms thick as the hams of wild boar.

"The question we've been avoiding," said Kliompte, "is whether we should be bleeding the guest's feet." Helia looked up sharply at this.

"They've never been cross-sawn before," said Scyrilla. "Look at that soft pink press of a foot. It turns the stomach."

"If she's capable of feeling pain, it might be just the thing to bring her round," said Kliompte. "It might be a blessing to her. Then we could ask her who she is and what she's doing here."

The goose had wandered off to hunt for breakfast. Time and the ocean waited.

"Oh, for the love of Maracoor, this is taking all morning," said Tirr. "Bray, help." Bray put down her heavyweight.

While Bray scored Cossy, Helia signaled to be lifted

to her feet. She put on her own wool sheathings and picked up a pair of sawgrass whiplets. Slowly she began to move across the floor to where the guest still lay, more or less comatose. But Mirka got there first. "We're not inducting this obscene foreigner," said Mirka. "Over my dead body, Helia. She's not one of us." She took off her blue veil and hung it like a curtain in front of the guest's naked feet.

Helia shrugged. Her authority was still valid, but she had neither tongue nor strength to reproach Mirka. She turned back, throwing the reeds in the basket for tomorrow. Bray, meanwhile, finished drawing blood from Cossy, and the brides readjusted their veils. With leather laces they strapped the brick-colored cloths to their feet. Kliompte wiped any drops of blood before they left the house. "We're just leaving her here?" asked Mirka. "All alone?"

"There's nothing for her to steal and there's no place for her to go," said Kliompte. "What else are we going to do?"

Helia's nod forward was mandatory. They left the green thing where she was.

Scyrilla poked Cossy, trying to provoke a race down the steps to see who could get her open sores into the salt water first and finish this worst part of the day. Cossy wasn't in a mood for games, though. She gave Helia a shoulder to lean on—as the shortest bride, Cossy was the best height to help—and they all made their way down to the amphitheater steps and the harbor. Wondering if today would be the day the coracle arrived, and wondering whatever they might say to the overseer if it was.

The goose had returned from its breakfast and it followed them down, as if it didn't trust them.

The malodorous hill winds spilled down from the rangy forests. The goats bleated on the heights. Seagulls made their redundant comments. The clouds turned over, thinned like pulled paste, massed into curds, turned again. The sky was an obstinate shade of forever. Little by little, Cossy's bled feet numbed in the salt water. And the brides sat down in a row, their feet in water, to net eternity into dailiness as it spun toward them over the endless sea.

The brides, the brides. As Cossy's tears finished drying, she glanced round, as if she were a green-skinned guest trying to figure out her hosts. What would the brides look like to someone who didn't know them? A novel exercise, pretending ignorance so as to see her world afresh.

They were sitting in order of precedence. Squat Helia, the hunched elder in her white veil at the far end. The others in blue. Mirka, shaped like a bottle, tall and narrow at the top and broad-hipped below. Tirr, so anthracite of skin that in some lights her lips looked white, next to Bray, the bull, scowling. Bray and Tirr had arrived the same year and behaved as twins or wives to each other. Kliompte, the princess of manners, as Tirr had named her—froth-haired, freckled, delicate, always starting with gasps of apprehension or horror or joy. Scyrilla, Cossy's one-time bosom buddy turned bane, an adolescent, much younger than Bray and Tirr. And novice Acaciana, called Cossy most of the time, in white, with her little butt perching on a stone hardly the width of a supper plate.

She had no way of knowing where the guest would fit in if she were to become an improbable, unregulated eighth bride. By age the guest was probably older than Scyrilla and Cossy, and maybe even Kliompte. But by order of arrival she was the newest novice.

When Helia or one of the older brides finally took it into her head to die, Cossy would get a baby of her own to raise, the way Scyrilla and the others had raised her. Cossy was ten; she was ready for her own baby. The green guest threw all these calculations out of whack. It gave Cossy a headache.

13

Halfway through the morning, Tirr tossed her length of net down to her feet. It swayed in the sudsy wavelets as if one of them. "We need to figure this out," she said. "Look at the sea. It's coming on time for the overseer."

They glanced up from their handiwork. Tirr knew what she was talking about. At a certain point every summer, the waves began to approach the mouth of the harbor in successive lengths of raveled froth. The dark blue showed between each white wave. The striped sea, blue and white, was called a ribbon tide. This was the favorable sea across which the overseer's coracle arrived annually. Tirr was right to be fretful.

"We have to figure out if we've broken code by

giving shelter to a guest," said Tirr. "What will the overseer say when he arrives? What will he do?"

"Maybe he can't count," said Scyrilla. "We'll line up, put the guest in an extra veil, and no one the wiser."

"Of course he can *count*," shouted Tirr. "He *comes* here to count, you moron." Tirr must have been stewing over this for a while; her voice was throttled.

Mirka glanced sideways at the old woman next to her. Helia just kept working her length of the net. It was a meditative act, this time of netting, this netting of time. It was why they were there, why they even lived. Helia wouldn't or couldn't be moved from her private calm. She didn't even look up. Prayer is its own reason.

"You're wrong to agitate us at our devotions," said Mirka in a voice smooth as thrice-pressed oil, "but, Tirr, you're not wrong to worry. This is the first waking moment we've had to ponder. Let's take the question into our hearts. Let us each bring her best thought to share at the table over the midday bite."

Tirr couldn't be stopped. "And if the overseer arrives while we're laying the table?"

"So it will be." If Tirr couldn't be calmed, Mirka couldn't be riled. Acting the queen bee already. She leaned down and grabbed where her length of net joined to Tirr's stretch, and lifted Tirr's portion back to her lap. "To your work. It will help, Tirr. Trust me. Work always helps."

Cossy didn't know if it would help. Tirr's gestures were raw and unthoughtful, more erratic than Helia's. The practice of the seven brides was to braid, knot, inch along; to sever yesterday's cords and retie them for today, in a balletic movement of hands. They repaired stripped or broken lengths and replaced rotten ones. Who knew how long the brides had been knotting nets? Or why there should be seven brides? Perhaps for no sounder reason than because that was how many the lowest stone step could comfortably seat.

Cossy kept glancing up at the ribbon tide. She wanted to be the first one to catch the coracle rounding the headland, should today prove to be the day. Instead, Cossy was the one to notice—again it was she, this singularity felt holy, this was nearly magic— and thus she was the one to be able to say, "Our guest is awake."

14

Cossy didn't know much about memory.

All existence measures itself in creeps and ticks, as far as she knew.

The tide came in and went out; that was regular. Storms came and went; vines grew full and fell back. Baby goats were born and older goats were eaten. Once in a while if a stupid boar managed to get itself trapped in one of the laughable cages that the brides maintained in the woods, they had boar ragout. You could notch the sequence of life by its menus if you had no other variables on hand.

The more notable movements of change in Cossy's ten years were social ones.

One year, for reasons beyond Cossy, Tirr had been so angry at Mirka's bullying the others that she had slept in the lean-to with the squashes, driven back to society only when the rats grew accustomed to her presence and began to run over her in the night.

Then, there was the time, not long ago, that Scyrilla had begun her bleeding. This a big change indeed. Cossy recalled it with minute detail. No one had made fun of Scyrilla; in fact, both Mirka and Tirr grew uncharacteristically tender. Or at least less caustic. Scyrilla had cried at night, and Tirr had warmed at the hearth a flat round stone, like an unleavened loaf, and wrapped it in a towel and brought it to press on her lower belly.

Cossy, remanded into the corner space with old Helia, hadn't watched. But she had lain awake, listening to the sobs. She dreaded her turn for that, whenever it might come.

Then there was the time that Kliompte had decided to try to hang rough curtains across the doorway, thinking they would move prettily in the breeze. She had spent weeks weaving the curtains with a goat's wool warp and a weft of yellowed grasses. As she was standing on the top rung of the ladder, however, the winds had wrapped the drapes around her legs, and Kliompte had fallen nearly twice her height. She'd spent half a year limping. Her failure to complain was deemed both a confession of her error and a sign of hubris. But in time she'd recovered and things had gone back to normal. The brides lived without drapes.

All else—the arrival of the overseer during the season of the ribbon tide, the planting, the harvesting, the moons, the menses—all else was the very definition of rhythm.

While Cossy loved Helia perhaps more than she did any of the other brides, even she was curious about what would happen when Helia died. Cossy would finally see a death. Then she would get a baby bride of her own to raise. She didn't want to say goodbye to Helia but her appetite for a dramatic occasion was immense. She had long ago understood that, eventually, time would have an irrevocable seam in it: life before Helia and life after Helia.

So for Cossy to turn and look at the green guest standing on the portico, one hand on the white column and the other touching the head of the goose, was to learn that there were other ways in which silken history could be torn by circumstance. Cossy's life was now utterly changed. Her calendar of memory had been hijacked by the castaway. Life before and life after the arrival of human spindrift.

The brides all looked, but their hands kept at their work.

"What are we to do?" asked Tirr.

Helia was wordless, watching, so Mirka said, "It isn't for us to do anything. We're at our station, performing our act of devotion. There's no rabid boar rushing us from the margins of the cove, no lightning storm. Maracoor requires that we assemble time at this place. We follow the code of custom."

But it was too much for Cossy. A guest on the steps of the house, her hand at her brow looking this way and that, and noticing the brides at their duties. This was just another version of lightning, a wild boar in a disguise.

15

It was then that Cossy broke time, ripped it at the hem.

She stood and let her end of the netting trail back into the water. She gestured again, this time with both hands: *Come down!*

"Cossy!" Most of the brides were appalled.

But, Cossy thought, So what that she broke the line? Time would survive. Newborn brides carried to the harbor's edge in their baskets hadn't been expected to do their share of netting with their unfurled infant hands, had they?

Cossy climbed three or four steps up the curved slabs of the basin. The guest was descending—walking slowly on her ugly, tender feet. The goose came with her.

Standing, the guest proved taller than Cossy had

expected. It had been hard to tell when she was laid flat on the floor. In fact, she wasn't unlike Kliompte in build—slight and strong—though where Kliompte was curves and curls, the guest was arranged on a stricter design. Shoulder-length dark hair whipped about her unveiled head. Above the maroon-striped tablecloth she had borrowed for a shawl, she seemed a green mask of exoticism; a walking pod of a maya-fruit tree.

Somehow when more clearly alive she seemed scarier. Cossy loved it.

"Acaciana," warned Mirka in a low voice. But there was no stopping the youngest bride now. Greenie was *her* guest. Cossy climbed the ranks of stone and waited at the top as the castaway descended, stopping a few feet away. They looked at each other. The goose squinted at Cossy sourly.

The guest spoke first, but the language was strange.

"You are our first guest. Ever," said Cossy. "The overseer doesn't count."

The guest listened with her head cocked. Then she put her hand on her breast and spoke again. This was, perhaps, her name, but no one could understand it.

The other brides had dropped their portions of net, all but Helia, who sat stoically looking out to sea. Everyone else stood up, breaking the code of custom. Tirr put her hands on Cossy's shoulders, as if to protect her from a curse. That was nice of Tirr, but Cossy shrugged her off.

The goose quawked again, and the guest spoke, and the goose quawked.

Cossy put out both her hands, palm out.

The guest reached to touch Cossy's hands. The brides all gasped and Mirka jerked Cossy back.

The goose let out a long complaint. It arched its neck and slapped its wings on the stones, but seemed to think better of attacking when the guest uttered a few syllables to it.

"Someone get me," said Helia. Holding up both of her arms. She had now dropped her portion of the net in the water. There was no one left to hold in time. The net could just sink or float away, and the world would be over. Easy as that. All because of a guest.

"It's magic, she's cured!" cried Cossy. "Helia can speak!"

"Get me up, my knees are rough today."

Bray and Tirr hoisted the elder to her feet. They helped her climb up to the lower step, where she turned around. "Don't you realize the goose is talking to us?" said Helia. "Isn't there a single brain among all six of you?"

"You've regained your tongue but lost your mind,"

said Mirka, trying to salvage her position as deputy-elder. "You'll go back to the temple and lie down."

Helia moved into position before the goose. "Speak. More. Slowly. Please."

The goose hissed, and garbled at a ferocious rate. The green guest seemed to advise the goose, who took on the serene if vacant expression of a heron. It positioned its head, as if to alter the pressure of wind from its lungs. It quawked once more, an odd, elongated sound.

Helia shrugged, but it was Bray who replied.

"You're welcome," said Bray, uneasily, maybe sullenly, but with courtesy.

"Did it speak? What did it say?" said Mirka, despite herself.

"It said you should go jump in the sea," muttered Cossy.

Helia said, "Shut up, everyone." To the goose: "Would. You. Say. That. Again. Please."

The goose looked fit to bite some of their fingers off, but it quawked one more time in a strange, guttery way. Bray repeated each syllable, rounding them into sounds they could better understand. The act of imitation made the goose's articulation less of a mystery. "What—is—this land?"

A talking goose. Well, a Goose. Scyrilla screamed. Kliompte fainted, but Tirr caught her in time to keep her from braining herself on the way down. Helia grinned. Cossy began to laugh and laugh. Mirka looked at the sun and scowled, as if expecting it to unfurl goose wings and fly away, why not, if the world was breaking apart anyway.

Bray looked blankly at them all. She was the one to answer the Goose's question. "Maracoor."

16

Seeing how they'd alarmed their hosts, the goose and Greenie turned to mount the path back to the temple. They soon paced out of earshot. Well, the girl had virgin feet.

Old Helia pointed at the nets. "Roll them up, we're done for today."

How her voice had come back, Cossy couldn't imagine. So what. A miracle. A sign. This was a holiday, and holidays happened only in the monsoon season.

"I don't know *what* you think you're playing at, Helia," said Mirka.

Bray and Tirr hurried through their sections so they could turn and support Helia under each arm. The three of them climbed the path to the switchback where the old tereboak tree tilted. Here Helia paused.

To catch her breath, she propped herself against a standing stone with a declivity at the right height for a tired rump.

Cossy helped Scyrilla and Kliompte store the nets under the droopy lip of a long rock. The three of them panted up the hill, arriving in time to hear Helia answer a question from Mirka.

"I suppose it was a spell," said Helia. She was making little effort to sound persuasive. "Some of you more senior brides remember old Bvaillura? She didn't speak for five years, until right before she died. Then she talked nonstop for two days until her heart gave out. Maybe it was like that.

"Not that you should start counting from today," she said to them. "I'm feeling quite myself. Only more tired. Besides, Bvaillura spoke fatal nonsense, and I'm for salty truth."

The guest and the goose had reached the temple and stood in the porch, out of earshot. "Greenie must be hungry," said Cossy. No one paid her attention.

"Helia," said Mirka. "What is going on here? Is this the beginning of the death of Maracoor?"

"I don't know any better than you do," said Helia. "We don't have much training in hospitality. We'll have to improvise."

"This is orchestrated madness," said Mirka. "I declare, Helia, you're up to something. Why did you fall mute just before the arrival of this interloper? You can't think I'm insensible to your cleverness."

"You credit me with foreknowledge? I know nothing of what will happen except, eventually, my death and yours," replied Helia. "An apple ripens on a bough, a cuckoo gets a cough. Accidents of happenstance. There doesn't have to be a relationship among miracles. Let's go see if we can interview this particular apple, this cuckoo. Get a grip, Mirka. We didn't ask to be visited, friends, but how can it hurt to offer this marauding army of two a slice of bread spread with tarragon honey?"

As Helia advanced up the hill, it seemed to Cossy everything was rapturously changed. The green girl in the blue-shadowed portico. The goose standing forward in the light so its breast feathers blazed like burning ash. Just for this passage of moments, as they climbed the mount, the temple housed a green presence. She was like a goddess. They were brides of a Maracoor different now than it had been at dawn.

That sensation passed, and Cossy was sorry. But there was too much to watch and hear to mourn it.

On one side of the temple stood an array of stumps and stools. Warmed by sunlight, the scent of resin from scattered pine needles lifted in the air. This was where old Helia led them, crooking a finger at Greenie to join them. To give the guest her own perch, Cossy squatted on the ground. Scyrilla brought some lemony water in an amphora and Kliompte fixed a tray with bread, yellow grapes, and goat's milk cheese. She offered some to the castaway, who fell upon it greedily. The goose raised its head and kept a lookout upon the horizon.

When Greenie had finished everything supplied her, she wiped her mouth on the back of her hand. She addressed the goose, it seemed. The goose snapped something back, adjusted its feathers and the tone of its quawk, and made an effort to translate.

Cossy couldn't understand why Bray, the simplest soul among them, was the one able to interpret the goose's speech. By now Cossy could tell there were words, but they came out so tortured, either clipped or lengthened, that she could only fix one possible meaning among fifty. But Bray, whose own spoken language was slow, seemed to understand the goose without much effort.

When the goose had fallen silent, Greenie looked about and opened her palms to the sky. Helia said, "Bray, we're waiting." With a great deal of blushing and stammering, Bray tried to recite what she could remember of what they had all just heard.

17

Her name, not Greenie. Her name, Rain.
       She come from far away.
Not boat like overseer.
She come in air. Like rain.
She has no wings. She cross sky—
Never mind how. Never know this.
Goose has a name, can't say it, too twisty.
She—the Rain—goose—they fall from the sky.
Flying for days and nights and times unnotched.
They see no island in the water before Maracoor.
They drop, they swim, they live.
They never know of us before today.
We do not know of them before today.
We are talking.
That is all I know to say.

18

B ray's brow was dripping by the time she finished. It was the longest speech of her life.

It wasn't enough for them to go on, but it was a start.

"Ask her where they came from," said Helia.

"You ask," replied Bray.

Helia did. The green girl turned her hands, palms flat up and empty, as if there was nothing in them, nothing to say. Then she pointed at the sky and made a wincing expression, which seemed to mean, *Sorry, sorry I can't be of more help.*

They sat in silence. The effort of using words to link up their lives on this outrageous day was too much for all of them. Helia waved a hand for more lemon water. "And for the Goose," she added, following the storyteller's custom of emphasizing the initial letter to indicate recognition of the rare creature as articulate. Sentient. For a Goose, anyway. So Cossy dashed inside and grabbed a saucer with a raised brim. She set it on the ground before the Goose. Kliompte squatted and poured some lemon water; the other brides waited till she straightened up again. Helia raised her cup and said, "To the world beyond what we know."

They all sipped, including the visiting girl—not Greenie, but Rain—and the Goose. They exchanged solemn glances with one another, but Cossy caught a fit of giggles and fell on the scratchy dirt in a fit.

She was still twitching there in some paroxysm of joy—or it may just have been surprise—when Tirr said, "Is that the coracle?" The brides stood, all but Cossy, who was still looking at the guest's naked feet from a low angle. How slender the edges of the foot, how unleathery the edges and soles. How could they support her height and weight? The green girl—Rain, Cossy had to practice that word, Rain—stood too and looked in the direction the others were looking.

19

The waters off the southwestern brow of Maracoor Spot, hidden though they were from harbor view, had always proven the safest place for a large seaworthy vessel to anchor. From there the overseer's coracle was lowered, from there he set out to approach the harbor, using the buoy to avoid treacherous rocks, to cross the sandy berm silted out of sight beneath the waves. To there he presumably returned after his inspection and a ceremonial meal. Occasionally the winds shifted and dragged the ship northward, as if against its will, and then the brides could catch a glimpse of the mothership's heavy white sails. Bridal veils strung up on gaffs and booms. This had never yet happened in Cossy's brief life, or not so she could remember. Until today.

The ship shifted in full view, bucking. Its sails were

being drawn in. The same wind that had brought down the goose and Rain was, perhaps, troubling the vessel. The coracle had already been lowered, though. A speck in the waves, appearing from and disappearing behind the hilly water.

Helia said, "Bloody hell, and this has to be today?"

Mirka interrupted her. "What are we to do? This Rain creature can't be found here, we don't know what would happen to her. To us!"

"What's the problem? Whatever could happen?" asked Scyrilla. Cossy flashed her a rare smile the older girl didn't notice; Scyrilla had voiced Cossy's question for her. It wasn't often they spoke for each other anymore. "Why don't we take Greenie behind the house," said Scyrilla, "take her up the hill? To the Mother of Olive, or beyond?"

"We have to let the overseer know of this aberration," said Mirka. "Not a moment too soon, his arrival. Bless the Great Mara."

"We should protect this Rain Creature," said Helia, by her accent giving the guest a title as well as a name. "Enough with this panic. We didn't break the code; it was broken for us. But we needn't sacrifice a human life for our protocols."

"Are you standing hip-deep in your own dotage?" shrilled Mirka. "We don't have the right to change the world. They'll make us pay for this. You know that, Helia."

"You're out of order, Mirka." Helia spoke with cold calm. "No one pays for a fallen tree or for a broken egg. That's just the world working in its way, sometimes lively and sometimes deadly. Go inside and begin to prepare the meal. Control yourself. And give me a chance to have a single uninterrupted thought, assuming I'm still capable."

Greenie—the Rain Creature—but Cossy would call her Rain—stood apart. She had lowered her brow and folded her hands in a crisscross pattern upon her midriff. The Goose was talking to her in such a gabble that Cossy could make out none of it. It gave her a crosswinds headache. "Helia, what *are* we going to do?" asked Cossy. "The overseer is coming. Will it be Lucikles again, do you think?"

"Yes, unless he's become sick or died or been put in prison," answered Helia. "My eyes aren't good enough to see that far. Can you tell?"

"No, he's rowing with his back to us. And I didn't look at him much last year, I was too scared. I won't be so scared today."

"That's my girl," said Helia. "Now go gather a few corn blossoms to arrange on the steps of the temple."

Cossy did as she was told. She picked them roughly.

In puffs of beige pollen, the moist mauve blooms released themselves from their stems. She had to lay the blooms gently in the crook of her elbow. They were so fragile, so easily crushed. And so quickly rotted—they wouldn't last the afternoon in the sun. So too this day would run out by dusk, and whatever happenstance might be rowing toward them, it would be folded into the past by tomorrow morning. The brides would return to their mission and net the new day, and the world would reinvigorate itself with normalcy. They would laugh about pompous Lucikles and imitate his snuffly hound, Cur. They would say their old chant:

Lucikles,
Bring the keys,
Free us please,
Lucikles.

But would Rain be gone, too—taken away in the rowboat, hauled away in the ship, brought back to the mainland, to Maracoor Abiding?

It would still take at least another whole year for a new baby bride to arrive, because they would remain the full seven brides. No one had died since last year.

Cossy paused for a moment on the margin of the path. She could see the rowboat—it was entering the harbor now, passing the buoy. Out on the ribbon tide, the mother ship seethed and turned this way and that, straining against its anchor chain. Below her, the brides were rushing to prepare for the emissary. Lucikles, or whoever it was this time, rowed his way across the harbor, his back turned to the procession. Little white footprints appeared in the surface of the water on either side of the boat as the oars went in and in and forward, back and out again.

Cossy found herself inventing a new magick, her very first.

Lucikles,
If you please,
Easy does it
Lucikles.

The newcomer stood poised in the light like a green statue perched on an outcropping of limestone. Cossy felt a sudden surge of alarm for the Rain Creature. She didn't know which she wanted more, the novelty of this green girl as her first friend, or the new baby bride that was eventually due Cossy to hold and raise herself. So Cossy was speechless and stuttery at once, till she managed at last, "Rain! Run!" and she beckoned with her hands, *this way, this way.*

Lucikles

1

He concentrated on his own family as he spaded the hills of water with his oars. This was his trick. It was how he managed to do his job. Probably most men did the same. In mind-numbing labor or in tedium, their thoughts returned to their homes: some petite fortress, a cramped set of rooms in a block of flats, that farmhouse squatting behind thorns. Those homely crofts that were the crucible of life. Where each day ignited, where each day burned into its ashes.

Lucikles, as Minor Adjutant to the House of Balances of Maracoor Abiding, knew that his chore today wasn't the worst of what he was called to do annually. This was merely the capstone of a tour of duty, the only task among his assignments to take him away for a chunk of time each year. Depending on the weather, his survey of outposts carried him off for two and a half months. This year, it looked more to be like eleven weeks, because of the unprecedented storms they'd just come through. An extra week of divorce from family life.

His son was nearly thirteen—dear Leorix—and his daughters, Poena and Star, were eight and five. His fatherly worry about them was distraction if nothing else. Of course, his wife and his mother-in-law could troubleshoot perfectly well while he was away. Both of them were in robust form, and the older lady was enjoying one of her spells of better spirits. But always the threats: the weather, drought, locusts, disease. So Lucikles hated having to go on his annual tour of the islands. Especially the final leg, this trip way out to Maracoor Spot. His requisite inventory of brides. It took too many days out of the mere clutch of years any father has to spend with his offspring. Childhood, which seems endless to children, is the most finite span of moments in the history of a life.

Cur was uneasy in the coracle, and spit a couple of times. Lucikles had never known a dog who could spit before. His hair being long and stringy, he often looked like a dirty mop. The flying spume didn't improve Cur's looks this morning.

"Easy, fellow, we're making surprisingly good time today," said Lucikles, pulling, pulling. He hoped the return passage this afternoon wouldn't prove as doubly hard as this seemed doubly easy. The winds ought to have turned about by then.

Cur growled, though not in a menacing way. He no longer cowered in the bottom of the coracle with his paws over his head, as he had used to do. Now he sat in the bow, sculptural, surveying the world as if he could settle the unruly water by growling under his breath.

Lucikles pivoted, locating between heaves of water the cork buoy bobbing on its chain. It was the size of a human head and he always thought, Man overboard— but still treading water after all these years. At one side of the narrow harbor entrance, he knew, lurked a treacherous submerged rock. The coracle didn't sit low enough, generally speaking, to be in danger, but if a gulp and swallow of the tides caused the level of the water to drop suddenly—it had nearly happened once or twice—a fellow might find himself in trouble.

"Here we go, Cur, here we go," he said. Even though the women he was looking in on were holy brides, unavailable in every way, Lucikles always found himself summoning strength for a strong finish. He didn't want to arrive seeming frail and panting. His survey of the island plantation was mostly pro forma, but a year was a long time—you never knew what you were going to find. He had his orders, his rituals; he sported a close-range short-bow with five arrows and he carried the latest in medicines. His work was cut out for him. There and back again in four hours, he hoped. A nice bottle of wine would be uncorked on ship at noontime so it could age properly in the oceanic afternoon air by the time he returned. His little reward.

And then, sails set homeward to the mainland for another year.

Set home to his wife, to his girls, to Leorix.

At about this moment, the lad would be having his midmorning reprieve from his lessons with Kerr Tompas or Kerr Misxou. He'd be spinning his top with the other boys in the marketplace, among the lemon-sellers and the scribes and soothsayers. He wasn't a natural leader, Leorix—a normal thumpy sort of boy, with limbs that bowed a little as if, as an infant, he'd been cured in the sun around the belly of a prize melon. But his was a heart of natural bloom. A sense of golden pollen spilling out of his good nature, his eyes, his simple words. He took care of his sisters, was decent to his mother and grandmother, and he seemed to be making better progress at the study of languages and the art of mathematics than his junior teachers had prophesied. (So much for their soothsaying skills!) It was for Leorix's advancement that Lucikles had stepped up his own ambitions and marshaled his strengths. Not at first, not when the boy was a mereling, a chunky and asthmatic infant—but eventually, as Leorix grew in strength and glory and a more potent innocence.

Cur growled a little, giving navigational advice. The coracle was about to rasp along the sandy approach. Even without turning, Lucikles could tell. On the margins of his vision, the water glowed sandy brown as the harbor shallowed and the floor sloped up to the shore.

He drew in with that sandpapery thrust of keel on grit. Cur hopped out and began to nose the seaweed. Lucikles knotted the coracle's lead to an iron ring cemented into a boulder, and turned to see who would approach. It wasn't proper for him to mount the slope until he'd been greeted and welcomed.

Most of them were standing beneath the portico of the temple, serene in their veils and reticence. They didn't line up as usual but clumped, informally and perhaps uncertainly. He couldn't count them from here, which was his practice. Odd. Usually the stout dame of them, the one called Helia, made her way to greet him, but he could see that she was seated on a stool, one hand rested against a pillar. Perhaps there was illness in the temple.

Helia's lieutenant, that pill called Mirka, was taking a deep breath and setting out toward him, swaying those wide hips beneath her narrow shoulders like the flare of a bell. Lucikles remembered her as contrary, a sour-cat, and he sighed through a broad fake smile. May this day be swift and return me to my wine, and may I deserve it, he prayed.

When she was about thirty steps away, Mirka stopped and intoned, "The mercy of Maracoor."

"Today is forever," he replied, hoping it wouldn't seem so, literally.

After a pause, Mirka admitted, "I'm not certain what is said next. Helia, my superior, has failed to offer training in the traditions. There is much she has held back from me."

"We aren't all that particular in the rhetoric," said Lucikles. This wasn't precisely true. Still, who would know? It was his report that went to the House of Balances, his and his alone; no one would question what he submitted. There was no one to gainsay him.

Cur came nosing along the sand, snuffling, wagging his tail. He'd been here often enough that he probably had preferential stinks to visit. He ignored Mirka for the time being, though Lucikles imagined that when the dog had finished swiping his nose through the sedge, he'd come back in for a warm hello, if Mirka could summon anything of that sort to her thin, gripped mouth. Were she less severe she might have been beautiful. Once. "What do you need to know?" she asked, as if she could bar the emissary from climbing the hill and making his enquiries in the portico of the temple.

"Well, where I can sit down, for one thing," he said equably. "I have to catch my breath. I'm a year older than I was when I last visited, and the waters are stronger today than was predicted. The heel of a storm, one you probably saw yourselves. I ought to have made landfall a week ago. Still, here I am now. For good or ill. Shall we?"

She looked at him coldly, as if she could refuse him by the cast of her eyebrows. "Then I'll lead," he said. "Come along, Cur." And the dog affably flopped ahead of them both, with Mirka following the overseer and probably making hex signs at him behind her back.

He didn't talk as they climbed. He'd been telling the truth about being winded. Besides, there was some domestic conflict going on here; he got that. Some power struggle between old Helia and the second, this Mirka character. They had always chafed against each other. He would have to be politic. His job was to assess the well-being of the brides of Maracoor, to return to the mainland, and to report on their status and their needs. But in and out, the faster the better.

As members of an established colony, generations old now, the brides were amazingly self-sufficient. Sometimes, however, a tool had broken, or a crop had failed, or a medical intervention was in order. One year he had returned in four weeks with a pair of female goats. The next year he arrived to find that one of the female goats had had five kids and the other goat had not been as advertised, had become a rogue male, escaped, and was busy eating through every edible item. The brides were near starvation. You never knew. He'd gotten there just in time.

He achieved the turn in the path and could see the waiting brides more clearly. There were four of them. The youngest—the girl younger than his own Leorix—was missing. Also the next one up, her nearest in age. This was an aberration. He was alarmed, as he would be for one of his own children. The old hogshead herself was now struggling to her feet and straightening the edges of her white veil. He decided to honor seniority. Perhaps her knees were bothering her. She was of an age now. That must be the simple reason Mirka had come to bid him welcome.

"Dame Helia," he said to her, and extended his hands in a sandwich of palms.

"Kerr Lucikles," she replied, repeating the gesture as best she could, given she was gripping a cane of some sort. To one of the younger brides Helia remarked, "Please bring forward the refreshment. Kliompte, will you lay the board?"

The one called Kliompte, she with the most rewarding form among them and the coppery corkscrew
tresses slipping from beneath her veil, she brought
forward the cloth. Then she added two stone goblets
carved over with sigils of piety. Mirka the battle-ax
retired into the temple shadows and returned with a
pitcher of water flavored with anise. With relief Lucikles sat upon the bench set out for him. Helia relaxed
onto her stool. The other brides stood back, hands
folded. Cur rushed into the temple and made sounds of
investigation and discovery.

"Get the dog the bones we kept for him," said Helia.
"Lay them out here in the sun where we can watch him
enjoy them. We'd have had soup from them otherwise;
we might as well see those bones appreciated."

Cur settled down on the porch steps with the largest
bone between his front paws. He went at it with relish.

"Not the full compliment of brides today, Dame
Helia," said Lucikles after they had finished their
drinks in silence. "Who is here, and who is not, and
where are they? I study up on your names before I leave
but I am forgetful after a hard row."

"We are Helia," she began, "and Mirka, who
greeted you. We are Tirr and Bray and Kliompte."
Each bride nodded her head when her name was
mentioned. "The youngest two, Scyrilla and Cossy,

they are up in the woods somewhere. We sent them for stonetree acorns this morning. It's an all-day task and we didn't guess this would be Visitation Day. But they're healthy. Thriving even. As usual."

"I'm supposed to wait until they return," he reminded her. "Can they be sent for?" He looked at the assembly. "Who is swiftest among you?"

"Usually I should recommend exactly that remedy," said Helia calmly. "But I note, as you do too, that the seas are high after the weather we've had. I'm concerned that the time it might take to locate those two dilly-dallies could cause you to miss the chance you have to return safely to your vessel. The tides have been stroppy in both directions all week."

"I should hate to have to come back tomorrow," said Lucikles.

"We should hate that too," said Helia. "Not meaning any rudeness of course."

They paused, at an impasse.

"Of course, we can testify on the Vessel that the younger girls are in fine form," said Helia. "It would be an unusual move, but it ought to satisfy you, no?"

"I don't know if that would be wise," he began.

"Bray," said Helia, "please make the proper blessings and bring the Vessel here."

The brides couldn't disguise their shock at this break

in protocol, but Bray did as she was told. Kliompte darted forward to whip away the tray and the cloth, and Tirr approached to lay down fresh branches of balsam and laurel upon the tabletop.

"You aren't in the habit of trundling the Vessel about?" he asked in what he hoped was an everyday tone of voice.

"Of course not," replied Helia a bit snappishly. "I'm making a point here."

"It seems an extreme gesture."

"Your staying overnight because you want to wait for the younger brides to return would be more extreme. We live with the Vessel, Kerr Lucikles. We live with it and for it. You are looking agitated. Be at peace. The mercy of Maracoor."

"Today is forever," he replied automatically. The commonplace exchange calmed him, at least a little.

Bray approached with the Vessel. It hadn't changed. An ironstone strongbox, wider than it was high or deep, whose front was about the length of his forearm. The Vessel's top was barrel-domed. Its sunken lock, though old, remained shiny and well oiled. The Brides guarded their precious totem with diligence, he could see. This was the unspoken point of his visit, but he rarely had to go this far to verify the correct pursuit of bridal behaviors.

He didn't like to be in the presence of the Vessel, but to back away would prove evidence of fear he thought it inadvisable to show. Cur, however, abandoned the bone as Bray set her heavy burden down upon the aromatic branches. The terrier backed away but emitted a low, menacing clearing of the throat.

"My, my," was all Lucikles could say. "Steady, boy."

With the help of her cane, and then Tirr at her other elbow, Helia came forward and put her right hand upon the lid of the Vessel. "I swear unto the Great Mara and Maracoor Abiding that the seven brides of our station are well and accounted for, though two are absent in the uplands today."

One by one the others came forward and made statements close to the same, Bray struggling with the words until Mirka supplied them for her to parrot. When all five had testified, old Helia turned and said wryly to the visitor, "Would you like to testify that you have heard what we have sworn, and that you accept it?"

"No need for that. You can take this away now. Blessed be the Vessel," he added, not to seem impious or overhasty.

Bray came to hoist the holy casket away, but as he had noticed once or twice before, the Vessel needed more strength to dislodge from a resting position than, apparently, to carry once it was in motion. As if the whole thing were magnetically secured to the tabletop. Tirr and Mirka moved in to help Bray. He would have helped but it would be unseemly. Anyway, he believed he might have strained a tendon coming to shore.

When Bray had dislodged and heaved the Vessel back into the temple, Lucikles exhaled through both corners of his clenched mouth. He said to Helia, "Let's review your year. You can itemize any requests you have. If they're urgent, I'll be back in a month. Otherwise, this time next year. As always."

Helia said, "I'll be blunt, Kerr Lucikles. We're likely to need a new bride before long. My health is failing. I suffer spells of blackout and tongue-stop. So far I always recover but one day I will not. The customary order of things is that Mirka ascend to take my place when I die. But I don't think she is suitable."

Helia said this right in front of Mirka, who flushed red with shame and anger.

"Is this a conversation we ought to be having privately?" asked Lucikles, knowing that witnessing Mirka's dressing-down would color his exchanges with her for the rest of his days.

"There are no secrets among us," said Helia. "My wariness of Mirka is commonly understood. We all live in relative concord despite it. But Mirka has a bitter and a grasping spirit, while the senior bride is required to be generous and wise. Not ambitious. You must understand"—and here she held up a finger toward Mirka without looking at her, as if shushing her before she had begun to speak—"wisdom and cleverness, often mistaken one for the other, are different branches of knowledge."

"I'm not aware that there is a protocol for selecting a chief other than the eldest," said Lucikles. "You, as our senior bride, would know that better than anyone else. I can ask the Magistrate but I might not get the answer in time. Before your death I mean."

"I know something of protocol. I know more of innovation," said Helia.

"Perhaps Mirka's special talents and character are just what Maracoor needs in the next congress of brides," offered Lucikles. "The world is smarter than we are. You collect our days for us, but you aren't expected to interpret their meaning."

"In time one can't help learning to interpret, unless one is a fool."

"I insist we should move on from this issue and consider the inventory of supplies, and come back to the matter before I leave. We can continue the discussion in sequestration."

Helia seemed to relax; he had signaled he was going to leave, after all. "Very well." She began to sketch a review of the incidents of the last year. Not much had happened. The seasons, such as they were, came and went. The brides had managed custody of the nets of time with devotion and regularity, only missing a couple of days in the winter when an uncharacteristic cold had lined the edge of the harbor with a lip of ice. And this past week of unprecedented weather. There's been one or two bouts of sickness. Bray had hit her head again—for a woman of such strength, she was useless about navigating under tree limbs. Not much else to tell, really. As to the readiness of supplies . . .

But now that the Vessel had been retracted from the porch, Cur had lost interest in his bone, and he was nosing about the margins of the temple. On the steps first, and then around the podium. Picking up a scent he didn't recognize, or maybe did and found compelling. He barked in alarm or wild hope of some sort. "Cur," said Lucikles, "you're a guest here, remember that. Behave yourself." Cur did nothing of the sort. He ran madly about in circles, making investigative feints into underbrush.

"The dog is in need of chastisement," said Dame Helia, but Lucikles wasn't under her jurisdiction and felt no need to call the dog to heel.

"He's a distraction to my thinking," she said as Cur's barking got louder.

"Let him run. He needs the exercise. Quite some days since our last port of call. Now, we were about to talk about foodstuffs and medicines . . ."

"No shortage of yellowspine tea leaves yet," said Helia briskly. Lucikles knew that particular dusty tisane served as the building block of all therapies, and that yellowspine ferns didn't grow on Maracoor Spot. Only the wetlands of Maracoor Abiding. It was cheap as mildew back home but precious here. "We ought to request some cotton bandages though," continued Helia. "We went through quite a portion of our stock when Acaciana cut her leg on a highland ramble and it refused to stop bleeding for a day. We thought we would lose her."

Lucikles made a note. "Emergency return, or will next year be all right?" he asked.

"Next year. But bring an ample portion. That child is coming into the clumsy age."

The dog now was lunging upslope toward the orchard, then coursing under its arching boughs toward the woods.

"What the devil is he on about?" asked Lucikles, despite himself. "Some rabid feral thing come out of a cave? I hope nothing big and skulky is lurking about that you haven't mentioned, Dame Helia."

"Nothing of that nature," said Helia blandly enough.

"Now let's move on to that happy juncture of medicine and refreshment, namely, wine . . ."

"I think that's a goose I hear," said Lucikles, "making a protest. I hope Cur is smart enough to steer clear. A goose could brain him, I mean assuming Cur has any brains to begin with."

"There is the random goose about, now and then," remarked Helia, "no matter. I suppose I ought to have guessed. Shall we consider the wine supply?"

But there was no denying the menace of an angry goose, and the sudden sounds of voices in the near woods, screaming at Cur to back off.

"Dame Helia, I think we'd better . . . ?" Lucikles raised his eyebrows.

Helia struggled to rise as he forged ahead. The other brides, in heed of Helia's command, stayed behind. He cleared the stone deck of the podium and jumped to the ground, and he labored up the slope of the orchard. He wove underneath the umbrella spokes of their canopies. Beyond, the deciduous forest leaned in shadow. His feet slipped on dried needles from last season, but he arrived at an outcropping of schist and rounded its broken brow.

Cur had a great gander or a goose at bay, and was closing in on the creature. This despite the small dog's being dwarfed by the furious bird drawing itself up. "Cur, back, boy, back!" shouted Lucikles. The company of brides, the younger ones presumed to be upslope, were shouting and waving their hands at his dog to deter him from attack. "Cur, you thug," he shouted. He swooped down to collect the dog around the belly. Cur gave him a nip before he recognized his owner, and continued to growl with theatrical gusto, but he was shivering too, as if afraid of what he'd started.

The goose backed up, and quawked, "Neutering is too good for that mutt!"

Then Lucikles came to his senses and saw that the two youngest brides were flanking a third, a foreigner, a green-skinned creature not yet two decades old, if he was a judge. She was a figure from myth and fairy legend. For a moment he thought, The fathers of Maracoor Abiding were wiser than they know; this is a holy island after all. For the first time in his life, he passed out cold.

He wasn't unconscious for long. The younger brides had sat him up and were patting the tops of his hands. Cur leapt in feints to lick his face. The goose was busy picking nits, as if proving no culpability in the matter. "Queen of earth and sky," Lucikles managed to say to the young brides on either side of him. "Do you see her?"

"Of course they see me," said the green girl.

He didn't know how to proceed in addressing a myth. "Who—who are you?"

"A maiden of little renown and no importance. Who are you?"

A peculiar nicety, that a deity should enquire after his particulars. "I am Kerr Lucikles, Minor Adjutant of the House of Balances, resident of Maracoor Crown on the mainland of Maracoor Abiding."

"A bit self-important, himself, don't you think?" opined the goose—no, a Goose!—to the green girl. "I suppose it comes from being the only human male among all these scratchy hens."

"You should talk, Iskinaary," said the green vision. "You might be making common cause with another of your gender instead of acting superior."

"I've heard tell of Animals who can speak," said Lucikles, "but I've never come across one. They don't frequent the capital city in this day. In fact, I thought it might be only old farmwives' chatter." He rubbed his eyes. "Unless," he continued, "you are some sort of spirit companion, an angelic confection in goose garb?"

"I like the sound of that," snorted the Goose, "but this isn't your lucky day."

"I hope your dog isn't having fits," said the green girl. "He's still shaking."

"Don't talk to him," the youngest of the brides told the stranger girl. "I don't know what you're saying but stop it!" She had her hands clasped before her like a child in a pageant singing about something sacred. Her name—he should remember—Acaciana. Cossy. And the other bride was Squirrel or something like that.

"Cossy," he said. "Help me up. You too, Squirrel."

"*Scyrilla.*" Oh, with such a foul expression did that one correct him.

"Can you *understand* her?" the youngest asked Lucikles, gesturing at the apparition. "You were *talking* to her!"

He didn't need to be interviewed by the most minor bride; he was the interlocutor. "Do you have a name?" he asked the green girl, and attempted a little bow.

"Please, not obeisance, no, I couldn't stand it," said the visitor. "I have a name but you don't need to know it. Leave these girls alone. Leave us alone. We were walking up to the ridge when your dog attacked Iskinaary. Go away."

"Where were you taking them?"

"The young girls? For a stroll. They were bored."

This didn't seem like the behavior of a deity, to be a rural governess on a holy mountain. "How—" His years of experience had failed to prepare him for such an interview. "How do you know they were bored?" was all he could come up with.

"They've been acting bored all morning and last night besides."

Lucikles began to come to his senses. "So you appeared to them last night too? Are you one of the Twelve Sleights of Grace? Why did you manifest yourself upon this island?"

The girl swiveled her head and looked at him slantwise. "You don't need to know what I do or why. You go your way and I'll go mine, and that'll be the end of this, then. All right?"

"All right," he said, and waited.

After a moment she asked, "Are you going?"

"I'm waiting to see you go first. Do you—disappear? Dissolve? Levitate? Do you become a zephyr, a bird, a blown thistle seed, some harmonic chime upon the air?"

"I walk on my feet," she said. "Iskinaary, come on. Goodbye to you all."

With a heavy tread that seemed improbable for a sacred entity from the holy poetry of the faith, she veered away. She took up a scrappy broom that didn't look competent to snag a cobweb from a lintel, and girl and Goose began to venture farther into the forest.

"Don't go," said the youngest, that Cossy, with a pulse of grief in her voice.

"Let the weird thing take herself off, she's nothing but trouble," said Scyrilla. "And I didn't like her mangy pet anyway. But Kerr Lucikles, how come you can understand her and we can't?"

Finding his voice again, Lucikles called to the green vision, "Come back. We'll return to the temple. Together."

"Have no interest in that," replied the departing stranger, over her shoulder.

"I have arrows and a bow," he mentioned, and patted the leather strapping the device to his side.

She stopped at that. This is how Lucikles knew for sure she was human, or at least somewhat human. No angelic spirit is wary of the human weapon.

So they began to make their way back down through the orchard, the four humans and the suspicious growling dog and the Goose. The Minor Adjutant had to get things back on track. There was more inventory to discuss. Such drudgery would buy him time to think things over while he was still islanded. Discovering this first-ever break in island protocol would either ruin Lucikles or make him, depending on how he handled it.

Dame Helia was unsettled at his return with the green visitation.

"I expect some clear answers," he said to her.

"Leave the old woman alone," said the green figure. "She's not to blame. No one is to blame. And there's been no harm done in any case."

He could tell that Dame Helia, too, couldn't quite follow what the verdant spectre was saying. He pressed his point with Helia, who shrugged and replied, without much conviction, "I didn't know you'd be able to see her. So I didn't know that she needed mentioning."

"Kerr Lucikles asked her if she was one of the Twelve Sleights of Grace," said Cossy, and nearly sniggered.

Lucikles continued. "You told me that there was nothing new here, Dame Helia. Quite the oversight to fail to mention a visitor."

With her pinky she dug for an errant sesame seed stuck behind a back tooth. "I said there was nothing huge and fierce and frightening to trouble us. As you see this evanescence is a slip of a thing, hardly worth the coin of conversation."

But he could tell that Helia realized this green stranger was no apparition of spirit such as he had taken her for. The other brides knew it as well. They didn't flinch at her appearance. She was strange but already something of a familiar to them.

"You took her for a sylph of the sacred winds. An expression of the mountain's holiness," said Helia. "One of the Twelve Sleights of Grace." Her tone was neither mocking nor appalled. Nonetheless, he closed his eyes to steep in his shame alone, as alone as he could manage. "It's no surprise," said the oldest bride in a more tender tone. "She isn't a regular feature of your visits, after all. Nor is she of our lives. I don't know that there's any reason to keep talking about her. Shall we return to the matter of soft-good stocks and food supplies?"

"You ought to have mentioned her when I first arrived," said Lucikles.

"An awful lot of yacking," said the Goose. Lucikles would have to mention the existence of a Goose—not goose, but Goose, a talking creature—in his report. This would raise eyebrows and generate gossip in the bureau. Oh, the headaches. The questions about his competence, his drinking even. The Goose quawked, "Let's leave them to their business, Rain."

"If you're not a holy avatar of the Great Mara," said Lucikles to the green guest, "where are you from?"

She twisted her thin lips in a wrinkled expression he couldn't read. "I can't say," she told him. "I just can't say."

"Leave her alone," interrupted the Goose. "We're going to go walk along the beach now. I need to introduce myself to a salt-minnow or two and have some lunch. Keep my strength up. Come on, Rain. Let's lose these losers."

"Don't go to the beach," said Lucikles. His coracle was tied up at the harbor. He didn't want the girl and the Goose fleeing in it, or setting it loose to float away, stranding him here overnight. "Go back and shelter in the orchard if you must. But don't go farther than that. I'll hold the dog here to keep him from pestering you." Cur had calmed down some but his expression of indignation remained.

"I'll go too," said Cossy. "This is boring for me here anyway."

"Manners!" Old Helia had a hard time suppressing a grin at Cossy's bluntness.

"How can you understand the green girl, and talk to her, when we mostly can't?" the child asked Lucikles. "And the bird too?"

"Your ear is innocent of accents, that's all," he replied. "She has an othersea accent that broadens her vowels. It also enunciates consonants that you and I tend to drop. If you played a game with her of naming common things, you'd see soon enough that our language and hers is the same, or nearly. It's a matter of

training your ear to hear through the foreign diph-
thongs and alternate stresses. If this, this peculiarity—"

"My name is Rain," said the girl again, coldly.

"—if Rain would spend ten minutes with you in the
orchard pointing things out, and naming them, you'd
soon get the hang of it."

"Good suggestion. That is, if I don't levitate myself
to some other picnic," said Rain with the scorn of one
not fully emerged from teenage ferocity. The lips of
several brides must be twitching at Rain's tone of voice,
he guessed, since her words were still largely unintel-
ligible to them. The tone of mockery in the young is
universal.

Lucikles felt himself blushing and turned his back to
them all. "Let's tear through our usual work," he said
to Helia. "Then we'll discuss what's to be done about
this audacity."

"We didn't invite this guest, she just showed up,"
said Helia, but Lucikles was beckoning to that harridan, Mirka. Helia had made a fool of him. So, brook-
ing Helia's disapproval, Lucikles told Mirka to bring a
chair and join the executive conversation.

Rain and the Goose disappeared off the temple's
porch, with Cossy wheeling after them. Her ten-year-
old limbs flashed beneath her swirled robes. The other
brides busied themselves in the kitchen nook, prepar-

ing the Minor Adjutant a lunch before he set out again for the ship.

Lucikles silenced Helia's muttered objections about Mirka and he began with his list and his pen. Cur settled nearby, but his chin stayed alert and his ears cocked for nonsense from any quarter.

When the work of inventory and the recording of general well-being on the island was completed— excepting the aberration of the Goose and the green girl—Lucikles put his ledgers back in his satchel. He sat without a pen or ink or scroll.

"What is to be done?" he said then. He tried to speak as if he knew the answer and wanted them to prove they knew it too, as a teacher will ask young scholars a question to see if they have learned anything.

"There's nothing that needs doing, Kerr Lucikles," replied Dame Helia calmly. "Have your lunch and go your way. We brides of Maracoor have devoted our lives to taking in the dailiness that the sea delivers, and to wrap with holy intent the ineffable into the particular. So what, that the sea shocks us by washing up something we've never seen before. Maybe the brides have kept vigil on Maracoor Spot for the better part of two centuries just so we can be here today to welcome this young woman, this Rain. Maybe we've been waiting. We are the brides, and this is our job. Now you've come and overseen us like the good overseer you are. So you can go. Leave us to our work, which we determine on our own."

"I beg to differ," said Dame Mirka.

"Petition denied," snapped Helia, but Lucikles stayed her objection and gestured for Mirka to continue.

The elder-in-waiting drew herself up behind compressed lips. She didn't speak till she had all her sentences lined up in single file in her mouth. "This is my opinion, Kerr Lucikles. We are to be seven brides, and only brides, and only seven. That is our sacred mandate. Perhaps Rain's appearance is precisely timed, by the systems of gods and fate, so that through your good offices the news of her arrival can get back to Maracoor Abiding. More to the point, if there is no way for the Rain Creature to leave—what, is she to float offshore in the wings of that Goose the way she arrived, and drift to some other island?—if there is no way for Rain to leave—I insist on completing my sentence, Helia— then it is clear she is meant to leave with you, Kerr Lucikles. The mystery of coincidence brought her here yesterday precisely so that she might be ferried to Maracoor Abiding in the overseer's ship. *Today.* I don't believe, Helia, that we can tolerate a shirking of duty on the part of our overseer, our better and master."

"I'm not your master," said Lucikles.

"You have the coracle," said Mirka. "Same difference."

"Mirka, you don't know what you're talking about," said Helia. "So shut up. For my part, I quote the prophet's reminder: Upon which matter one does not know, upon that matter one ought not speak."

"Mirka may have a point," said Lucikles. He didn't like the upstart bride with her needle nose and her poison squint, but he was still angry at Helia for showing him up as a fool. "But it's out of the question for me to bring this creature back to the mainland. The sailors might rebel. Not having been told about this cargo in advance, they'd object. Anyone who goes to sea for a living is superstitious and has salt on the brain. In any case, the ship isn't outfitted for a female. I couldn't vouch for her safety. No, that will not do."

"I insist there are to be seven brides on Maracoor, not eight," said Mirka, stabbing the tabletop with a finger.

"The officiousness! See what I mean?" asked Helia of the overseer.

"Yes, Mirka has a *point*," said Lucikles again, "but I'm not in a position to make any such decision today. I'll have to yield to you on this for the time being, Dame Helia. I will sail from here and leave—what did you call her, the Rain Creature?—leave her with you, for now. I'll explain what's happened to the Magistrates in Maracoor Abiding and they'll instruct me. They may tell me to come back in a month and haul this arriviste back to the mainland. Or they may send an assassin. Or a small present tied up with ribbons. I can't tell you what will happen next. Mirka is right in that the tradition allows only seven brides of Maracoor. But for good or for ill, I'm leaving Rain here, swelling the population. Perhaps when I return in a month, we'll find that this aberration, this Rain, has already disappeared. Despite our expectations to the contrary."

"*Levitated,*" said Scyrilla in a spooky tone. Lucikles hadn't known she was lurking nearby.

"Scram, you," said Helia as the Minor Adjutant closed his eyes again. Mortification was supposed to be good for the soul, but it felt like nausea.

"All right, I'll just *evaporate,*" muttered Scyrilla tauntingly, and made a kind of twirl on her toe, just as Lucikles's own young Poena might do.

Lucikles scratched an eyebrow, which perhaps was becoming weary of arching in surprise so repeatedly. "Dame Mirka, I will now ask you to give me a moment alone with the senior bride."

Mirka stood and bowed briefly to him but not, he noticed, to her superior. She left.

"Farther off," barked Helia. Mirka stomped up to the orchard in a rage.

"The thing is," said Helia, leaning forward and lowering her voice, "you and I know that Mirka is riven with an appetite for authority. She's always been like this. I fear her state of mind when she is given access to the key to the Vessel. What if she should forget she is only the chief guardian, and become exalted with the notion of such—such a totem? Inebriated by her elevation, undone by its significance?"

"Are you becoming crabbed and suspicious in your dotage, Dame Helia?"

"I will admit you this, Kerr Lucikles. A few days ago I spent a short while feigning a spell of thick-tongue. I watched and I listened. My fears were borne out. Mirka's devotion to duty is as real as mine, I give her that, but her singularity of focus is not. Should she ever fall prey to some temptation—to use the power of the amulet, to trade it to some successor of yours, or some unanticipated delegate more threatening than an off-color adolescent girl—I fear the sacred mission of Maracoor Spot would be placed in jeopardy."

"Is this an old woman's paranoia about death?" he asked. There, that was a stiletto to sink under the skin of her shaking wattles.

She was not set athwart by his strike. "Perhaps.

Let's not find out, though, shall we? Beg the Bvasil for permission to elevate one of the others in my place. If this is our final interview, I leave you with this counsel. It isn't a curse but a prophecy of a danger that I hope you can avert: keep Mirka from the position. It would destroy her and might do Maracoor grave damage as well."

He stood and made an unconvincing bow of respect to Dame Helia. "Come, Cur," he said.

"But we have your luncheon to serve," said Helia, making no effort to rise.

"I'm not hungry," he replied. "I'm leaving. Cur, come."

The offense he had taken was now public and rank. The brides stood back, uncertain of themselves. Usually they declaimed holy verses in an adenoidal monotone while he broke bread with Dame Helia. Being unstuck from protocol unnerved them. He didn't care. He didn't salute them or accept a blessing.

Putting out into the harbor, with the prow of the rowboat facing the open water, Lucikles couldn't help but focus on the diminishing temple on its mount, and at the ridge of cypresses closing in behind it. In this high noon light, he could see the green girl returning to the portico of the white stone structure. She stood out like a virus, like gleaming mold on the skin of an orange. She turned the brown and white brides disported around her into a setting, a housing against which she glistered.

He maneuvered around the clot of cork daubed with red to make it stand out in the blue-brown water. Even the misshapen buoy seemed castigatory, swiveling on its anchor as if to watch him, to make sure he was on his way back to the ship.

One way or the other, that green girl would have to be removed. His professional reputation depended on it.

2

The barque had swung around on its anchor, so its three masts now lined up one behind the other. The sails whispered and snapped and settled again. It looked like its own island, a small liveliness of brown and white in the field of cold and opaque blue, sharp spearheads of sunlight darting on the water all around it. The *Pious Enterprise* was well into her fourth decade and in keen fettle still, thanks to the harbor crew that managed the upkeep. Kept her ready to welcome even the august Bvasil of Maracoor, male avatar of the Great Mara, should he ever present himself. Which was unlikely.

The crew wasn't expecting Lucikles for several hours. The dozen and a half of them were likely tucking into lunch in the shadows of the staysail. No one was

leaning over the port side to lower the leather pouch
for Cur. Lucikles didn't holler for anyone. He tied up
the coracle to the trailing lines and tucked Cur into the
breast of his ocean coat. If a dog could purr, that would
be the sound Cur made when he found himself out of
the wind and close to Lucikles's heart. Then the overseer legged the gap to the side of the *Pious Enterprise,*
and he drew himself up the knotted ladder.

The wind caught him when he reached the taffrail,
as it often did, and without a crewman's arm to steady
him, he swayed. But while he had expected Cur to be
scratching to be released, the little dog kept silent in his
haven. Lucikles put down his satchel and crossed the
cedar deck between the accommodations fore and aft.

His guess had been correct. The crew was sprawled
in positions of repose around a mess of salted bread
and hard cheese, cured meats and oranges. One was
playing a guitar with a witless sense of timing. Herkile,
the timoneer, was enjoying the prodigal and welcome
sunlight, his right arm cast over his eyes. The crew
didn't hear Lucikles approach, they didn't see him.
They chattered on. He paused in the shadows, curious.
In that their work was to help him conduct his annual
review, they were answerable to him. Still, he was a
land man, a bureau chief, while they were men of the
moods of water and wind. The advantages of class and

profession could break either way, depending on how far from a harbor wharf they found themselves.

"Don't say that, he's not so bad," one of the fellows was remarking.

"He's a small portion of mere cabbage spooned on a golden plate; don't know how *he* earned the privilege."

Lucikles knew they were talking of him. Everyone else on the voyage was on deck and within his sight. He held back still.

"You see him plying his prayers of an evening? I pass his hammock on my way to the head. He's like an old woman, murmuring with his eyes closed."

"I murmur with my eyes closed in my hammock too, but it's not the gods I'm thinking about."

"What kind of a man visits an island of seven virgins and comes back as buttoned up as when he left?"

"We all know what kind of man manages such a trick, but Lucikles has got a wife and kids, so it's not that. Give him some credit. It's a boring job and he's not a firebrand." It was Herkile defending him, after a fashion. "His assignment gives us work, and so we get our weight of minastres from the scales when we drop anchor in home port. What is it? Does his very mildness scare you fellows somehow?"

"Nothing to fear, I'm back," Lucikles said jovially,

before this went on too long. He stepped into the light. Cur caught scent of sliced salted pork and he nosed his way out of the buttoned sea coat. Through what Lucikles had overheard, Captain Gargios Nitexos had remained silent, signaling neither agreement nor disapproval at the insolence.

"Ah," said Nitexos now, with a drawling calm, "you surprise us, Kerr Lucikles. You usually come late afternoon. I hope you found nothing to concern you?" The Captain didn't gesture for Lucikles to join them. Lucikles could guess why; his own quick return to deck provoked a fear he might be bringing on board a germ that had felled the population of Maracoor Spot. Such a disaster had been known to happen before. Some years back, that instance of the *Hind of the Sea*. When that luckless vessel had washed up on Ithira Strand, all hands were dead and the crew members black and pitted with decay. The recovered Captain's log had noted that in their putting into the harbor at Lesser Torn Isle, they'd found a population of rotting corpses, and no clue as to what had fallen from the sky or washed ashore to infect and fell all human life there.

Islands were their own worlds, like dreams and visions, like separate childhoods.

"Everything in order, all seven alive and accounted

for," said Lucikles. "We're fine to set for the mainland. That was the last of my missions, and it's completed earlier than usual. Be grateful for that. Nothing to worry about. We can turn sail for home."

"You mean before we've finished breaking our fast?" asked Nitexos.

"Enjoy your bite. I'll have nothing, I'm surfeited," said Lucikles. Having skipped the meal offered by the brides, in fact he was famished. But his sense of personal dignity had been roused. Let them make faces behind his back as he passed them to head for the locker where he stored his notes. "Come, Cur," he said to his boon companion, but the dog chose instead to linger in the neighborhood of possible tidbits.

Whatever outbreak of pique or ridicule he'd witnessed, it had subsided by first bell, when those who rested first had settled into the warm and noxious dark. Lucikles swung there too, a sweaty lump of middle-aged man in his porous cocoon.

Damn, he couldn't turn to his prayers. Those snarky remarks must have hit home.

So he relied upon his other evening mental exercise. Tonight it was a pleasure more than usual. After the aborted inspection of the brides upon Maracoor Spot, his tour of duty was complete. The *Pious Enter-*

prise, even now, was prow-bent for Maracoor Abiding at last.

Every night of the past eleven weeks before going to sleep—or, if in stormy seas, lying awake lurching and dizzy in his hammock—he had spun visions of his wife and children and their home in the capital city, Maracoor Crown. It kept him sane.

But tonight, now that there was nothing left ahead of him but home port, he indulged in a review of his journey. Mostly to postpone the greatest pleasure of this mental meander: the thought of home.

They had slipped from the quay all those weeks ago in the teeth of a late winter freshet, icy rain and indecisive winds requiring the maneuvering of sails with exhaustive attention. He'd been sick upon the launch, which wasn't common for him; Lucikles prided himself on his seaworthiness. But by the time they'd reached the first island, North Orgole, he'd recovered. From the governor of North Orgole, a patient if idiotic grandfatherly type, Lucikles had received tribute, and then he'd dispensed blessings and eighteen kegs of harmseed oil.

On for two weeks in the anonymous sea, nothing but stars and hunches and an inferior old-style astrolabe by which to steer. But Captain Gargios Nitexos was a cunning man, and his instincts stood in when the skies were clouded. The *Pious Enterprise* was scarcely a day behind schedule putting into Skeleton Harbor, the only navigable port on the hulking landmass of Great Northern Isle.

Lucikles in his hammock lingered over memories of the blandishments of Great Northern: the hot apple wines with butter, the sweet cream delicacies of a dessert buffet. The formality of the colonists in their gold braid and promenades and quadrilles. The concerts in that gilded corridor of crystal lancets, all the scented powder and pomp incapable of cloaking the elemental hardiness of this population. These people didn't merely survive; they thrived in perhaps the harshest climate in all of Maracoor and its outposts.

The Great Northerners were proud. They were also independently minded; the size of their landmass and abundance of natural resources afforded them this. They emphasized their particularity by insisting on local customs. It was always a gas, though the Minor Adjutant could get tired of observing their traditions. The *Pious Enterprise* harbored ten days or so in Great Northern while Lucikles traveled to four or five of the midsize towns higher up and inland, to see if rebellion against the governor was in lively or quiescent mode. For his daughter Poena, Lucikles had found a beautiful painted doll made of jointed porcelain limbs and cornflax hair. When secured by the iron stand it came with, the toy would stand as high as Poena's waist. For Star he had picked up a stuffed plush silkie, that creature with a seal face and a mermaid's tail. For Leorix, bless him, a small dirk in a leathern scabbard decorated with Great Northern runes. Lucikles couldn't wait to deliver all his presents, and to greet his fond and reliable wife.

He would not soon sleep tonight, he could tell. The humiliation of having been bested on Maracoor Spot by the brides and the green visitor burned in him still. So, having started now in reverie of his recent journeys, he continued, as slowly as possible, dragging it out.

He retraced his steps from the heights of Great Northern Isle back to Skeleton Harbor. The port itself was a virtual city of swaying masts and clapping sails. Through the congestion of ships one couldn't see from one side of the U-shaped harbor to the other.

That tedious final banquet at which Lucikles gave a tedious farewell address, nearly verbatim to the one he delivered every year. No one minded because no one listened.

The *Pious Enterprise* left Skeleton Harbor on a morning of brisk running winds and hail-hero light. Whether Lucikles and Gargios Nitexos breathed deeper sighs of relief or the addled governor did—for having side-stepped any incendiary incident of one sort or another during the annual visit—there was no saying. The Great

Northerners took honor to extremes, and dying by duel was second only to frostbite as the highest cause of death among men over the age of fourteen.

For days the ship heaved around the upper edge of Great Northern Isle. Despite his annual survey of that vast and forested land, Lucikles was always shocked anew by the reaches of wildness and the icy casing that made those deepwater coves unnavigable.

Once in a while the travelers spied the candle-gleam of a lighthouse on a spit of treacherous coast. The satisfaction of knowing there was human life even across the reaches of cold water was assuring at the moment. But how keen human self-knowledge could be, that there was even a word in sailing argot to describe the feeling of despair and loneliness experienced when a ship sailed beyond the last lighthouse, even if into safer waters. That word, *ephrarxis,* from a nearly extinct language once widely used in the Hyperastrich Archipelago, had come into colloquial use as a way of expressing the kind of regret one feels at passing a simpatico stranger on a pavement or in a café. The life we might have lived together, O passing stranger. Ephrarctic moment. (Often followed up by a stiff drink.) Nostalgia for something that never had been.

Lucikles had missed the several lighthouses this trip, by dint of the cycle of winds and sleep schedule.

He took his turns on deck every fourth night. Though he was useless at sails or navigation, he helped out by talking other sailors into staying awake at their posts.

Once Great Northern Isle was a disappearing smudge in the horizon, the *Pious Enterprise* tacked across the doldrums of the outer calm. Some years it could take half a month to traverse, and Lucikles then would be that much later getting home. This year luck was with them. They made it in a little more than a week. When the citadel of Panic was spotted—a weird stylite pillar of an island, with its rabid monks and rancid wine and its rabble of heretics and mystics—Lucikles knew that whether unpleasant or rewarding, the remaining stops on his mission would come more quickly. The worst of tedium was behind him until his final northwestward voyage from Maracoor Spot to Maracoor Abiding.

Panic Island, he told himself, ticking it off on the itinerary, but he didn't bother to summon up into memory the wild-eyed patriarchs and penitents who thronged like brigands up and down the punishing steep trails. Panic Island, then Lesser Panic. Soon enough: Trosse, and Antitrosse, and Penultimate Trosse. (Ultimate Trosse had disappeared under the waves a century earlier, but no one wanted to change the names of the islands—who wants to claim the ultimate island as home?)

How welcome, the entangled canals of Astrich itself, its nearly numberless hillocks among brackeny marshes no longer certifiably original or constructed—each canal dug out gave foundation to the next landmass of private holding. The reef that surrounded Astrich, the capital city of the Hyperastrich Archipelago, made such civil engineering possible, though if the gods grew annoyed at the rearrangement of their world and eventually smote the reef with a storm from the south, which had never yet happened, goodbye to the spun-sugar pillars and the private water gardens and the balconies and the local singing of romantic lullabies, and to the happy exercise of ephrarxis in all its poignant pleasures.

Tonight Lucikles didn't indulge in the recollection of his four nights in Astrich and the accommodating woman who'd shrugged and said why not and stayed with him. It didn't award her any kind of social cachet to sleep with the Minor Adjutant from Maracoor Abiding. The Astrichians, like the staunch residents of Great Northern Isle, thought themselves well above the boorish powers that governed them from the mainland. The Astrichians were fascinatingly polite, scholarly, insolent, and dismissive all at once. In Astrich, alone of any port on his journey, Lucikles had always found he could manage to be a private citizen, or nearly. He didn't pay for the woman's company. He didn't know if she had a husband or kids on some plop of an island a half hour away. She was there, merely and fully. She did her nails in the light coming over the balcony rails, she sang a little bit and brought pastries and wine from the market. She was talented in bed and not demanding. She relished clove cigarettes, to whose smoke he had proven allergic, but to find at least something unpleasant in this interlude made him recognize it wasn't a daydream, but an interlude of middle-aged life, such as one might read about in memoirs. If one were a reader. Which Lucikles was not, particularly, and especially not on board ship. It made him sick to read on a rocking vessel.

After saying goodbye to—well, he'd choose not to remember her name, out respect for his wife—after saying goodbye to the energetic companion and reboarding the *Pious Enterprise*, he'd fallen into a mild state of something he jokingly named to himself antiephrarxis. The regret you feel when you *don't* pass up the beautiful stranger, and it still isn't, ultimately, lifechanging or even terribly rewarding. When you come right down to it. He'd stayed in his berth longer than usual, more than a day, feigning a stomach thing, but it was a disconsolation of the spirit. He often experienced something like this midway through his mission. It didn't always have to do with taking a lover. Regret could disguise itself in a thousand veils; you could perish before having the strength to drag the last one away.

The Hyperastrich Archipelago spun itself out in a long series of fingerlike islands, configured upon the ocean in the same way that a dashed paintbrush can sprawl a trail of dots much the same general shape, if varying in size and in distance one from the next. There were four subsequent towns to visit, whose names Lucikles could never keep straight because they were so alike. On the last island a curse of some sort had rendered all the inhabitants blind, and no intrepid travelers would intermarry with them. The population was dying out, but more slowly than Lucikles might have imagined, as one thing that blind people could apparently manage to do as well as anyone else is sleep together. Lucikles hated visiting the tiny two-vessel port of that harbor more than anyplace else on his trip, but it was his job to check on the production of poxite in the mines that snaked well below sea level on the island's far side. Another thing the blind can do fairly well, he learned, at least these Hyperastrichians, was to mine poxite, whose presence was detectable by a certain sulfury odor.

Leaving the Archipelago behind, the *Pious Enterprise* then steered southeast. The crew was accustomed to finding this leg of the journey a breeze along the apron folds of a steadily brightening and more cerulean sea. The sun strengthened by dint of latitude and also the season.

Usually. But this year an army of belligerent winds swept up from the south. The ship fought the resistance of a dry but ominously clouded atmosphere far longer than usual. It was five, maybe six days before the *Pious Enterprise* found the climate returning to its ordinary ease.

As he swung in his truss of netting, Lucikles relived those final days of making easy progress though hospitable seas to the farthest outpost island in the maritime provinces, Maracoor Spot. Fish grew more colorful. Schools of golden spangles and emerald, dolphins carving rings into the air around the *Pious Enterprise* on all sides. The water even smelled different, to Lucikles anyway. Less rank, sweeter somehow, though it was still salt.

Then the anchoring off Maracoor Spot, and the coracle into the harbor, and the interview with the chief bride. The counting of the brides and a hasty glance at the Vessel, to make sure it was intact and untroubled, and the amulet still locked inside.

The only tribute he received from the brides was the same they gave to the nation—that ritual harvesting of time in benefit of the whole world. If they served him a meal, it was only common courtesy. He did his job. He counted the brides. Upon his return he delivered his account to his superiors. Sometimes when it was necessary he returned a month later with a baby bride to replace one who had passed away since last year. There must always be seven brides. He didn't know why. Perhaps because there were seven days in a week, more or less. Maybe it was as simple as that.

Lucikles tried not to think of the interloper, that green girl, that Rain Creature. Though she wouldn't easily be unseen.

Still, here he was, rocking in his hammock, finally reunited to himself, memory joined to the present moment. Except for the unseasonable storm from the south, it hadn't been a difficult trip. He'd recorded no assassinations of tribal leaders or elected officials. He'd witnessed no murders of crew members in pub brawls (that seemed to happen every second or third year). He had not fallen ill. Except for that aberration on Maracoor Spot, no one in the islands had proven substantially different from how they'd seemed last year. There'd been no murmuring of mutiny.

So now, having delayed his pleasure for so long, he allowed himself to imagine forward. The next eight days rolling out under warm spring skies. Pray the gods: no thunderstorms on this leg of the trip—bad weather on the homeward leg of a journey gave the superstitious crew the collywobbles.

Lucikles put off picturing the final approach, trying not to rush it. Extending the foreplay, as it were, before breaching the harbor. He lingerered instead on the sight of the mainland at last, off the port side as they sailed northwest. How it grew from an undecipherable smudge into specificity as they approached. Great beech forests below, the rockier highlands beyond, bare and goat haunted. Then the first few fishing ports, and the scatter of whitewashed houses, built leaning close to one another like sheep around a crib. The occasional smokehouse a bit farther along the shore, close enough for convenience but distant for stink. Little by little the villages became towns, and then around the elbow of the Orageous Promontory, and slipping into the harbor at last. Though noticed by the harbormaster, of course, who would signal with a pennant which berth the pilot should take, the *Pious Enterprise* would otherwise be just another anonymous ship jostling into this largest and busiest of all known harbors. (The pilot would be white with nerves for all the traffic.)

It would take clerks an hour to do the paperwork, and in that time, news of the ship's docking would have gone out to the legislative courts and to his home up in the garden neighborhood of Piney Quarter, near Temple Houranos. By the time the wayfarers were given leave to disembark, dear Oena might be in the sunlight or huddled in the covered shelter, with Leorix beaming at her hip, and Poena at her other hip, and little Star fussing in her arms to be allowed *down* so she could run meet her papa. Her flyaway blond hair a nimbus, suggestive of that sanctity of childhood when childhood wasn't in its demonic mode.

The cost of this happy vision was the acid twinge of anxiety. What if something had happened in eleven weeks? Though hardly a long time in the life of a marriage (except at first), that much time was forever in the life of a child. One year while he was away, Star had gone from being a sucking infant to a chattering baby gibbon.

Poena would have a new comb or a new hair-twist of some sort or another, and he must remember to notice and comment.

And Leorix, sweet Leorix. Growing in inches and pride at this stage. The boy's chin had been smooth and his voice still tenor when Lucikles had left, but already his son's limbs had begun to lengthen and his boyish fat to evaporate. In this passage toward manhood, a boy needed his father more than ever, even while rejecting help ever more fervently. Each year Lucikles's chief

worry about his annual mission was that in his absence
the boy would have outgrown his father, would be un-
recognizable, perhaps unrecoverable. Established too
much independence. There would be no winning him
back.

The rest of the Minor Adjutant's anticipations faded
away. All he could see in the dark bolt of sleep closing
in on him was his family approaching from the quay-
side wooden shelter with open arms, bright smiles, their
unity another kind of lighthouse on the horizon.

Two or maybe three days still to go, the *Pious Enterprise* was visited by a shocking storm of birds. Proof
that landfall was imminent. Usually this was a terrific relief. The land birds who sung the returning
ships to harbor were considered emissaries from one
of the sky gods. The old legends of the harpies and
the paxitreen, those scolds and saints of fate, vari-
ously, had probably grown out of the thrill ancient
sailors had felt upon seeing proof of the mainland.

But this visitation of pale blue songbirds was arrest-
ingly strange. These were not the gulls or the terns, or
wheat-ears, or swallows. They weren't in numbers of
a dozen or so, a flitch off the larger flock. Those more
usual emissaries were upland birds from the eight hills
that made a semicircle around Maracoor Crown, birds

that commonly scissored about in pairs or quartets. This conclave of songbirds from a higher elevation—what were they called, no seaman could remember, were these cloud-birds, maybe, because their feathers were cloudy blue-white?—arrived in a number of several hundred. They crowded on the ratlines and the rigging. Their signature call, pretty when heard as a duet or a chamber piece, was raucous when broadened into an oratorio chorus. That they shat the deck slippery was the least of it. They were prophecy, they were augury, they were a mob shrieking alarm or common grief.

Captain Nitexos did his best to quell the superstition that gripped the crew, and Lucikles, too, though he tried not to show it. The sailors could scarcely hear themselves over the cloud-bird din. For more than a day the avian assembly swooped and circled the ship, a twittering density that matched the ship's steady pace across the water. Finally Gargios Nitexos had the huge iron laundry kettle hoisted up from below-decks. There was no bricking upon the deck for the safe building of an open fire, so Nitexos ordered kindling and charcoal stacked in the kettle itself, and lit. As the smoke grew stronger the birds began to fly more madly about. When more than half of them were aloft at once, some unidentifiable ringleader turned west, and enough of them followed that it suddenly became an emigration. They departed as quickly as they had arrived. The silence they left behind was unnerving in itself. Nitexos ordered the fire kept lit for a few hours, but when there was no sign of a return of the cloud-birds, he had it extinguished.

For a day, things returned to normal. The sailors began to arrange their kit sacks, readying for a quick scattering toward their families, perhaps, or away from the law, once the vessel had docked and the salaries were doled out.

Finally, at dawn, when the winds were just so from the west, the first aroma of earth arrived. Forest breath of balsam and perhaps even sweet flaxflower of the meadowland. The horizon couldn't yet be seen but the birds and the scent of fauna had done the trick. The travelers were close, and closing in.

The great height, Mount Ontexos, showed its broken shoulders at last, and a cheer went up. It was only a matter of hours before the green of woodlands skirting the ocean would become visible to the naked eye. The *Pious Enterprise* drew in to hug the shore as near as possible. Only Gargios Nitexos had a spy-glass, and he husbanded it jealously, occasionally scaling to the crow's nest himself to give a report. This was the best part of his job every year, and one he cherished. If he wanted to command a good crew next time out, he needed to leave this crew happy as they disembarked. Word got around. He knew how to do this.

But his reports were terse today. "We're making good time," he would say, "better than usual, perhaps." The mutterings of the crew put this skeptical tone down to the Captain's having been spooked by the ambush of the cloud-bird chorus. They kept to their work with renewed initiative, polishing every fixture and swabbing every inch of decking so as to deserve a bonus if the Captain and the receiving Board of Governors were pleased with their service.

Lucikles tried to suppress the growing unease he felt. Suddenly the arrival of the green girl upon Maracoor Spot and the subsequent interruption of normalcy by the cloud-birds seemed of a piece. You're falling prey to the superstitions of the uneducated, he told himself; get a better hold upon your emotions, man. You aren't a teenage girl or an old monk screwing his one good eye for messages from divinity in the chicken entrails. You're a man of some learning. You rely on reason. Not the ineffable pox of mood.

But he stood as close to the rail as any of the men who were not on post, longing for the land as it steadily became clearer in outline.

"Better speed than usual, today," announced Captain Nitexos. "That southeasterly wind, which may have riled up the cloud-birds, is now doing us a service. Instead of arriving at dawn tomorrow, we may well arrive late afternoon this very day. All hands on deck for final review."

Lucikles went below to finish his own packing. He wouldn't shave until the ship had berthed. In the hour that the paperwork and inspections took, and because the ship would be relatively still at last, he would risk the razor.

Matters took a creepier turn when the *Pious Enterprise* drew close enough to the shore—at the Orageous Promontory—so the monument to the godlings of the currents appeared in its severe lines of pale marble. The temple was the first sign of built civilization that ships returning from the southern reaches ever spotted, and often at this moment in the voyage, a keg of better brew, reserved for the occasion, was tapped and drained dry. Today, however, the roof of the Promontory Oratory, as it was affectionately known, seemed not its usual verdigris but an odd, muted brown. The body scent of homeland wafted even stronger here. The better noses among the sailors could detect the decay of leaves from last autumn, and mud from snow-melt, as well as new growth and sexy bloom. It was intoxicating, but the adjustment to the look of the Oratory disconcerted everyone, Lucikles included.

Then the roof flew off—or seemed to. It was another flock of birds, a different sort. It swarmed like evacuees from a beehive. Out over the water. The birds veered to the south and then approached the *Pious Enterprise* on the strong wind, gaining in speed. The first birds to reach the sails smacked into them, as if they were flying blind, and eight or ten fell to the deck, senseless.

They were owls. A parliament of owls. This wasn't the time for owls to flock, not in mating season, and anyway, owls usually avoided any water deeper than a puddle. They had no defenses if they settled in water; they couldn't propel themselves out again. "We're cursed," barked a sailor, and others took up the cry. They began to swing at the owls, who showed no sign of malice. Just, perhaps, a kind of need for human company?

It was too much work to haul up the iron kettle again to try to smoke the parliament away. In any case, it was unnecessary. The owls seemed to sense the cold reception they were getting, and they didn't alight the way the cloud-birds had. They just circled the masts of the *Pious Enterprise,* hooting as they flew. This too was unusual—owls in flight kept silent, as a policy, so as not to alert their prey, and probably to save their breath, too. They were known only to broadcast a sound when encountering an enemy they wanted to scare away.

The sailor who brought forward this gem of bird lore managed to grab one of the owls that had stunned itself on a mast and fallen to the deck. Though it was still alive, it was a little dazed. This sailor—a strapping kid named Chorkos—grabbed the bird around its talons, pinning them with the strong grip of his right hand. With his other hand he gripped the bird's head from the back of the skull so it couldn't pivot and bite him. "Bring a coal, we'll show them," he yelled, and others saw the sense of it at once, though not Lucikles.

Someone hurried up from below with a copper soup pan and its lid, and a couple of hot coals from the kitchen stove smoking within it. That seaman smashed the bird's face with the lid of the soup pan, and Chorkos forced the bird into the basin of the pan. The lid clapped upon it; the bird beat and screamed and burned to death.

At this, the owls abandoned the *Pious Enterprise,* all at once, flying behind the ship. The Orageous Promontory was already receding, out of sight. Whether the parliament was returning to the temple of the godlings or fleeing to someplace safer, none could venture a guess.

Now the shore of Maracoor Abiding would unfold in its holy beauty. At midday the sky was nearly cloudless.

Creamy in its tenderness, the light seemed investigative of every budding tree and rocky outcrop. Occasionally a clot of midges would appear and then disperse, more fullness from the land. Evidence of fecundity, of all the alarum and hubbub of spring. The far tableland of High Chora to the west etched a pale blue wainscoting above the shoreline.

The travelers caught sight of that stretch of homeland where the forests fell back, and the first villages to the south of the capital city began to show, hunched at the shore, their docks with their paws in the water like beavers washing their catch. The villages were low and humble, in whitewashed or rye-flour-colored stone. While fishing vessels close to shore were in slighter number than customary at this time of year, from this distance it looked like business as usual, more or less. For too brief a moment, the sailors realized in retrospect, they relaxed. It would be the last they knew of calm for some time.

When the *Pious Enterprise* veered easterly to accommodate the raw protrusions of rock known as the Stripes, for how they made narrow, parallel streaks in the relentless tides, the voyagers were out of sight of the mainland for another hour. Rounding the last of the Stripes, they would tack across the swift north-running current in a series of three or four maneuvers, positioning to come about at the right moment and slip in the deep but snug harbor of Maracoor Abiding. Done badly, they'd have to reposition to the south and try again. In a tough wind it could take all day. In tougher, they might go aground and join the carcasses of shipwrecks on North Tooth, as it was called. Today the weather was challenging though not impossible.

Having sensed something untoward all day, they now could smell it. At first it seemed a mockery, a return of the stench of charred owl. But this new affront was deeper, a downright scorch. Coiling over the tapering ridges of the Stripes to greet the *Pious Enterprise,* the foul and smoldering air seemed an omen of disaster. The sailors ceased their chatter. Captain Nitexos lit his pipe, as if he could singlehandedly annul the reek from the mainland. The tendril of cherry tobacco, however, proved nothing but a joke.

Then the noble profile of the capital city of Maracoor came into sight, Maracoor Crown, like a courtesan waking and rubbing her kohl-smeared eyes. Acrid smoke wafted horizontally, black bandages unraveling. Thicker at harbor level, more tentative the farther upslope. The domes of the House of Rule were smeared to the eye but seemed undamaged, lapis blue and silver. Shiny baubles found on a corpse, Lucikles found himself thinking. But it can't be as bad as that.

The harbor, usually busy at this time of day with shipping vessels returning before the fall of dark, was ghostwater.

Captain Nitexos bit the end of his pipe clean off and threw both pieces overboard. "We're coming into the harbor of a place we do not know," he said with unusual clarity of tone. "We'll take the precautions we take whenever we make landfall in a strange harbor. Men of Maracoor, to your posts."

Lucikles had no post. He picked up Cur and cuddled him. No one onshore was raising a pennant to direct the *Pious Enterprise* to an assigned berth. There was no sound from Maracoor Crown at all but the clang of harbor bells and the shriek of seagulls.

The crew worked with an efficiency and precision beyond any they had demonstrated for the past eleven weeks. The *Pious Enterprise* swung about like oiled clockworks. The ship zigzagged to accommodate the play of tide and of winds, and cleared the North Tooth, Lucikles thought, almost with an air of insouciance. There being so little harbor traffic, the *Pious Enterprise* pivoted to sail parallel to the wharfs and the quay, the better for Captain Nitexos and the others to survey what was going on.

But what had happened wasn't expressly clear,

except that the capital city of the country seemed largely emptied of its population. Here and there, a man with a wheelbarrow or a woman with a passel of children running behind her, or a few men conferring in the waning sunlight. Several had their arms in slings or their heads in bandages. They paid so little attention to the *Pious Enterprise* that the ship might as well be invisible. In ordinary days few would be hailing a returning ship anyway, not in a harbor as busy as Maracoor Crown's, but in this day of silence Lucikles would have expected some gesture of welcome. Or warning. Something. The small number of citizens present had other matters on their mind, it seemed.

Or perhaps the cursed crew upon the ship had become invisible.

But this was dream logic, and he dismissed it. Anyway, just then Cur barked once and a dog onshore turned and barked back, so that finished the matter.

Gargios Nitexos found a pier left of center that was clear of commerce and traffic, and the pilot stabilized the *Pious Enterprise* in place. Since there seemed to be no wharf crew to rope them in, the Captain ordered the lowering of a lifeboat, and four sailors rowed in to perform the necessaries. When they were ready, the ship came about. No harbormaster with his manifest and his documents was standing ready to interview the

Captain. So Nitexos just alighted and looked about. The crew, used to an hour's embargo, broke protocol and swarmed the ladders, but on the wharf they huddled together, afraid of breaking up and going their separate ways—especially before being paid.

Lucikles joined them with Cur. He carried his diplomatic pouch, his personal kit, and the roped bundle of souvenirs for his wife and children. He was unshaven and unkempt, a disgrace to the government. But there was no one to report him, and he didn't want to remain onboard alone.

"We'll walk the wharf till we can find someone to tell us what has happened," the Captain said to the Minor Adjutant, and they set off on their land legs.

Close up, the government and commercial district, Maracoor Centre, showed little sign of damage—no torched buildings—but the evidence suggested a rapid evacuation. Some waterfront buildings stood with windows and doors open wide, signs of looting or even scavenging. By humans, maybe, but also by dogs or gibbons. The shutters of most buildings were secured though, and unbreached.

Scat everywhere. The most evident life was cats, for cats refused to comply with instructions in the best of times, and they saw to their own safety faster than the ordinary human narcissist could blink. Neighborhood cats padded along, as if open for business as usual, though Lucikles thought he noticed a feral suspicion deeper than usual in their daggered eyes.

It was hard for Lucikles to add everything up, and harder still for the quarter-sawn-oak sailors, over whom phantoms and the minor deities held more sway. Captain Nitexos glanced at Lucikles.

The Minor Adjutant squared his shoulders. "I'll find out what has happened and come back the moment I do," he said. "Captain, will you stay with your men?"

"I'll come with you," said Nitexos.

"Then you, too, Chorkos," said Lucikles, selecting the beefiest and least merciful of the younger men. "We may not go out of your sight, or we might," he continued to the rest of the crew. "In any case, guard the *Pious Enterprise* and wait for our return. Do not break company."

The men weren't inclined to obey him; many had family in town, or women anyway. But Captain Gargios Nitexos stopped their muttering with a shorthand command. Lucikles, Nitexos, and Chorkos walked the length of the pier and crossed the cobbles of the quay to the promenade along the curved harbor. "We saw stray indigents, we saw walking casualties," said Nitexos. "Where are they?"

Maracoor Centre was built for crowds. A half-dozen

market plazas opened one upon the other. Lucikles led his two companions through an arcade, past a parade of boarded-up shops and private concerns, until they rounded a corner into the largest open square, Government Agora. The quiet of it, the emptiness at this hour, spoke of slaughter or plague. Still, there was no smell but that of smoke and of such rotting food as dogs and monkeys and birds hadn't yet fallen upon.

"By the spears of Mirinos, we are surrounded by death," said Chorkos, and made peasant gestures to ward off evil.

"There's a noise down that alley, a human voice," said Lucikles drily. "Let's find out who has something to say."

They walked a few feet apart, as if striding a polished corridor toward an appointment in the law courts. Such insouciance, so false; he felt the right fool.

The alley yielded to a dead-end courtyard. A wretched toss of jumbled junk. By an open door, a middle-aged man in blacksmith's leathers sat on a stool in the light, talking to himself and testing for balance a delicate hinged utensil of some sort. Cur's nose went into spasms at the thrill of it all.

The blacksmith didn't look up at them when they hailed him, at first, and when he did, he seemed not to see them. His eyes were red-rimmed and crusted with gunk. When he spoke, it was gibberish. He wasn't quite addressing them, Lucikles guessed. "We are newly arrived," said the Minor Adjutant with what he hoped was authority. "We've come from abroad, to find our home in strange guise. Nothing is right. What has happened?"

The blacksmith babbled some nursery jingo. His eyes leaked; he wiped his forearm against them, which seemed to drive more smut and ash against his eyelids; they watered some more.

Captain Nitexos said, "Chorkos, find some wine inside; there must be a cupboard." Chorkos did as he was told in short order, and brought out a beaker of sour yellow plonk reeking of pine resin and dust.

The blacksmith took a cup of it but dashed it onto the ground. "Nothing here is safe to eat or drink," he said. At least he didn't throw it upon us, thought Lucikles, and then remembered he had in his own pouch a flask of better brandy from Great Northern Isle.

"I've brought this from over the water." Lucikles handed the small flask and hoped the blacksmith would neither smash it nor empty the whole amount into his mouth. It was good stuff, both rare and dear. "This is clean and it will help."

The blacksmith sniffed it—plum and pistachio at its base, if Lucikles's own palate was reliable—and the blacksmith took a sip. He scowled but took a longer swig. Then he handed the bottle back. Lucikles pocketed it without passing it around further.

The blacksmith sniffed a couple of times and rubbed his eyes.

"You're not about to lop off my head if you offer me a swallow of that," he conceded. He studied them a little more rigorously.

"We're in from the islands. What are we finding here? What happened, and when? Where is everyone?"

The blacksmith shook his head and puffed out his lips, trying to get the enormity of it into some sentence to start. The Captain said, "Quick, man!" but Lucikles stayed any further remark with a slice of his hand.

"When?" asked the Minor Adjutant. He hoped a short question would be easier to answer. "How long ago?"

"Eight days," said the man, "nine, ten. I'm not sure."

"What happened first?"

"It was just toward the end of that storm from the south, whenever that was. Did you get that monster far out to sea the way we did here?"

Lucikles glanced at Nitexos and they nodded. "We got something," said Nitexos. Lucikles remembered the spell of foul weather, broken only as they were approaching Maracoor Spot. Yes, ten days ago, if the weather had behaved itself here the same as across those hundreds of miles.

"What happened first?" said Lucikles again.

"Attack just before dawn. Before the fishing fleet was out. A navy appeared at the mouth of the harbor and positioned itself there somehow. I don't know how, the winds were terrific."

The words were intelligible but the thought was not. "A naval fleet?" Captain Nitexos's tone was nearly mocking. "A *military* fleet? From where?"

"Far as anyone could tell, someplace south. The winds were blowing from the south. They must have sped a fleet so quickly north that it passed any lookouts on the southern cliffs under cover of darkness. Had to be the south. No fleet coming from the north could have made headway in that gale."

"The Lomarians? They couldn't launch a tin boat in a hip bath. They're agrarian but for their love of smelts."

"Not Lomarians—some more distant people. The like we've never seen before. Pale and evil—long legged, big bellied, bearded, and fanged."

This sounded the stuff of nightmares, not testimony, but Lucikles rolled his hand: give us more.

"They surprised the city at dawn. Two or three advance vessels were equipped with catapults. They attacked us with flaming shot. The first two volleys sank most of the fishing fleet and quite a bit of the coast patrol. If you just came into the harbor today, you sailed over the flesh of fishermen and the bones of their boats."

"The alarm—?" asked Nitexos.

"Raised too late, and too confused."

"And—where is everyone?"

"Dead. Dead, or fled. We would all be dead but for a miscalculation. The marauders didn't account for the slackened winds once they could venture between the North Tooth and the South. They aimed their second volley to the south of the city centre, probably expecting the gale would correct its course and land it squarely on the government buildings. But the winds had died down and the trajectory was more true than they'd figured. The south-end warehouses and the abattoir district took the brunt of it."

"And then?"

"They came ashore. They had short iron daggers for the fist, and glaives with serrated blades that they could heave from the forearm. They ran people through, they sliced throats."

"They were after the treasury? The senators? Did they kill the Bvasil?"

"No one interviewed them about their aims and ambitions in life." The kick of the liquor was settling in, good. "The Bvasil and his guards fled before the palace could be breached. But to those of us lucky enough to stay hid, and there are more of us here than you probably spied, it seemed they were concentrated on breaching the armory."

"The armory."

"They broke down its doors with a battering ram. They didn't stay long. Either they found what they wanted or they didn't, but they were gone by midafternoon. The quays and the docks were pooled with blood. We who remained have been tipping bodies into a pit to the south of the city and burning them." He held up the implement he'd been forging. "This is a pincers for extracting gold teeth from the dead. No, we don't steal them; we give them to the survivors, if they have brought their corpses in for burial."

"Why didn't you flee yourself?"

"For what?" said the blacksmith. "I had a woman but she was a cheat. She cheated on me by sleeping with her husband. I was glad to see them both receive their due."

"Everyone can't have died," said Lucikles. He was unbuckling at the knees now, his resolve eroding.

"Of course not. People have an instinct. The roads

out were massed with fleeing cowards. Those who had carts and whips made better time. Much the greater part of the city escaped death, I'd wager. But they've dispersed. Some come creeping back to collect valuables and run away again."

"Did they leave a message, do you know?" asked the Captain. "The invaders?"

"Am I ambassador?" said the blacksmith. "They left no message with *me*."

"And you don't know who they were or what they wanted."

"I don't. They came from the south, at least that is what we have to suppose, given the winds. They were pale the way southerners can be, though they didn't resemble Lomarians, nor the clans of the Pomiole Estuary. Though perhaps they were distant relatives of the Pomiole peoples. They had wide jaws and thin lips."

"We'd better get back to our men," said Captain Nitexos. "They'll need to know all this, and decide for themselves what to do."

"You both go back, and luck to you," Lucikles replied. "But I'll want to know where to find you, Captain—I mean, supposing I need to make a return visit to Maracoor Spot a month out, as we sometimes do."

"Luck will allow you to find me or not," said Nitexos. "In any case, who knows if we'll have a crew or a ship or a capital city at our disposal when that moment comes. The fates alone decide. I'll try to leave word about my whereabouts in the harbormaster's cabin if it's still there—I didn't even notice. Where are you going? And what about your clobber on the quay?"

"Take it, put it in storage if you can, give it to someone, leave it there, anything," said Lucikles. He began to back away.

"Where are you going? Where will I find you?"

"My family," he said, no longer able to control the gasp. "My own . . ." He rounded himself on a heel and took off, his mission for the House of Balances abandoned.

Piney Quarter, in the district of Temple Houranos, was a densely built neighborhood on the slopes due west of the harbor. In good days it was a thirty-five minute stroll from the heart of the city centre. He made it in fifteen. It was the nicest of the midrange neighborhoods because the Temple stood in a substantial park, amidst a spring and some bosky dells and dramatic protrusions of rock. The lanes nearby, though narrow, allowed for slender cedars and poplars as well as the spreading canopies of salt tamarix, so Temple Houranos—as the quarter was called—was shadier and cooler at midday than much of the city. And less trafficked. A donkey and a narrow cart could get along, but any carriage drawn by a pair of horses had to pause on the gravelly aprons of Temple Houranos to await or discharge its passenger there.

Lucikles's own house, if small for five people, was smart and shipshape, with the benefit of a tidy front garden and side terrace. Not to mention out back, a walled courtyard in the crook of the building's L shape. Whitewashed. Fitted with green-grey, sun-battered shutters his family kept closed against the sun and open at night for the breeze. The overhanging, shallow roof bright with tiles of native orange clay. In ordinary time the whole ensemble would be dashed with the color of spring pansies and early dill and lavender, life immortal, in pots standing on doorsteps and windowsills.

He had become more aware of human activity as he pounded his way up the switchbacks of the Great Evening Road. People lurked behind shutters, disappeared at the sound of his approach. They *were* here. Perhaps more of them than the blacksmith had even realized. But they were staying hid, at least in daylight. He could hear the sound of cisterns being pumped, of someone sweeping, of others wailing quietly. He saw no one. The pretense was of total abandonment of Maracoor Crown.

He veered left off the Great Evening Road and began the zigzag approach to Temple Houranos. Of the commercial corners serving the residential area— everything locked and boarded up. No barrels of olives on a merchant's doorstep, no crates of persimmon or apricot, no tankards of salted goat cheese or corked cruets of olive oil. He approached an old woman on a bench. She was talking to herself and fingering prayer tablets strung on a coil of bailing twine. He nodded at her as if it was an ordinary evening and he was returning to his family. She looked up and said, "You again?" and then began to sing to herself in an obscure tongue. Some peasant grandmother come down from the hills and stuck in her children's home, no doubt, and unable to see the need to keep out of sight. Her feet were hardened, a lifetime in the orchards and fields, and he wanted to kiss them. He passed by without doing that.

At the park, he saw some goats from the uplands who had wandered into the strange quiet of the city. They were nibbling at ornamental shrubs and drinking from the Fountain of Dread Need, and standing on the stone walls and the steps of the Temple like guard dogs. Survivors ready to rule in the next age of creation.

The more residential the streets, the more like a

plague this seemed. Neighborhoods are containers for children, and the children were silenced.

Finally, his house, on its little thump of a granite outcrop. Like all the other buildings, his house was boarded up, as if readied for conveyance to a new owner. But the key to the wooden garden door was still in its hiding place, behind a votive urn in a niche in the wall. He worked it with trembling fingers and pushed through.

The toys in the garden, left in skelter. A wheeled pull-toy on its side, the little child-size pushcart stuffed with an old blanket and some dolls in need of hospital attention. The pansies were wilted onto the lip of the pots, but not yet dead. Some scavengers had been paying call on shoots of vegetables; the plot was torn up and would remain barren till he or Oena replanted it.

He could tell no one was here. They weren't in hiding behind some chimney stack. Absence sends out signals no harder to read than presence. Cur dashed about sniffing and whining, as if sensing traces of panic in the corners of the place, the way a skin augurer could read a person's touch upon an iron sword or a copper spoon.

But had Oena taken the children down to the quay to enquire of the harbormaster about the *Pious Enterprise*? Ships that passed close enough often traded news from one bridge to the other. If that volleyed information involved an update as to a ship's journey, such information could sometimes make its way back to home harbor. The *Pious Enterprise* had been more than a week late as it was.

Perhaps Oena had been in danger while waiting for news of Lucikles. But even in the ordinary course of things, Oena and the children might have been arriving in city centre, if it was market day. They could have been looking in the antique stalls for a present with which to welcome Lucikles home. They might have been among the first to die.

The kitchen table was set for the next meal, and a half loaf of bread was greened and sour. He threw it out the open doorway into the yard and pressed beyond the kitchen, into the living circle with its alcoves and bedding.

The bedding was all folded up and put on high shelves, as was normal in daytime. So they hadn't been surprised by this disaster in the middle of the night. But they had been thoughtful, he saw. The chest with their clothes stood open, and the warmer shawls were removed, and winter leggings.

The ikon of Ferona the Defender was gone from its nail. The larger bas-relief of Houranos remained in its place leaning up next to the hearthstone in the living circle. It would have proven too heavy to be moved quickly.

So they had at least made an effort to flee.

He hesitated, but then he threw open a high window over the marital mattress. The breath of wind brought up the smell of sleep and the luxury of dream next to Oena, that happiest dream of security. The light was a lance, and picked out a bit of paper on the floor that he hadn't seen in the gloom. Perhaps it had blown off the kitchen table when he first unlocked the door. He grabbed at it.

Oena's handwriting.

We will head for Mamanoo's.

Her mother. She had taken the children to her mother's home in the country.

He sat down on the edge of the bed and shook with dry eyes, relief that they had had time to make it out.

But which way to follow them? There were two routes to Mia Zephana's small holdings in High Chora. The quicker route followed a rising set of switchbacks between the brows of chalk fields and low cliffs. But that route was open to sight of any other traveler, including the highway robbers known as the Wolves—and their actual wolves, semidomesticated beasts for whom exuding menace was the same as breathing.

If there had been a mass exodus, Oena might have chosen safety in numbers and fled with the children along that high road.

The other way was more taxing, longer, but also less often used. It was forested nearly the whole long looping way, with any number of dense shrubs, standing stones, even small cliffs and lodgments in which to hide should trouble arise. If Oena was traveling without him, she sometimes chose to take the longer route through untended forest rather than the broadway across the bluffs of pink and white stone and scrub meadow.

She left no clue in her note. Perhaps she didn't think of it, or maybe she was afraid someone meaning her family harm would be able to tell which way she intended to go.

Or maybe she didn't know as she was setting out.

He pulled himself together at last. He closed the shutter again in the marriage alcove. He didn't bother to check if all the food had been taken from the keeping-room alcove. It seemed more urgent to follow her at once, to protect her if she were in trouble, and to reunite with her at her mother's. To hold his children in his arms again, to worship at Oena's knees, thanking her for her courage and swift action.

Locking up the kitchen door, he glanced around. The shallow iron cauldron—more an upturned stovetop lid than anything else—showed no sign of a recent augury. A few bird feathers, as if maybe a cat had caught a meal, but nothing more. No blood, no bones, no char.

The feathers, Lucikles saw, were blue and ivory. Cloud-bird feathers.

He then remembered the two visitations at sea—the flock of cloud-birds, and then, nearer in, the owls. Had these populations been disturbed from the mainland by the smoke of the attack, the burning warehouse district? Only now did he realize that the aroma of persistent burning was everywhere. In the garden, in his nose, on his clothes probably.

He went back into the kitchen and removed a butcher knife from a drawer, and sharpened it on the whetstone. He wrapped this in leather and secured it with strapping and put it in his shoulder valise. Locking the garden gate and returning the key to its hidey-hole, he looked this way and that. Still no sign of anyone. Closer to city centre, the less wealthy citizens were hiding in place—protecting their treasure from looting if nothing else. But the district of Temple Houranos was truly desolate of human inhabitants. The neighborhood usually rang with the peals of childish play or alarm from dawn to dusk. It was that kind of place. Today it was as still as the City of the Dead.

He walked, without the desperate urgency of his earlier trot, back toward the Temple. In a few moments he would have to make a decision about which track to take to Mia Zephana's, and he wanted to stretch out the time in which to study the options.

But his mind instead went to the remarks of the blacksmith. The same burst of wild weather from the south that allowed some vandals to travel from so far away that they couldn't be recognized—that same burst of weather had brought the green girl down into the waters off Maracoor Spot.

Just as the Maracoor Spot protocols were being broken by the intrusion of an eighth bride, the hitherto impregnable defenses of Maracoor Abiding had been breached. Perhaps on the same day.

Lucikles had always kept to himself a healthy skepticism about the practices of government and faith, especially as they intertwined. Sure, he would conduct the odd augury if Oena was uncertain about how to proceed on a matter of some importance. He attended rituals and prayers at the Temple with perhaps less frequency than others, but he wasn't an apostate. Not really. He prayed more out of habit than conviction. He had always figured that doing his job for the government was a kind of service to deity. The lack of his own personal capacity to believe deeply was a failure he could work around. It hadn't interfered with his work. Perhaps, he secretly wondered, it had made him one of the more efficient Minor Adjutants, and a certain tepid agnosticism had helped him advance. It certainly cleared away the distractions of the dreams of old women, who loved nothing better than to tell how the divine Houranos or some other luminary from myth had deigned to appear to them at night and give them a cooking lesson of history.

But now, as he struggled to keep central the question about Oena's state of mind, and which route she might have chosen in her flight to Mia Zephana's, he found instead he was thinking about a second set of contradictions.

There was the practice that many believed inviolate, that seven brides of Maracoor kept the working of the world in order by harvesting dailiness from the eternal sea.

There was the deeper truth that Lucikles knew about, the other mission of the brides, of which they were largely ignorant. They, and most of the nation.

And then, on the opposite side of these realities, was the question he rarely asked himself. What if the faith of his country, that faith he found a hard time crediting, had more basis in reality than he countenanced? What if his failure to remove from Maracoor Spot that—aberration—that girl called Rain—had alarmed and offended the gods? What if her arrival there was a harbinger of the invading navy? What if he had judged wrong in leaving without her? What if he might have saved history himself by removing her onto the *Pious Enterprise,* and restoring the balance of seven brides that tradition had deemed necessary to peace and prosperity?

Arriving at the north edge of the grounds of the Temple Houranos, he paused one more minute and cast his eye back. The sea between the columns of the Temple—blue as new grapes in sugar water. Blue-green, really. The smoke from the warehouse district drifted north like morning fog across the breadth of Maracoor Crown. He was above the smoke now, mostly, though he could still smell it. The capital city was dead—or paralyzed at least. Not so much sacked as kicked into unconsciousness. Who knew if a navy would return, a navy bringing an army, and what they might do when they arrived.

He couldn't manage the whole country. He could only manage his family, if even that. He turned and, on instinct rather than logic, made a left turn at the tavern, choosing the lower, more winding route, the woodland meander. He would be better hidden himself there. Better protected, to live to serve his children and wife, if they had survived the exodus, survived the wolves on the highlands or the elements in the forest, if they had made it to his mother-in-law's farm.

He wouldn't get far tonight—the first lean-to, maybe. But to have made a small start on the journey to find and perhaps rescue his family was better than to have huddled at home, paralyzed with their absence.

He was half a mile out before he remembered that Cur had been close at his heels all along. "Good boy," he murmured. Cur ignored the praise, more intent on the aromatic intrigues of the evening.

Rain

1

In the mornings, this is what she noticed: that the world relied on three shapes to take form. Blocks, slices, and currents.

The blocks were earth and structure, and human forms walking around her. This was where gravity lived. The heaviness of stone and footfall. The heaviness of silence.

The slices? The lateral pools of light and air in which she stirred, sat up, across which she walked. Where movement happened. Where color happened, too, and shadow. The scent of lemons, pepper. Gardenias.

The currents of the world, then, must be wind and time, and, she supposed, tidal surge and slackening. Corridors of unceasing sound. (Those birds. That pipe made from reeds.) Processes of change.

Walking back from the privy, she noticed a little brown bird. It was examining something at ground level, something invisible to Rain's eye. It fluttered up and settled again eight feet ahead, in the center of the path. As Rain approached, the bird hopped forward yet again. The bird and Rain repeated this six or eight times. She didn't believe the creature was leading her back to the temple—she didn't need an escort, she could see the temple roof over the brow of the hill—but why didn't the thing just frisk itself into the bracken and wait till she had passed? Could a single bird want company?

So much she didn't know.

The reality of loss. She still recognized *that* concept. It took her a while to remember the name of the syndrome.

Amnesia, that was the doctor's term for such an affliction.

She could recall little from the time before she woke up on this island. Hence, a diagnosis of amnesia, she supposed. Some trauma to the head. Or to the heart. A kind of sedition against herself, maybe against her own history.

Winds and lightning and fog, and lashing torrents. That much, yes. All of that, muddled, but urgent, and recent. (A cloudburst over the sea seemed pointless. The sea already had enough water.) But for how long had she flown on that broom, for how many days and nights? How far had she and Iskinaary come?

And from where?

Rain was aware she had the answers inside her— they hid around corners. Like the memory of a dream suddenly glinting, then tucking itself away again.

Was there *ever* such a storm as the one that blew her here?

She felt she had somehow conjured it up herself.

But she had no power—had she? The power to fly on that broom, but that had seemed more the broom's efforts than hers.

Besides the weather, she remembered beginning to pass out with fatigue, after what had seemed like characterless days and nights of clinging awake to the broom. It was at that point that the broom, and Iskinaary beside it, banked low and dove beneath the clouds. Perhaps the Goose knew enough to help prevent her dying should she slam into the sea from any kind of height. Between ocean and low, obsidian cloud, only a thickness of wet air. The sea had become more and more muscular and sculptural as the travelers dropped, until they were beside it as much as above it, skirting the lifting mounds of brine, in which fish and vegetable matter could be seen, suspended at eye level, before subsiding again.

A stinking tumulus of water heaving, with something like a dead mermaid raised for Rain's inspection, then collapsing.

Iskinaary struggling ahead, and then tugging with his beak at the top end of the broomstick to keep it higher than the brush end, so that whatever else happened, Rain wouldn't go into the water headfirst.

But the actual moment of contact—that was gone. And Rain was glad of it. The next thing she had known was waking up in the temple among those serious and exotic women. Her broom somehow salvaged, too.

That was all she knew for now. Everything else either changed beyond recognition, or hidden, or gone for good. She was exiled from her own past.

2

Her grasp of their accent was better than their grasp of hers. Maybe she had traveled in her past—her ear seemed to have some nimbleness. When the brides spoke, she got it. Understood the words anyway if not the society.

She struggled to put it together.

"It's a cult," said Iskinaary, ducking his head close to his breast so he couldn't be heard. The islanders seemed to be able to decode the Goose's speech a little better than they could hers. That one called Bray, though slow of tongue, possessed the keenest ear.

"A cult. Hmmm. No men allowed, except for that fellow who returned to the boat." Rain scratched Iskinaary's neck, which he tolerated because he recognized it was a sign of affection. But he wasn't a dog and he snapped at her when he had had enough.

"It's a female haven," said the Goose. "A punishment, or a refuge. Only I don't see what sort of life it is for them."

Rain didn't admit that she had no basis of comparison. She hadn't yet confessed her memory loss to her traveling companion. She wasn't sure why not—certainly the Goose was her trustworthy friend? He appeared to have dragged her waterlogged body out of the open sea and into the harbor where she could be found and revived by this sorority. Perhaps she was merely ashamed?

If she could identify shame as an emotion, she must have known it in the past.

What a place to start.

"Can we sort them out?" she asked the Goose, concentrating on the here and now.

"Who these hens are as separate souls? I think we can manage to do that. The old one, with the stiff hips, that's Helia. I think she's the boss."

"The boss by age or by wisdom? What do you think?"

"That's your call. Human wisdom doesn't mean much to *me*," said the Goose. "But she makes the others pause when she speaks, and they stand back. So I bet she's in charge."

"Okay. The starchy upright one? With the disapproving expression?"

"*M* something."

"Mirpie? Mirkie? Mirka."

"That's it. Mirka Berserka, by the looks of it."

"Pretty clearly the second in command, that Mirka."

"She looks as if she sat on a cactus and couldn't get it out of her regions, and she's trying to pretend she didn't, so what is everyone looking at her for."

Rain laughed just a little, and was relieved to hear the sound of it in her own ears. Laughter was the sound of health; that was another thing she knew.

But these women didn't seem to laugh at all.

"I can't easily tell the order of the next few," she said.

"The big woman is called Bray. She's strong, and she's silent."

"And she's friendly with that one called Tirr. I can't tell anything about Tirr."

"Some people are born with character deficit."

Rain looked at the Goose. "I mean," he explained, "like being born without a sense of smell or a sense of pitch. Some people are born without much yeast in their dough. Tirr seems kind of vapid to me. Not stupid, not confused, just, sort of, you know. A cheese from the keeping-room not completely brought up to room temperature."

"You're in a nasty frame of mind."

"I'm never nasty about human beings, I mean nastier about one than any other. They're all pretty dreadful. Except you, but even then I'm making an exception out of duty and history."

What duty has bound the goose to me, wondered Rain, but thought: not yet. "I think the curvy one is next youngest, though I don't know her name. The one running around with a whisk broom, and lemons in her pockets? Picky. A little nervous."

Just now the Goose couldn't remember her name either. "Then the younger two," he said. "The yearling— I'm talking about the young teen. What's she all about? Her name has some of the sounds of mine. They call her Squirrel?"

"Scyrilla, that's right. What a memory you have, Iskinaary!"

"And me with a brain the size of a walnut. Who would have guessed it. Evidence of deep mystery in this universe, if not downright magic."

At the sound of that word—*magic*—Rain felt uneasy and morose, a shadow from an invisible cloud over her. If there could be such a thing as an invisible cloud.

"And the youngest is Cossy," she finished with triumph. "I like her best."

"She hasn't had enough time to go off yet, that's all," said the Goose. "She'll disappoint you in the end."

"Are you always this cheery?" she asked, but in a mocking tone, to disguise the fact that she wasn't really certain of the Goose, when you got right down to it.

"I have to work at it," he said, nipping at a bug in his breast feathers. He swallowed. "Ah, I remembered. The obsessive one. Kliompte, I think. Is that right?"

"You *do* have a memory."

"Test me on the names of my goslings and I'd be put in prison by my wife."

But again, the tone was mocking; Rain couldn't tell if Iskinaary had a wife, or goslings. "What do you think we should do?" she asked.

"We're stuck for right now. We don't dare try to launch ourselves in flight. Not yet. You need to regain your strength. Flying too soon might be a mistake. In any case I don't know how far we are from the mainland that the overseer was returning to," said the Goose.

"Why didn't you ask him?"

"Why didn't you?"

"I didn't think of it. Anyway, the man seemed flustered."

"We're the ones who should be flustered. Dropping out of the sky into the ocean." Iskinaary raised his wings over his head; in the dusk he looked like a grey flame quivering on the ochre ground. "Besides, I don't know if your broom has lost its capacity to fly. Maybe salt water killed it, as it kills so much vegetable bounty that grows in the good earth."

The broom stood leaning up on a pillar, an ordinary broom. Indeed, Kliompte had borrowed it to sweep the steps of the temple but found it so misshapen and contrary as nearly to be useless, so she had put it back.

3

After Lucikles had departed with a haste both unseemly and perhaps offensive, the seven brides of Maracoor and the newcomers sat down to break bread and consider what next was to be done. If anything.

Under the shadows of the portico roof they ate in silence. When the meal of mackerel paste on toasted flatbread was done and cleared away, old Helia signaled for her oakthorn staff. Mirka pretended not to have understood the command, but then she sighed and went to get the thing. Iskinaary, who had settled on a patch of wild thyme just beyond the edge of the temple steps, turned his head and exchanged a glance with Rain.

Helia thumped her stick three times upon the stone floor. "All right, it's time. We'll now consider the dilemma we're in," she said.

"We've been considering it since the moment it began," said Mirka briskly, "and it seems to me—"

"Let's limit our remarks to those that are useful or kind," interrupted the oldest woman. "In other words, Mirka, shut up. I'm about to lay out the matter for us."

The brides sat erect, with their hands in their laps, except Bray, who leaned her head against Tirr's shoulder and played with the plaited strands of her companion's hair. Perching on an extra stool at the far end of the table—the overseer's seat, probably—Rain let her elbows rest on the table in a casual way. She wasn't a convert to their coven, and she wanted to keep it that way. At least for now.

Helia looked around at the others, including Rain in the sweep of her gaze, though not the Goose, who seemed inattentive. Rain noticed the strategy. Geese are like cats, she thought. They have an advantage in that they look narcissistic by nature. This would make them good spies, if they were so inclined.

"First things first. We're turned by circumstances from seven brides to eight," said Helia.

Rain had decided to flatten her vowels and to leave a little cushion of air around every word. It might help them to understand her. "I am not a bride."

Mirka got this, and she held up her hand. "Are you married, then?" Mirka delivered this reply with a flush of self-approval. "It's essential for us to know how we are to *deal* with you."

Rain didn't believe she was old enough to be married; but then again, how could she be sure? Interesting how she knew some concepts but not how they pertained to her own life. "I'm not married *here*," she offered them, which seemed valid enough. Iskinaary had no eyebrow to raise, but the angle of his head suggested surprise at her wit, or perhaps her witlessness.

"A forbidden element, this arriviste," opined Mirka.

Mirka's breakthrough in comprehension of Rain's speech seemed to have been contagious. The brides became more engaged, leaned in to listen. They also spoke more slowly, though Rain hadn't found *their* accent a problem. "We are eight here today, in any case," said Helia placidly. "Let's not be tricksy with the terminology. The issue, my sisters, is this: we're breaking the convention of ritual life that goes back hundreds of years. Whether this is indeed a problem, or maybe not, we need to be of one mind about it."

"Why should it fall to *us* to do anything about this disaster?" asked Mirka. "We didn't cause it to happen. The Rain Creature did." The lieutenant jerked a thumb at Rain.

"Seven brides are called for, that's the custom," admitted Helia. "But so what?"

"If you'd died the other evening, Helia, and taken yourself out of the picture, we'd be right as rain," said Mirka. The other brides were horrified at the effrontery, but Rain caught the youngest bride sliding a glance worriedly in her direction. "Right as rain" had a censorious tone to it, or perhaps incendiary. Or prophetic.

"Eight brides, not seven," said Helia, "may not be the end of the world."

"And don't forget me. What am I, chopped liver?" asked the Goose. "Not to put ideas into your head."

They ignored him. Perhaps now that they could understand Rain a little, considering the opinions of a Goose seemed less necessary. "Still. We may need to evacuate you, Rain," said Helia. "Somehow. For your own good. I don't know."

"I'm a strong creature," said Iskinaary, "but I can't carry my companion on my back."

Helia turned to him. She sighed. "You carried her this far, didn't you?"

Rain thought it was time she spoke for herself. "I had my own method of flying," she said, "but it isn't working anymore."

The community clearly didn't believe Rain and regarded her with that certain sympathy reserved for the deluded. It was Kliompte who replied. "Perhaps we roped in this Rain. Maybe we brides have been here netting time into segments of dailiness for decades, devoting our lives to our mission of keeping the world running, just to be ready to do some new work right now. Now, when the moment is ripe."

"You, you just like it when everything is lined up. History and fate as well as our garden shoes paired off on the temple porch," said Mirka.

"And so what?" asked Kliompte, brilliantly unfussed. "Either one adheres to order and trusts in it, or one doesn't."

"No one invites a lightning strike," said Helia, with some weariness in her voice, Rain thought. Helia thumped a forefinger in her palm as she made her points. "No one schedules a plaguey pox. History is brittle, my sisters. It breaks its patterns through accident and contingency. So it's the job of the brides, and indeed of all humans I suspect, to rally together after the unexpected happens. To set things to rights. If it's possible to do so." She turned to Rain. "Is this your opinion, too?"

"I'm not sure I understand the question," said Rain.

"Is it our job to maintain order, or are we to embrace disorder as somehow organic and natural, and part of life?"

"That's *way* beyond my ability to answer," replied

Rain, relishing that her youth allowed her to duck the question. "I hardly can name my colors yet."

The Goose raised his head. "Well, no one asked me, and what is the opinion of a Goose in matters of the human heart, anyway? But to me it seems a very human thing to consider this as an either/or choice. Maintaining order and embracing disorder are strategies with less contradiction in the great world than you might suspect."

Scyrilla gave one of her customary scowls and picked up a stone, as if she wanted to pitch it at the Goose. Rain thought, oh, the ignitable adolescent. But the youngest, that Cossy, caught Scyrilla by the forearm and made her drop the stone. "You've never even told us where you're from," Scyrilla said to Iskinaary and Rain. "With your funny accents and all." Suddenly that was the question, and Rain could see the other brides had been reluctant to raise the matter before.

"Well?" asked Helia at last, gently. "Are you from the mainland? Are you from Maracoor Abiding, or some other state on the mainland, or from one of the islands?"

The Goose looked at Rain. Rain shook her head; she didn't want to admit that she didn't know. Iskinaary quawked a wordless enquiry to her about her reticence, but he went along with it. "We're from away," he said. "In your binary system of thinking, isn't that all you need to know?"

Mirka said, "I don't appreciate being lectured to by a Goose."

"Rest your insteps in goat butter, Mirka, that's not the issue here," said Helia.

But Mirka stood, which was both rude and aggressive. "Look, you," she said to Helia. "We aren't to be more than seven here. This is *sacred tradition*. We live our whole lives to safeguard that tradition, and to preserve life here and elsewhere in Maracoor. This isn't a—a *hobby*. This is life and death. Not just for us, but for the world. You're jeopardizing our very existence, and that of—of everything."

"May I remind you," said Helia, "that in the natural course of things, a bride occasionally dies? Either old age, or illness, or there was the time—before the time of some of you—that two brides drowned when the cliff edge they were standing upon suddenly crumpled into the sea?"

"Or they threw themselves into the sea," intoned Kliompte.

"When we brides are met with death, we wait until the overseer comes to assess our number and our well-being, and he returns with the proper young novices to fill out the roster. That's when Bray and Tirr joined us, in fact."

Tirr and Bray smiled at one another. Their affection nearly derived from the cradle, then.

"My point," Helia concluded, "is that perhaps ours can become a more . . . a more *porous* arrangement when necessary. We adhere to tradition but we can be flexible when required. We needn't come to blows. Now sit down, you're giving my neck a crick, having to peer at you up like this."

Mirka wouldn't sit down. She walked around the table. She looked demented, thought Rain. Her shoulders went back and her breastplate curved, as if she were trying to touch her elbows behind her back. She clamped her palms upon her waist at the sides of her apron.

"There . . . are . . . to . . . be . . . seven brides," she said, throwing her voice as if speaking to someone behind a stone wall. "Have we dedicated ourselves to this holy commitment only to be told the constellation of brides is *arbitrary*?" She said some more, perhaps quoting scripture or the law; Rain couldn't identify the references. "It makes a mockery of our entire existence for Helia to tell us it doesn't matter. Oh, it doesn't matter, Helia? Shall we, what, put up a guest-house somewhere and take in paying customers? Shall we rent out our fields for some money-spinning gambit run by—by pirates? My dear friends," she said, spinning around and waving her hands now, "I tell you: note with alarm the casual attitude of our senior bride toward this aberration, this—this monstrosity—"

With one hand she singled out Rain as the monstrosity. Nice, thought Rain. Very sympathetic.

With her other hand, Mirka pointed to Helia. "For some time I've been dubious about the capacity of our senior bride to head our community with wisdom. My suspicions are confirmed now. Her mind has lost its way. We have no choice but to remove Helia from her standing. I call for your voice in my own election to the position of elder bride. Age notwithstanding."

"You've been practicing dramatics behind our back," said Helia drolly, but Rain thought the stout old woman wouldn't defuse the situation as easily as that.

"Perhaps I should leave so you can finish this matter in private," said Rain.

"Makes no difference to me," said Mirka, "as you have no vote."

"One doesn't vote on history," advised Helia, "any more than one ordains an early sunset for one's own convenience. But we can open for voices on that matter. As long as we're all clamoring to be heard?"

"I think it's better I absent myself," insisted Rain. "I'll take a walk. Come on, Iskinaary."

"Hey, wait, this was getting fun," said the Goose. "If they're warming up for a wrestling competition, I want to watch."

Rain turned away from the table and left the portico. Iskinaary waddled alongside, chuckling a little under his breath. After a moment, Rain felt a small hand slip into her own. "Cossy, isn't it," said Rain.

"Acaciana," said the youngest bride. "Cossy. Yes."

It was an invasion, that child's hand in her own. Uninvited, but perhaps not unwelcome? Rain didn't know how she felt about it, so she let it be.

They walked around the temple to where they wouldn't be seen by the other brides, all now deep in discussion. The olive grove was arranged in a wheel, concentric circles of smaller trees in a semblance of obeisance around a colossal specimen known, Cossy told Rain, as the Mother of Olive.

The tree was sixty or six hundred or six thousand years old; it was hard for anyone to be sure. Three grown brides with their hands linked would just barely be able to encircle it. To Rain's eye, its trunk twisted like the spine of a basilisk, or several basilisks living in erotic formation upon one another. Rain was loath to approach this tree. "It's hard to take in," she said to

Cossy and the Goose. "It looks grotesque. It might as well be from a different species."

"*Grotesque* is a condescending word," said Iskinaary. "She begs your pardon," he continued, as if to the tree.

Cossy giggled. "The Goose is talking to her?"

"The tree is a she?" asked Rain.

"She's called the Mother of Olive, so that's usually female, right?"

"Oh, how right you are," said Rain. "Well, Iskinaary is right, *grotesque* is the wrong word. Especially for an ancient mother. Formidable, perhaps. Arresting. What would you call it? I mean, her?"

"Big," said Cossy. "I mean, bigger than big. *Big.*"

"The Mother of Olive accepts your apology," said the Goose to Rain. "And she isn't from a different species, any more than Helia and Cossy are from a different species. Just a different time."

"Is the Mother of Olive talking to you?" asked the young girl. "How?"

Rain was as curious as the girl though hid her eagerness for the reply.

"Listen," said the Goose. They paused in their footsteps. The air off the sea was lazing up the slope, catching its fingers in the thinned but regular gown of leaves the Mother of Olive still sported. It was such a large tree that the breeze could raise dimension in it.

Soft assertions and rebuttals, like that of wind instruments in a trio. An improvised and complex melody.

Rain didn't know if the Goose was having them on. The sound was both secret and subtle.

"The Mother of Olive *is* terrific," said Rain, squeezing Cossy's hand, and signaling to Iskinaary to lay off the dramatics.

"What is she saying?" asked Cossy.

"She's saying, you're too young to have a voice, but when you have one of your own, you will understand hers," he said.

Rain didn't like the possibility that the Goose might be misleading Cossy, being fanciful with her. In this hardscrabble place, fancy might very well be dangerous. But before she could work out for herself how to cut off Iskinaary, a sound bubbled up from the temple. "Cossy, Cossy, come," called one or two of the brides. The voices were threads in the purple dusk, sounding less assured than the voice of the Mother of Olive.

"We'd better go back, I guess," said Rain. "This was only brief exercise, but thank you, Cossy, for introducing me to this Mother. I think she must be a bride, too, don't you?" So Rain was entering into the rhetoric, too. Maybe it was contagious.

Cossy shrugged. Verbal play, thought Rain, maybe not often exercised here.

At the temple, the brides had rearranged themselves. Helia still sat at the head of the table. She was working with her colored threads, making a picture upon a white napkin. Her stitches were ungainly because her eyesight was poor. It was a small performance of complacency that fooled no one. Kliompte stood behind her and Scyrilla lurked, sullen, beyond. Opposite, Mirka was erect, leaning with her hands on the table. Bray and Tirr hovered at her right and left shoulder. Most of the brides seemed ashamed, but not Mirka, and not Helia. Mirka appeared furious and Helia amused, or skeptical.

"We've raised our voices," said Mirka, "and Cossy, we need you to raise yours, for we are at an impasse. There are three votes to jump me to senior position, and three against. Your voice is needed to break the tie."

Rain tightened her hand in Cossy's. But the youngest bride surprised everyone. Cossy lifted her chin and spoke in a slight but carrying tone. "I believe I am too young to have a voice," she said.

"You must vote," said Mirka.

"I'm not old enough. I won't," said Cossy. "So there."

Kliompte's sense of domestic order required that Iskinaary sleep somewhere else than in the temple proper. Besides, he was male, even if a Goose. So, near the open door, Rain settled down for the night on a pallet of blankets the brides had assembled from their store of extras. Across the threshold, she could talk to Iskinaary a bit before going to sleep. They were too far to be heard by the others. The brides had agreed to allow their Rain Creature to sleep unsupervised. Helia had returned to her own bed in her own private screened corner, and Cossy to the floor next to it.

Rain said to the Goose, "I like that child."

"The youngest one."

"Yeah, Cossy. She has spunk."

"She hasn't been broken yet."

Rain thought about this. "Do you think the others have been broken?"

"Well. Not broken, but drained of a certain sap, maybe? They seem so complicit. So beholden to their rigid rule of praxis. But being able to yield to change is a healthy skill to have. You don't believe me, ask any wing to have flown over an ocean. Ask the Mother of Olive."

"I think you're mostly talking about the harridan? Mirka."

"She's an obvious candidate for obstinacy. Watch her, Rain. She's bad news. But they all seem—well—wedded to their tradition. One has to wonder why."

"There's a lot to wonder about here."

Iskinaary didn't reply.

Rain thought she might have briefly fallen asleep. She roused herself back to thought. To the extent she could hear them, the other brides were breathing softly. Their breath made a cloud of confusion over them, in her dream-picturing mind, but above her were stars, out the slant doorway, and she felt she knew what she had to say next. It had come together for her.

"Iskinaary, are you awake?"

"I am now."

"Were you asleep?"

"Once upon a time. It doesn't matter. What?"

"Do you know where we are?"

"On this island, you mean? No, not really."

Rain still didn't want to admit to the Goose how much of her past life was blocked to her. She couldn't work out why, but it seemed urgent to keep her condition of amnesia to herself for a while longer. So she thought craftily before she said, "I wonder if we are dead."

"It only feels like death," said the Goose, making no effort to suppress a yawn.

"No, I mean it," said Rain. "How would we know what death is? It may be like this. It may *be* this.

Wherever we came from in our past, here we are in a secret and puzzling present. Could death be like this? How would we even know?"

"What did you have for supper? Is it disagreeing with you? You're sounding deranged, you realize."

"You are my guide," said Rain. "My spirit guide. Is that it?"

"My mama didn't raise me to be anyone's spirit guide but my own." The Goose was huffy. "I don't see you paying me a salary for this, by the way."

"Then why are you sticking by me? You could fly away and leave me here. Are you going to do that?"

The Goose said, "I don't know any more than you do what tomorrow will bring. I assume we'll be a little bit surprised—that's what tomorrows promise. Something unexpected. That's about all we can believe in, most days."

"Did you really talk to the Mother of Olive, or was that a game?"

"Would you be still and let my Goose brain rest?"

Rain closed her eyes but her ears and her heart remained alert. She thought about moving through this new world with nothing more than a sense of her body, her skin, her name, her prior relationship with the Goose. But how little else she had brought with her. Her clothes, such as they were. (As her apparel had been reduced to rags, she now dressed in borrowed bridal habiliments.) Her broom. A satchel of leather, which had withstood being drowned in the ocean and was slowly drying out, with a pattern of salt pox upon it and a quirky misshapen aspect. Nothing in it but a lumpy seashell. Everything from her prior life emptied out like that satchel.

The seashell a souvenir from some forgotten shore.

What did she know of death, really? What did anyone know?

"There are mosquitoes," said Rain.

"Is that you again? *Please.* Anyway, I can't eat all of them," said Iskinaary. "I have my limits."

"I mean, should mosquitoes exist in the Afterlife? Do they?"

"If that's where we are," said the Goose, humoring her, "I got to eat too, honeycake. It's not all goat cheese and apricots and pistachios for us Geese, you know."

"Is there—is there *need* in the Afterlife?"

"I'll tell you this," said Iskinaary, with the slightest modulation toward gentleness in his tone. "I may not know where we are, or why. But I'm not leaving you, or not for a while. If I decide to do so, I'll let you know. Unless I'm felled by a fox or an arrow or a virus of some sort and I can't get back to you. But meanwhile

I need to sleep. That's a given. So shut up already and get some rest."

Rain grimaced in the dark, but couldn't stop herself from adding, "If you can be killed, you're probably not yet in the Afterlife. If we were, all that mortal danger would be behind us, right?"

The Goose emitted a fake snore and wouldn't remark further.

She put her arm over her head. The Afterlife, if this was it, must have some pertinence to the life she'd left behind. Otherwise, how could she identify anything? Herself, a Goose, a temple, an ocean?

The Mother of Olive. It was itself, on the slopes beyond the corner of the temple that overlooked the harbor of Maracoor Spot. But it was also the very idea of tree—huge, protective, aromatic, hulking, bringing to mind every tree that had ever existed. She didn't need to be told what a tree was in this Afterlife. She knew.

Maybe she could work backward from what Maracoor provided as template. Slowly uncover what she had left behind.

The sweet girl that Cossy seemed to be—she was Cossy, the youngest bride, to be sure—but maybe she was also Rain, as Rain might once have been at the age of ten.

"Iskinaary," she whispered one last time, thinking of the bird she'd seen hopping before her on the path that morning, that ambassador, that guide, "did you lead me here?"

No reply. A soft breeze swept in, and the smell of cypress and of malthusia blossom, and Rain abandoned this Afterlife for the other kind, the one reached through gates of ivory, the dream world.

Cossy

1

It was darktime. Cossy had rolled over, awakened, and fallen asleep again several times. This moment, though, seemed a little different. She felt a little more alert.

She listened for the small orchestra of night breathing. She knew whose breath was whose, and which bride might be asleep and which not. It was a game she played from time to time.

She lay in the dark, naming the snores, when a voice spoke her name. "Acaciana."

Oh, that's why she was more awake. She'd been summoned. She lifted her head. "Helia? Are you all right?"

"Never better, never worse."

"What's the matter?"

"I need to tell you something. And then I need you to do something for me."

"Now?"

Helia was sitting up in bed. It was rare she could raise herself on her own anymore. "I think now, before it is too late."

"What do you want?" Cossy was on her knees beside Helia's bedstead, reaching for her hands.

"I want you to be very still. I don't want anyone else to wake up. Are they all asleep? I think they are."

Cossy listened. She clocked their stupor. "I can't speak for the Goose, but everyone else, even Rain, seems to be fast asleep."

"I thought so. We haven't got much time. I need to tell you where the key is."

"What key?" But of course Cossy knew what key. Not the key to the wine cupboard, which lived on a string around Kliompte's neck. The other key. The key about which Mirka had been agitating for so many months, and the more so after Helia had gotten sick for a day. The key to the heart of the temple. The key to the Vessel.

It was hidden, had always been hidden, and should remain hidden. Because it had such utmost importance, that key, though none of the brides knew exactly why, perhaps not even Helia. Back before Scyrilla had gone all moody and snitty, back when the girls were true friends, she and Cossy had used to guess where it might be stove away. Under one of the massive floor stones of the temple. In a hollow bole high up in the Mother of Olive. Hanging by a string off the highest of the marine cliffs on the far side of the island. In a rude place on Helia's very person.

How they'd laughed themselves sick over that one.

When Cossy was younger and had asked how come the famous key needed to be hidden, someone—Helia, or maybe Mirka, someone with a strict voice—had rounded upon her and asked Cossy if she could speak the same language as the Great Mara.

"Of course not," said Cossy. "No one can."

"Why not?"

This rhetorical questioning, so tiresome. "Because-the-Great-Mara-created-the-earth-and-the-heavens. And the Great Mara would be bored by conversation with us mortals. So we can't say a word to her."

"More or less, that's right. And suppose you *had* a key to the language of the Great Mara? Suppose you could understand the complaints of the dew and the boasting of the winds and, and—the endless litanies of genealogy articulated in, no, *spluttered* by every apricot and bean, would you choose to use it? To address the Great Mara herself?"

This was a trick question. The correct answer was "No," and that's what Cossy said, because that was the quickest way out of such a browbeating. But at that stage of her young life, Cossy's real if unspoken answer had been, "Why not?"

The key about which Helia was talking now, in the middle of a moony night, wasn't just an idea, an idea-key to unlock the language of the Great Mara. But it wasn't a mere wasp in the lemon drink, either. It was central to everything, somehow.

"I'm going to ask you to get the key for me. In case I die, in case something happens to me. This arrival of Rain, it may be about to change everything. We have to be ready."

So bizarre. Cossy couldn't summon up a response. Helia looked a little wild in the moonlight, but who didn't? Her hair was galloping right off her head in a twist, a kind of spooned white flame.

"Sometimes one must act at once, or lose everything," said Helia with urgency. "So listen carefully. I want you to go down to the harbor. Uncover the little rowboat we use for dragging nets. Pull the boat into the water. Get the oars, too, or you'll be washed out to sea."

"And what for?"

"To row out. The key is in the buoy."

"What?"

"Don't make me repeat everything. There's no time," hissed Helia. "Listen. The buoy at the mouth of the harbor? It has a cork plug in the top, stuck in very tightly. You'll have to bring a kitchen knife to wedge into the seam. You can work it back and forth to inch the plug out. Then reach inside and grab the key. Are you attending? You must put the key in the bottom of the boat so it doesn't accidentally drop in the water. Replace the plug as best you can, and row back here. It won't take you long unless you have trouble with the cork."

"I can't do all that."

"You can row. I've seen you fishing in the harbor. Look, it's a calm night tonight and a bright one. You can be there and back before someone wakes up to use the pot. I've been lying awake counting the minutes to our safest stretch of sleep, and this is it. Do you have any questions?"

Cossy had a thousand questions, but none she could put into words.

"Good," said Helia. She beckoned. Cossy leaned down and the oldest bride kissed the youngest on her forehead. "Go to it. Be quick, be safe, be silent, be strong."

"But, Helia. Why must I do this in such—secrecy?"

"That isn't yours to know about. But I see why you

ask. Mirka is next in line but she is *a dangerous creature*. The knowledge that will come to her in the normal course of events is too much for her. It would break her, and perhaps more besides. Much, much more. You have to trust me, Acaciana. I am the senior bride."

"That means you're the oldest," said Cossy, thinking: not necessarily the wisest. Even if I love you the best.

"As far as you're concerned, I'm the closest you get to the Great Mara on this earth. You have to trust me. Whom else can you trust?"

"Everybody?" she proposed.

"You're young enough that foolishness is not yet a crime. It's just ignorance. But do as I say. Exactly as I say. It is for the best. Go now, little marmoset. And never tell a soul what you have done."

Cossy nodded but she didn't promise anything in words. She wished she could wake Rain up and bring her along. Nonetheless, she kept her unspoken promise and tiptoed away from the temple alone.

2

Cossy had never been out fishing on her own. She was usually paired with Scyrilla, who was stronger at the oars. Sometimes if they went out before dawn, they could be back with enough fish for a midday meal even before the daily scarring of their feet and the braiding of the day.

How Cossy loved doing this, and for a while how she had loved doing it with Scyrilla. Early morning on the harbor, so weird, a kind of seizure. The world holding its breath. Nothing was yet as it would become. Almost magical.

To be out alone in the harbor at midnight was such a different experience. The stars and the moon cast a diffused glow across the slope of the sky. The top of the water was sharded with light. Cossy rowed into the moonstruck path, relishing and regretting her independence.

She wasn't asleep but she felt as if she were. Everything seemed so calm, so easy. She had no agency. The light everywhere she needed it to be. And the island behind and around her, seen from this midnight vantage for the first time, was little more than a cloak of grey felt dropped upon a spangled floor.

She missed Scyrilla out here, and wished she'd come along. Then Cossy hated Scyrilla again because she would have been no fun, not anymore.

The buoy was attached by iron links to some stone dropped to the floor of the harbor. The bits of the corroded chain she could make out, hooked to the buoy's bottom, were lumpy with barnacles.

Cossy slowed the boat and looped its rope in a lazy noose around the buoy to keep it close. Seen up close, the bobbing cork sphere proved indeed to be made of two pieces. A plug emerged shallowly, centered as a stem on top of an apple. Was Helia the only one who knew about this?

At first Cossy had trouble trying to insert the kitchen knife into the seam. She worked the knife back and forth against the cork's resistance. She stabilized upon the buoy itself when she came near to overbalancing.

The plug released all at once, with a perky, popping

sound. The inside of the sphere was irregular, scooped out quickly with a serrated spoon perhaps, as Kliompte might do to the interior of a squash. But, as promised, Cossy's fingers could feel a heavy key on a leathery cord. It was dry and cold. She withdrew it, and remembering Helia's advice, she set it flat down in the well of the coracle.

Replacing the plug was harder than removing it. There was no way she could force it all the way back in. Someone with more strength would have to hammer it into alignment. But she did the best she could. About three quarters of an inch stood up, a rising crust on a pan bread. Higher than before she'd arrived. Would it be visible from the shore? Probably not. Anyway, even if one of the eagle-eyed brides did note that the buoy looked different, and rowed herself out to investigate, there'd be nothing to discover here. The prize had been claimed.

The passage back to shore was swifter than coming out, as if the sea itself approved of her mission. The knife and the key lay parallel, like a pair of brides lying down to rest. A knife always carried a message of danger along its blade. The key was more obscure, maybe reticent.

This wasn't the kind of thought Cossy usually had— she wasn't a child who thought in figuratives. But once when the knife slid over upon the key, covering its wards, its shoulder and shank, as a blanket covers a sleeper, Cossy put out her foot and tiptoed the knife away. She needed to keep her eye on the naked key.

She beached the rowboat and tied it up. She replaced the oars. She clenched the key on its cord in her left fist and held the knife, blade down, in her right. As she padded up the path to the temple, she thought she saw the Goose raise his head an inch or two and cast an avian eye in her direction. But perhaps he had been as deep in sleep as the brides remained—even Helia, bless her—for he just settled that nodule of weird intelligence upon his spine again and shuddered a couple of feathers. Then all was still.

She put the knife back in the kitchen and couldn't think where to put the key so that someone, waking before she did, might not find it. Finally she tucked it under her night shift, between her thighs, and pulled her legs up the way she'd seen Rain had done. She fell into a sleep of rocking waves and hard black water.

3

"Where is the key?" said Helia in a mutter. "Did you get it?"

Cossy rolled over. She'd slept late. It was first march to the foul-shack and the brides were taking turns as they roused themselves. "Good morning to *you*," said Cossy.

She didn't know quite where her tone came from—it was more Scyrilla, or even supercilious Mirka, than it was herself. She sat up. "What a dream I had."

"No dream, I trust," said Helia, "unless it was my dream and you barged into it. Stop playing around. Did you get it?"

Cossy could feel the key under her shift, neither warm nor cold, pressing against a knee. "You never told me what it was for."

"It's for safekeeping. Let me see it."

"First tell me."

The brides were used to Helia and Cossy chatting in the morning, and didn't notice that their voices were lower than usual. A refreshing simpatico between oldest and youngest, something sweet about it, even eternal. The older brides could all remember their attachments to their own senior bride, the one in office back when they were novices. They let it be.

Helia's jaw went the opposite way of her nose, as if she were grinding down on a pistachio shell to break it. Cossy could tell that although the key was within two feet of Helia, it was more lost to her than when it had been bobbing about in the buoy. Because now Helia wasn't sure where it was.

For once Cossy knew something that no one else in the world knew. Not Helia, not the overseer, not even her erstwhile intimate, that scabby Scyrilla.

"We should get going or we'll miss breakfast," Cossy said, stretching with false languor.

"Cossy," murmured Helia, "let me give you something to help your feet today. You've been working very hard. You deserve a little soothing."

The girl was wary. Helia had always been kind to her, more than kind, but if the old woman possessed some protection against the daily scarring and hadn't ever bothered to offer it before, wasn't that sort of rotten?

Helia scootched her stool back toward her bed. She glanced around to make sure she wasn't being watched. Then, from under the mattress, she pulled a small flat clay jar with an ill-fitting lid. Affixed with a pin, the top swiveled to one side, revealing a shallow declivity holding an opaque yellow unguent. "I use this when I'm in distress," she said. "You deserve to try it today. You've earned it."

Cossy knew this was true, even if Helia couldn't quite be sure herself yet. "What is it?"

"Quick. Let me smear a little on your insteps. You don't need much."

"It looks slimy. What does it do?"

"It dulls the nerves for an hour or so. It'll get you through the worst of the scarring this morning."

Cossy had no reason to doubt Helia, but why had the old woman never offered this balm before? "Do you hog this all for yourself?"

"It's a benefit for the senior bride. I only use it when I fear that the blisters will begin to suppurate. At my age, though, I don't feel much in my feet anymore."

Cossy said, "Won't it come off on the floor?"

"You'll have to sit for a while. Let the skin absorb

it. It doesn't last long, so when we get up, we should rush our breakfast and hurry to the harbor." She took Cossy's foot in her hand, as if to rub a knot away, and cunningly she slipped a thumb-tip's worth of salve onto Cossy's instep.

The girl felt a tingling in her skin—not unpleasant, but rare and creepy because she didn't know if it would turn and become a different kind of sensation. "If this works, why don't we all use it?"

"Acaciana," said Helia in her loving but improving voice, "learning to suffer is called growing up. If we postponed all our sorrows, could we be capable of doing the work we're called to do?"

"Nobody called me," said Cossy. Argumentative today, and with her beloved Helia!

"The Great Mara called you, and that's enough of that. You're starting to sound like Scyrilla, all sass and posture. I hope you're not turning childhood's corner already."

"Okay, okay. But just tell me, where does this magic ointment come from? Do you make it yourself without anyone knowing?"

Helia tilted her face to regard the other brides, all bustling about, and she looked with one eye at the youngest girl. "The Minor Adjutant brings me a small supply. It's intended only for the senior bride, so only she needs to know about it. There, now, you have learned a secret."

I have learned more than one secret, thought Cossy.

They made their way to breakfast. Cossy had hidden the corded key in the pocket of her shift. "Quick, eat up," said Helia in a public voice. "Cossy, brush your hair. Straighten your chiton, it's dragging. You can help me down to the harbor today."

"What's the rush, we'll all go together," said Mirka. "As usual."

"Don't question the moods of an old woman. I've a strange yen for the sight of open water. Perhaps I'm dying, ever think of that? You should be so lucky. Bring your orange, Cossy, let's go now. We'll score our feet at water's edge today."

The brides and Rain watched as Cossy guided Helia toward the portico. The oldest and youngest bride each picked up a few rushes from the pile set aside for this use. As they descended, Cossy was beginning to see what Helia had promised about the salve. Even the small stones digging into her naked soles didn't hurt as much as usual.

"I can't believe you've kept this from me for all this time," she groused.

"It's a small supply, so it must be husbanded for emergencies. Hush and don't question me."

"And what kind of emergency is today?"

"I need to see that key," said Helia. They reached the shore. "Now you'll learn how much easier this is. Do you want me to cut you?"

"If the ointment works the way you say it does, maybe I can manage by myself for once?"

"There's always a first time. Might as well try."

Cossy put her hands behind the folds of her apron. She took up three rushes and looped them around her protected palms. Gulping, she glanced at Helia, whose scrutiny of her was loving and sad.

"There's always a first time," Helia said again. "It'll be all right. You'll see."

Then Cossy began to saw the grass along her right instep, at a certain diagonal for ten strokes, at the reverse diagonal for the second ten. The welts obediently arose, and the red skin glistened. But Helia was right. The pain was numbed. Cossy felt as if in a dream, doing but not feeling, or not fully feeling.

Her gratitude was so great, it spilled out of her. "Here is the key," she said, crying. "It's in my pocket. Oh, Helia."

"Put it away," said Helia, once she'd glanced at it. "No, I needn't hold it. I recognize it well enough."

"But what is it for?" asked Cossy, when she could

speak again. "Quick, the other brides are coming already. Why did you have me get this for you?"

"Didn't I tell you last night? Don't you remember? It's the key to the Vessel. The strongbox sequestered in the temple sanctuary. Hush now."

4

For the rest of the morning they prayed, and braided time, and bled for the cruelty of the world. Rain and Iskinaary arrived at one point to watch them, but found the ritual pointless and upsetting. "You're hurting yourself on purpose?" asked Rain. "Doesn't the world do enough to you, that you have to add to the insult?"

"You don't need to understand," said Mirka, "and that you don't get it at once is proof of your alien status here."

"No arguing; we're in prayer," intoned Helia.

Cossy just shrugged at the Rain Creature. *Grown-ups.*

So Rain and Iskinaary set out along the rising bluffs to the south to explore a little more of Maracoor Spot. With envy, Cossy watched them go.

Their offices completed, the brides returned to the temple to receive their orders for the day. As Helia could no longer get out easily to inspect the fencing for the baby goats, to see to the repair of the olive press, she had to rely on reports. Giving out daily assignments had become more collegial as a result.

Today, however, with more dispatch that usual, Helia sent the brides out for foraging—even Kliompte, who with her fair skin usually tried to loiter under a roof by offering to take on the floor-washing or the laundry. "Out, even you," said Helia. "We need a fuller cupboard now that we have a permanent guest. I don't want any argument. Go."

"We've made no decision about harboring this Rain Creature indefinitely," began Mirka. "I'm not sure it's wise."

"Oh, for the love of Mara, go when I tell you to go," barked Helia. The brides picked up wicker baskets and sauntered away, each of them in a private snit. "You," said Helia, when Cossy was at the door, "you hang back, a little. I need some help first at the wash basin."

"Allow me," said Kliompte with an urgent smile, but Helia just shook her head and made a rude gesture. Kliompte disappeared with the others.

"What?" asked Cossy. Now they were alone. They

couldn't be overheard. They were a secret pact of two. It was thrilling.

"I want to show you the Vessel," said Helia.

"That's—that's impossible. They won't understand. I don't understand. Why? Isn't it Mirka's place to receive the key when you go, and take care of the casket and whatever it holds?"

"In the normal course of affairs," answered the old woman, "if Mirka weren't ambushed by her own ambition, I'd have inducted her into the secrets of the treasury already. But I don't like her."

"I don't think that's supposed to matter," grumbled Cossy, much to her own surprise. She didn't realize she had opinions of this nature.

"Okay, let me put it like this: I don't *trust* her. The brides of Maracoor must be led by a woman of probity. That means everyday moral sense. But Mirka is too impressed with her own coming power. She doesn't know how to take the high road for the greater good. So I'll be blunt. Her approach to the problem of this green girl and the Goose has finished my thinking on the matter. She's rule-bound. She's contemptuous, she's scared. She's dogmatic. Scheming. That's a dangerous mix. Volatile and unstable."

"She's just having feelings, same as me," said Cossy,

amazed to hear herself defending Mirka. She'd never had much good to say about that old bag. But even so . . .

"We weave time, we collect history in increments of dailiness," said Helia with stolid patience, as if she'd said this a hundred times before. As probably she had. "I've been doing this for more than seventy years, my little marmoset. I know dissent when I see it. Now you listen and listen well. I feel my time is nearly over. I've had signals, I've had spells. Mirka isn't the right person to trust with the key. I want you to have it. At least for now. I want you to know what you are holding."

"A key? I know what a key is."

"The Vessel is too heavy for you to bring to me," said Helia, "so we'll go to it." She indicated that Cossy should help her rise. When she was on her feet, she leaned on Cossy's shoulder heavily. They crossed the great room to the windowless sanctuary at the back of the building. To the west, the door: breadth, light, everything. Maracoor Abiding over the sea. To the east, in this chamber of shadows, a single stone block, carven with obscure pattern. And sitting upon it the treasurebox, of some rare dense metal, in a gloom somehow sour but organic, too.

Not a speck of dust. Kliompte saw to that every day.

Helia breathed heavily and transferred her weight

from Cossy to the corner of the altar. "Take up the key and open the Vessel," she said.

"I hardly dare."

"Do as I say."

So Cossy did. The key slipped into the lock as if it lived there and was only coming home. It turned smoothly, though the lock emitted a screech of protest. The latch fell open. "Lift the lid, girl," said Helia. She seemed almost to have forgotten who Cossy was. Her eyes were glazed and gluey.

Cossy had to use both hands to raise it up. The hinges attaching the lid to the chest made a sound like the splitting of dry twigs. Once the lid was fully upright, it rested in place.

From the inside of the box rose a dull and dusty radiance. No warmth, as from a flame or the inside of a blossom in sunlight, but something else. A kind of chill glow, the likes of which called into question everything that Cossy knew about light.

She didn't ask what it was, but peered a little closer at what was inside.

She could see its shape, more or less. A sort of implement. Maybe a crude hand-axe. Apparently made of one solid piece of something. Stone, or iron. Or some dense and light-absorbing wood. Longer than it was wide. A neck that one might grasp with a strong hand,

and a knob on the other end like a mushroom head, or a misshapen hammer. Coal-purple or ebony, the darkest shade. And—it was hard to figure this out—although the instrument or totem seemed a sinkhole of black space, as if nothing on its surface could be seen, the air around it glowed, faintly, perhaps even reluctantly.

"What is it?"

"Now you've seen it. The treasure of Maracoor," said Helia. She leaned forward. Pulling from her pocket the cloth napkin upon which she had lately been embroidering designs, she dropped it in like a pretty veil upon the amulet. "I've been wanting to do this for a long time. Provide a shroud and hope for the best. Close up the box. Lock it. We will leave it be. Use that leathern cord and tie the key around your waist so no one will see that you have it."

"Don't you want the key?"

"Not at the moment."

5

Perhaps to thank Cossy for acquiring the key in the middle of the night, Helia told her that she could spend the afternoon roaming the heights of Maracoor with Rain. The Goose refused to accompany them. Walking up slopes was not his idea of recreation. "Just don't fall off the cliffs, Rain. The winds are striking strong up there," said Helia.

"Could be the Rain Creature will stumble to her death and we'll be rid of the overcount," muttered Mirka, in a voice that Cossy wondered if she was intended to hear. Maybe Mirka was giving Cossy a secret license to tumble Rain to her death. What a viper.

The day had begun cloudless, but by the time Rain and Cossy reached the last approach to the higher peak, the horizon was thick with statuesque clouds.

Whether ornamental or full of weather, Cossy couldn't tell. She'd begun the climb hoping to get more from Rain about her mysterious past, now that the twists of the stranger's accent seemed easier to parse. But Rain diverted all questions back to Cossy, and Cossy wasn't interested in talking about anything *she* knew—it was too boring.

In any case, Cossy seemed not to have answers to the questions that Rain was asking—like where they were, *really*. And what the mainland was like. None of the brides could remember the mainland—they'd all been inducted as infants. Or, Cossy wondered, maybe the other brides knew more than they were telling her? She herself was only ten, or something like that.

She asked Rain how old she was. Rain shrugged, as if she didn't care.

But as the slopes got steeper, the girls linked hands to balance on wobbly stones or hoist each other over tricky stretches. That was a kind of conversation, too, hands joining and dropping and joining again. Until recently Cossy had enjoyed a complement of bridal hugs and kisses, but now that she was older, Scyrilla cried cooties and shied from any touching. So the easy warmth of Rain, warmth uncomplicated by hierarchy, made Cossy feel different yet again, for the second or third time since she'd gone to bed last night.

At the top of the climb, she imagined they'd sit and talk. Maybe Rain would open up about the world from which she'd come. Maybe she could answer questions that Cossy would never get the chance to ask the Minor Adjutant, not until all six senior brides had died and it was her turn to rule the temple and its brides.

But while Rain might have relaxed some, the wind on the heights made talking impossible. They crouched down in the noisy air, and scrunched forward on their bottoms, coming within three feet of the dangerous cliff-edge. Oh, little risk of falling over here. The west wind was pushing up at them. It seemed as if they could have leapt off the cliff and been held in place in the air.

Rain threw her arms out. "It feels like flying," she said, "except we're not moving."

That was it. That was all Cossy got. But the expression on the green face was tortured and ecstatic.

When they turned to make their descent, Rain scanned the horizon. "No other islands at all?" she said.

"The Minor Adjutant says there are quite a few islands to the north, a sort of sloppy group of them. Some are together in clots, others more isolated. We are one of the smaller islands, Helia tells us, and the farthest out. There isn't anything beyond us."

"There is somewhere beyond you," said Rain, but

she wouldn't answer any more questions about what that somewhere was.

"Can't you tell us where you came from?" said Cossy. "You can tell *me*. I won't tell."

Rain ran her hands through her hair for a while. "I can't tell."

"That's no fair."

They picked their way across a rushing brook. "I'm just, I guess, halfway," said Rain at last. "Between what I don't know and what I can't know. I feel as if I'm dead, or dying, or on my way to death. Do you know what that feels like?"

This was heady stuff for Cossy. She took her time to ponder before she spoke. "Everyone is on the way to death, aren't we? I mean that's what they all *say*. But I have no idea what it feels like. How could I? I always wonder, all the time."

"I thought everybody knew about death but me."

Cossy sighed. It was easier to squabble than discuss stuff. "I've seen goats die, I guess. And fish. And trees fall down. I've squished bugs and stepped on bees with my sandal. And watched birds fall to the ground and limp for a couple of days before they inch under something and go still."

"You've known other people to die? Maybe you watched them flicker out?"

"The whole world had only had eight people in it till you came—us seven brides and the Minor Adjutant. Sure, there were other brides before me, I know. They died. And Helia is the oldest and will croak pretty soon, I guess. Then a baby bride will come to be novice, and I'll be second youngest. I'll be like Scyrilla and be nasty. Except nobody can be as nasty as Scyrilla. Why do you think you're dying?"

This was the longest speech Cossy had ever made. She could hardly believe she still had breath left with which to go clambering down the hill.

But Rain wouldn't answer the question. She just glanced at Cossy with a sad sort of wince, a smile that wasn't at all hopeful. Cossy let it go. They made the rest of the descent in silence.

The cumuli that had threatened the western horizon brought a cloudburst shortly after supper. The spell of good weather had been such a relief, especially after that long assault of storm last week, that some of the brides became upset. A few of them threw on shawls and went out to spread panels of light balsa upon garden shoots to keep them from being washed away.

Rain offered to help. She wouldn't take a shawl, she didn't seem to mind the water. "Well, with that *name*," observed Mirka wittily. "Ought we conclude you're some sort of rain-whisperer, here to drown us?"

"Don't be absurd," said Rain, a note of annoyance shooting into her voice for the first time. "Meaning no disrespect, I won't be made a scapegoat. That's just not on."

Mirka grimaced in overdone astonishment. "I see I've struck a nerve," she said pointedly, but acquiesced at the sight of Rain's darkening brow.

Cossy wanted to join them in the vegetable patch, but once again Helia held her back. When they were alone in the guttering of the oil lamp, the senior bride said, "You must keep that key very safe upon you at all times, Cossy. Have I made myself clear about that?"

"I don't really know why," replied the girl.

"It's a dangerous item in that treasurebox," said Helia. "I'm afraid that if Mirka finds the key, she'll open up the box and put inside a handful of tarragon or witherwort. Herbs locked in that dark space with the artifact take on a certain power. See how frightened Mirka is of Rain. I am afraid Mirka would use the herbs to mix into Rain's food somehow. Maybe stirred into the vinegar dressing for the root vegetables, something like that. If Rain ingests a small portion of herbs tainted by exposure to the treasure, she might not even survive. She has a constitution bred elsewhere, you see. I wouldn't put it past Mirka to try to nudge Rain out of this situation by poisoning her."

"Oh, Mirka's a pill, but she's not a demon," cried Cossy.

"I do hope you're right," said Helia. "But let's not give her the chance to prove you wrong, shall we? Keep that key close to you."

"I would rather you have it."

"If it comes to me, it will go to Mirka. I have explained this. Mirka isn't sound in her judgments. You heard her wish that Rain would fall off the cliff-edge this morning."

"She was joking!"

"Was she?" Helia's expression was gentle and her old hand reached out to touch Cossy's palm. "Mirka is hidebound, rulebound, and frightened. Even if I were to die tonight, Mirka would not be able to tolerate a green foreigner taking the place of a native Maracoorian. She'd rather wait for the overseer to bring a suitable replacement. And I so don't want Mirka to try to hurt Rain. A quarter cup of chopped herbs that have spent a night in that box—I am afraid that is all it would take to do away with Rain. Then when the overseer comes back, we'd be only seven again, and the problem would be solved. Unless of course perhaps you think that having Rain—slip away—is a good idea?" she said with concern, gripping Cossy's hand with her own, a surprisingly strong grip just now.

"Are you nuts? I'm thrilled that Rain is here," said Cossy. "I won't let Mirka do a thing to her."

"That would be my hope, too," said Helia. "But watch Mirka like a hawk, my cunning marmoset. She's a sly one. She has her ways. That key must ever be in your care."

"Helia," said Cossy quickly, for she could hear the brides and Rain splashing back from the gardens, "what *is* that thing you showed me? The treasure?"

"It's an amulet, I suppose," said Helia distractedly, "an ancient totem of great and unknowable power. It's called the Fist of Mara. I don't know anything more about it. Hush now, and put together the salad plates. And sing me a song while you're at it."

Cossy began to arrange the eight portions of green on their clay squares, warbling a devotional rhyme about the Great Mara. Helia didn't seem to be paying much attention to it. Her eyes were slits, watching the brides coming in the portico of the temple, while nodding absentmindedly to the split rhythms of the hymnody.

6

The deluge slanted into the portico too heavily for the guest and her Goose to sleep on both sides of the open doorway. The brides punctuated their sighs with arched eyebrows and flared nostrils, and afforded Rain and the Goose a space on the floor near the dish cupboard. Then they repaired, the seven of them, to the gathering mat before the hearth on the other side of the room. Kliompte had lain a small fire against the damp. What with the torrent upon the roof and the surf pounding in the usually gentled harbor, the brides could talk quietly without being overheard.

"Far be it from me to promote discord, but all this is insupportable," said Mirka.

"Are you going to start? Stop already," said Helia.

"My aching bunions have a headache, and my headache has a migraine."

"I'm talking about the weather that brought her to us," hissed Mirka. "Don't you remember? Eight, ten days of monsoonerie? Not normal for this time of year. A few days of calm, and now it seems to be back. Do you refuse to see a correlation?"

"A girl named Rain bringing the rain with her? Is that what you're gassing on about?" asked Helia. "I'd say you're making a bit much of word association, Mirka. I can't blame it on your high feeling of the month—we all know you've arrived at the great dryness. So you're supposed to be reasonable now. Might even become serene if you put your back into it. Like me." She smiled, making fun of herself. The other brides bit back their smirks. It didn't help matters if Mirka sensed she was being made fun of. "So what is it, Mirka, that makes you think our visitor is in charge of cloudbursts?"

"You're denying what's right in front of your face. It's too intense to be a coincidence."

"Everything is a coincidence. You, me, the deep blue sea. Stop angling for advantage, Mirka."

"You don't understand." She stabbed her finger in the air. "Something needs to be *done*, Helia. Stop averting your eyes. You're ducking responsibility. The whole balance of the world is upset. Every omen shows it. Your inability to take this in, I declare, is stinking proof that you've outlived your time as the senior bride. The ferocity of this situation requires new leadership. I'm calling on you again to step aside. You've become incompetent."

Helia put her hands together in her lap and looked at them. "Would you holler mutiny, my dear Mirka? Over a random summer storm?"

"This is no ordinary storm. This is no ordinary time."

"We *make* the time happen," said Helia. "Have you forgotten why we're here? This is the time we braided at the seashore, so this is the event we have roped in."

"For ten days it was too stormy to fulfill our obligations," replied Mirka. "*Ten days.* That's never happened before, Helia. Even in winter we usually manage to thread the hours for a short while every day. The longest we've left it before this is, what, maybe four days in sequence? I don't mean to be smart when I say that we've lost the thread. It's escaped us, so this is where we are left. You must step aside. It is a new time. I so announce it—"

"We sleep on it?" asked Bray, ever averse to conflict.

Mirka folded her arms across her breast. "I call for a voice vote."

"You tried this already. I might remind you that we don't vote. It was an amusement last time, but you're becoming unhinged. Cut it out."

"It's a new moment," insisted Mirka. "Who would *like* to vote?"

This time Cossy thought voting would be fun, so that she could vote against Mirka and wipe her out for good. She raised her hand. She wasn't alone—everyone but Helia and Kliompte raised a hand.

"That's all very well but we don't vote," said Helia, though perhaps less confidently than before.

"Excuse me, but we've just voted to vote on the matter," said Mirka.

"Well, *I* didn't vote, and if we were to vote, my vote would outweigh all of yours anyway. I'm the senior bride. I have advantage."

Cossy thought there was clarity in this line of reasoning, but Mirka just laughed and held her ground. "We can't be eight on this island. The world has gone awry. Something needs to be done. If you don't rectify it, Helia, I will. Vote or not."

"All right," said Helia at last. "I'll allow a vote, but on my schedule. And it won't be at night. Bad decisions are made in the dark. We'll hold out for clear weather and for sunshine. So the spooky old rain doesn't sway our thinking."

On her pallet next to Helia's bedside at night, Cossy thought back upon the day, and on the notion that Rain might be halfway to dead—dying, or in a dead state. Certainly the Rain Creature's color was strange. Maybe that green was the color the soul took on passing into another world. How could the visitor smell so real though, and look so sharp and intense, seem so full of feeling even if she couldn't name what her feelings were? How could she be so much like a person if she was on her way to being emptied of personhood?

To help Rain if she was trying to die—but then Cossy would lose the first new friend she'd ever made. Still—what did friends do for one another?

"Did you hear what Mirka said?" murmured Helia in the dark. "Something drastic needs to be done. I fear what she has in mind."

Something drastic needs to be done, thought Cossy. What a grown-up thought.

The storm continued through the night. While it slackened some in the morning, the skies didn't clear, and the downfalls pounded and paused and began again. The brides avoided catching either Mirka's eye or Helia's. For her part, Rain seemed to have picked up on the communal prickliness. She took her morning ration onto the portico and shared a mumbled colloquy with the Goose. "She couldn't have overheard us last night, could she possibly?" asked Kliompte, whose domestic ambitions recently had begun, tentatively, to include hospitality.

"Don't be a ninny. In that weather? The Great Mara herself couldn't have heard her own heartbeat," said Helia. This remark, so casual as to be nearly blasphemous, made several brides flinch. Cossy thought: how *would* a vote go, if we took one?

"You don't know what Iskinaary may have heard, though," murmured Tirr. They all slid their eyes Goose-ward to see if his head twitched at the mention of his name. That would clinch it. But the Goose either didn't hear or was too smart to let on if he did.

The brides finished their breakfast and then began their morning oblations, wounding themselves first. For the first time Cossy saw that the scars of sawgrass made a kind of braided pattern on her own soles. Like the weaving of nets, except upon her own self. She didn't linger on that thought. Having been introduced to the secret unguent, she was cross to have it denied her. But she saw Helia wasn't using it either, so she didn't feel she could ask for any. "Why do we even do this anyway?" she grumbled.

"You're becoming Scyrilla, full of disapproval," said Helia placidly. "It was bound to happen, though I will miss my innocent marmoset."

"But really. What good does it do?"

"It's a sacred gesture, a sacramental sign that we have agreed not to walk away from our holy obligations."

"Where could we walk to? We live on an *island*."

"It's a symbol, Acaciana. But it's also a practice of

piety. We rake our feet to blood as a symbol of what we are willing to give up for the world. It's called sacrifice. If you don't understand, ask the next chief bride after I'm dead. I've been explaining this for years and I'm bored from the repetition."

"Maybe it *is* time for someone else—" Cossy hadn't meant to say that. It was just the next thought she had. Helia's lips tightened and whitened a little.

They walked together on raw feet to the harborside. No one mentioned the occasional rain, the clouds, the pending vote.

Once seated, Helia became her usual self, unsteady, placid, ruminative as an elderly nanny goat. Mirka was more brittle. She twisted the net-lines too vigorously, snapping them.

Meanwhile the clouds sorted themselves but wouldn't head home. The air warmed a little anyway. Squirrels at their morning panic, bees on the whirl, and a turtle out for a stroll along the margin of the tide.

When the ritual was complete and the day's chores were to be assigned, Helia told Cossy to head out to gather eggs from the hen yard. "Can't I go and ramble with Rain again?" she asked. "It's drizzling but it's not awful."

"I ought to be given a task," suggested Rain. "I don't

want to rely on hospitality anymore. I need to pull my own weight."

"It may come to that," said Helia, "but not yet. We're still figuring out what is most sensible to ask of you. Enjoy one more day of exploration while you have it. The Goose can go with you."

"I'm not one of your minions, to be ordered about," quawked the Goose.

"Oh, you, you're free to leave, aren't you," said Helia. "Take to the wing and head for Maracoor Abiding if it pleases you. If you stay, though, you'll acknowledge the way we do things here. I need a space to clear my head, so in other words, and I mean this nicely, get lost."

"I'm not a tourist," said the Goose, and added, "I won't stay where I'm not wanted, though."

"Rain, you and your cranky crony can take the path over the southern headland. You'll find wise-moss meadows and oak-apple trees, easy walking and pretty. Possibly a few early oak-apples. You could bring back half a dozen in that apron we loaned you, if they're windfalls. If they're too riddled with worms we feed them to the donkeys."

"We're not partaking of any apple *she* brings to the table," barked Mirka, as if she couldn't help herself. "Poison apples aren't to my taste."

"I'll do what I'm asked, and if you don't want something I haul in, don't have it," said Rain without rancor. "Though it would be nicer if Cossy could come with us to show us the way."

"It's impossible to get lost on an island this size, Rain. Cossy will be here when you return. Take some bread with you in case you meander for longer than you expect."

Rain did. Iskinaary kept his beak closed. He preferred bread to grubs and wasn't about to be rude enough to have his portion held back. They left in a mutual splashing of puddles. To Cossy the temple seemed emptier when they were gone. A foretaste of how you might come to feel if someone died? The shock was that the place now could seem emptier, when all seven brides were still bustling about just as they'd always been. How quickly the functioning of the world can readjust. Decay, improve, whatever it might be.

The other brides were set to tasks farther away from the temple. When Cossy returned with the eggs, Helia cocked her finger to draw her close.

"Now I want you to go to that patch of stony ledge north of the harbor," she said. "Where the worts grow. The part we call the Giant's Forehead."

"What for?"

"I need some redweed and some witherwort."

"Redweed is for cooking," said Cossy, "I know that. Tomatoes and onions. But witherwort—that's awful stuff."

"Do you remember your worts? Groundwort is useless—neither toxic nor tasty. Leave it be. Rangewort is nice for about two days but gets woody too soon and becomes indigestible. Witherwort is the tricky one, it comes halfway up your shin. Slightly shimmery and more pinky-brown than the others. Can you remember?"

"But we're supposed to avoid it, aren't we? It's toxic. And it looks so much like rangewort. We're not supposed to get it mixed up."

"It's horrible stuff," agreed Helia. "If Mirka were to pick some and chop it up and leave it to dry overnight in the Vessel with the amulet, who knows to what uses she could put it. Mixed in a cup of oil and vinegar with tarragon and rangewort to mask the taste, and served on a lettuce leaf, no one would know she'd been dealt a nasty portion. That's what I worry about should Mirka get hold of that key, now. Mirka believes we should be seven here on Maracoor Spot, not eight. A troublesome salad for the Rain Creature. So keep it safe and let no one else know you have it."

"You've told me that four dozen times. But why do you want witherwort if it is so dangerous?"

"I like to put leaves of it in my pillow slip," said Helia. "At my age I suffer from bad dreams. The witherwort leaves keep the dreams away. It's simple as that. But I don't like the other brides to know because they'd call me for a fool. An old dame beyond managing anyone else. They're already ranged against me, I can feel it. In the past I always collected witherwort for myself but these days, my knees, you know. Will you do that?"

"Will it hurt me?"

"Bring a small knife. But no, to touch it will not bother you. To eat a small portion would make you queasy and to eat some that had spent a night steeping in the dark next to the Fist of Mara would, I think, make you sorry. Why should Mirka do that to poor Rain?"

"Does Mirka even know what is in the Vessel?" asked Cossy. "If she does, she has never let on."

"You ask too many questions," said Helia. "Do what I say, and get back to me before the high noon sun so I can strip the leaves and arrange them in my bedding before the others arrive and call me an idiot. Do you understand?"

Cossy looked balefully at Helia. The old woman's eyes were rheumy, her lower lip soft and caving, her eyebrows raised in an expression of openness and hope. The red in her cheeks suggested health, but a palsied motion of her hands, gripping each other, supposed otherwise. "You are a good girl," said Helia, "and everything you do is for the good. Don't forget it. I love you and I have raised you well. You understand right and wrong. Now will you do as I say?"

The youngest bride didn't quite answer, just shrugged, picked up the paring knife and one of the smaller herb baskets, and set out in the sunshine.

That evening, because the rising moon was making an unusual formation on the horizon—conjoining with a couple of celestial bodies so that it formed the shape of a hunting and snarling snout of some sort—Cossy was able to find a few moments alone. She chopped up a handful of witherwort and put it in the bowl of a spoon. Then she unlocked the casket and laid the spoon down carefully upon the embroidered napkin that Helia had dropped along the spine of the amulet. She locked the box again, secreted the key on the cord around her waist, and rejoined her sister brides to watch the moon on its prowl. It looked menacing, distended. Some freak of celestial design. An omen, or just another ugly accident of nature.

"This is your first Xiroton moon, isn't it?" said

Helia to Cossy. She reached out her hand and squeezed Cossy's. "It's frightening to look at, but marvelous. You'll be lucky to see it a few times in your life. I think for me it is the fifth sighting, and it is surely the last. Hail, Xiroton," she intoned, "god of the hunt, the snare, and the net; pass over us in your mercy, and leave us to live another day."

Leorix

1

Cur beside him. The mangy thing there all along, panting, sniffing. Loyalty on stumpy legs. "Onwards, laddio, we're taking the longer road," said Lucikles. "Sniff out danger, there's a good dog. Let me know a few seconds before the arrow strikes my heart or the stone my skull, will you, boy?"

Cur whuffled a kind of assent, and behaved himself for a few moments, until the gutters of the road called to him. A rich hunting ground tonight for a dog newly returned from the high seas.

Eight or nine major arteries snaked out of the city. Any number of tracks and trails over the southern farmlands, into the wild woods and highlands due west, and through the scrubby barren bluffs and alluvial swamplands farther north. But since the city had emptied itself of so much of the scrap and society that lived there, those fleeing from the marauders would have used every available route. This low forest road was filthy with abandoned food—shells of nuts, skins of fruit, broken firkins and sandals, and the scat of donkeys and cart horses.

More proof of panic, for in general the citizens of Maracoor Abiding prided themselves on civic order.

Still, a paradise for Cur.

Lucikles convinced himself that the rustle in the undergrowth was nothing more than local populations in their everyday work of murder. Weasels, stoats, foxes. Sounding only like dry leaves slipping over themselves. Humans could rarely move with such delicacy. The larger beasts of the forest—the tomb cats, mostly nocturnal, and manticores, mostly mythological—would avoid a blundering noisy human being unless cornered. Deer fled; bears froze; wolves tended to prefer the highlands where it was easier to pick off prey. At least peppy little Cur could growl off your standard feral dog at twenty paces.

No, as usual, it was humans mostly to be feared. Lucikles found himself grateful for one thing: if he had to go chasing his family through the Thalassic Wood, at least the human exodus had largely passed by before he got there. The woods seemed full of everything but living, stinking people.

He knew there were three or four hamlets to clear

before the winding route turned back on itself and began to climb to the tableland known as High Chora. On excursions when his family had traveled this route, on their way to join his mother-in-law at the family farm, they'd often taken shelter in some humble inn with little to recommend it but supper and fleas. That the fleas often departed the inn buried in the collars of lodgers suggested that they too felt the accommodations wanting.

Here and there patches had been cleared for those vegetables that could thrive in shade: beetroot, carrots, cabbage, skullroot, chard. Lucikles came upon the first such holding an hour or so into his walk. The wicker-wrought fences had been smashed to splinters, and most of the harvest yanked away. Not the work of beasts, he thought, unless one's accounting of beasts included the human variety. Ah, for the poor peasant in the forest whose food supply had been so ravaged. Then, perhaps the peasant and family had already fled at the news of an alien invasion, and were busy ravaging someone else's holdings farther up the track.

He spent the night in a lean-to woodshed with rats and spiders and Cur.

It was high afternoon the next day when he came into the first hamlet. A few cats sat on windowsills.

He heard an old woman's voice crooning tunelessly from inside one of the cottages, but when he shouted a hallo, she stopped singing. No one came to a window either to hallo him back or to rain stones upon him. The place seemed deserted otherwise, and locked against trespassers. So he pressed on. He knew the second hamlet was only half again as far. Without children or a cart to slow him down, he could get there before nightfall. Should that place be abandoned, too, he'd break down a door and find somewhere to settle himself for the night. Assuming he could actually break down a door. More likely he would just find a goat shed and come to a stop upon a thump of moldy hay.

Cur kept to heel happily enough, having done enough exploring for the time being. Once in a while he lifted his nose, keened a bit, but nothing ever emerged from the bracken to threaten them. Lucikles thought Cur might be suffering from a disorder of anxiety.

The shadows lengthened. The forest greens turned purple, brown, black.

A howl and a roar, off to one side in the woods—which side he couldn't even tell—but whoever had been threatened had either safely fled or been slaughtered. Silence, that uneasy hesitant silence of woods, returned.

2

At the second hamlet, which was large enough (six buildings!) to have a name—Midasoor—there was a little more human activity than at the first. A family with too many young children to evacuate, he guessed, was roasting a rabbit on a spit. The children laughed and shrieked in circles in the road, but fell silent as he approached. The paterfamilias looked up from the fire and neither frowned nor protested a stranger's arrival. Perhaps having so many children had inured him to human aggravation. "Behold a straggler," he said to Lucikles. "And at an hour when he will be hoping for a bite."

Cur went dashing up to greet the children with licks and little yaps, which they loved, except the smallest child, who screamed bloody death. "Cur, back," shouted

Lucikles, for the gesture of it, though he knew the dog would pay him no mind. "Yes," he said to the father, "and at this hour, if you've a notion where I could bed down for the evening, I'd be grateful. And I have coin to pay."

"It'd be a curse upon our family's honor for us to take coin during a crisis. Wife will be out with something to drink in a moment. Wife?" he called. "A tankard of something? We have a guest."

He grinned at the look on Lucikles's face. "Don't fuss me with your city ways. Her name is Wife, her parents called her that at birth. Her sisters were called Maid and Abbess, so you see I got the pick of the lot. Though Maid is married four times now and unwed Abbess has twelve children. So names only go so far. At least they didn't have a fourth daughter named Husband."

Wife emerged. She too seemed unperturbed at a single wanderer at this hour. "Here you be," she said, handing him ale in a pewter mug. "How is it you are lagging behind the others?"

"I was away at sea," he said. "I only just returned yesterday to find the great city evacuated. When did people come through?"

She replied, "Began ten days ago, perhaps, didn't it, Fippios? It was a solid three days, though not in a single parade. We're sure the broadways were as thick with crowds as on pilgrimage days. They took the brunt of it, the main roads. But most city dwellers don't like a dark forest, so while we had a steady stream come by, it was no flood."

"Where does a whole city go to?" It was hard to number the population of Maracoor Crown—he'd never tried—but it had to be close to a hundred thousand people.

"Do you know anyone who doesn't have relatives in the villages?" asked Fippios. "With an inland as deep as Maracoor's? If it's too crowded here, and too crowded there, you can always go farther from the sea. I suspect after the first few days the crowds thinned out, family groups turning this way and that, each toward its motherwomb or fatherfield."

"Would you have seen my wife and children?" he asked.

"We fed every mouth that came our way, but we didn't stop to draw their pictures or to register their names," said Wife. "That is, we fed them as best we could. Our stock is reduced, but rabbits do come out of the underbrush, so stay with us tonight. And if you choose to leave a coin, we wouldn't throw it back at you."

"Wife!" said Fippios.

"We're not charging for our warmth," said the woman, "but we're not going to refuse a charitable gesture." This sounded like a theatrical bit between them that had been rehearsed many times. It was effective. Lucikles found some coin in his satchel and laid his offering upon a bench, where it glinted in the sun. Neither Fippios nor Wife looked at it, but she refilled his tankard as soon as it was empty. He was thirsty, he was tired, and it was good to sit down.

"Did they speak about the attack?" he said. "I have had so little information."

"Most were too tired or shocked to talk," said the husband, "but not all. A fleet of armed vessels arrived at dawn and began to burn the city. That's what I heard. I have never been there so I can't picture it. But apparently there was no discussion, no mandate or ultimatum, not that I picked up on—just a wild and unprovoked attack by a population no one could identify. The home guard was unprepared. It capitulated before everyone's eyes. A mortal shame. Those guards who survived will be taking their own lives if they haven't already. But if the marauders destroyed the city or if they moved in to squat in the mansions and temples, you know better than I do."

"They did neither," said Lucikles. "The destruction was incidental and, I am coming to believe, superficial.

The rumors of mayhem are somewhat exaggerated. But I didn't stay long enough to learn what they may have attempted to do. They must've had a mission."

"Sack the treasury, steal the women, take slaves, that kind of thing?"

"Who knows. Perhaps all of that, and more. I couldn't wait to find out. I am hunting my own family, who fled along with everyone else. A woman named Oena, traveling with three children, ages five to twelve? I don't know if she'd have been with neighbors or traveling on her own."

"Can't help there."

The little children had grown used to Lucikles by now and were sitting nearby, glad for the change in routine. One brave lad even climbed into his lap and pulled at his mustache. Ache for his own son rose so suddenly that Lucikles almost tumbled the babe onto the ground. He governed that whiplash and bounced the kid on his knee.

Soon after that, he accepted their offer of a pallet in a kitchen corridor and lay down. All night the mice in the area beneath the stove rustled like a cove of manticores. He didn't believe he slept, but look, there was a cup of steaming chicory by his shoulder. He hadn't heard anyone set it down.

The children didn't want him to leave, and hung

on to the hem of his tunic. The little boy, nothing like Leorix when Leorix was that age, cried when Lucikles got up to go. Faithlessly he promised to return, eager to get on the track. Fippios and Wife were done with him, and barely managed to wave him off. They had handed him a loaf with a moldy crust and some soft cheese wrapped in grapevines. Perhaps they'd hoped for a larger token of coin.

3

For a while the track seemed easy, even welcoming. Cur loped along, his tongue out, his appetite for the day exactly as eager as it had been yesterday. Three birds followed them for a little while, darting from branch to branch in a weaving ornamentation, singing. For a few moments he pictured the spirits of his three pretty children, and again he was enlivened; but then he imagined the birds as the souls of his children, making a final visitation to their father, and a gust of howl rose out of him so bull-like, stentorian, that Cur turned a puzzled head at him and whimpered in solidarity.

So they walked faster.

Coming upon the next small hamlet—this one at

a kind of crossroads, though he didn't know where the diverging tracks went—he was appalled at a sight of ruination. This village was burned to the ground, at least those parts that weren't stone. Immolated, abandoned. There was a stink of carnage. He went by quickly, looking neither right nor left. If he found a survivor, he'd be obliged to help, or he'd deem himself guilty of abandoning someone. The survivors he needed to find were Oena and Leorix and his daughters.

Maybe the villagers had refused to offer succor. Maybe the desperate refugees had been attacked by locals and had fought back. There was no one left to tell, or no one with a voice. The stench of an abattoir.

He was all but pelting now. There was a fourth village, he knew, the last in the lowlands before the forest track reversed course and began to climb the slopes. If he could avoid it he would—but of course—and only now it occurred to him—what if Oena and the others had been hiding in the rubble of the burned village, groaning their last breaths as he'd hurried by?

Too many choices of horror in this world. Taking in Maracoor Spot, and all the islands, and his homeland of Maracoor Abiding, and the countries of which he knew and those of which he was ignorant, all of earthly

Peare—from side to side—seemed a hopscotch blanket of miseries. There could be no haven in which heartache was unknown.

More sounds of distant distress in the forest, one creature losing the battle against another.

4

At the fourth plantation of homes, something different: a full complement of residents. A few men with crossbows tracked him as he sloped along a loop toward the first of the buildings. "You'll keep going and you won't stop, or if you stop you'll never go again," said the nearest.

"We're giving up nothing," said another.

"I ask for only safe passage," said Lucikles. "I need nothing from you but the next few moments of life till I'm beyond your concerns."

They were cautious but permitted him by. The buildings were all boarded up at the ground level. One flight above, every windowsill was supplied with heaps of stones and broken glass. The villagers on upper floors didn't bother to hide, but jeered at him as he hurried along. From flat rooftops groups of youths hammered at drums and made hoarse shouts, and their sisters and mothers ululated. A means of driving off danger. Primitive, but effective. At one point, to a tender younger woman with a heart-shaped face, Lucikles dared to call up, "I mean no harm, I'm of your country and of your blood," and she smiled liplessly and aimed a tray of night soil in his direction.

He slipped that town like a minnow through reeds, and left it behind. He was shaken and cold. Cur stumped along with his head lowered, as if equally demoralized.

Lucikles paused by a rank stream that smelled of sulfur, the perfume of the underworld, and he put his feet in the water but didn't sip. He ate some bread, and offered a little cheese to Cur, who turned up his nose and went to hunt something more appealing in the underbrush.

As the Minor Adjutant rested, and felt his heartbeat return to a quieter rhythm, he began to think about the questions that Fippios had asked. What had the marauders been seeking, that they had pushed off as suddenly as they had come? What sort of operation had they been on? If they'd meant to conquer the capital city, it was theirs for the asking. But they'd come and gone. To return with a greater fleet? They'd apparently left behind no force to maintain the foothold they'd established. No, they must have gotten what they'd come for, at least for now.

Gotten it, or found that it wasn't there for the taking.

He pulled himself to his feet and began the long slow final climb that, with little reprieve of flat stretches, and full of switchbacks, would bring him to the tableland, perhaps by nightfall if he didn't slacken his pace. He marveled at how the world could empty out. Then, in the deepest heart of the deep green woods, his mind skipped, unbidden, back to Maracoor Spot and the improbable arrival of that green-skinned stranger.

That girl, that Rain Creature, had come in on the tail end of the long strike of unseasonable storm, old Helia had told him.

The same weather. Could it be? A storm that drives a fleet of ships up from some settlement so far to the south that it was virtually unknown to the capital city?

Maybe the vandal armada had been waiting for a signal to strike, to secure whatever advantage they sought. Maybe the unprecedented pattern of weather had been that very sign. Their navy captains had read the winds and harnessed them, had raced their ships from the far south so quickly that, even had they been spotted by lookouts in watchtowers, a warning signal couldn't have been relayed to Maracoor Abiding in time.

The marauders entered and left the capital city with such dispatch either because they found and stole what they had come for, or because they'd determined in short order that it wasn't kept there at all.

And his mind went back to Maracoor Spot, and the temple above the harbor, and the sanctuary, and its locked ironstone Vessel.

He remembered how the brides of Maracoor spent their patient and dedicated lives in braiding time together for the world. Had the arrival of that green girl caused them to carry on their work in new and embittered ways?

Then again, did he really believe they were doing what they were enjoined to do, there at the edge of the harbor of Maracoor Spot? Did *they* even believe it? Did it matter? Wasn't time enacted regardless, even in spite of possible apostasy? Did the gods actually *need* the faithful to believe in order to ordain the world with dailiness? Could gods be that petty?

5

The woods thinned. The dense, gnarled vinewood of the Thalassic Wood gave way to taller trees with higher canopies. The air grew aromatic. The light of later afternoon seemed to boil with the activity of the insect universe. He grew a little light-headed.

When the sky through cedars had begun to glow pink among the cobalt shadows of the woods, Lucikles found his vision a little blurred. He paused and gulped some water from the canteen that Fippios and Wife had supplied. He rubbed his eyes. Scattered volleys of tiny and fiercely energetic birds swooped down from the treetops, feasting on bugs at the level of the crown of his head. But the birds became agitated. They began to pester him, to make small feints, as if wanting threads of his thinning hair to weave into their nests. Several of them scraped him with their beaks as they passed.

They were a species unfamiliar to him. Blue and silver—it was hard to tell. Blue in the approach, silver in departure, or blue and silver in turn, or separately? They moved so fast he could hardly see the wings, like hummingbirds. Blue and silver hummingbirds. Maybe the blue was male, the silver female? What were they after?

Blue and silver witches in a swarm.

The moment he thought that—though was it poetry, premonition, or observation?—he became weirdly more serene. If the world of folktale were cracking open, and if manticores were indeed waking up from the stone sleeves in which they slept, and if the djinni-harpies of nursery legend were at play, what good would the panic of a mortal do? Or what harm, for that matter? The djinni-harpies would bat him forward, toward rescue or doom. He was going that way anyway.

For the first time since pulling into the harbor of Maracoor, he felt liberated from the sense of agency. This relief would be fleeting, he knew, but he enjoyed it. What would be would surely be. Blue and silver witches, homunculae-harpies, pester me forward. Stir my feet more quickly along the path. Bring me to what I must in any case come to know, whether it be the safety or the sabotage of my family life.

When he cleared the tree line and began the stonier final ascent to the tableland, the hummingbird-witches scattered. Now he thought he could hear them singing in lacy, buzzing voices, though whether blessing or invective, or nonchalant nonsense, he couldn't imagine. But as he reached the plateau of High Chora at last, with its slightly richer volley of winds, its scattered and shabby farms coming into view, Lucikles thought back to the approach into Maracoor Crown of the *Pious Enterprise*. That first weird infestation of birds upon the prow of the ship—had the flock been an omen of some resurgence of fantastic population? Or was this a mere fancy of his, only a misremembering, also born of hunger and worry?

6

The world opened up its spaces but closed down its daylight at about the same rate. Lights began to burn sporadically in distant farmsteads. A sound of cows, and goats, a doubling of choirs. Healthy, normal, unfussed. Kitchen fires across fields. He would be there by the rise of the moon.

And then the moon appeared on the edge of the plateau. Its visage was mendacious, its usual sphere augmented with several adjacent pale stones of the sky, lining up to look like a brow, a hunting profile. He had seen this rare effect of heavenly adjacency twice before in his life. Any calm he had been suckered into feeling now leeched out. He began to run.

The snout leaned over the horizon, then rose in a sky washed with vitreous green. An effect of moonlight upon clouds too thin to be seen, he guessed. He could be wrong.

The domestic smell of cows having wandered not so long ago in the roadside meadows, a tonic.

He stopped to piss. Instinctively he moved in toward the trunk of a tree, as if a man urinating in a country lane could offend the society that wasn't there. The tree clenched itself in a squeeze and the sound of wood against wood was a rhetoric he couldn't decipher. A potential trap. An arboreal embrace. He backed away, still spraying. He was losing his grip on reality.

Around a few stacks of sweet early hay, pitchforked into heaps for collecting tomorrow. Farm tools left to stand as were, without a farmer's fear of their being pinched—that's how isolated the place was.

Here, a stand of tender teenage willows, their dendritic wands trailing toward the surface of a pond. In the half-light they looked poised in a dance-step. Two ducks emerged from the bank, moving away from him but without haste—pretending not to notice him, but veering off anyway. It seemed to Lucikles that they were each ridden by a homunculus in a cap of red felt, or something like. It was unclear what gender the hobbins were, if any. He almost hailed them, to catch their details, but thought better of it. What if some farmer were lurking about in the shadows, and questioned his motives? He moved along, though Cur kept casting backward glances and growling in the deeps of his throat.

Tricks of the light, tricks of the mind.

And finally he was in terra cognita, on the apron hems of known territory. Oena's family's farm, such as it was. Oena's father was dead a decade, but her old mother, Mia Zephana, kept it up as well as she could, with the help of a loutish cousin or two, when they showed up. There, the great oak, its swing swaying in the wind, as if someone had just jumped off and run to hide in the undergrowth and leap out at him and shout Boo! There, the hedgerow to keep the cattle from eating vegetables, and the green gate through it. His breathing grew panicked and noisy in his own ears.

He pushed through the gate, making a clatter. The farmhouse door was open to the yard, and the yellowy glow of a hearth-fire patched the dirt and grass with promise.

They had heard him approach, they were there; they were at the door. Oena, her hair in a rag; and the girls, his Poena and Star: the girls halting to adjust their vision to the dark, and then, in recognition, rushing at him across the yard.

He pushed forward, his heart in his throat. "Oena?" he cried. "My son! Leorix!"

Oena put a palm up in the air. The girls halted, confused. He saw the look in their eyes, that he had not greeted them; he saw that they had seen his confusion and taken it for preference, and he saw that they would never forget this. They never did.

7

After he had visited Leorix in his sickbed, and felt his wounds, Lucikles turned back to his wife. The girls had pretended to forgive him and they accepted his hugs, and he had tucked them in bed. He had shared a glass of whiskey-musk cordially with his mother-in-law. Then he repaired with Oena to the yard for a few moments, for privacy. She told him about the attack of wolves upon the party—they had risked the quicker, upland route after all—and how Leorix had tried to defend them—how he had probably saved all their lives with a huge and unwieldy dead tree limb.

Above the couple, the leering creature in the heavens lolled its jaw and slavered its invisible tongue.

He talked only about the walk from the city, not about his trip. He told her about the witches. "Witches, a flock of little witches?" she said, thinking he was joking. "You mean the upland sparrowlarks?" He told her about the hobbins riding ducks like steeds across the pond. About the tree that had wanted to encase him in its bark. He laughed as he spoke, but when he looked up, he saw a look of resignation in Oena's face. She tried to hide it, she laughed, she held a finger to her lips to shush him, she took his hand. But there wasn't any doubt. He had left his children young eleven weeks ago, and sure enough, they had grown older during his trip. They always did. They had grown older, but he saw now that he, he Lucikles: this time he had grown Old.

PART·TWO

The Fist of Mara

1

The green girl and the Goose, up earlier than the others, walked to the harbor. Rain perched on the ledge where the brides would fuss with the netting that caught the shallow tide and let it out again.

It was agreeable for them to be on their own here. The horizon that she faced was still indistinct with the dregs of night. As if her own uncertainty and imprecision about herself was pasted upon the world.

The Goose occupied himself with his toilet. What a talent for abstinence from idle blather.

She dropped her chin in her hands and stared at the shell that she had found in her satchel. She was like this empty shell—whatever had lived inside her once had escaped—or died. Was it alive somewhere? Could she find it, could she forge access to herself?

Iskinaary made his martial sort of promenade over to her and, as if answering her unspoken musings, remarked, "Have you forgotten your nerve? I've been patient, Rain, waiting for you to initiate a plan. Things with these brides are getting testy. Maybe we ought to talk about what happens next."

"I've been unsure how to say much of anything," she began. Aha, she suddenly got it: she'd been afraid of abandonment. "I don't remember much from before. There, I've admitted it."

"It's a start. In any case, your vigor is restored, at least somewhat. I mean, your color is good. Relatively speaking. For a green human being. You can walk without limping. Did you even notice you were limping the first few days?"

She shook her head. "I lost my sense of a lot of things. I've been waiting for it to return."

"You and me both."

"I had a dream last night," she began.

The Goose quawked. "Human dreams! Spare me. Pointless. Endless. Always skirting the subject. Like the work of certain human composers I could mention. How something unhummable can be called a melody is a tautology I can't bite."

"I think it was important, though. I mean, in that I had a dream at all. My memory may be coming back."

The Goose lifted his beak. His expression was keen and frosty, yet perhaps also somewhat kind? It was hard to tell with a Goose. "Well, if you're ready to face this collapse of your precious fund of memory, we're getting somewhere."

"Have you known all along?"

"Sweetie," said Iskinaary, "I made a promise to accompany you over the water. If you met with some sort of dementia because of our wipeout on the sea, I wasn't going to leave you. But now you seem to be coming around a little, it's time to consider what's next."

"I dreamt of men and women," she said. "So we come from a place of men and women, don't we?"

"After a fashion. But like most of your kind you're anthropocentric to a fault. We also come from a place of bucks and roes, queens and drones, rogues and herds, heifers and steers and geldings and a few creatures that don't fit into neat categories. Just for starters. What did you dream of, you with your fitful obsession over your own kind?"

"I don't know," she said sadly, "just that they existed, and they weren't the same people as these brides, or as that man from the mainland. Lucikles."

"Do you remember your life at all before we got here?"

"I hardly remember how we got here. And I don't remember why."

"We were flying," he said, clearly cautious about how much he ought to be filling in for her. "We were flying, my gosling. We encountered a ferocious storm, and you came down into the sea, and I came down beside you so you could cling to me and keep from drowning."

She shook her head. "I don't know very much about the world as it was before I woke up here. But I don't think people fly. As a matter of daily practice."

"Not without a broom like yours, no, usually not. But you need some native skill of your own. The broom won't give a talentless rider a single grasshopper leap."

She cocked an eyebrow. "Tell me more."

"Certainly not. You'll remember what you need to remember. Or maybe it's better that you forget. Anyway, I don't want to cause you suffering."

The horizon now rimmed with phosphorescence. A green pulse in the blackness. Behind them would be the gelid white-blue of the predawn sky. "One day I might insist you fill me in on my past," she declared. "But for now—"

"This is where you are, for now," said the Goose. "This is where you've ended up. For good? Who knows? As humans go, you are young. That stout old creature, Helia, she's four or five times your age, I bet. *You* could grow to be that old. Is this the beachhead you needed to storm? Are you to stake your life here among these women? Quiet, out of the way, safe from assault by life?"

"I don't know."

"If you decide this is it," he went on, "I suppose I'll go back. Go home."

"Home, where is home?" Not a question, more a philosophical shrug.

"But if you want *out*," he continued, "and if you can't fly anymore, then I should go on ahead, and find someone to come get you. For I can't carry you off this island. I'm strong but I've seen some years, and you're too lumpy to be a passenger."

"I'm not lumpy. But anyway, it would be unseemly, riding you."

"Now you're sounding like these crabbed women. Beware false piety, Rain. There would be nothing indelicate about my carrying you, if we could make it work. I am a scholar and a gentleman. A gentlebird, that is. The scholar part is an exaggeration, though I can work an abacus with my beak and do celestial navigation without an astrolabe. Still, that's beside the point. I haven't the strength to bear you away even if I wanted."

"Could the broom be persuaded to fly again?"

"Maybe it still needs to dry out from the seawater," said the Goose, "but frankly I think it requires someone who knows how to pilot it. As you've forgotten so much, perhaps you've also forgotten that skill."

"When we have a moment today," she promised, "I'll take the broom somewhere off on my own and—well, how do I even begin? Do you know?"

"*I* start with wings," said Iskinaary. "A human starts with something in the mind. Or the spirit maybe. I've never been sure and it seemed impertinent to ask."

"So others have flown before me?"

But the Goose would say no more on the subject.

So they turned and headed back to the temple, where the breakfast coals had been unbanked and honeycake was beginning to scorch in a skillet. The quiet sounds of the women at their ablutions ratcheted toward panic before Rain and Iskinaary reached the bottom step to the portico. "She's not moving, she's not breathing!" they heard Kliompte say. "Oh, brides, come help, am I wrong, is she in a faint? I think—"

The Goose and the girl looked at each other.

"She was old," said Iskinaary. "She could hardly stand up anymore."

But it wasn't Helia, they learned.

To escape the wailing of the brides, and the mess of preparing a body for a funeral pyre, Rain fled up the slope. She ran under the generous limbs of the Mother of Olive in the low orchard, and then through the grove of apricots beyond. She found the track that she and Cossy had climbed to the brow of the mountain.

The broom was over her shoulder like a rifle.

Though she hadn't thought the word *rifle* before. What a concept, a rifle.

She'd glanced only briefly at the figure dead in her sheets. It would have been prurient to look more closely. Lacking in respect somehow. Had Rain ever seen a corpse before? She could conceive of worms, and the oozing of organs, the drying of the skin, the hysterical insistence of hair to stay attached. But this wasn't proof of experience, just information. The dirty news of death.

At a level promontory she turned and looked at the temple roof and at the curlicue of harbor. The little buoy blinked in the sun, the knuckles of treacherous rocks near it showed themselves between the crashes of waves. Up here the wind was considerable, so the sound from below, of the brides' keening and their consternation, was mercifully cloaked. The horizon was filament of glass. How high would she have to get before she could see some land other than here? What other land could there be?

She needed a safe place unpestered by crosswinds. Ah, this: a high hollow between stony rises. A small stream beside her crawled with its watery whisper to a place where it collected in a pool before continuing. Here, she unshouldered the broom and put its brush upon the ground. She felt as if she were patting the shoulder of a child only two-thirds her size. Someone the size of Cossy.

Dear Cossy. Poor Cossy.

She wasn't sure how to proceed. The shaft of the besom was a trimmed limb of a tree, its nodules and spokes sanded away. A sort of bitter twine braided with a filament of metal, a tightening wire, clenched the brush to the handle.

She upended the object and put her face to its sharp bristles. She was hoping to breathe in life, but not the past life of broom corn. The organic life in the implement was as dead as the bride below, now being cleaned and dressed in her own bedsheets. Rain wanted to detect a different sort of life.

A life of flight.

Passage through the air. A flight forward, or a flight from something.

What was I fleeing, why did I fly?

She cradled the bony skeleton in her arms, almost cooing to it. Take me up, lift me from here, she said to it. Get me away.

What did she expect? That the broom would grow a mouth and begin to give her good counsel? That it would move of its own accord? "Oh, broom," she began, and then her words continued as if she were channeling some old ditty.

Oh broom, with whom I linger
O'er many a chore and any floor,
Would that your banded skirt and sanded finger
Drag me out my housemaid's door!
I would be flag and banner bright
And you my stag in the day and night.
Parana, palexus, norrex noritopsis.

For a brief moment she almost believed the broom shuddered in her hands. But perhaps that was just a gust of wind along the narrow canyon. The surface of the incidental pond ruffled into lines of script, but she couldn't read their meaning. The broom's agency was only her imagination. It still smelled of flotsam and dead fish.

"Damn," she said.

Oh, so she could swear now. Life was getting back to normal.

"Who's the bigger fool, you or me?" she said to the broom. "Me, I guess, for even talking to you."

Some small residual respect for housework kept her from pitching the tool into the pond. But what a temper she had as she turned back. She'd give the fool broom to Kliompte. For all Rain cared, that fastidious bride could feed the useless thing into the fire they'd be banking up for the immolation of Mirka later in the day, once the flames grew high enough.

When Rain turned the corner of the vegetable garden, she found Cossy was lurking there, hunched under the bean poles with her teary face in her knees.

She'd been wordless all day, the child. Rain didn't wonder at it. Death comes as a shock even when it is inevitable. The world reasserts itself. It says, I keep going whether you do or not. I am indifferent to your need for constancy, says the world, and my indifference is shown in my own constancy.

"So have they figured out what happened?" Rain spoke with a certain brusqueness she hoped would be useful. Cossy shook her head and sobbed.

"As I understood it," Rain continued, "everyone thought that it was Helia tiptoeing along the final margin. Poor Mirka. What happens next, Cossy?"

The child still couldn't answer. While Rain felt

tender, this wasn't getting them anywhere. She took Cossy's damp hand in her own and they circled back to the portico of the temple.

The others had wrapped Mirka's body in her bed linens. Kliompte, who cared the most about such matters, clued Rain in with singsong asides. "We'll burn her later, when the afternoon winds can carry the horrible stink upland and away from us. She's finished her mission here; she's lived her life harvesting time for the world. There's no reason to dignify her with psalms of regret or other dollops of excess. This isn't our way. We are only missionaries for the world, after all, and when our work is done we really don't exist. Do we? Can it be said for anyone?"

Tentatively Rain picked her way along a strand of thought. "If you're making an argument in defense of such plain practice . . . you must . . . be able to conceive another way of doing things?"

"Oh, we can all imagine," said Kliompte, raising her hand to the air. "That's our strength, isn't it? We can imagine the roof blowing off in a gale; therefore, we keep supplies for immediate repair on hand. We can imagine a great many things being done differently— thread of gold for the temple, more solemnity, richer incense to burn in honor of the Great Mara, all that. But not for ourselves. We're laborers for eternity. We fulfill our function like any fruit, and then we rot and die. No one sings a dirge for an apricot deliquescing in the sun."

"Would it be different were it Helia who had died?" asked Rain. "As the senior, I mean?"

Kliompte shrugged. "Maybe a little. But not essentially."

The oldest bride was on her feet, using her oakthorn staff in the customary way. But her shoulders were thrown back and her brow lifted higher. She stomped the ferrule of her staff on the stone, making a ringing sound, and everyone gathered around. Mirka in her shroud had already been moved to the floor of the portico, where her feet faced the harbor and her head pointed toward the Vessel in the dark sanctuary. "Come around, everyone," said Helia in an ordinary voice, the tones she might use deciding which vegetables ought to be gathered for the evening meal. "We have to talk about what next, now that things have changed."

The brides circled closer, and Rain was with them. Iskinaary waddled nearer too. "Not you, you're not invited," said Helia, but the Goose stayed where he was, and they let it go.

"No one knows how and why Mirka chose this moment to die." Helia's voice was taking on a grave tone for the first time since the body had been discovered. "She had seemed in good health. But all life is mystery, and death is a sister to life, and so also mystery."

"Mirka was threatening your authority, Helia," said Tirr.

"That was her job as second in command, don't you think, Tirr?" answered the old woman. "I'd have worried had she been too docile. But it wasn't yet her time to rule, and now it seems it's not her time to live. Perhaps she wanted the elevation a little too much. I wasn't dying fast enough to accommodate her."

"The Minor Adjutant left us just a week or two ago," said Kliompte. "He won't know that we need a new bride."

"But do we?" asked Helia. "Look, we have the Rain Creature. Given to us as a gift from Mara, a gift from the sky. Rain is given and Mirka is taken, and so we are seven brides as ordained."

Rain started to raise her voice, but Iskinaary behind her lunged forward and nipped her heel, and she took his message: be still, and listen first.

"But brides come from mainland?" said Bray, making it a question.

"That's what we've always known. But we're not in charge of holy mystery. This is just how things have unfolded. You might argue that *this* is the time that we have been harvesting. The variation is new, it is fresh, and perhaps it is right. I think perhaps it is."

"Don't you think Lucikles and the Bvasil to whom he reports will have thoughts about all this?" asked Kliompte.

"Well, they can afford to have opinions," said Helia. "We give them the time. Meanwhile, we'll keep to our work even on this day of mourning. We'll start the funeral fire and then we'll go down to harvest the day. Rain, you won't need to scar your feet this morning—you can stay and feed the flames until we return. We will be six brides at service today instead of seven. That's how it usually goes—we've never before had a ready novice standing by at a death."

"I don't want to scar my feet," said Rain. "I wasn't brought here for that."

"Something brought you here," said Helia, without an argumentative tone.

"A great storm, no more than that. But stoke the fire, that much I'll do. At a time like this, I can see all must pitch in."

"I give you our newest bride," said Helia, nodding to Rain.

"I haven't agreed to that."

"Oh, your agreement is incidental. After all, here you are among us. One of seven. And we are the brides of Maracoor. So thank you for helping out. Bray, would you and Scyrilla and Acaciana begin dragging the deadwood from the heap?" She nodded to a ring of boulders to one side, blackened with char and ash from decades of who knows what kind of ceremony. "You know what to do."

After the regular morning rituals, Rain watched warily as Helia stumped her way to the corpse on the long table in the portico. Helia took from the pocket of a housework apron a curving needle about the length of a thumb. She threaded its eye-slit aperture with a twist of grey-green cord, perhaps made of vine and seaweed. "You can look, you can not look," she intoned to Rain, without glancing up.

"What are you doing?"

"It's the final bleed, that's all." Turning back the hem of the shroud, Helia drove the needle into the smallest of the corpse's toes, which had grown purple. Red beaded up the arch of the needle and dripped along the cord and onto the porch floor. "We stitch the toes together, all ten of them, a symbol of the sacrifices the bride has made in life."

Rain was revolted and her gorge surged. She managed to control it, just, before saying, "Death isn't reward enough?"

"No reason a vengeful spirit should go traipsing about making complaint," said Helia. "Here she lived, on Maracoor Spot; here her spirit will remain, because it will not be able to walk across the water to see what else life might have held for her."

The youngest bride had come in and was watching, her expression costive and wasted.

When the pyre had been readied, they used a pair of planks as a ramp to slide the corpse upon it. Ropes attached around the ankles and throat helped the brides to position the figure centrally upon the fagots. Somehow, thought Cossy, the body in its winding sheets wasn't Mirka any longer. It was something else. Something unsavory, and needing dismissal.

Though Kliompte had promised a minimum of ceremony, in fact Helia did strike a moment of solemnity before the lighting of the tinder. The Goose, wanting no part of this, wandered off to express his indifference to malarkey of this nature.

The brides and Rain stood equidistant from one another in a loose ring around the band of boulders. Helia made a signal. The brides lowered the veils off their heads. The wind flew their hair about—no one had taken much time this morning at her toilet.

"We consign the body of our sister Mirka to the skies of Maracoor," said Helia. "In service of the holiness of life, we worked beside her. Now we will work with her memory beside us. Should she intervene with the Great Mara on our behalf, may she remember our kindnesses to her." No one shot a glance at any other. The kindnesses toward Mirka had not been plentiful. But who had kindness to spare in this hardscrabble life?

Helia began to sing an ancient threnody. Cossy had not heard this text or tune before. Some of the older brides took up a raveled refrain. The prayer, when Cossy could make it out, sounded archaic both in language and in accent. She supposed that the younger brides learned it one death at a time. By the time in her life that Cossy would be the senior bride of Maracoor, she'd know this by heart, too, without ever having had to be taught it.

A taper was lit. Helia made a pious gesture above it, and nodded to Cossy to take it to light the pyre. "Me?" said Cossy. "Why me?"

"Who better?" asked Helia. "Who more pure?" She steeled Cossy with a look commanding obedience.

"Let Scyrilla do it, she always wants to do everything."

"I'll do it, I'm not scared of bones or fire," said Scyrilla. "Give it here."

"Cossy will do it," said Helia. "This is beyond discussion. Acaciana."

So the youngest bride, having no choice, took the taper and threw it into the tangle of desiccated old root. At first the flame seemed to go out, but then from the thicket of shadows came a hiss, as of rainwater falling far away. A tendril or two of smoke, snakeheads lifting. A snap, two or three more. One small heart of fire beating against the cave in which it had been lit, hungry for more air. Mirka went up in smoke.

Some of the brides stood with Rain to watch the stinking corpse crackle and sizzle in its inferno. Cossy, though, had seen all that she cared to see. Obeying orders, she set herself to peeling boiled eggs in preparation for the evening meal. Nearby, Helia laid out a planchette of lettuce leaves sprinkled with opened tuskweed seed and apricot slices. They worked in silence until Helia finished with the forks and the butter knives.

"Well, well," said the old bride. "If there is a reason for this day, I don't know what it is."

"What's the reason for any day?" Cossy's tone was sullen.

"I know you're upset," said Helia. "It's a normal re-action. But isn't it strange that Mirka should die just like that? With so little warning?"

"Is death all that strange?"

"When you've finished peeling those eggs, I want you to halve them with a knife. Scoop out the yolks and mash them. Add some soft butter, spring onions, crushed peppercorns, and stir it all up. Put it in a bowl."

"Why?"

"We'll use the discarded white half-eggs as spoons, to scoop up the mash."

"Why?"

"Why the fuss, do you mean?" Helia rested her knuckles on the table and looked kindly at the child. "Someone is dead, Acaciana. It's only proper that we acknowledge the loss by doing things a little different. It's what she would have wanted."

"She would have wanted mashed eggs? Why couldn't she have them when she was alive?"

"It's difficult, I know," said Helia. "Death is always hard for the young, and a first death the hardest. It gets easier, my sweet. Death is a part of life."

"I thought death was *not* a part of life, and that was the difference."

"You know what I mean."

Cossy didn't answer. She felt hopelessly lost in her white tunic, a rope of twined herbs looped around her neck. It raised an aroma of sanctity she couldn't feel. She cried a little. Helia put a heavy hand upon her shoulder and said, "There, there."

"Should it have happened like this?" said Cossy. "I mean, Mirka was a terrible person, but she was one of us."

"Who knows how it should have happened," said Helia. And then, more deliberately, "Or how it did happen. It's a mystery."

"It's not that much of a mystery."

"Cossy," said Helia. "If you had anything to do with the sad final illness of Mirka, I certainly don't want to know about it."

Very slowly, almost monotonically, Cossy said, "If I . . . had anything to do . . . with the illness of Mirka . . . you certainly don't want to know about it?"

"That's what I said to you, yes."

"What do you mean by that?"

"I'm sure you're worried about what is to happen next," said Helia. "Your little world is shaken, your mind is unmoored. You don't know what is from what isn't. It's quite possible for someone so young to get mixed up with fanciful and unreliable memories and dreams. Let's focus on what's going to happen next, shall we?"

"What's going to happen next," said Cossy, "is, I

suppose, that you're going to die. Whether or not Mirka is here to cheer at the prospect, you're old. You're going to die next."

"There was never very much doubt about that, my honey." The old woman sat on a bench and rubbed the sides of her thighs and then the sides of her hips. "We've seen spring lambs butchered for the feast day and old ewes stumble in their sleepwalking and give out right before us. Do you remember the time the goat leapt to snap at a butterfly and dove right off the cliff into the sea?"

"I wasn't alive yet."

"You were, but I guess you're too young to recall it. Death happens with such dailiness that we can hardly even perceive it. Of course you're alarmed at the change of situation here. You ought to be—that's how you learn you can survive change like this. Survive it and still be yourself."

"I'll never be myself again," said Cossy, starting to cry.

"Nonsense. Perhaps you're more yourself than ever. The truth is, sweet marmoset, that we'll go on as before. Just without Mirka. Rain's existence here is no longer threatened. Can't you be happy about that?"

Cossy couldn't answer, though she would be happy if Rain's safety was in any way secured.

"You ask what's going to happen next. I expect that the Minor Adjutant will return with instructions from the Courts of Balance or from the divine Bvasil himself. Lucikles may want to take Rain away with him. But now we're only seven brides, not eight. He can't evacuate one of us seven, even if the new installed bride was delivered unto us in an unorthodox manner. Choosing to reduce the number of brides would break with convention. It could threaten history, it might revoke Maracoor's pact with the Great Mara. It can't happen. Mirka's death has restored equanimity and balance to our plantation here, and I'm using my own seniority to resolve the matter. I will not be brooked."

"You will die next," said Cossy. She sat next to Helia and let the old woman slide her fat and wobbly-skinned arm over her own skinny shoulder.

"Probably I will," said Helia, "in the ordinary course of things. And then the person to lead the Brides will be Tirr. Or Bray. I don't know which."

"Can you imagine Bray as the chief bride?" Cossy almost started to laugh despite herself. A plug of snot shot down and caught in her necklace of herbs, shining like excessive dew.

"More likely it will be Tirr. She's likely the older of the two even if they arrived in the same boat. But that will be okay. Don't you see, the Great Mara has a way of working this out for us? We had one bride too many, and now we don't. It would be undignified to offer an anthem of thanks for our delivery, but in our hearts we can be grateful. Don't you think?"

Cossy did think this. She nodded and put her thumb in her mouth.

"You're too old to be doing that." Helia slapped her hand away, but gently. Then Helia slipped her own clean thumb in Cossy's mouth. "There you go, if it's any comfort. For a moment. Then mash those eggs as I told you to do. We need our strength. It'll take hours more for Mirka's body to be consumed, and we have to keep diligent. We don't want the fire escaping the ring of stones and threatening us all."

Around Helia's thumb Cossy mumbled, "That would be just like Mirka."

"Don't I know it," said the old bride, and made a gesture to ward off evil. "We'll dump her ashes in the harbor soon enough."

2

Lucikles put his girls to bed. They clung to him with a ferocity that was near to anger. Little Star regarded him with cool appraisal, like a housewife doubting the age of the slab of trout being proffered by a fishmonger on the make. But Poena's knobby hand gripped Lucikles so tightly around the wrist that he had to ask her to slacken.

The girl peppered him with questions. It was as if his older daughter needed his tales of travel to take the center stage; these could crowd her own recent adventures into the shadows. Star just listened, but with more doubt in her expression. She was of an age that took other people's lives to be pretty fictions, useful merely for adorning the invisible membrane that contained her own singular and glorious existence.

"Was there *really* such a storm?" said Poena. "Did birds really come and roost upon your masts that far out at sea?"

"That's how the story goes," he replied, singsong and with a wink; a family custom.

"We had a storm too," said Poena. "Star was scared to death."

"Was not," said Star.

"Star thought she was going to blow right off the roof when we went up there to look for the cat."

"What did happen to the cat?" asked their father.

"She blowed off the roof. Mamanoo says she landed on her feet in another world and it takes her some time to scratch her way back, so not to worry." Mamanoo was their name for Mia Zephana, their grandmother.

"You have to go to sleep now." He blessed them and sang them a night charm to keep away bad dreams. "Papa is here now and all is well."

"That's *pretty* good," said Poena skeptically. He didn't know if she meant that his singing wasn't up to snuff or that his return was only a moderate improvement in their circumstances. In any case he accepted the chastisement of his eight-year-old, and escaped the loft under the eaves.

Below, Mia Zephana was laying out a late supper. Oena let her mother do the kitchen chores while she labored at the repair of an item of clothing, holding it close to her nose in the hearth-light to study her stitches.

"How do you find everything?" she asked in a low voice, lifting her eyebrows to the ceiling, indicating their girls.

"Changed; shaken; the same. Resilient. Are they angrier at me than usual?"

"They're angry you were away during the storm and the catastrophe of the invasion."

"I'd hardly have left if I'd known either of those things were to happen."

"Lucikles. They're children. They have a right to be angry at circumstance. I'm angry, too, though I know how little reason I have for such an anger. It's just a feeling. But it's real."

"Tell me about Leorix."

She sighed. Mia Zephana moved farther off to the corner of the room and started clattering copper pots; perhaps she couldn't bear to hear the story told again. Lucikles looked at Oena. She had such an elegant brow, and her hair escaping its pins framed her profile with a dark halo effect. Her face was flat, a common enough aspect among upland stock. A rural face, passed down among generations spent staring at the flank of a dairy cow. Her nose was patrician though. Why do we temple our gods and goddesses, he thought, when they sit here in the lamplight with us on a nightly routine?

"Leorix," he prodded.

She told him about the storm, briefly. How at the start it was almost like a festival, the thrill of it, until it went on too long. Then, when the winds died down at last and the sun returned, how she had left the girls at a neighbor's. So she and Leorix could go to the city centre to look at the damage. Try to locate some fresh fish and leeks for supper. They'd headed to the main market, hoping some of its tables would be open to display their wares. At least the ancillary stalls established under covered parades would have been sheltered from the worst of the winds. They might be doing a brisk business on a bright morning. Halfway there, at the place where the Well of Istripis was cut into the flank of a boulder, they began to see considerable storm damage. The statue of Istripis had fallen over into the basin. Her arm was broken, her face was broken, she was in seven or eight pieces. Leorix, a sensitive boy, was in tears at the sight.

At nearly the same moment, screaming began to sound through the thin trees of the boulevard that circled the slope and debouched into the market piazza. Citizens ran toward them, pitching their straw baskets and purchases helter-skelter as they fled the city centre.

Without waiting to learn what was happening, Oena and Leorix had turned, too. They hurried home. The noise behind them grew louder even as they retreated from it. Smoke billowing from the factory neighborhoods suggested some sort of terrible accident, a firestorm of volatile materials. Maybe a lightning strike from last night had taken this long to smolder to explosion? It was impossible to tell.

Once home, and the door locked, Oena ran to the roof and called to her neighbors. Soon enough she heard word of the landing of a foreign armada in the harbor, and bulletins of slaughter and rapine.

They locked the house and left, taking nothing with them but a loaf of hard bread. Oena was too panicked to bother to hitch the donkey to the cart. If Lucikles hadn't seen the donkey and cart in the stable shed, someone must have pilfered it. Good luck to them; that donkey always was a stubborn cuss.

They made their way via the more exposed route, hoping, Oena insisted, that the number of people fleeing the city at the same time would make the road safe from brigands or wolves. However, a kind of clannishness developed on the road as people segregated themselves into family units. To have chosen to travel without a donkey and cart had been, it seemed, a mistake. By the end of the first day, Oena and the children had been outpaced by other family groups and clots of friends, and they found themselves alone on the path. A glorious dusk, full of spring green and the smell of wild lemon in the wind. And then wolves.

"Leorix did his best," she concluded. "And we survived. We got here. He will be all right. We will be all right."

She repeated, "Won't we, Lucikles? Won't we be all right?"

She held up the item of clothing. A tunic of Leorix's. She had almost finished replacing a back panel that presumably had been clawed or bitten away.

"We will," he said.

The reunited couple ate in silence while Mia Zephana chattered. Like her granddaughter Poena, she wanted to hear everything about Lucikles's recent voyage. It helped her to put current worries aside, she said. So women never do change, thought Lucikles, if tender Poena and tempered Mia Zephana rely on the same strategy to get through a hard hour. But then, do men change, either? He couldn't say. It wasn't the type of thing about which he usually spent time thinking.

When his meal was finished he told them both about his trip, and about the presents waiting on the slip of the *Pious Enterprise* that likely would be lost to looters already. For some reason, he didn't tell them about the arrival of the Rain Creature on the island of Maracoor Spot. His interest in her might be misunderstood.

Before sleeping he went in to sit with Leorix. The boy was not precisely comatose, but was languishing in some half-state of illness. His eyes blinked and his lips pursed to take water or soup, but he didn't yet speak or groan or even turn himself over. He had made it all the way to the farmstead, helped by mother and sisters, but once there he had collapsed. Recovery would take some time.

Lucikles held one of his son's hands in both of his own. Under the thatched eaves a wind soughed plangently but also, it seemed to a weary father, kindly. "No harm will come to you, no harm can come to you, I am here," he said, but that was a lie. His presence didn't legislate against the possibility of harm. Even the youngest child, Star, looked at him grimly, as if she now understood.

They were glad he was there anyway. But he had lost his heroic stature in their eyes.

As he sat there, almost nodding, he heard Oena prepare for sleeping and then crawl into the bed they shared in the inglenook downstairs. Usually the first night he returned from a voyage was joyful for both of them. With so much rawness abroad in the world, though, it was hard to imagine either of them approaching the other under the blankets tonight. Maybe he would wait until he was sure she'd fallen asleep.

Then it seemed to him as if the roof was busy with presence of some sort. At first he thought, rats in the straw? Normally Cur and his best friends, the farm dogs, kept them away. Certainly not thieves in the night—again, the dogs would be rowdy with alarum. He tried to still his own breathing to listen more closely. There was a sound of—but what was it? The movement of wing, a padded foot, a ducking of heads together in the dark, an assessment, a determination, a hesitation. Benign or criminal? He didn't know. He couldn't breathe now. It was something from the other world, something tentative, perhaps neither malicious nor beneficent. Then it was gone, in a flash; a normal rustle of wind replaced it.

He left his son, crawled into bed with Oena. She was still awake after all, but he turned his spine to her and pretended to sleep at once, and wept silently into the mattress.

3

The pyre burned well into the early evening. White ash and brownish-black smoke and a feeling of grey hopelessness sank upon the slope and appalled all the brides, each in her own way. Rain and Iskinaary loitered at the harborside, where the air was freshest, since the smoke tended to roll upslope in the breeze.

Eventually Rain ventured to the necessary, a lean-to built over a pit. She washed her hands and then her face in the tin basin, to remove the stink that had settled upon her. When she got back to where the Goose was waiting, looking serene as a statue in bronze, she said to him, "Now that the body is nearly consumed, they're turning to a more celebratory mood."

"Fancy that. What do you mean?"

"Kliompte is soaking lemon slices in a puddle of plum

juice and honey. Bray is dragging the board out to the portico so they can eat in the fresh air. The old one is muttering a hymn and waving a bundle of smoking herbs, myrtle and mycassandra together, I think. And while they're not going to slaughter a lamb—apparently Mirka isn't *that* widely mourned—they *are* rolling out a better cheese from a keeping-room dug into the hillside."

"And the sullen child?"

"Cossy isn't sullen."

"Sorry. The dear thing?"

"She seems the most stricken. Though I guess that's to be expected. She's such an innocent. She's never come upon human death before. She's nearly mute, and sticking very close to old Helia."

The Goose made a sort of muttered quawk, deeper in his throat than usual. "This is a warning sign, Rain," said Iskinaary.

"What, this death? Warning about what? More death?"

"I see you're feeling more and more like yourself. A bit spirited. That's what I'm looking for, and it makes what I am about to say easier."

Wary, Rain tucked her chin into the collar of her borrowed tunic. She looked slantwise at the Goose. "You're afraid they're going to catch you and roast you because it takes too much time to bleed a lamb?"

"Thanks for putting ideas in my head. But no. I think that we need to be more alert about what's to happen next. Now that you've told me the broom won't respond to your petition to fly, or not yet anyway, we have to rule out an escape from the island by air."

"*Escape,* that's a powerful word. Escape from what, except the hereness of it all?"

"Escape from having no other choices," said the Goose. "Let me put it in words of one syllable, if I can. I'm sure you can see that the brides have only one way out of this life, and that way is to go up in smoke? Is this why you flew across the ocean? To land here as a young woman and then rot in place with these prisoners?"

"I don't think of them as prisoners."

The Goose was silent. "Perhaps that's because you still can't remember what life is like anywhere else."

"Maybe," said Rain cautiously, speaking as much to herself as to her friend, "that makes me a good candidate to stay here? For if the brides all arrive as infants, learning about life here as if it is the only life possible, maybe this *is* where I am meant to be."

"That's total nuts-and-shells. As you continue to regain in health, your memories will return. Mark my words. You'll find yourself living in an impoverished world. And you'll be trapped."

"It sounds as if you are afraid *you'll* be trapped."

"Ah," said Iskinaary, "but I have wings still."

Above them the brides began to chant a litany of some sort.

The Goose continued. "Rain, I've already proposed that maybe you aren't remembering the world you left behind because it was too painful."

"If it was all that painful, well, smart for me to stay here and not aggravate those memories. No?"

"Ah, but whether you remember it or not, there *is* a real life behind you. And whether you can yet picture it, a real life ahead. Something other than this— fortress of constipation."

"So glad you're casual enough with me to tell me how you feel. I'm honored. You're working up to make a suggestion, I can tell."

"I'm of two minds," admitted the Goose. "If you're determined to stay here, Rain, I can return to where we came from. I accompanied you on your journey out but I'm nobody's slave. I have other matters to attend to. Now listen: if you plan to escape this prison without bars, I propose to fly west and try to locate this so-called mainland. I'll find a way to hire a sailing vessel to come and retrieve you, to haul you off this outpost and drag you to someplace with more opportunity."

"You speak as if there is danger to me here."

"The danger of paralyzing sameness? Yes. But also—"

The wind had shifted. Rain detected the embers of the pyre; the scorch of human bone—at least that is what she imagined she was smelling. She had no frame of reference for that.

"—but also," continued Iskinaary, "if you become inconvenient to them—if they decide your green skin has brought them ill luck, for instance—who is to say you will not be the next to roast, like a witch upon a bonfire?"

Rain laughed. "A witch! These are holy women. Look how they tend to each other, look how they manage their religious habits and devotions."

"Look how Mirka died. Suddenly, strangely. The pink of health one day, and the next day stiff, and as putrefying as a bad clam."

"I don't know a lot about it, but I don't think any death can lay claim to being, um, gorgeous. Can it?"

"We haven't time to go into aesthetics. I'm talking about the ethical ugliness of murder."

"What in the name of O—" She stopped. She had almost said something, some phrase from her past, it had almost slipped out between her teeth to peg her to her own past. But the ball of air in her open mouth had held still, and the word had not formed. So *this* is emotional lockjaw, she thought, and took a detour around the shock of it. "*Murder?*"

"I can't say. What do I know of murder?" said the

Goose nonchalantly, and then answered his own rhetorical question. "A lot. What I propose to do, Rain, is not to return to our own homeland but to go on to the mainland of Maracoor. I'll try to resolve the issue of how to spirit you away before it's too late."

"Who would want to murder one of the brides?"

"Perhaps someone who would prefer to see you take her place. In this case, someone else is making the decision for you. This might be easier for you now, when you're vacant of both memory and responsibility, but it won't be something you can live with in the fullness of time."

"So you want to make the decision for me instead?"

"I'm listening to what you say," the Goose pointed out. "Now, look. If you forbid me to try to help, I'll obey you. I'll set out eastward instead, hoping to return to where I was born. I'll try to live long enough to see my home again before I die. But I think you're not going to refuse my help."

"Why do you think that?"

"You're still too alive, is what I think."

They were balanced in a moment of choice. So, thought Rain, this is the choice that the Goose is talking about. He is asking me to make a decision. He is also reminding me, if I ever knew before, what choice feels like.

What an operator.

"All right," she said. "I'm not saying I'd even get into a boat if you're able to convince one to come for me. But I can't stop you from trying."

"You can stop me," said the Goose. "Just say 'don't,' and I won't."

Her mouth again made an airy sphere out of some possible word that she didn't say—but this time her silence was a more conscious choice.

"Very well. I'll leave before dawn," said the Goose. "If someone doesn't murder me in my sleep tonight so they can serve Goose porridge for breakfast."

Did she want to be a bride of Maracoor? To learn to submit to the authority of routine? To bully her own feet into bleeding, to give up choice, to take up a mission in which she couldn't yet believe?

Even put that way, Rain wasn't sure. Perhaps she did. Perhaps this was what she had been seeking.

Passivity. Regularity. A dulling of other pains. Distraction.

A further shedding of her identity, even deeper than amnesia had yet achieved.

The animal unblinking stillness of a hare in a trap, as the poacher draws near. The paralysis before the inevitable.

Choosing death before death chooses you.

4

Until he stopped traveling for a few days, Lucikles hadn't fully grasped how this period of his life had ensnared him in campaign and compromise. Now, largely motionless for three nights, Lucikles recovered at his mother-in-law's holding. He slept like an old dead dog, without dream or appetite. Indeed, when he woke up, he didn't even need to empty his bladder. It was as if his body had become inert with dread.

Oena and her mother worked in the barn with a few farmhands, distant cousins from neighbor holdings. It was the season to dock the tails of the new lambs against blowfly strike and to preserve their older siblings from other parasites by rotating them to pastures with taller grass. Lucikles appeared one day in the surgery lean-to eager to help, but Oena and Mia Zephana sent him away.

When he was feeling stronger he entertained his daughters, but he didn't want to go far from the farmhouse while Leorix was still recovering. The womenfolk didn't trust Lucikles to change the dressings. So, at night, while the boy lay with his half-lidded eyes looking drugged and dysfunctional, Lucikles told him stories of Maracoor's fabled past—the Great Mara, the dryads of Thanatos Wood, the rise of the Bvasils. The comic exploits of Aspirotle, messenger to the minor deities. Young Leorix neither laughed at drollery nor winced at the tragic consequences of messages misapprehended or gone astray. He neither squeezed his father's hand nor pursed his ghost-lips to return an evening kiss. The girls hung about their brother's sickbed waiting to be put under covers themselves, to glisten at the stories, to theatricalize their own responses. He gave them what he could. He sensed it wasn't enough.

On the morning Oena announced that, the lambs all having been tailored, she'd be working with her mother to put up relish of spring onion and malarisk berry, Lucikles summoned Poena and Star. He needed to get out, he needed to repair things with the girls. "We're going to go hunting for something wonderful," he said. "I don't know what it is, but it's time to find something terrific in the world."

"Can we have treats?" asked Poena. She was told she

could wrap in a towel a few sweet lemons and cheese biscuits. Star wanted to invite along all of the household dolls—the battered survivors of earlier childhoods on the farm—which, because of their number, would hamper their expedition. So Lucikles proposed that the dolls might be sat upon a branch of the collapsing wisteria tree and arranged to view the prospect. Beyond the derelict stone wall was a meadow, a patch of jungle-fern, a small shrine to Regina Marastar. A pond and the stump of a long-dead tree. "They can watch, and can call through the loft window and let your brother know what we are up to," said Lucikles.

Cur plowed ahead, invisible in the tall grass. They followed, setting out for the shrine first, which was only proper. At what point in a child's life, wondered Lucikles, does the imitation of devotion convert into genuine piety? And does it convert the other way, too, on the far side of maturity, so that all one has left at the end is practice, and the hollow echo of deep feeling that once colored one's more impressionable and less rational days? He sometimes wondered if he suffered a nostalgia for belief.

They knelt on the paver of threshold granite, made their oblations, lit the oil lamp. They rearranged the family story stones. Star giggled. More sedately, Poena lowered her beautiful lashes. Was she casting slitted glances at him to see how he did it? He modeled fidelity to the sacred traditions of family and nation, not sure if he felt faithful at all, or a fraud.

Then they tramped four dozen yards and, still able to see the rooftop of the farmhouse, stopped to unpack their snacks. "They'll taste better now than later when we're less hungry," said Poena. "Because we already ate them." Lucikles didn't try to decipher the sense of that. Star unwrapped the scarf around her neck and she laid it on the ground like a runner for a trestle table. They lined up the humble snacks, sat down, and consumed every scrap of them.

"Are we going to live here for good?" asked Poena. "With Mamanoo?"

"I don't know," said her father. "But for now, yes. She's very kind to us. Do you like her this time?" (Poena could turn derisive or devoted at the cast of a die.)

"She smells too much of sheep. I wish she'd leave her barn clothes in the barn."

"And walk across the yard naked?"

"She walks to the pond naked."

"Oh." He shrugged. "It's her farm. I guess the sheep don't mind. But don't get any ideas. It's too cold to go swimming."

"Maybe for you it is."

"For you it is too."

It felt ordinary to be fatherly, it felt consoling to be omniscient in minor matters. He was big, they were small. His strong arms lifted them across the stream, and when one of his feet slipped and got wet in the bargain, and he cursed, they screamed in delight at the collapse of patriarchy.

The therapy of the domestic.

They arrived at the pond, which was a wiggle-shaped vernal pool, so rich in algae its depths were choked with healthy green fur. Fish winked and turned, a few smears of red-gold. Star on her stomach reaching for them. Poena on her knees next to her, ready to yank her baby sister's hands back in time to allow a glint-eyed torpie to escape.

Birds made their calls by rote, no urgency. Cur collapsed with a hardwood stick in his jaws. The world at rest. A few birch trees nodded at their own reflections, broken white puzzle pieces in the green water.

Nearby, the remains of a bigger tree, a sycamore perhaps, felled with an axe long ago. The low grey stump remained, displaying its memorializing rings of time. It made a level seat. A flat, slender upright still rose from where the tree had split as its weight had crashed the trunk forward. One could sit on the stump in comfort, lean against the pinnacled backboard, and face the water. Rule like a Magistrate over the algae and the mosquitoes and the torpie. The children always called it the throne tree, and took turns being princess or prince (or bvasil) when they came to pay homage to the spirits of the pond. Oena never joined them here. It was their own game.

He oughtn't have been so surprised—yet he was—to glance that way, as the children splashed and dabbled, and to see a naked man disported upon the throne. It surely was an effect of light and shadow, or of his own continuing exhaustion? He didn't want to draw the girls' attention to the stranger, but he couldn't help glancing again, and then staring.

It seemed to be Relexis Kee, the immortal consort of the Great Mara. The god was her signal messenger, as she didn't deign to appear to mere humans, apparently, nor ever to address directly her human subjects in the everyplace-world of Peare. In the origin myths Relexis Kee was the consort of the Great Mara, drawn from the side of her one exposed breast. (In popular figuration, her other breast remained hidden by her military shield, often fashioned of opaque glass.) In some variants of the ancient stories Relexis Kee was her son. Another confusion of family dynamics best not to question too closely. Parents at hearthsides tended to gloss over the implications. ("Ah well, you know, families, they're complicated.")

Lucikles would have suspected this was Relexis Kee by his beauty, his perfect musculature, his indolence alone; no mortal male could affect that kind of naked unguarded languor once his balls had descended. The spirit sported a martial helmet of bronze with a brush of horsehair dyed military-red, raked up like a coxcomb. Standard archaic mode. The clincher identifying him was his other item of raiment, a wide collar of brass fit tightly around his neck. Perforations in the shapes of the phases of the moon turned his cherry-brown skin into a diagram of lunar moods. Only Relexis Kee wore that circlet. A signature item.

The deity knew he was being adored. Lucikles shifted on a diagonal so that if his girls turned, he would be blocking the god's nakedness from their tender eyes. The Minor Adjutant of the House of Balances lifted his hand to shade his eyes against the glare of god-in-shadow. If this was something more than a fever dream, or a tricksy mirage born of Lucikles's anxiety and dread, Relexis Kee was here to deliver a message. Lucikles knew he had no choice but to receive it.

"Not that one, *that* one," Star was saying.

"What?" said Lucikles, though not to his daughters.

"The other one, you idiot," said Star, pointing out something in the depths.

Relexis Kee arched his noble feet in the air, as if even

gods in their appalling beauty could get cramps in their insteps. He put one arm upon the seat of the throne sycamore, knuckles down, for balance, and leaned forward. His brow furrowed as he stared at Lucikles in some terrifying moment of judgment. Then with his other arm he pointed away through the woods, to the left of the path back to the farmstead. He was indicating where the country road led, and it led away from High Chora. Back down the palisades of rock. Down to where the capital city sat, with its eyes to the water and its docks and quays knee-deep in harvested time.

There was no mistake about the instruction.

Lucikles winced, and thought about nodding to signal that he had perceived the command. But gods don't need a stamped receipt. Lucikles blinked back a mawkish tear of appreciation for the apparition, and dread of what might come next. During that blink Relexis Kee and his golden eyes disappeared.

Cur was sitting up, his ears cocked, his nose aloft, his limbs and throat frozen. He was attentive in the direction of the throne tree, but didn't stir a muscle.

The girls had reached the stage of annoyance where one of them was about to get dunked, so he corralled them to their feet. They continued on their circuit of the pond. Interesting that today, of all days, they all walked past the throne tree as if not noticing it. Perhaps the girls picked up on their father's reticence. Or they had other things on their mind. Cur kept glancing over his shoulder toward the tree but didn't leave Lucikles's ankle.

By the time they started back, he was beginning to doubt himself. Perhaps he was suffering some lagging effects, symptoms of a seasickness he hadn't encountered before. He wasn't generally given to fancies. Or to devotions strenuous enough to call forth deities. For the love of Mara! He was a midlevel civil servant.

Working to recover the normalcy that made him feel competent, he said to the girls as they headed back to their lunch, "So did you see what you wanted today? Did you see anything new? Did you miss anything you usually look for here?"

Poena said, "Oh, Papa," meaning, Your questions, really, even now; what do you *want* of us?

But Star replied, "Yes, we saw the Queen of the Mermaids."

"We did not," said Poena witheringly. "It was a big old fat glint-fish, a torpie, that was all."

"You didn't look close enough," said Star. "You were too busy being stupid."

"What did she look like, then?" asked her sister.

"You know. You saw her."

"Tell Papa, if you're so sure."

"She looked," said Star, her voice growing in volume, "like the *QUEEN OF THE MERMAIDS*. What do you think, like, a, a, a duck?"

"Now, now," said Lucikles, with too much docility to be effective.

"You're so stupid you don't even know how stupid you are," cried Poena, and then the kicks and scratches began.

Back at the farmhouse, Star recounted the story in tears. Mia Zephana said, "None of us know how stupid we are, come to that." She glanced at Lucikles.

"I'm going to check on Leorix," he said, having had enough of the females in his family for at least the next half hour. Cur bounded to the bottom of the loft ladder and waited below for Lucikles to return.

The boy was still lying in bed, but his head was off his pillow for the first time; he was raised up on his elbows, staring out the window.

Lucikles rushed to him and took him in his arms. The boy relaxed in his father's embrace and, after a moment, returned it. Someday, thought Lucikles, I'll have had the last embrace from my son as a boy, and then it will take a decade, if I live that long, before my first embrace from my son as a man. Let today not be our last embrace during his childhood.

"Are you feeling well enough to talk?" he asked, when he could manage to speak.

Leorix remained silent and shook his head, as if to clear the thatch of thoughts and dreams away. His straight hair, bowl-cut, looked damp and fatigued. He did lift a hand, though, and point through the window. For a dreadful moment Lucikles wondered if Leorix had seen Relexis Kee too, and if so, what command the god had given the boy. To steady himself, Lucikles turned and glanced. The dolls belonging to his wife were still visible on their limb. From here they looked suspicious. Engaged in military surveillance. Implicated in espionage.

"Your sisters," said Lucikles with false cheer, "and their ways."

"They want so much of everything," said the boy, in a voice crusted from disuse. Whether he meant his sisters or the dolls, Lucikles didn't know, and didn't want to ask. He was afraid for the state of his son's mind, and didn't want to encourage him in fancy.

"I'll get your mother. She needs to know you are awake at last. I'll be right back." At the door he turned. The boy was still gazing out the window. He looked aggrieved. Or perhaps father was just witnessing in son the birth of a healthy and dispiriting skepticism.

Lucikles waited until well after supper, when the girls were asleep and the mother-in-law out checking on the gates of the sheepfold and the disposition of the dairy cattle. Oena's face had relaxed thanks to a touch of sweet ardeur-mint served in a green glass. Lucikles summoned his resolve. He told her that, now he'd made sure his family was safe, he'd need to return to the capital city in the morning.

Oena's moment of calm eviscerated at one strike. "For what earthly reason?"

"I have obligations to the court of the Bvasil. As you know."

"You have obligations to your family. In any case, the way you told it, the court is dispersed and the Bvasil himself disappeared into hiding."

"No country runs itself. Those who hew to their posts will be rewarded with honor, and after honor often comes cash. I have no useful skills but diplomacy, Oena. More to the point, the homeland needs its defenders."

"Lucikles of the House of Korayus is to become a soldier? My my."

He'd never heard her speak with such mockery. "I've given my word to the Bvasil and his court. Besides, I have an inkling about why this catastrophe has come upon us. My conclusions might inform the court about how to overturn the threat and thus preserve us all."

"I'd never credited you with an affliction of such self-importance."

"I don't want to be an advisor of strategy, Oena. Listen. But if I alone am positioned to do so, it would be a crime as well as a danger to us all for me to refuse. I will leave in the morning. I will take Leorix with me."

At this she lurched from the table as if to strike him. "You don't know what you'll meet on the road or in the city! The boy is safer here with me."

His calm was theatrical only but he kept to it, using a measured voice when he replied, "And was he safer with you when the wolves attacked him?"

She snorted with contempt and, he guessed, a little fright. "He is with us now, he is still alive, he is bruised and broken but not buried in maggoty soil. I won't let you take him."

He couldn't really say why he needed to—it was to keep the boy safe. That look in his eye when regarding the dolls—as if they had been talking to him. There was too much malevolence abroad in the land, and Leorix had come close to the precipice once already. "He'll help me in my work. We'll return when I am done."

"And if the Bvasil shoots you off on another diplomatic mission? You will, what, send him back here on his own, whistling for the wolves?"

"Things won't remain in disarray for long. The citizens of Maracoor will come back to their city to defend it. You're alarmed only because you have no vision of how society works. Leorix and I will leave, we'll stay in our house, I'll conduct my business at the House of Balances when they are ready—they may already have reconvened, for all I know—and the boy and I will return here as soon as we can."

"I forbid it."

"Mama." Leorix was at the door. His sleeping sheets had slipped off one shoulder and the mark of a wolf claw showed red and scabbed around the bevel of his torso, at about elbow height. "Mama. I will go with Papa."

"I forbid it, didn't you hear me?"

"I need to go." Leorix didn't elaborate, for which Lucikles was relieved. He didn't want to hear it said aloud, whatever the reason was, nor that Oena should hear.

"You will do as I say," said the boy's mother, in tears of rage.

"Leorix is twelve, he is nearly of the age for the

lyceum. He is starting to own his own life. He can be trusted to make his own decisions."

"He doesn't know right from wrong, or menace from mercy." She had lost, she knew it; her face was in her apron.

"You're right. I am 'starting to own my own life,'" said Leorix, nodding to credit his father for the turn of phrase. "I have the strength to make my own decisions. Besides, I turned thirteen while you were away."

They left before dawn. Lucikles was armed with a pouch of pepper sand from the storeroom. If thrown in the eyes, it could blind any wolf who might brave to come that close. Leorix kissed his sisters and went to hug his mother, but she turned away from the clasp. Mia Zephana walked them as far as the mill, and gave them some dried shredded ham wrapped in lettuce leaves and tied in string. "These are trying times," she said with an admirable neutrality; she had resisted weighing in on the disagreement between her daughter and her son-in-law.

The girls wailed. "Don't go don't go don't go!"

As he stumbled along with his son, Lucikles couldn't get that apparition of Relexis Kee out of his mind. A portent of his own impending death? Or maybe just a normal spasm of anxious imagination in a time of panic? Just the same, he didn't question Leorix about whether he too had seen a god, in case it meant the same thing. That Leorix should approach death at so young an age was a possibility Lucikles couldn't tolerate considering.

5

Cossy was the first one to notice that the Goose was missing. She kept it to herself, even as she slid glances at Rain for some clue about what was really going on. But Rain was still largely a cipher to Cossy. To all of them.

True, in some ways Rain was allowing herself to be folded into the life of the brides of Maracoor. She kept to one side of Cossy—Helia held prime position at the other shoulder—through most of the day. Rain was learning to duck her eyes, to speak with less variability in volume or pitch, like the other brides, at least when at their hymnody or their labors. She joined the hemming of the harbor every morning. She insisted on being assigned work in the afternoons, after the brief rest following a noontime repast.

But Rain wouldn't agree to have her feet scarred, or not yet.

"If you're joining us, you join us," said Helia, but she said it only once, and without the thunder of command.

"I join you as best I can. I'm picking up the slack left by Mirka's death," said Rain with a conscientious air. "But I'm not worthy to submit to that sacred ritual. I come too late to it, or you suggest it too soon. I'm not sure which."

"Sagacity and cunning, what close cousins. But we're patient. We net the days as they wash to us," replied Helia. "One morning we'll harvest the right time for you to join us more fully, as it has been ordained."

"We aren't at odds with history, are we, in letting her work beside us without having been initiated?" asked Kliompte.

"History has brought the Rain Creature to our fold," replied the senior bride. "I'll tell you when the time is right for her further induction into our sorority."

"I don't want to scar *my* feet anymore," murmured Cossy, but in too low a voice for anyone else to hear. She was just trying out the thought in the humid air of a morning in early summer. "I want to learn to walk on the sea or on the air."

Still, she remained amazed that the other brides were so blind. No one asked after Iskinaary. No one said, "Where is that fool companion of yours, Rain?" Cossy supposed that, with the death of Mirka, normal processes had all gone lopsided. The hours had been shaken to their core. The change was so vast for the brides that they didn't seem to notice the missing Goose. Perhaps the brides thought he had grown as bored with them as they sometimes grew with one another.

"Where *did* he go?" asked Cossy, when she and Rain were coming back empty-handed from the blueberry bushes—it was still too soon for edible fruit. They were swinging the basket between them. Cicadas hummed an urgency in the heat, like metal wires tightening.

"Lucikles? Well, to the mainland, isn't that the practice?" replied Rain.

"Don't be silly." Cossy tried again. "Don't be a silly *goose.*"

"Oh." Rain laughed with a nonchalance that even Cossy could find artificial. "Well, Iskinaary comes and goes, that's the way of a wild creature. He isn't beholden to me."

Cossy didn't have the experience to question this. "What is the difference between wildness?"

"Between wildness and what?"

"Between wildness and—" Cossy flexed her free hand, opening her palm. "Whatever this is?"

"Civilization?" ventured Rain. "Society?"

"I don't know. Us."

"Wildness, I don't know, I guess, maybe, maybe wildness has more freedom?"

"Freedom to just go away?"

"Like Mirka, free to go away. Any way you can find."

"Is there anyplace really to go to?"

Rain's face was soft-hard. Cossy felt her own face redden: she'd asked something that Rain couldn't or wouldn't answer. She pivoted the thought. "Well, wherever he went to, is Iskinaary coming back?"

"I don't know. Right now he might be at the portico steps, looking for grubs. You can't tell with wildness. It doesn't obey."

Cossy put that thought and hung it on the string inside her tunic, where it swayed invisibly, a counterweight to the iron key. Wildness doesn't obey.

One evening, four or five nights after the burning of Mirka, Bray came rushing back from a visit to the necessary. She claimed she had heard the roar of a creature high up on the slopes to the south. Among the brides Bray was the least fanciful, perhaps, and also the least easily frightened by the larger land creatures. So they took her alarm to heart, most of them.

"A mountain cat, perhaps fighting another?" proposed Tirr.

Scyrilla inched closer to Cossy, but Cossy pushed her away. Now that Cossy had Rain, Scyrilla didn't rate high enough to cozy up to. So the second-youngest bride scowled and took on that acid quality the young sometimes display when practicing moral judgment for the first time.

"Cats go tenor in battle," said Bray. "This was a bass."

Then they all heard it. A thrombosis shaking the architecture. The brides glanced at Helia, who maintained a look of disregard, and dragged her bread through the plate of olive oil. "I shouldn't worry," she said, "we're all here."

"All except Mirka," said Kliompte with a note of hysteria. "Mirka wouldn't be sitting around as if nothing was happening."

Helia snorted. "Get up and bar the door then, if you think a manticore has been born among the root vegetables and is coming to sting you to death."

Kliompte looked around, not certain if in moving she'd be setting herself up as an insurrectionist. Rain, perhaps taking pity on her, rose to her feet and did the job of locking them in. "Is that a normal sound?" she asked.

"I've heard it before. I paid it no mind," said Helia.

The sound began again, but lower; almost a rumble. Earth becoming animal.

"I hope it doesn't eat Iskinaary," said Cossy, provocatively.

Rain lifted her chin at the youngest bride.

"Perhaps you'd better call the Goose in," said Kliompte, which was kind of her, given her lust for a state of total antisepsis.

"I haven't seen him in a while," said Rain, with a nonchalance that was, perhaps, ill-judged; the brides thought her scheming.

"He's your creature, your thingy, what do they call it. Your familiar," said Tirr. "He doesn't leave your side."

"He's a Goose, he has his own ambitions. I always knew he might leave, and I suppose he has." The roar occurred again; it was nearer and now glottal, somehow. "Could this be an earthquake rather than a creature, do you think? Helia?"

Helia crossed her wrists on her lap, a familiar position she often adopted when given to a pronouncement. "Perhaps the island is preparing to give birth to a savior of some sort, who will restore the irregularities of this season."

"And bring back Mirka?" asked Scyrilla. "That'll be tricky, since she's only ashes and smoke, or knobs of scorched bone bobbing in the harbor."

"I think you should be careful what suggestions you put into the air, Scyrilla," said Helia. "You with your womanly state, you're stronger now. And you never know which god, disturbed of his or her rest, will play with a notion. You could be sorry. For all their power, gods are highly suggestible. Almost like children."

The roar of the basilisk, the birth of the hippogriff, the uneasy opinion of boiling lava beneath the crust of Maracoor, whatever it was—or everything at once—it stopped. When Cossy went to bed that evening, she broke convention and pulled her pallet nearer to where Rain was sleeping.

Helia lay alone in her corner. Scyrilla proposed to drag her sleeping mat to the elder's side, taking Cossy's place, but Helia growled, and Scyrilla skulked away.

In some loamy level of apprehension between deep sleep and midnight, Rain was aware of lowering and rising. She was flying. The unseen world below was heaving beneath clouds that ripped apart and clotted again. There was no light, though she sensed the Goose nearby. Behind, or to one side. Perhaps she said his name in her sleep, and that was what woke her up.

Helia, part sarsen stone, part maiden aunt, was paused over the pallet. The other brides were asleep.

"With the young one removed to your side, I have no one to see to my needs this night," she said crustily. "I was going for water."

"I'll get it for you." Rain sat up and stepped over Cossy, who in her blankets looked hardly more than five years old.

Rain filled a lopsided goblet and brought it to the old woman, who said, "Well, we're up, let's have a look about." Helia made a flipping gesture with her hand, and Rain unbolted the door to the temple. They stepped out into moonlight.

The configuration that had made a snout in the sky was corrupted by now. The moon had stopped growing and the other heavenly bodies that had lined up to shape a predatory profile against the blackness had already begun to drift apart. Astral menace against the world and its creatures no longer seemed immediate, just—tentative. Just maybe. Just a rash of possibility.

"So where did that Goose go, then?" asked Helia. "Back where you came from?"

"I am not so good with answering questions," said Rain.

"You aren't from nowhere. You aren't just born in a raindrop. You might scare the others because of your vegetable aspect, but I know better. You're keeping something from us and I want to know why. If you're from Maracoor, you can tell us about it in ways the Minor Adjutant never will. If you're from somewhere else in Peare, give us an advantage by sharing what you know. That's the price I exact for providing you a safe harbor here."

Rain said, "I don't see any reason not to be frank with you. There are things in the past I don't know because I can't remember them. There are things in the future I don't know because I can't see them."

"Perhaps we should conduct an augury, and that might help you remember."

"He's gone, he's gone," said Rain, "that's all. He told me he was going and he left."

"He?" said Helia. "Do you mean the Goose? Or someone else?"

When she received no answer, the senior bride leaned against a column and put her head back. She closed her eyes, an ancient martyr resigned to the arrows, or maybe even eager for them. Rain couldn't take the measure of this figure. The old one was more complicated than all the other brides combined. Maybe, Rain thought, this is what happens to the brides; they move through the stages of their lives until they are unreliable and contradictory. Like Rain herself—a woman trembling between girlhood and womanhood, not one thing or the other.

"I wonder why you and Mirka were so antagonistic," she found herself saying.

"That's a poking sort of question," replied the old woman.

"Turnabout is fair play, I seem to remember hearing."

"You tell me where you came from and maybe I'll come clean, too."

Rain shrugged. From behind them a cloud came over and scattered the ground with small handfuls of wet, and moved on; some unseen frogs who had been silent made thirsty comment.

"She wanted too much," said Helia. "Too much and too soon. Enough to do me in to get to be chief bride. Mirka thought my practices were getting sloppy, my attention failing. Though she was second in command, she didn't have the wisdom to know that this is also what happens. We braid the world each to our abilities at the time, and the ability of every bride is called for. We span the ages of women. So she thought me merely failing, and I thought her opportunistic and grasping. I've had the good of our holy mission at heart my whole life. Concern for the individual bride here or there hasn't been urgent. And that's what was between us, nothing more. Fairly standard stuff."

Rain said, "Helia, I'm sorry I can't tell you where I'm from. I wish I knew. In any case, thank you for welcoming me here. Not everyone would. You have a large spirit—you and the girl. The others are wary but not unkind. Still, as long as we have this sudden moment, maybe I should ask you directly: what do you see for me here?"

"I only see a day at a time, as we shape it in our ministry at the shore," said Helia. "But yesterday I saw you beside us, and tomorrow I do too. That's enough for me right now. We need someone here to guide the others when I'm gone."

"Now that Mirka has died, you mean. But isn't Bray or Tirr the next in line?"

"Tirr is probably next in line, but neither she nor Bray are adequate to the job. They are lacking in conviction. They are diligent, they are bees in the hive, they have no vision. It isn't their fault. You—you have flight in your bones. So who knows?"

"Surely you're not saying—but I'm a young woman. I'm younger than Kliompte. I don't even have a memory, so I have no—no scope."

A distant echo of that frightening roar from earlier in the evening. Now it sounded like an underground cavern collapsing, or a small posse of rogue creatures of the wild—something bigger than wolves, stranger than the sea lizards who sometimes got beached in a high tide and couldn't rescue themselves without help.

"If I believed in minotaurs . . ." said Helia. "Let's go inside, I'm getting chilled."

"Why not believe in minotaurs? You believe in roping destiny for the world—minotaurs aren't half as far a stretch of faith."

"So you know what a minotaur is," remarked Helia, grumblingly.

"I suppose I do, in the abstract."

"Wake the fire a little. Stepping outside has iced my bones more than I expected. We kept a few coals from the pyre banked under ash; you can stir them up."

The other brides didn't twitch as Rain followed Helia's command. When a small blaze had begun to throw heat and to flicker light across the temple floor, Helia pulled a stool forward. Rain squatted on her haunches with a poker, to tease the flames higher.

"I don't know how to respond to your suggestion," said Rain after a while. "I don't know if I'd ever be ready to be a senior bride, or a senior anything."

"It was no suggestion," replied Helia. She seemed disinclined to continue. Well, the other brides were so near, and might be lying awake, eavesdropping.

Rain stirred the tinder. "I only ask you one thing— can you really believe this, this ritual you perform daily? Do you really think you and the other brides are doing something essential—I don't know how to call it—scraping time into daily segments? I thought the sun across the sky did that. If we all were to die of, oh, a plague, an attack by that creature we hear growling, wouldn't history keep on mounding upon the land, in its incremental way? One speck of incident at a time?"

"You don't know, you can't know. Just as you can't know what it is to be on the other side of breathing until it's your turn. Most of us can wait to find out."

"It seems—I don't know. Proud?"

"Proud? Our humble work?" Helia considered. "I suppose it is proud work. Do you fail to believe in human agency, then, young Rain? Do you think that what we do in this life doesn't matter?"

"Of course it matters. But can we change the world by it?"

"We'd better," said the old woman. "And we may rely on you for help, if you catch my drift."

"I might not be up for it."

"Time will tell."

The clutch of fledging minotaurs or the belch of subterranean thunder sounded once more, in a rumble with voices at several low pitches, but farther off. "I'm ready to go back to bed," said Rain.

"Me too," said Helia. She gestured with her staff. "Help me up."

As Rain did, a certain suctioning wind from the chimney flue raised, out of the sweet applewood and sycamore limb, a scarf of smoke. It twined about itself diaphanously, pale charcoal and nearly white, with a cowl about its neck. Then from popping wood two sparks spit directly up to chin height or so. They hovered an instant, long enough to gleam like eyes glaring in judgment. But the difference that caused Rain's blood to jump was this: light from any source was usually warm, yet this spectre cast, for a moment, a bitter cold luminescence. Saturated moonlight, hanging from a shoulder bone.

The figure turned its shrouded shoulder; its alabaster ankles tapered together into a single narrow flickering stem.

Helia started and her voice choked some horrible sounds, as if she were expelling dice from her throat. "Dyani!" she said. "Be gone!"

For a venerable woman with lumbago, the old bride moved with startling haste. She grabbed the tin bucket and doused the fire into a fit of hissing. The apparition vanished in a puddle of ash.

"Dyani?" said Rain.

"Did you see her?"

"Who is Dyani?"

"A dyani, a spirit. A smoke-ghost. Mercy upon us. A bad sign."

And still the brides slept on, as if drunk.

"Tell me," insisted Helia, "did you see her? Did you see the dyani?"

"I saw something," said Rain, "but I'm no more convinced of its reality than I am convinced that the moon and its companions become a heavenly jackal, or that a cloud in the sky that looks like a horse with wings is any such thing. I am open to likenesses, that's all. So what. I am not a fool."

"You'll learn just how much of a fool you are," snapped Helia, the mood of collegiality dissolved. She'd been badly shaken. Rain lay down at last, but Helia didn't return to her pallet. She sat before the hearth with the rest of the bucket of water on the ready, in case the embers reignited themselves out of spite, and the dyani returned to curse them all.

Rain didn't go back to sleep right away. She tossed on her lumpy mattress pad. There were no more sounds of mystery from outside, but the image of the dyani played upon her mind. Is that all it took for a soul to believe? One moment's exposure to a transitory presence? Had a visitation actually happened, or was she just being suggestible?

And if a dyani—if there were such a thing—what did it want, why had it come, what possibly could have put it in such a bad frame of mind? It looked for that one instant as if it had wanted to spit coals at both of them, Helia and Rain, specifically. And with malice.

Return of the
Pious Enterprise

1

The wolves in the wild didn't circle Lucikles and Leorix as they made their way from the farm to the track that zigzagged from tableland to coastal plain. Harder to avoid were the bands of refugees displaced from the capital, however, or locals protecting their property. Still, Lucikles had learned a lot from his career in diplomacy and Leorix was clearly a child in need of a father, so some mercy was shown them in dicey moments. Father and son slipped clear of the worst of the danger.

Going downhill was faster than climbing, of course. The more open route was also more direct. They were offered a ride in a cart by a farmer taking produce to the city to see if he could charge exorbitant prices.

One way or another, Lucikles and Leorix reached the outskirts of Maracoor Crown just after nightfall.

No horde of foreign invaders squatting in Maracoor homes, though evidence of upheaval, to be sure. Looting, probably inevitable, and an acrid stench still hung in the air. But also signs of cleanup. Brave lights in upper windows, dogs barking. Here and there a tray of extra garden produce put outside a gate so the hungry could help themselves (and pass by). Lucikles felt restored in his sense of civic pride.

The farmer left them off not far from the Temple Houranos. The district seemed chaotic. A yowling chorus of house cats gone mad from deprivation. A pack of hounds delighted to make the lives of cats more miserable still. Reaching Piney Quarter, Lucikles approached his own home, dreading the possibility of ransack. An untethered cow from beyond the city limits stood in front of his gate, gazing at him with turned head, chewing. "It's about time," said the cow, or so Lucikles thought. I'm losing my mind, or the world is hexed throughout. But as the cow ambled along the cobbles, a human came into view, sitting on his doorstep. She wore the sash of a military messenger. She stood. "But better now than at midnight. I can deliver my instruction and get back to barracks before being locked out for the night."

"Do I know you?"

"You are Lucikles, no?"

He nodded his head. She continued. "I haven't been posted here to guard your property, but my hanging around didn't hurt matters. No harm seems to have come to call. Look, my message is simple. You are to report to the House of Balances tomorrow between second and third bells. News of your return from the islands has reached the Bvasil. Your report is overdue. I suspect there will be penalties, but that's not my affair."

"I had family matters—in this crisis—"

"Don't spend breath on me. It's not my concern. Do you understand the command? Good, then I'll be off. Welcome home."

"Won't you take a scupper of water or something before you leave?" asked Leorix. Lucikles scowled at him, but the messenger just smiled and began to pelt away into the darkness.

They went in and made themselves at home, but without Oena and the girls the place felt lonely and cold. Leorix dropped off almost at once at the foot of the marriage bed. Lucikles kept awake for quite a while, listening for the sounds of break-in. They didn't happen. So he slept.

In the morning, Leorix insisted on joining Lucikles. "But this is a professional meeting," said his father.

"You told me I was old enough to choose my own path, and I'm choosing it," said the boy. Lucikles relented, assuming the boy was frightened to be left alone in the house, even on a sunny morning.

Relying on Cur to stay and guard the property, they walked down through neighborhoods a little more prosperous and a little better defended than their own. More men and some women had returned to supervise their homes. By the time Lucikles and Leorix reached the city centre, sounds of children and of commerce were beginning to be heard. Fear of a second attack seemed slight. But Lucikles didn't stop to barter for news in case it would be frightening for Leorix to hear. The lad was just thirteen; in the sliver of time called *now* remained the most precious last drop of his childhood. No need to tilt it out upon the ground. It would fall or evaporate of its own accord in good time.

The great stone House of Balances stood in a paved broadway opposite a municipal exchequer and beside a sensibly situated bordello. The ladies of commerce called out to Lucikles with pretend familiarity and they admired the stripling lad. Without comment Lucikles guided his son past them and up the broad sweep of steps to the guarded entrance.

His immediate supervisor met him in the corridor with a bored flick of the fingers, as if Lucikles had just returned from a smoke. "The boy will have to go wait outside. He can't be party to our conversation," said Kerr Porox.

"Surely he can wait here. He's got a small schoolbook to study with."

"No."

"There are too many enticements next door, Porox. He is only a lad."

The man shrugged but gave in, and he made Leorix sit on the floor outside the chamber. Porox then closed the door firmly behind them and drew Lucikles as far from the doorway as he could get.

"I wonder if you might be requested to present yourself to the Bvasil himself," said Porox. "I'm still waiting to hear. But in the meantime I will catch you up. The return of the *Pious Enterprise* was duly noted despite the disarray in the harbormaster's offices. Your failure to appear immediately to make your report is counted against you, I'm afraid." At Lucikles's sputtering protest, Porox lifted a hand. "We have more important things to discuss, my good man. I am told that Captain Gargios Nitexos is being held in harbor awaiting your return to his ship."

"I need to let you know what has happened."

"I believe I know something of it already. A Goose appeared in the port yesterday and tried to make arrangements for a vessel to make a run to Maracoor Spot. Apparently there has been a—a castaway? Washed ashore?"

"It seems so. I was going to say—"

"And a very peculiar story has come out of Lesser Torn Isle about a small cohort of strange flying creatures arriving there in search of a green girl. An adolescent girl, I mean, not a child."

"It's part and parcel of a very strange set of developments—"

"While at the same time a pugnacious naval party has landed in Maracoor Crown for the first time in living memory. Under such circumstances, you choose to take a holiday with your family out in the country?"

"And what did you do, Porox, when the marauders arrived? How did you behave?"

"No business of yours. But I can't chastise you as you deserve; we need to get your briefing." A side door opened and an underling passed along a written message. "Ah. I see. You are to proceed to the Court. Please follow this page."

"I'll bring my son with me."

"So out of order that I can hardly bring myself to reply."

"I won't speak to anyone without keeping him by my side. You can lock me up for that if you must."

The Court was waiting, so Porox capitulated. Leorix leapt to his feet. Father and son were led up a grand staircase that Lucikles had been permitted to mount only two or three times before in his career in the Courts of the Adjutants.

He felt his face pale and his center of gravity pivot like a wobbling top as the page led them past the great double doors of the Adjutants' Hall to a black onyx door, smaller and off-center. It was surrounded with a decorative frieze of silver laurel leaves. The salon reserved for the Bvasil himself, should he be in the building. "Oh, Leorix." Lucikles squeezed his son's hand. "Unless I am mistaken, you may be about to have an encounter vouchsafed to very few of us." He brushed the dust of travel and sleep off the shoulders of the boy's tunic. "Straighten your spine. Remember that you asked for this."

"I didn't ask," Leorix reminded him. "I told you I was coming."

The page opened the door and led them through a dark vestibule that opened into a higher room. Windows with stone mullions ran below the ceiling on all four sides of the room. Beneath them, between pale beige stone pilasters, the vertical panels of wall were upholstered in royal velvet, now blue, now violet, now nearly plum red. Across them, the whole length of the room, a banner of saffron gold hung from regular pairs of poles lodged in clay pots filled with sand. A table of gilded oak stood across from the doorway. Behind it, on a chair with tasseled gold cushions, the Great Mara—the Bvasil himself—straightened from a lounging position and lifted his double chins at them. He was newly shaved and a spot of blood still glistened at the side of his mouth like a ruby.

"Lucikles, lately returned from his annual review of the Ephrarxis Isles and the Hyperastrich Archipelago," intoned the page, and withdrew.

The Bvasil—the Great Mara of Maracoor, in human form for this generation, which tended to a little pudge—leaned on his forearms and squinted. "The light is dreadful in here. It's all to impress guests, but at this hour highly impractical. We can't make you out at all. Come nearer. Is that a boy or a girl? Heavens, a child in any case. Save us. Are you lost, child? Don't answer. Stand there. No, that's too close, back up. Yes. That'll do."

Lucikles and Leorix positioned themselves as directed and waited. The Great Mara was an ordinary-looking round man with a lopsided quiff upon his head, raked forward from what remained of his grey thatch. On his desk to one side, cast there as if it scratched, a wreath of bronzed laurel leaves and berries of pearl and jet. "State your name and briefly deliver your report. We haven't patience for niceties." From the shadows in one corner a scribe emerged with a codex, a quill, and a pot of ink. The scribe sat on a bench to one side and poised his pen to take dictation.

Lucikles cleared his throat. He was so shocked at an audience with the Great Mara that he could scarcely recall the proper form of address. "Your Beneficent Servant—I am Lucikles—second born of the House of Korayus."

"*You're* the beneficent servant. Get your facts straight. We are Your Magnificence. We mean, when you address us, we are, we're not *your* magnificence. In any sense. Heaven forfend. We wouldn't know where to begin." He rolled his eyes at the scribe. "We can see this is going to be a bit of a damp diaper, as proceedings go. Forgo with the niceties, man—Lucikles, was it—and tell us what we need to know."

"Accustomed as I am to delivering my report to the Courts of the Adjutants, I scarcely know the form in whi—"

"Stop sputtering. Tell us what's going on in Maracoor Spot, you fool."

Lucikles didn't like being called a fool in front of his son, even if the speaker was divine on his mother's side—his mother having declared herself divine about

forty minutes before she expired in an apoplectic con-
vulsion of self-admiration. "I first present my son.
This is Leorix Korayus."

The boy nodded with the terse self-control of a civil
servant three decades in the administration. He'll go
far, if he survives this madness, thought his father.

Gathering his strength, Lucikles plunged ahead.

"Your Magnificence, if you please. There's concern
about an aberration to custom in the sacred habits of
the brides of Maracoor. What I know about it is scant
indeed. From some unknown origin, a young woman,
really scarcely out of childhood, arrived on the shores
of Maracoor Spot shortly before our annual inspection.
She was accompanied by a talking Goose."

"We've heard tell of such things, but we never really
believed it," said the Great Mara. "Well, we take so
much on faith. We can scarcely fathom that human
beings manage to string eight words together into a co-
herent thought. They look so idiotic, most of them. Go
on. You met these creatures? This girl, this Goose?"

"I did. The brides made an effort to hide her from
me, but I saw through their bluff." This was overstat-
ing the fact a little, but the Great Mara didn't seem to
notice. Or mind.

"You were late in arriving on Maracoor Spot, we understand. We mean relative to your other ports of call."

"I was. There was a week of tremendous weather. Unprecedented winds from the southeast. We nearly turned back, but we feared the repercussions if we had been charged with abandoning our mission."

"That weather, too vexing. We lost an entire flock of singing pigeons, the ones we train for holy days. They went up in a vortex, their little throats raised in harmonic terror, and that was the end of them. At least so far. We live in hope for the miracle of their return. The sweeties. Also we were invaded, did you hear? But we digress. We want to know in what ways the green apparition has upset the regular practices of the brides of Maracoor. Their regimen is strictly dictated by long decades of sacred orthopraxy, so the introduction of a foreign body to their number can't have been met with cries of joy."

"It's hard for me to comment. I visit Maracoor Spot at best twice a year—Your—Your Divine Magnificence." The addition of the adjective was inspired; the Great Mara simpered a little, and relaxed against his cushions. What a belly on the fellow. Lucikles said, "I can come to no conclusion. It's for minds wiser than mine to interpret fate."

"And you just left her there, diddling away and making trouble?"

"I had no license to remove her."

The Great Mara puckered his lower lip and made a sucking noise. "Has it occurred to you that this creature and the navy that invaded our capital city were borne, perhaps, by the same great storm?"

Oh, it had, it so had, but Lucikles kept his mouth shut.

The Great Mara spoke as if he was musing aloud. "There are reports of mad upheavals inland and coastal. The heavens are disturbed and the earth responds in aberration and cunning. The great lizard of the chalk slides, you know the one?—it emerged from its slumber, did you hear that? It sloughed itself down the coast and ate a village and a half and then burped and returned to its lair. People had forgotten to take it for real, it hadn't happened in so long."

This accorded with the several strange sensations Lucikles had had himself—like that of Relexis Kee manifesting himself bodily upon the trunk of a dead tree and giving travel advice.

"And upon Lesser Torn Isle, we're reliably informed, a small coterie of winged simians made landfall, having come from some unknown island across the sea to the far east. They claimed to be looking for someone named Rain. No one on Lesser Torn Isle knew of your having found a green child on Maracoor Spot, so they directed the monkeys to the mainland. The creatures haven't shown up yet in the capital city. We don't know if they made landfall on the mainland or if they aborted their mission and returned to their primitive unknown home. We don't know; we can't really see the details. It would take the very Oracle of Maracoor, no less, to tell us what all this nonsense means. But we hope those monkey-birds don't come here. They sound spooky.

"In short," said the Great Mara, "this disaster of our time, in its multiple varieties, seems to be centering upon the appearance of this importunate visitor to our shores. So we're directing you to return to Maracoor Spot. Remove the offending article before more of our history becomes unhinged. Bring the green girl here so she may be questioned. The galleon in which you just returned is at the slip, waiting with crew and captain to take you out again. Goodbye, heave-ho and all that natter. I'll have a few grapes and, perhaps, some meats of walnut?" he told his scribe.

"May I go?" asked Leorix. The boldness of the boy!

"You must go; I've had quite enough of children."

By that final exchange Leorix claimed authority to join his father on board the *Pious Enterprise*. Lucikles couldn't deny that "You must go" could be interpreted as a sacred order for Leorix to accompany his father to Maracoor Spot, even if more likely it had meant

"Get lost." In any case, there wasn't any time to return Leorix to the safe hold of Oena and her mother in the upland farm. After receiving further muttered instructions from Porox on the other confidential aims of the next mission, Lucikles hurried away. The ship was to sail at sundown.

Father and son scarcely had time to return to the house in Piney Quarter. They scrabbled for clean changes of clothes. As instructed, Leorix tried to assemble some niceties of food to vary the tedious shipboard fare. Cur leapt about at the commotion. Lucikles dug out a few more coins hidden in the underfloor safe. On their way to board the ship, they flung a silver tribute into the coffers of the Temple Houranos for safe passage.

With Captain Gargios Nitexos at the helm, fuming at the assignment he had no permission to decline, they set sail. The boy stood at the rail, watching dwindle the only world he'd known. The eastern sky was shutting down, the western glazed with hysterical sunset. But more lights showed from chinks in the shutters of Maracoor Crown than Lucikles would have imagined. Dozens, perhaps hundreds—apparently quite a few people had chosen not to flee, but had hunkered down and hidden in their attics and storeholds. Or had returned after only a brief absence. He felt proud of them, though he guessed their presence was as much greed as it was patriotism.

Still, the city lights upon the harbor seemed brave. Three hundred separate tiny lighthouses.

The boy was too thrilled to go below-decks. Or maybe he was timid of the rough crew. He was still an innocent in every way, his Leorix. Near the prow of the ship Lucikles stayed with him, each of them looking in a different direction. The wind was fair. Once they'd cleared the harbor the run promised to be smooth, at least initially. A little light chop, but refreshing. Leorix laughed as the spume reached up and felt his face.

Circulating the deck, the Captain joined them for a few moments. He wasn't happy at being sent out again so soon, though it was cash in his wallet. The *Pious Enterprise* was due for some overhauling below waterline, and needed to spend several weeks in dry dock. But Nitexos didn't foresee problems, provided the weather was cooperative. A straight haul to Maracoor Spot and back could be accomplished in less than two weeks, assuming no trouble.

"I went up the ratlines to study the sky before the full night set in," he said to Lucikles. "Pittance to the gods for a safe journey. I thought I saw an underwater escort on both sides of us, for a bit."

"Dolphins?" Not impossible this close in, but rare. "Surely—you don't mean a whale pod?"

"It was hard to tell. Too deep. But movement, shadow, keeping pace with us to either board, for sure."

Lucikles glanced into the depths; it was too dark now to see much but the light from portholes below-decks puddling in oily yellowness on the surface of the water. "I was inattentive."

"I thought I saw something, too," said Leorix. "Earlier I mean."

"What did it look like?" asked Gargios.

"Oh," said the boy thoughtfully. "Nixies?"

"Looked like nixies, or were they?" pressed the captain.

"Well, I never saw a nixie before, so I don't know." How easily the boy seemed to possess his ignorance. It was like a coat he hadn't outgrown.

"First night at sea, fancy strikes," said his father, ruffling Leorix's hair.

"I'll teach you to scale to the crow's nest tomorrow, lad," said the Captain. "Catch some sleep. If the men get too crude, have a word with me, Lucikles. They're not used to juvenile company on board."

2

The days settled into a new pattern. Rain found herself wary of the hearth, unhappy to recall the spectre of the dyani even if it had been largely a figment of her exhaustion. For her part, Helia seemed to have taken up a permanent post over the coals. She abandoned the fire only during the morning rituals and for meals and sleep and to visit the privy. She kept a pot of water at the ready and a poker across her lap, as if for defense. "Do you intend to read the ashes of our dinner fire?" asked Kliompte once, approaching with a broom and pan to give the hearthstones a good going over. "If so, do it now and let me get to my housework."

"I don't need to read ashes to know what ashes say," replied the old woman, but she seemed troubled. She chased Kliompte away and told her to go pickle some radishes if she needed a chore.

Not far away, Rain and Cossy were settled upon a rag carpet, playing a game of sticks. Scyrilla hovered near, wanting to be involved, but Cossy kept turning her shoulder.

"I'll play the winner," said Scyrilla.

"We're busy," said Cossy.

"We can do two against one, I'll be the one, I don't mind. I don't even mind losing." Scyrilla was magnificently insincere. "I like it."

"Go away."

Rain said, "We can figure out a way for three to play, can't we?" but Cossy threw her such a look of contempt that the green visitor fell silent.

"You can help me slice the radishes if you want," called Kliompte.

"No, *I'm* going to read the ashes," said Scyrilla. "Why not."

"Get away, you're not wanted here," scolded Helia, but she had dropped her poker on the floor and she couldn't bend to reach it and ward off Scyrilla.

Scyrilla knelt at the threshold of the hearth and leaned down. Her chin was at the level of the andirons. In a self-satisfied singsong she chanted:

Fire of fate in the filthy grate,
Tell us what's wrong before it's too late.

"You fool, you idiot," cried Helia, trying to kick the girl. Scyrilla blew very faintly on the dead fire. The embers glowed and winked red, but no dyani appeared. The ash merely rose in a low puff, and fell down again upon the flat stone.

"Now I will tell you what I see," said Scyrilla. The room had gone still—Rain and Cossy poised over their sticks, Kliompte paused with a paring knife in her hand, and the others looking up from their evening occupations. Even Helia seemed paralyzed. Scyrilla wasn't used to commanding attention. She mused over the pattern in the ash. Finally she straightened her spine and sat back on her haunches. "I'm not too good at this," she said in an ordinary voice. Staring at Rain she continued, almost ruefully, "But I think you're trouble. You're big trouble."

Rain felt a chill flush her from forehead to shins. "You're a silly girl."

"Probably I am," said Scyrilla. "Even so."

"What did you see?" asked Helia in a low voice, more terrified than menacing, but Scyrilla would say no more. She'd improved her standing enough not to want to jeopardize it, mystery being a more alluring perfume than clarity.

That night Rain woke up but, afraid of encountering Helia again, she lay on the pillow with her eyes squinched closed. A splash of longing was muscling through her somehow. She was missing something dreadfully without being able to name it. Perhaps it was like wanting to have a child, she wondered, but this was more precise. It wasn't mere loneliness; it was thwarted affection. She was missing someone she had once known and could no longer remember.

Tell me what's wrong before it's too late, she found herself praying.

I f the *Pious Enterprise* really had an underwater escort, either beneficent or malicious, Lucikles never saw it. But the ship made such swift passage through the southern sea that he couldn't help entertaining that notion.

Leorix stuck close by his father's side until he could no longer stand. He then soldiered through his bout of sickness in his hammock as the waters roughened. And the boy was still recovering from the attack of the wolf, after all. He swayed, pale and quiet, not even kicking his limbs. Lucikles thought that if his son should suffer and die at sea, that would be the end of his own marriage for sure. But this was an unnecessary worry, for Lucikles himself would have already died of grief.

Still, as they breasted the coastal current and set

across stiller waters for Maracoor Spot, the boy began to revive. After he spent a few afternoons under a blanket on deck, color returned to his cheeks and brow. The crew hadn't wanted a simpering child on board but had grown to consider him a mascot. They shared with him their daily portion of citrus and the occasional horehound sweet.

On a day of broad clarity, the type of day where the blue at zenith looked nearly black and at the horizon pale as thinned milk, Maracoor Spot came into view. Leorix shouted with excitement and ran back and forth to tell everyone. Cur yapped at the commotion, too, as if he could smell fresh hunting in the wind.

"We'll drop anchor as usual and proceed tomorrow morning in the longboat," Captain Nitexos informed him.

Lucikles was surprised. The longboat took half of the crew to maneuver, three to the thwart. "Not a coracle, as usual?"

"You may want some strong-arm if you meet resistance."

"We're not going to steal a woman against her will," said Lucikles though, in fact, was that what they were about to do?

"I'm coming too," said Leorix. Lucikles began an argument for him to remain on ship, but then thinking about the occasional assault upon cabin boys by frisky crew members, he changed his mind.

Before they set out the next morning, he laid down the terms of the engagement. "Once on land, I am the authority," he reminded the Captain and the crew, including his own son. "I will negotiate with the brides for the removal of the stranger. You will wait at harborside unless I signal for your help. In all instances you will keep your hands to yourself. Is that understood? You sure of that? These women have seen no men in their lives except me and my predecessors, and then each overseer always approaches alone. I don't believe there has been more than a single man on the island at one time in the entire last hundred years. Are there any questions?"

Oh, did the men have questions, but in deference to the sensibilities of the boy among them they made do with leers and gestures behind his frail and scarred shoulders.

"Oh, and also, when we return to the *Pious Enterprise*, we'll be carrying with us a few items for safekeeping."

4

The brides had finished their morning ritual. They were drying their bruised and salted feet, the better to keep from tracking sand into the temple. Kliompte could be fierce about that. Rain, the only one to take part in the daily ceremony without having bled her feet, was always the first one dry. Now she went twirling about on the strand in a sudden state of giddiness. She didn't quite know why. She had once loved someone enough to be lonely about it, maybe that was all. She knew in her heart it was someone other than the Goose—though she missed Iskinaary too.

"Such nonsense, it isn't seemly," groused Helia. "Help me up, Rain."

"You skipped a few toes," said Rain, and went on dancing.

The Goose had gone away, he would come back—oh, sure, he would come back! Rain trusted in Iskinaary's capacity to argue a boat out of nowhere and return for her. What would happen next she didn't imagine. She might even reject the hard-won offer of rescue. But to sense that there was something to anticipate—that, however blank and featureless her life stretched behind her, it yearned forward with healthy avarice—it was like recovering from a long fever. And there would be more to understand, as long as she paid attention.

"She'll raise that basilisk from the lava throats, at this rate," said Helia.

"Ah, she's raising more than that," said Tirr, and pointed to the headland at the harbor's left side.

So soon, that was the reason for my elation, I could feel him coming, thought Rain. The harbor was picked out with a dark lozenge, a low boat of some sort, larger than the coracle in which that overseer man had arrived, with a number of oars being wielded by a crew.

"Away," cried Helia, grabbing so hard at Tirr's chiton it almost ripped. She pulled herself to her own feet without even use of her staff. "Quickly!"

The brides began to collect the bolster of net they'd woven. "Leave that!" barked the oldest woman, and they did. They scrambled up the path. Tirr and Kliompte were moaning. Scyrilla tried to catch Cossy's hand, but the youngest girl batted it away. Cossy reached for Rain's hand instead. Scyrilla's voice danced a scale of terror to a high, prolonged note.

No one had to explain to Rain that this was an unprecedented turn of events, as unique as her own appearance upon their shores a few weeks ago.

Once in the temple, Helia all but fell on her knees before the fire and began to stir the embers. Though it was a bright day, with the door slammed shut the temple was sunk into the gloom of a sudden dusk. "All right, if you're there, you dyani, make yourself seen so you can defend us from this assault!" she cried. But the dyani made no effort to compose itself in the smoke, by which Rain thought—well, if there is any truth to this, and the dyani is the essence of Mirka somehow, wouldn't that be just like her.

From a clerestory window at the roofline, reached by an uneven ladder, Cossy was calling out what she could see. "They are beaching their vessel. I can't even count that high, it's more than seven. More than eight. Maybe twice seven? I think one—yes—yes, one of them is the Minor Adjutant. That Lucikles."

Rain said, "Is Iskinaary with them?"

"Maybe they left him back on the ship. I don't see him. But there's—there's a small man."

"A dwarf? Or maybe it's a boy," said Rain.

"I don't know the difference," said Cossy. "But we'll find out soon. Lucikles and the smaller one are starting up the hill. The others are waiting with their oars all raised to the sky."

"Damn you to the underworld, you dyani," hissed Helia. "Oh, I forgot, you're already there. Well, serves you right. Get down from there, Acaciana, and reach me my purple robe. I'll admit him an audience in the most formal vestments."

"But what is happening?" cried Kliompte.

"Change. As far as I know, it's called change."

Cossy was frightened to see Rain go up and stand behind Helia as the old woman ordered the door unbolted. It seemed a risky maneuver. "Stay here. I don't need a second," said Helia.

"Don't go out there," pleaded Cossy. Helia flashed her a wry grin, which faded when she realized that Cossy had been talking to Rain.

"Close the door behind me and lock it," said Helia. The brides drew near the brilliant doorway as Helia left, and heedless of the instruction, Rain accompanied her onto the porch. The other brides didn't follow Helia's orders either but hovered in the doorway, gaping.

Lucikles and his companion were at the steps to the temple. It *was* a boy, Rain could see that. Probably the son of the Minor Adjutant. He sported the same tapered chin and a certain asymmetrical arch to one of the eyebrows. Man and boy looked like a pair of relatives who were congenitally quizzical.

"Your Reverence," said Lucikles, bowing to Helia. He nudged the boy, who made his own clumsy attempt at a bow.

"Kerr Lucikles, I will have this discussion with you in private," said Helia. "If we must. But it is untimely."

"Untimely is right. We'll talk here, Dame Helia," said Lucikles. "We have no time for niceties. We start the return to Maracoor tonight. I've come to remove the green visitor from your midst."

Helia drew herself up, as high as her crookback and arthritis allowed. "You have no call to do that."

"I am under order of the Bvasil himself."

"By what argument?"

Lucikles had guessed the senior bride would try to command the terms, and he was ready to stand up to her. "The Bvasil doesn't supply arguments even to a reverence such as yourself. But as you know, the Brides of Maracoor are designated to be seven. An eighth member upsets the tradition. Havoc is being seen throughout the land, and I mean the mainland and the islands. This isn't a matter I am at liberty to negotiate." He turned to Rain. "If you have anything like belongings, collect them now. You're returning with us."

"She can't leave," said Helia. "She is now the seventh bride. You can't deprive us of one of our number. By your own word we're designated to be seven."

Lucikles winced. "I don't understand, but I don't care. She's coming with us."

"Let me explain. Shortly after you left," said Helia, "one of our brides died. Suddenly and without warning. A terrible loss. Mirka, you know. The poor dear. We still grieve. But the Great Mara supplied us Rain in advance of need. You can't upset history by removing her. Nor dare you go against the fate we have twisted for the nation. I won't have it. You'd best take yourself away."

"We require the Vessel, too," said Lucikles. "I am going to call my men up now to retrieve it. We will take the strongbox, and we will take Rain."

"That never can be—" began Helia, but a noise from inside interrupted.

"She didn't die." Scyrilla, from her place in the shadows of the doorway. "Mirka didn't die! She was killed. She was murdered. She was poisoned. If you have to take someone, take the murderer."

At the voice of the girl in the darkness, they all turned. She was a sooty silhouette clenching her own elbows, but her eyes were gleaming with rage. "The child is mad with fear, look what you've done," said Helia, her voice guttural, contemptuous.

"I won't say who it is," said Scyrilla, "but Helia can tell you."

Lucikles glanced down at Leorix, whose eyes were wide. The boy had inched to stand closer to his father. These women were alarming to Leorix. They seemed competent but wild—not the herd of docile sheep he'd expected. More like a riot of gibbons. Or a spray of anarchic dryads loosened from the deepest woods.

"I will sit with Helia while you make your good-byes," said Lucikles to Rain, with a coldness he didn't feel, but needed to project. "You others? Dismissed."

They obeyed him. Most of the brides ran toward the Mother of Olive. Rain and Cossy dove deeper into the temple. Cossy was weeping with such a tempest of feeling that there was no possibility of Lucikles's words being overheard.

Helia summoned a stool and seated herself. The boy sat at her feet as he might have done beside Mia Zephana, perhaps a bit obsequiously. Lucikles remained standing.

"It's Mirka, then, is it," he said. "The thorn in your side. She's passed on to the Groves of Salanx. May her spirit find peace there."

"Little chance of that. Mirka wasn't known for tranquility in this life, that's for sure," said Helia. "I won't pretend to be in mourning, Lucikles. I haven't the time in life left for that kind of hobbledey-noise. I suspect the Groves of Salanx remain in something of an uproar if Mirka has moved into the neighborhood."

"And unexpected? What is this bandycock about her being killed?"

"The first I've heard it said. The girl is hysterical. Pay her no mind."

"Where is Mirka's body?" As Lucikles spoke, he saw his son flinch. "Do you want to go exploring?" he asked Leorix, out of grudging respect for his innocence. He waved at the domesticated slope around the temple. "Take Cur with you."

Cur was slavering to find that Goose again and rejoin the battle.

"Well, yes, but first, I never saw the inside of the Temple of Maracoor Spot before," he said, and bounced up and crossed the threshold. Across in the orchard, several cries of alarm fluted up from the watching brides, but they stayed where they were. Lucikles held his tongue.

"I had a glance at the place the key is kept," said Lucikles to Helia. He, Helia, and one other functionary in the Courts of the Adjutants were the only ones to know about the key's hiding place. "It appears to have been disturbed."

"I haven't been out there for years," said Helia evenly.

"Is the key still there?"

"It isn't given to me to be sure."

He tried again. "Dame Helia. Tell me. What did that child mean, Mirka was murdered? An act of that sort on the sacred isle? Who? How? We both know the power of the amulet. Has it been used against one of your own number? Helia, have you gone mad?"

"You and the Bvasilry have put us here and dedicated our lives to this aim. We do what we've been raised to do, and no apologies. No, I didn't murder Mirka. The idea! For that matter, you yourself could have secured the key and come stealing into the temple in the middle of the night and made—some arrangement of poison. You're the only other one who knows where the key is."

"That's not true," said Scyrilla. Oh, the wiles of young girls. Lucikles thought he'd been keeping watch, but she'd left the grove and returned to the temple and stolen around the side of it. She'd been listening.

"You! You're a tissue of hothouse fancies, Scyrilla, you're stricken with your monthly crazies. You haven't learned to manage the upheavals yet. Go away," snarled Helia.

"Someone opened the casket with the key and closed it up again," said Scyrilla. "In the middle of the night. I woke up. I saw it happen."

"You saw who?" asked Lucikles.

"Her," said Scyrilla, but didn't point with finger or expression.

"Rain? That stranger, Rain?" Then: "Do you mean Helia?"

"Call her," said Scyrilla to Helia. "Call her or I will. It doesn't matter now, but it would be better if you did."

"Tirr, Bray, come drag this mosquito away from us!" shrieked Helia.

No one moved, pinched in the stalemate of competing authorities.

"Cossy did it," said Scyrilla. "Cossy," she repeated in a louder voice.

Helia's silence was judgment and conviction at once. "Cossy," she said at last. "Come forward."

So there were six on the porch, party to an impromptu arraignment for indictment. Lucikles. Helia. Scyrilla, who was flushing stray tears from the corners of her eyes. Cossy, who had approached from the depths of the temple, clinging to Rain's hand and elbow. Rain herself. And Leorix in a fluster of confusion, loitering nearby.

Helia said, with an air of aggrieved weariness, "It is suggested, Cossy, that you made plans willfully to steal the hidden key to the Vessel in the treasure-room, and you did use it to make poison somehow which, I don't know, you wrapped into food to be served to Mirka, or stirred in her portion of wine, or some such inanity."

Cossy couldn't speak. She wept as if she were on a scaffold with a noose for a necklace.

"She's a child," said Rain, "no such thing could be possible, surely?"

"Your opinion isn't sought, so don't provide it," said Lucikles.

"Someone must speak for her," said Rain. "Look, she can hardly speak for herself."

"Do be quiet, you. You are still a guest here, and a guest unfamiliar with our customs," snapped Helia. "Now listen, Lucikles. It *is* true that I told the child where we had secreted the key to the strongbox. I had been having spells and was afraid that I might go to my death without letting anyone know."

"Surely Mirka was next in line?"

"Perhaps I had a foreboding," said Helia. "Perhaps a dyani in a chimney hearth let me know Mirka wouldn't live long enough to need the information. Anyway, she wasn't trustworthy. She was an insurrectionist. In the long run, a threat to our mission. We require strict compliance as brides. Her death was a loss but it wasn't a sad loss."

No one argued against that conclusion.

Helia went on. "A child, though, even if she had

procured the key, how could a child decide to use the totem with such malice? The notion is fatuous. Hysteria has flooded in to take the place of normal grief. I won't hear anything more of it."

"Ask where the key is," said Scyrilla. "Go on, why not?"

"I assume it's in its usual repository," said Lucikles drily.

"If you're actually accusing a child, Lucikles, then ask the child." Helia jerked a thumb at Cossy.

"This seems like panic and hysteria—" began Rain, but Helia cut her off.

"What's that you have on a string around your waist, then, Cossy?" asked Helia. "I caught a glimpse of such when you were dressing. We aren't given to private jewelry in our ministry of fate."

Cossy's eye bulged and she made to lunge at Helia, but Rain and, after a little hesitation, Leorix, too, held her back. Cossy snarled at the boy.

"Well, that would be interesting to see," said Scyrilla. "Nobody ever gave me a little secret cincture for my waist when I turned any number of years old."

Helia pointed to Lucikles and said, "Show him whatever it is, Acaciana. If you did something, admit to what you did. No one will fault you. You're too young to understand moral algorithms."

Cossy pulled the cord, and a heavy key emerged. She dangled it, a pendulum; it swayed between her and Helia. She went to pass it over, but Helia shrank away.

"I haven't touched that key in decades and I don't touch it now. Lucikles, if you still speak to that alchemical augurer on the mainland who can read the presence of human oils upon objects, I recommend you apply to him for his services. I suspect that unless you touch it yourself, you'll find that there is no recent human oil upon that item except that of this child. Now if you open the Vessel and find any evidence of a deposit of herb, perhaps even still a little green from our heavy spring rains, I concede that Scyrilla may have proven a point she had no permission to raise."

"Did you treat herbs by storing them in the strongbox with the totem, and then did you feed the herbs to your sister bride?" asked Lucikles of Cossy.

"She is beside herself. She won't speak," said Rain. "How could she?"

"The Great Mara alone knows why she might do such a thing," said Helia, clapping her hands.

"You hated Mirka," said Scyrilla.

"I did," admitted the old woman, "but I didn't kill her."

"Cossy was afraid that Rain would have to leave," said Scyrilla, "because she was one bride too many. If

Mirka were gone, Rain could be the seventh. She could stay. Cossy was doing your bidding, Helia, whether you knew it or not. She was also trying to get what she wants. She hogs Rain all to herself."

"These are dreadful heavy charges to state," said Lucikles, "and you're a silly child to do so."

"I woke up and I saw her coming out of the treasure-room in the middle of the night, carrying a spoon of something," said Scyrilla. "And a day later Mirka was dead in her bed."

Helia shrugged and made a conceding moue of possibility. Some foul complicity here, thought Rain, but she didn't know these people enough to guess where it ran.

"Let us go to the Vessel," said Lucikles. "And see if there is evidence of anything being placed there adjacent to the totem, with the intent of being charged with a spell of poison."

"You can't come into the temple," said Helia.

"All the rules are broken now, haven't you heard?" said Lucikles heavily. "Mermaids are swarming the tidal pools and dying in heaps; tree spirits signal to each other by waving the limbs of their trees when the air is breathless and still. You, little girl, come with me, little girl; let us look in the casket together and see what we see, little girl."

He didn't want his son near the dangerous item. "You and Cur stay here and mind the door. Let no one approach," he said.

Leorix swelled with the assignment.

Three brides—Helia, Scyrilla, and Cossy—accompanied Rain and Lucikles into the umbrous temple, and then to the sanctuary at the far end. A smell of tombs, this deep in, thought Lucikles. Stone has its own opinion about eternity and perfumes it accordingly. "Here—Acaciana, am I right? Acaciana. Cossy. You have the key. You show me how the lock works."

"A lock only works one way, anyone could do it," said Cossy, rather cagily thought Lucikles. In the quiet of her own mind Rain was thinking the same thing. The girl produced the key, drove it into the keyhole, and turned it. The key performed its duty and the hasp fell open.

They all leaned over to look while Lucikles put his fingers on both ends of the lid and lifted gently, as if there might be some asp or scorpion or coiled dyani within, ready to spring. But despite an eerie undersea glow from the box, it was still too dark to see.

"Get a taper," said the Minor Adjutant. Scyrilla dashed away and when she returned, they leaned forward again.

The amulet, the Fist of Mara, lay somnolent but ready to strike. Rain thought it ominous but she couldn't guess why—it was a strangely shaped stone, like a weapon found in nature. Conformed by accident or by sacred design to fit the human grip. A stone that had given whoever first found it an entirely new notion of weaponry.

Beside it lay a crumpled, embroidered handkerchief, the one Helia had put there. The flickering of the flame showed that a few flecks of witherwort leaf, still olive green so recent enough, gathered in the folds of the cloth. As if in a daze, Lucikles licked his forefinger and reached in to tab the shred, perhaps to taste it, but Helia knocked his arm. "Are you mad? That will kill you, or make you very sick indeed."

"Yes," he said. Recovering. "And I suppose it is evidence, too." He lowered the lid and nodded to the youngest bride to lock the Vessel up.

"Evidence?" asked Rain, Helia echoing the word an instant later.

"I'll take the key in a leather fold," said Lucikles. "Your idea about the scent augurer, Helia, is a good one. If the girl is the only one who touched the key in these past dozens of years, she's likely to be the one to have put herbs there. She will be investigated for the murder of your sister bride Mirka."

"How could that be, she's a child," said Helia. "I won't have it, Lucikles."

"The world seems to be breaking in pieces," he replied, "but justice in small matters remains as important as justice on the world stage. You should know that while I was here interviewing your new arrival—Rain—Maracoor Abiding was attacked by a hostile navy assault."

Rain bristled. "I didn't arrive as a diversion for some military maneuver," she said. Though she realized that she wasn't certain about why she'd arrived at all.

"If we forgo matters of right and wrong on a human scale, we invite disaster in every door and window and via every mountain pass and harbor. I've come to take Rain to see the Bvasil, and to commandeer the Vessel and return to the mainland with it lest you, too, be overwhelmed by a vandal landing here."

"You mean other than the one you bring with you today?" Helia shot back.

"I'll take the child too. She'll be interviewed by the Magistrate at the House of Balances for the crime of which she's been accused."

Cossy could hardly follow all this. "She told me how to do it!" she said, pointing at Helia. "She told me about how the totem could magic itself upon simple herbs and render them deadly."

"Oh, I did do *that,* I confess," said Helia mildly. "I needed Cossy to know how Mirka might misuse the power of the amulet for her own aims. Someone has to be on the lookout after I am gone. Look, if the key is stained with human oil from only her fingers, as I'll warrant, there will be evidence of her agency in the matter, and none other. But she's a child. Leave her be. You can't possibly—"

Lucikles said, "I need a leather wallet that has been wiped with fresh water inside and out." Scyrilla hopped to obey with too much eagerness for anyone's taste. When Lucikles had it, he opened it and said to Cossy, "Deposit the key."

The girl looked at Helia, whose expression was sad and loving. "Do as he tells you, child."

Cossy bit her lower lip and began to settle the key upon the fold of leather, but Rain leaned forward and took the key in her fingers and felt it up and down.

"There," she said. "Now my human oil is upon it, too. So there's nothing exclusive about your proof. The idea, to charge a child with murder! I find I don't know much about the world, but this is cruelty if not madness. Let her go. You're taking me away anyway; I'll deal with the accusation."

Helia looked startled at Rain's behavior, and Lucikles admitted surprise himself. In her own locked strongbox, deep beneath her breastbone, Rain felt a surge of something fiercer than she'd known since waking to find herself on this island. Maybe this is what Iskinaary meant by choosing, she thought. Why did I implicate myself without thinking it over? Acting on—some instinct toward—what?

Cossy's face, frozen in a rictus of uncomprehension, was why. It seemed a mirror to how Rain had felt since her arrival.

Fellow feeling with a pre-adolescent girl. That such a thing even existed . . .

Lucikles wrapped the key up and the group moved back toward the light of the open doorway and the portico. "If we lose sight of small morals, we have no hope of remembering large ones," he said. "Sympathy for the disenfranchised is admirable but murder is not. I am going to ask you to join your sisters in the arbor, Acaciana, until we're ready to leave."

"Don't move," said Rain to the girl.

"I'm not going anywhere," she replied with spunk.

Lucikles raised his voice. "Very well, but I'm in a hurry. I'll have you removed. Leorix—run down, summon Captain Nitexos to approach with four men."

"You won't have them touch the girl!" Helia swore at him, and then turned her head. "Bray, here. Hurry!"

The big woman arrived before the soldiers could scale the slope. At Helia's instruction, she lifted the scrabble-limbed child and hauled her down the temple steps. The girl cried and kicked, and Rain lunged to accompany her, but Lucikles raised his hand. By now the sailors had arrived. Two of them carried ornamental glaives for show, but the weapons had a mean utilitarian gleam to their polished blades. Bray fell back.

"One thing more before we go," Lucikles said to Rain. "I find your concern for the girl's well-being touching. Captain Nitexos, come closer so you can witness this exchange. You may be asked to testify to what you hear if we need corroboration."

"At your service," said the Captain.

"A question," said Lucikles to Rain. "The girl is too far away to hear you. If you've just set yourself up to spoil the investigation into Mirka's death, your testimony will have to be consistent. I assume you are positioning yourself to have been a possible murderer of this woman, thereby to cast doubts to a Magistrate about the girl's culpability?"

"I could say that I put the herbs in that stone box, that I did it all myself."

"Very well. Then where did you get the key?"

Rain looked blank.

"The key was hidden. In order for you to be implicated in this crime, you'd have had to find the key and open the box yourself. Where did you find the key?"

Rain could say nothing.

"Where has it been hidden all these decades?"

"Lucikles!" protested Captain Nitexos who, not privy to the full rationale surrounding the brides and their practices, wondered if the Minor Adjutant was losing his wits.

"It's too late, Nitexos. The amulet is coming with us," said Lucikles. "Just tell us, Rain, where the key was, so you can plausibly be supposed a suspect in this crime. If that's what you want."

Rain could not answer.

"Your lack of a reply is construed as an admission that you do not know, so you can't have masterminded a deadly attack upon one of the citizens of this holy island."

"I—I could have taken it from Cossy when she was sleeping."

"But you didn't," piped up Scyrilla, "because I saw her creep into the treasury and come back out again, and you slept the night through."

"We're done here," said Lucikles. "Rain, either you will walk with us to the *Pious Enterprise* on your own two feet with dignity or I will have these men take you forcibly. It is up to you."

Helia turned a plum-colored face to Rain. "I didn't bring you here," she said. "Look at all the harm you have caused by choosing our island to be swept ashore upon."

"Where is the choice in any of that?" said Rain. "Making choices only begins again today."

"How will we perform our duties with only six brides?" asked Helia.

"Five," said Lucikles. "We are taking Cossy too, so she can be charged with murder in the court of the Magistrate of the Bvasilry."

5

Before third bell, the longboat was slipping away from the shore of Maracoor Spot. The harbor water looked still as glass, hardly a tidal ripple, as if it had frozen in shock at this turn of affairs. Most of the other brides were weeping in the temple, terrified that the men would change their minds and come back and abduct them, too. Only Helia had descended to watch them leave. With her oakthorn staff she stood immobile, inert, a crude effigy to be sacrificed in fire at some ceremony.

Rain's own hand was upon her broom, and she turned the handle up in imitation of Helia's crook. They were like two chieftains saying goodbye silently as the water widened between the stern of the longboat and the horizontal stones that stepped into the harbor. The morning's nets were still cast aside in a heap. The temple began to look less massive. How like a mountain was a temple, and how unlike too. The verticals of the columns, so magnificently set, a forest of ancient stone groomed into rectitude, putting barred and sacred face to the arbitrary world. Though Rain had seen the temple from above, its roofs had not seemed as magnificent. Now, the farther out she got, the more perfect the architectural proportions seemed—and the more insignificant.

She had approached the island through the harbor. Iskinaary had dragged her that way. But she had been insensible. Maracoor Spot wasn't the whole world it had seemed when Rain woke up there. It was only a dollop of soil thrown against the roiling blue-black waters. And smaller by the moment, as she watched—smaller in proportion to the sea and to itself. Just an accident of earth's backbone poking out of the waters.

She turned to Cossy, who had buried her face in Rain's side. For the time being the girl was done weeping. "Take a last look, then, to hold you," she murmured.

The girl shook her head. "Nothing held *you*," she replied, "no matter how hard you looked."

Rain said, "It may yet come back to me. More is happening than I can credit, to myself and to you, too."

The boy, whose name was Leorix or something like that, was watching Rain and Cossy without the slyness and prurience of some of the sailors. "Those who leave can also come back," he said.

"Tell that to Mirka," said Cossy savagely. The boy shook his head; this story was beyond him. His kindness went unwelcomed.

The angle of the longboat shifted in the stronger seas. They had gotten beyond the forearms of the harbor, and the temple seemed to be sliding on the hillside. First the peg-like form of Helia, and then the temple itself was lost to view. From this spot, the island sported no evidence of human habitation.

But if Iskinaary returns with a boat for me, thought Rain, Helia and the others will tell him what happened. He will come find me wherever we're being taken.

Then, around another hump of the island, anchored in a sweet spot out of the currents, the great profile of the *Pious Enterprise* rose its stand of masts and slapping sails.

The winds were favorable for Maracoor Abiding.

Captain Gargios Nitexos gave up his cabin for Rain and the girl child to use. Lucikles appreciated the generosity, but the captain brushed off any compliments. He didn't want to be responsible for assault upon the female guests by randy crew members, many of whom had worked the long trip he'd just returned to port, and had had too little time to satisfy their needs with their wives or otherwise onshore companions.

Furthermore, the Vessel with the amulet was stored in the Captain's room with them, secure in the Captain's large iron safe. As Nitexos found the obligation of carrying that sacred object troubling, it was easier for him to avoid the whole idea while he could. The Captain was open about the skittishness he felt. If the ship should go down carrying the totem, what would become of any of them? Either in the chambers of the House of Balances, or in the regard of the Bvasil—or of the Great Mara herself? So Nitexos strung a hammock above deck and tried to ignore those possibilities that fate might heap upon his head.

Cossy had retreated into a stage of mute disbelief about the turnabout life she had scraped into somehow. Rain stayed by the child's side. With Leorix as a third, they played sticks, and also bones and dice. The younger girl found some consolation in the fact that if her green companion had ever traveled by oceangoing vessel before, she couldn't remember it, so everything on board ship was new to her, too.

Leorix was a better player, and he teamed up with Cossy against Rain.

As the days progressed, they tried to give voice to their amazement. The way the horizon refused to resolve into precision, giving the ship a sense of floating not in water but in space and time, too. The arias of the winds, the cloud armies storming far away, once or twice coming near but then, luckily, skirting the *Pious Enterprise* and skittering off elsewhere. Dropping rakes of summer lightning toward other targets.

"Do you know what will happen when we get somewhere?" Cossy asked the green girl.

"I never know what we are going to have to eat at eight bells. What will happen tomorrow is beyond me," said Rain. "If you're cold, come under my cloak. The wind is a tyrant today."

Cossy steered clear of Lucikles as best she could, as well as all the sailors and the Captain. But she didn't hold Leorix in special contempt. After all, he was only a few years older than she was, to guess it. And as he had a level and open expression, Cossy concluded that he wasn't to be blamed for whatever wicked campaign his father was conducting.

Leorix looked like a younger version of Lucikles, but he was himself, too. This was a mystery to her. She came to realize that, in her short life, Leorix and Lucikles were the first two people she had ever met who were related to each other.

"What does that feel like, to have a parent?" she asked Rain.

"Maybe like this," said Rain, and drew her closer to shelter her from the wind. "Though to be honest, I can't remember." The realization made Rain fall quiet. But for the child's sake Rain tried to lighten the moment. "Look, seagulls, and new ones—they're partly brown. It's not the four or five who have been following us from Maracoor Spot."

"They're mainland gulls," said Leorix, fresh from the head, flapping his wet rinsed hands in the wind, joining them at the rail. Enjoying the authority of prior knowledge, he looked smug. "It won't be much longer before we see the continent."

"Tell us about it," said Cossy. She realized that she liked him, even though he wasn't a bride. He was something else, not a girl, but he wasn't one of those men who smelled so rank and bristled at the chin, and shouted over the winds as if they could holler them to silence. Well, she knew Leorix was a *boy*; she understood the concept. This entity wrapped in the package of "boy"— she was intrigued, she was alert. She hadn't expected to notice, much less to care.

"The world?" he said. "Tell you about the world? All of Peare, the known and the unknown lands, and the heavens and seas too?"

"That's too wide," intercepted Rain. "A slice of it is enough."

"A story of it, then. Would that do?"

Cossy shrugged. She couldn't judge whether it would prove equal to her appetite until it was over.

Leorix began with an apology. "I'm used to telling my younger sisters stories about the adventures of Houranos and the Centaur. Do you know Houranos? The fiercest hero of the Fabled Age?" The boy lurched into an entrapment of plot, backing and forthing among characters whose central attributes he presumed were universally known. Rain and Cossy stayed rapt regardless, Cossy because she had too little experience with this kind of thing to be critical, and Rain? Rain was enthralled by the boy's kindness.

Whatever task Houranos had been enjoined to achieve—it had something to do with a plot of revenge and rescue, involving an underground anvil and a goddess who had been turned into a golden persimmon—he eventually managed it. He was rewarded with a promotion to immortality, there forever to caper with other immortal companions who sounded, frankly, a bit out of control. It didn't matter. Cossy was intrigued. Her face glowed in the lowering sun off the port side. The final lines of revelry and honor and filthy riches were scarcely delivered when a bell rang from the Captain's perch. A different pattern of strike in the air. They all lifted their heads.

"Land," cried Captain Nitexos. And so it was, a few dark smudges above the mist of the horizon.

The three younger passengers learned it would be half a day or more before they would drop anchor in the port harbor of Maracoor Crown. Cossy's moods shifted among states of excitement, dread, and regret for the closing of this period of suspended judgment. Rain was quieter in her expressions but clearly agitated too.

Leorix tried to calm them both. "You'll be treated as honored guests," he said to them. "In all of Peare there are no people more hospitable than those of Maracoor Abiding."

"You sound as if you've traveled widely," said Rain.

"No, but I've been told." His tone was momentarily waspish for a young boy.

"What is Peare, what do you mean?" Cossy asked him.

"Peare," he explained, as if that was enough. Then he revolved his wrists so his open palms welcomed everything that could be seen or imagined. "Peare, where we all live. The world."

"Oh, the *world*," said Cossy dismissively. "I'm not sure yet if I love the world."

"Oh, nobody's sure of that," he replied with insouciance, "that's normal." He meant to cheer her up, and he managed it. "You'll like Maracoor Abiding, though."

"If they think I've done something wrong?" she pressed him.

"They won't think that. You're only a girl."

"They must think that," said Cossy, "or they wouldn't have kidnapped me and made me come with you."

"We're a reasonable sort," said Leorix. Lucikles, passing, wondered at his son's equanimity, and whether it was born of ignorance or of a deeper knowledge of the species than Lucikles himself possessed.

"The House of Balances will likely conduct an investigation," Lucikles commented to the three of them. "Under the circumstances of the national alarm, the process may be brief and superficial. And that you are only a child will provoke a sentiment of mercy in the Magistrate. No point in worrying about it ahead of time."

"Oh, fine, I won't then," grumbled Cossy. "Thanks for the tip."

Rain got up and followed Lucikles toward the prow, where he was headed to sniff the wind for a breath of earth. In a low voice she said, "I'd be grateful to know if you were just being kind, or if you really believe that no harm will come to the girl."

"Well, it depends on whether she did what she's been indicted of, I suppose," he replied. "Mercy is essentially a process of mathematics. The great Polytheus teaches us this. If murder is allowed as an accusation, and if the child is convicted, I imagine punishment would be commensurate to the consequences to the body politic of the murder she committed."

"Can you really propose to accuse a child of murder?"

"Oh," said Lucikles, "it won't be up to me to make that decision."

"But you're busy hauling this child to a place where such a decision might be made about her?"

"That's my job here," he said. "It's my only job. The application of justice? That's a transaction beyond my capacity to determine. Leave it to the courts."

"I'm uneasy about this child," said Rain.

"Spend some time being uneasy about yourself," advised Lucikles. "I have a much poorer sense of what is in store for you. There's no precedent for what you've done."

"What *I've* done?" asked Rain, astounded. "What are you talking about?"

"It isn't for me to second-guess the thinking of the Bvasil and his minions. But nothing is normal now. Haven't you noticed?"

"Nothing in my life has been normal since I woke

up to this life—this apparent second life of Maracoor. What else do you mean besides that?"

"I mean—the turmoil under the skin of things. The rash of—of aberration. The appearances, the once-in-a-never-evers, the hollow stories taking on actual figure and form." It was the first time Lucikles had talked to Rain as other than a prisoner of sorts. The first time he was putting into words his alarm about the heightened vivacity of the material world.

Its diaphanous spirit-curtain shaking visibly before them all.

Well, before him anyway.

Maybe it was just him.

He slanted a look at the Rain Creature to see if she was taking up his meaning. But she was too much a foreigner for him to be able to read her expression. He had thought her divine when he first met her. Maybe he had been right after all.

"I can't care about the misbehavior of the earth and sea and sky," she said, "but to torment a young child is insupportable."

"Young children don't feel the torment we do, they haven't the goods," he said, and looked over her shoulder at the horizon again. How peaceful the mainland seemed at this hour, in this light. If armies were hurtling on the coastal plain toward the capital city of Maracoor Abiding, they were invisible from this distance.

"I ask you, since you're a father, to take care of her as if she were your child," said Rain suddenly.

"How impertinent." Suddenly he found himself irritated at her tone. "As if I would treat her with anything other than correct equity. You offend me."

"You are tender toward your son," said Rain in a softer voice. "That's all I'm saying. You have the capacity of a man of mercy."

"My son is my son, heir to the house of Korayus. Now if you'll forgive me, I have preparations to make before we land."

He left her and looked neither left nor right. He wanted no cloud-birds, no harpies. There was only so much spirit-world folderol a man could be expected to take.

The House of Balances

1

The *Pious Enterprise* drew into Maracoor Harbor for the second time in a moon. The bustle of the port was reasserting itself with vigor and clamor, almost back to normal. As the ship drew near to berth, though, sailors and passengers alike noted the congeries of military armament. Catapults and pots of boiling pitch at the ready. A martial presence of cuirassed soldiers making a show of their plumes and pluck, stomping in formation up and down the quay. Beyond them, commerce was rollicking along with a merry gurgle. Fear of war, it seemed, had brought merchants back to life.

"A second surprise," murmured Gargios Nitexos, "but this time we can't be as surprised as the first. We don't have it in us anymore."

The harbormaster sent an envoy to the ship to review

papers. Within the hour, a military guard assembled at the end of the gangplank to escort Lucikles, Rain, and Acaciana to locked chambers where they could freshen up for an audience with the authorities, which would convene after the noonday meal. Leorix and Cur were allowed to tag along only after some harsh words were exchanged.

In the House of Balances, Lucikles found Kerr Porox, his immediate supervisor, prowling the halls outside the Courts of the Adjutants with a bored nonchalance, as if he'd been at his post for months and was due a holiday soon. The Minor Adjutant begged leave to escort his son home. Oena would surely have returned to Piney Quarter by now. She'd be furious and panicked over the disappearance of her son and her husband without so much as a note. Indeed, Lucikles knew that his marriage might never recover. Still, he owed it to Oena not to leave her worried for an hour longer than necessary.

But the Sergeant Adjutant declined the request. "This enquiry is central to everything," declared Porox. "You are ordered without fail to attend the hearing this afternoon. There is no time for a frolic to the home hearth. If it all goes swiftly and there are no questions as to your own comportment in this matter—"

"*My* comportment?" said Lucikles. "I did what I was told, exactly. Furthermore, I took immediate action when I encountered a gross anomaly in the arrangements at Maracoor Spot."

"Why so defensive? I'm merely saying," continued the Sergeant Adjutant. "If the Magistrate's judgment is swift and your help isn't needed, and if you aren't found complicit in any way, you may be able to be home in time for dinner. For all I know. If you're concerned about the boy, sling him in a cart and pay someone to bring him to Temple Houranos." He glanced at Leorix. "Hardly an infant."

But somehow Lucikles couldn't risk even this. He couldn't haul their son across the wide ocean and back again, only to deliver him into the hands of a stranger. Gargios Nitexos might have helped, this once, but his presence was required at harborside, to corroborate the details of their journey. He also needed to hand over the amulet to whatever authority would show up to claim it.

"You'll have to come with me to the courtroom when I make my report," said Lucikles to his son. "You'll sit in the far back, you won't speak, you won't contradict anything I say, you won't gasp or cry or make *any indication* that you are there. You aren't to cast a shadow even. Do you understand? I suppose you think that you ought to be allowed to pace the streets from city centre to our home on your own, but—"

"But I don't want to do that," said Leorix. "I'd rather be at the proceedings. I would."

Lucikles was stupefied. He looked at Leorix, as if seeing him for the first time since leaving him more than three months ago on the annual survey of the colonial islands. The boy's physical state, lying shattered and silenced in a cot in Mia Zephana's farmhouse, had absorbed every scrap of his father's attention. But as Leorix had regained his health, Lucikles had been so relieved that he'd failed to take stock of the other changes.

There was a more sober cast to his son's eye, a steadier gaze. Yes, and he was taller; he was admittedly thirteen. The thighs had begun to lengthen and to muscle up already. Usually ready to look for such transformations upon his return from a long trip, Lucikles had been blind to them this time. The scars of the wolf attack had diverted his attention from the obvious.

"Very well," he said. "But mind what I say. A misstep could throw a Magistrate's mood in the wrong direction. No broken egg yolk has ever yet been turned back into a golden orb again."

And, once the innocence of childhood is lost, no adolescent has ever regained it.

Although some corridors of the House of Balances were busy with military men, the wing of the Courts of the Adjutants, where cases were heard, was comparatively quiet. A few birds flew in the open windows and ate crumbs off the unswept floor. Lucikles and Leorix presented themselves at the door of the chamber a few moments before the Magistrate took his post. They were examined at the forearm and calf and thigh to make sure no scabbard or knife was buckled out of sight. That they both were admitted to the chamber meant Leorix's name was already on the manifest. Strange.

Generally, Lucikles made his reports to his superior and one or two specialists in a cozy debriefing salon, over a glass of tea or a snifter of spirits. Though he worked near the court chambers, this was only the second or third time in his life he'd had reason to enter them on business. He thought he was ready. Courtesy of a pavement barber, Lucikles had taken time to have his facial hair trimmed to a neat, close-fitting sleeve. When the Magistrate entered sporting an unruly tangle of beard, clear evidence of crisis in the capital city, Lucikles feared he'd be considered self-absorbed, unconcerned with the panic facing the nation. There was nothing to be done about it now, though. He squared his shoulders and followed the courtier's beck of entry.

It took a moment for Lucikles to recognize the Magistrate. It was Borr Apoxiades, not Borr Xanon as Lucikles had expected. Apoxiades was thought fair and rigorous, most of the time—though rumor had it that when his wife was roaming the agora with a come-hither look daubed upon her countenance in kohl and rouge, his judgments could be peremptory and, more often than not, harsh. Lucikles felt a sly twinge of hope. The wife of Borr Apoxiades wouldn't be likely to be hailing sailors at a time like this. The Magistrate would prove judicious, surely.

Though the Minor Adjutant caught himself then: if he was sensing in himself a twinge of hope—hope for what? He wasn't able to voice a best-case outcome for the brides, for Rain, for this sliver of a young girl thought a suspect in a possible murder case. He only wanted this entanglement of problems to be behind him so he could reunite with Oena and, at last, see his family safely together at home. Whatever was to happen to the amulet, to the brides—who knew? Beyond his obligation to the satisfactory fulfillment of his assignment, he didn't care. And he wouldn't spend a pair of mismatched coins to find out.

Borr Apoxiades arranged his judicial bulk with care, the better to focus his judgment upon the case at hand. He had a bad knee and favored it as one might a slightly dim grandchild. When he was comfortable, he recognized the court scribe, but stressed the need for absolute privacy. Pain-of-death type of affair, understood? Good.

He opened a blue lime neatly, almost prissily, with a clean thumbnail, and he segmented the fruit. Lucikles watched blandly until he realized that Borr Apoxiades had already begun his presentation by arranging the flotilla of fruit canoes on the bench before him. "This was the invading force," he stated. "It entered the harbor a half hour before dawn, we're told. Most of our fishermen had already launched, but the lazier ones were still messing about with their cordage and pots. That morning the harbormaster was awake but inattentive, perhaps hungover from the night before. He'll be hanged on Gallows Corner for irresponsibility tantamount to treason if we catch his sorry carcass—he's disappeared. Anyway, around the edge of the southern headland they sailed, these two in the lead, see." He arranged a crumpled napkin to approximate the coastline. "Perhaps to draw fire if a quick defense were mounted. The easier, maybe, to signal to the rest of the fleet to stay back, or withdraw. The other eight or nine having fanned out in the morning mist a mile out, like so, where they couldn't be spied by those on the quay or in the harbor. Later we learned four or five fishing vessels had indeed detected them, but they'd been quietly and efficiently sunk before a single one of them could turn back to raise the alarm. All fishermen were presumed drowned or taken prisoner, and the boats capsized. Though pieces of them washed ashore in the subsequent days."

Borr Apoxiades ate one of the invading ships. Blue lime juice beaded on his rubicund lower lip. "Our job today is to investigate if there is any relationship between, on the one hand, the appearance of an alien woman who infiltrates the community of brides in Maracoor, and, on the other hand, the arrival of an alien fleet in our waters."

"Yes, Your Dignity."

"Determining this will help the court to decide the proper course of action in the disposition of the woman held in detention. And determine whether this is a civil or a criminal matter, if either. I understand her name is Rain? Has she a surname of any distinction? Well, any surname at all?"

Lucikles's moment. "Your Dignity, the young woman has suffered some sort of mental disorder—amnesia, I suppose. Most of her memories of her time before arriving on our soil are blurred. She told me she believes there was another name but she can't recall it."

"Very sensible of her. And convenient. It makes her hard to question. A little stress and unhappiness while incarcerated might improve her memory. But let us hope we don't have to open the door to *that* chamber. Kerr

Lucikles, please make a short statement as to your findings. Keep in mind that while I have employed a scribe to take notes, the findings of this investigation will be kept as private as possible. You needn't worry about rumors getting around of any inappropriate actions you may have taken."

"I don't have to worry about such rumors. My actions are above reproach."

"Yes yes yes. Of course they are. Proceed."

"Your Dignity. Before making a statement, I present my son, Leorix, whom you must have requested to have present at this hearing."

"I must have? Well, if I must have, then I probably did. I do what I must. Good afternoon, young man. You will be sworn to secrecy before you leave the building. All words spoken here remain custody of the state. Go ahead, Kerr Lucikles. We haven't all day."

"Very well. But before I proceed with the facts as I understand them, can you confirm that the Vessel is safely in the keep of the Bvasilry?"

Borr Apoxiades nodded the least vigorous of assents ever displayed by human head.

"Thank you," said Lucikles. "My signal obligation was to deliver that item to the court of the Bvasil. If it is successfully received, everything else is polished potatoes."

"Street talk is not allowed. Keep your argot professional."

"My apologies, Your Dignity. I suppose relief trips my tongue into sloppiness. But no matter. Let me report on my most recent trip, and make some select observations. It isn't mine to draw conclusions, but my son who is present was a witness to the events and to the pertinent exchanges." Lucikles glanced at Leorix, who had turned oddly pale. How strange it must be to see one's father in a professional light for the first time, thought Lucikles. Something Lucikles himself had never been able to do, his own father having died before Lucikles had reached the age Leorix was now.

The Minor Adjutant found that the story needed to be told from the start. He described how, when he had first arrived for the annual inspection of life on Maracoor Spot, the brides of Maracoor had concealed from him the presence of a green-skinned girl, perhaps seventeen years old or so. Hard to pinpoint the age exactly. His little dog had flushed her out. She was said to have fallen from the sky and washed ashore, clinging to a broom and accompanied by a talking Goose—

"A talking Goose," said Borr Apoxiades, and snorted. He had heard this bit in chambers already, but it delighted him, the nonsense of it. "Of course we have only her word for her mode of travel. That, and the misapprehensions of the cloistered brides. Perhaps she really was dumped overboard near the shores of Maracoor Spot from a ship organized by the marauders, whose compatriots even then were approaching our capital from the south."

Lucikles gave a shrug and continued his recitation. Uncertain what to do, he had returned to the mainland for instruction. Learning that the city had been beset by a fleet of berserk foreigners, he had endeavored to determine what his next obligations to the Bvasilry might be—

"Let's be blunt, you fled to the hinterlands," said Borr Apoxiades, without apparent disapproval, but pointedly. "Remember you're under oath here."

"Of course, Your Dignity." A misstep on his part. "For efficiency I was narrating solely on the story of Maracoor Spot." Lucikles tucked in a line about his family and then guided the narrative back to his mission as set by the Bvasil himelf. The Minor Adjutant was ordered to return to Maracoor Spot and to pluck the stranger from the midst of the brides. He was to deliver her to the capital city. Perhaps more important, he was also instructed to evacuate the Vessel and its contents from the temple. Which mission he had completed with duty and dispatch.

Lucikles detailed how, in so doing, he'd learned that

one of the brides had died, leaving a gap. He told how the senior bride had already begun the formation of Rain to fill the vacancy. When a slight tussle among the younger brides revealed an accusation of murder that involved the amulet, he had—

"Stop there," said Borr Apoxiades. "Your son is not privy to these state secrets."

"He was there, Your Dignity. He knows what I know."

The Magistrate sighed. "Very well. But we're now at a crucial point of this hearing. We must take this very carefully. I need you to detail for me who had access to the amulet, and how, and why."

This matter wasn't decided in Lucikles's own mind, but he did his best. "It is hearsay, nothing more, but I believe that the youngest bride, a child of ten years, named Acaciana, was in sole possession of the key to the Vessel. Either alone or in collusion, she may have carried out a murder through poison. It's possible she didn't mean to kill her sister bride. Children of such tender years don't always understand what they are doing, nor even why."

"*I* did," said Borr Apoxiades. "I was hardly a moral genius, but I knew right from wrong. I had it slapped into me. But we'll leave the matter of her guilt and any punishment till later. Is it possible, do you think, that the foreign agent planted among them had talked the gullible child into the murder?"

"The agent . . . ? Oh, you mean Rain. I couldn't say. The stranger seems befuddled with a memory loss that it would be difficult to feign. Even if she'd intended to spy on the brides or to hunt for the amulet, in the crisis of her arrival the Green Creature—that's what they called her, sorry—Rain—apparently surrendered any sense of mission. In any case, I can't see that the death of one of the senior brides could have anything to do with the amulet—I mean apart from the object's possible toxifying influence upon an ingestible herb rumored to be the cause of death."

"You think these are separate campaigns? The murder of a Maracoor bride, the invasion of a fleet from hell?"

"My opinion is sadly uninstructed, but, yes. Yes. I think the events are unrelated."

"No wonder you're only a Minor Adjutant. It takes a capacity of vision to force contradictory stories together into complementarity. But that's my job, and why I'm here. Did I read in your report that this Rain had actually thumbed the key herself? In order to prove her human oils detectable upon it? Thus to corrupt the definite identification of the child as the culprit? Isn't it likely she did that in your presence to mask the fact that she had already held the key?"

"I'm out of my depth, Your Dignity. I'm no investigator of crimes. I'm a civil servant reporting on procedures of state. In this instance, to wit: the supervision of the brides of Maracoor, who by their holy mission secure the daily commonwealth of the nation in the name of the Great Mara."

The Magistrate shifted on his haunches. "Spare me. I know your brief, Kerr Lucikles. But I'm trying to discover a relationship between the arrival of Rain on Maracoor Spot and the attack by a foreign fleet on our city at the same time. It seems to me that the central item of interest in both campaigns has to be the amulet. Coincidence isn't quite so uncanny."

"I thought by definition that is precisely what coincidence is," said Lucikles, though Borr Apoxiades might well be right. "In any event, the amulet is returned to Maracoor Abiding for the first time in our lives. For the first time in several hundred years, as I understand it. I don't know if it's in your purview to determine how to fill the openings caused by a death of one bride and the removal from Maracoor Spot of a second. My guess is that the girl Acaciana will be deemed blameless and returned to her post. An infant bride can accompany her at the same time. Unless you think that Rain, being odd but probably not involved in espionage, might be returned to Maracoor Spot to serve as the seventh bride?"

"I'll confer with my estimable colleagues about all that bosh. Anyway, it may be I'm not the one to decide," said Borr Apoxiades. He banged his gavel. "This hearing is over but the matter is not closed. Come back in three days' time and we will interview the young woman and the child before making a determination as to their fate. You are free to return to your home. But I will not have you lighting out for the uplands under any circumstances. Should you disappear you will be held in suspicion of collusion with the enemies of the state. The usual unpleasant penalties. Do you understand?"

"I am kept by the conventions of deference from expressing my outrage at such a suggestion," said Lucikles clearly and coolly. "My son and I will repair to our home and return on the appointed day."

"I don't believe your son is needed any longer. I found I didn't need him to corroborate any of your assertions," said the Magistrate, groaning as he prepared to rise.

"But may I be allowed to attend?" said the boy. "Your Dignity?"

The official turned. He nearly smiled. "The firstborn

of a Minor Adjutant speaks in court, and without being recognized. What temerity. Your offense is probably not actionable, but it is droll. And risky. Now, tell us: what interest do you have in this matter?"

"Cossy is my friend," he replied.

"He doesn't know of what he speaks," sputtered Lucikles.

"Oh, come," said Borr Apoxiades, demonstrably cheery, now his workday was done. "If there's one thing the young know, it's the value of friendship. Maybe that's the only thing they know. All right, young man; you may accompany your father when he returns in three days."

They left the building like pickpockets tearing away from a ransacked market stall. Lucikles didn't bother to speak until he had first governed his fear and then— and the second effort took a while longer—his irritation. When their pace slackened enough for the throb in Lucikles's forehead to lift, he said, "Before we get home and the next tempest breaks across our prow," he said to his son, "I'll remind you that you weren't to speak today in the Magistrate's presence. Yet you did."

Leorix shrugged and puffed out his lower lip. A trifle.

"You might have done great danger to yourself or to me. You don't know the complexities of this situation."

"I only said something quite simple."

"You had no right. I'd forbidden it."

The main road was returning to something close to everyday commerce. Barrels rolling on cobbles, cart horses neighing. Merchants shouting across the way one to another. Leorix waited until they'd turned into a quieter boulevard before answering his father. "You told Mama that I was old enough to make my own decisions as an adult."

"Maturity is a level of degrees, and it is a fault of the young to grasp for an adult status before they are ready. You are only twelve."

"Thirteen, actually. I've already told you. You were away for my birthday."

Lucikles grimaced, feeling the sting of the rebuke. "You haven't had your initiation at the Temple nor your training at the lyceum or gymnasium. You haven't spent a night in the wilderness to be inspired by the threaded ghosts of your ancestors."

Leorix twisted his mouth. Oh, the first appearance of sarcasm on the boy's brow. Withering superiority. It had happened now to Leorix: the ugliest human look the species could manage. The boy said, "On the road to Mamanoo's, as we ran away from the invaders, the House of Korayus was assaulted by a band of wolves. As you have heard. I hurt king wolf badly enough that it skulked away, and the others joined it in submission. There was another one, a Minor Adjutant wolf, maybe, the one that jumped my back. I killed by braining it with a heavy bole of grapevine root I found at the side of the road. That was my spirit fight, Papa; that was my gymnasium. My lyceum will be the rest of my life, I suppose."

The boy had certainly gained confidence in rhetoric, Lucikles conceded. "Be that as it may, you risk so much by speaking up for Cossy in the interest of *friendship*? I don't think you know much about friendship."

"I don't think you *remember* much about friendship," replied the boy. Then, as if realizing for the first time that he had grown in his power to wound his father, he said, either in tact or in guileless curiosity, "And where are they now, for the next three days and nights? Rain and Cossy?"

"It's not for me to know," said Lucikles. "There are hospitality cells for women in trouble with the state."

"Surely Cossy doesn't qualify for *that*," protested the boy, so it was Lucikles's turn to shrug.

2

Rain and Cossy were taken to a seedy district to the south of the city. A stench lingered from the fires the area suffered weeks ago. The place was called a House of Detention, but it was more of a mud-plastered prison. Four long, blocky structures joined at their corners, closing in the courtyard. The three buildings containing dormitory cells were several stories high, but the fourth, which housed the entrance hall and the kitchens, was only one level. The institution was nearly vacant at the moment—maybe its usual occupants had been evacuated during the invasion.

But it was clean enough—even Kliompte wouldn't have had much cause to complain. Rain didn't need to wield her broom in the interest of housework. The floors were sanded boards, the lime-washed walls swept of cobwebs and neither damp nor scabrous. The slatted windows near the ceiling let in air and shifting trapezoids of light. The house matron had supplied cots and faded bedding, a table and two chairs, a slop bucket. When requested she even brought forth a deck of playing cards for Pixie or Seven Card Snuff, amusements Cossy talked about but whose rules she couldn't fully remember. So to pass the time the prisoners played a Peek and Guess nonsense of their own devising.

Rain didn't share the degree of restlessness she noticed in Cossy. The room was a twenty-foot cube, large enough for them to dance in had they been of a mind. But Cossy paced the edges and chewed on her thumbnail and, when she wasn't holding her own shoulders and shuddering, cried out repeatedly to Rain, "But what is to become of us?"

Once when Rain had tired of being posed this unanswerable question, she replied, "Would you stop, please? You don't have anything to worry about."

Though Rain had no conviction that this was certain.

"I'm locked up, that's enough to worry about," replied Cossy. "Do you think that Kerr Lucikles will let us out soon?"

"I don't get the sense that he can decide one way or the other."

"His son will talk him into it," said Cossy. "I trust him."

"Leorix? He's only a boy," said Rain, and saw immediately that she had made a mistake.

"He's *only* a boy? A boy will stand with us. Don't you see that?"

"You can't have that much trust in him—we spent scarcely seven days together on the *Pious Enterprise*."

"What do you know about boys?" said Cossy. "If you ever knew anything, you forgot already."

"I'm not that old to forget—" But that was wrong. Life, whatever it was, had made her that old. "Tell me about him," she said, a calm voice admitting humility and defeat.

"Well, *you* know," said Cossy. She was an innocent, she was ten, she was out of her depth all at the same moment. "He's the nicest boy I ever met."

"It's nice when there's a nicest," said Rain, skipping over the obvious, that for Cossy, the *nicest* and the *only* were in this case interchangeable.

But Cossy went on, a little more cogently than Rain had expected. She was ashamed of that but she listened hard as Cossy said, "He played at sticks fairly, and didn't treat me like a little baby who had to be allowed to win, the way the brides often do."

"I'm sure they are just being considerate and loving."

"It's better to be honest. Also, you know, he's different. He's braver than the brides."

Rain said, "I don't know if that's true. Maybe we're only each as brave as the circumstances of our lives allow us to be. Maybe that's all the brave we *can* be. But he is different. What did you two talk about when I wasn't with you?"

"Everything. The sea, and the Goose. And Cur. And his family. He has a family, you know, real parents. The father we know, but he has a mother too. And sisters. I don't have parents, only brides."

Rain didn't want to conduct a lesson on human conception. For all she knew she had it wrong herself. But the girl rushed on. "I suppose you have parents, maybe?"

"Maybe," she said. The way it hurt to admit this—oh, it made Rain understand why Cossy had clung to her so early, so insistently. Cossy observed in Rain's ignorance and lack of memory a twin condition to her own. For different reasons they were equally devoid of certainty.

Cossy said, with pride, "He tells me everything. He told me about his sisters, how much he loves them. But they are younger, younger than me."

"Maybe he could talk so comfortably to you *because* he has sisters of his own."

"I think it was more than that," she said. "I don't

think we could be friends just by accident. It feels more like fate. Don't you think that's what friendship is?"

Well, of course, to a girl raised to twist happenstance into daily portions, everything was fate. And why not? "Friendship may be fate, but it's more than that," said Rain. "It's also—it's also a gift. I think. Not just an accident, a coincidence, but something of a choice. You make a decision to lower your weaponry. You decide to trust the enemy agent."

As she spoke, clouds that had blocked the late afternoon sun blew away and the light came pooling in at a new angle. It must now be rushing past a tall but slender tree outside the compound, for the shadow cast upon the opposite wall seemed nearly human. Like a young man, older than that Leorix kid, standing with one knee bent, adult hips at an angle, something nearly like a profile of a face in the shifting pattern of the topmost leaves. Oh, Tip, thought Rain, without knowing what that meant. Oh, Tip, where are you?

A cousin cloud came to cloak the apparition. The room dimmed.

"What is Tip?" asked Cossy. "Or who is Tip?"

Rain must have spoken aloud without even hearing herself. Cloud formations of memory and forgetting shifted behind her brow. She couldn't answer. But she knew now that the answer was there inside her.

So she would find it.

Watching the green stranger, Cossy didn't have the words to express what she sensed. After all Cossy's sacrifice, her devotion: Rain knew something that she wasn't sharing. That she wouldn't share. She had a separate life from Cossy's. The younger girl adored the older one, but for the first time Rain felt wary of the differences. So many hidden parts of their lives that they could never admit aloud.

The privacy of Rain's life, whether through amnesia or selective silence, meant Cossy was excluded.

Cossy was locked into this prison room with a false bride from whom she was locked out.

As if to shake herself from a reverie, Rain said to her, softly, "Cossy, you've never told me whether you did what you're accused of."

"What do you care?" replied the girl, and turned her shoulder.

3

Arriving in the neat if modest neighborhood of Piney Quarter, Lucikles and Leorix were cheered to note the bustle of householdry from other homes. So normalcy was still possible. He and Leorix, having settled into the silence of truce, rounded into their lane at a pace and clacked the gate against the post, announcing their arrival.

Oena emerged from the open doorway with a small pail of chicken feed in her hands. The seed flew to heaven as Oena ran ruin over a stand of lavender in the center of the garden, the more quickly to reach her son and take him in her arms. Her head fell on his shoulders. She revolved her body, as if to conceal from her husband's eyes the evidence of her relief. Lucikles didn't mind. Mothers were allowed exclusivity in nearly all the parental operations, and in any disagreement over child management that resulted in a tie, their votes were heavier and carried the day.

The girls came running out. They paid him enough respect to buckle his knees with their embraces, but as soon as they'd fulfilled their obligations to their father they turned to Leorix. The boy kidded with them and almost immediately began to ignore them, which was normal behavior and put everyone at ease.

Lucikles found himself almost pleased, upon entering the house, to see Oena's mother straining yogurt through cheesecloth. He hoped her presence would silence any spousal invective. "Well," said Mia Zephana, anticipating, "you couldn't expect me to let Oena and the girls brave the trip home alone, bereft of both husband or brother, not after what happened on their way out to High Chora?"

"I knew you wouldn't let that happen," said Lucikles, making the proper gestures of respect. He had collected his belongings at the harbormaster's cabin, after all this time—and his baggage hadn't been rifled or stolen after all. Evidence of a certain slackness on the part of roving harborside thieves. Or maybe they'd fled for their lives, too. From his satchel Lucikles drew out the doll for Poena and the soft silkie for Star, and he made a quick decision to present to Mia Zephana the scrimshaw brooch he'd secured for his wife. Oh, he was good; Oena flashed him a glance of respect at his choice, guessing the wherewithals of it. That appreciation was the first sign of rapprochement, or at least he hoped it was.

Leorix looked at his dirk in its scabbard, shrugged, muttered, "Oh, this. Thanks."

The house hadn't been vandalized. Other neighborhoods had offered better plunder. While their home was suitable for Lucikles and his family, the place was bereft of special graces. It was just theirs, with its blandishments of familiarity: the common stains on the ceiling, the unevenness of certain flagstones, even the redolence of occasionally balky drains. Within an hour the family members were all pushing about the rooms, in and out of sunlight and shuttered shade, as if the nation had not been attacked, the family had not been separated. How much longer does this last, thought Lucikles. No single day of family life promises that there will be another one to follow. How blessed that the young are too blind to know this. They would go mad if they could correctly estimate the peril of daily life.

Needing a moment to himself, and huffing upon a small cylinder of wrapped clove and valerian, he took out the hall carpet to beat it upon the dark-leaved simitra bush.

The dust flew up in clouds. He paused for a breath and exhaled a small emission of scented smoke from his lungs. For an instance, in the slant sun of the hour before supper, the suspended dust he'd clobbered from the carpet was joined by a separate, more slender column of clove and valerian exhaust. Father and son, he thought; one is beaten near to death, the other comes aromatic to life out of paternal lungs.

A silly conceit, which he found himself relishing. In part, he realized, because there was no sense that these emanations were correspondences of the spirit world. Neither hints nor warnings nor mysteries of any sort. They were just dust and smoke, the processes of normalcy. They had nothing to say to him, in a loud and welcome way.

4

Cossy and Rain were housed in confinement. They were allowed to take exercise in the courtyard. It was featureless but for one affrighted fig tree cowering in the middle, too anemic to provide much by way of shade. If the hour was near noon, and way too cloudless, Rain and Cossy crouched against the one wall whose overhang provided a lip of shade.

Rain could hardly bear to talk to Cossy now, though talk she did. The green prisoner wanted to spend every waking moment turning over local impression for its deeper harmonic—does this set of stones remind me of any other set of stones; does that scented breeze from the rooftop seem like—seem like what? She felt like a chick about to hatch. Outside this pale membrane of memory-breakdown she could sense her lived life. The membrane was thinning all the time, and the only question was this: could she survive long enough to break through?

But Cossy *would* go on and on about Leorix, about how nice he was, how good, how she half expected him to climb over the rooftop of the compound and drop down for a visit, or even smuggle in a purloined key to rescue them.

"Haven't we had enough of purloined keys?" asked Rain at one point, and Cossy sulked.

Rain relented. The child was only a child. She needed hope. Still, Rain wouldn't play the game of guessing how long it would take. "We are here until we are released. This is a new job, to test patience," she said to the girl. "Isn't this how you lived your whole life on Maracoor Spot, imprisoned with no possibility of parole?"

"I didn't think of myself as being jailed until after we left," said Cossy.

"Maybe that's what dying feels like," said Rain. "Leaving jail."

The girl just blinked at her. "I wouldn't know."

Then for a moment Rain thought that Cossy's trust in Leorix had been more legitimate than her own skepticism, for there came a sound at the peak of one of the courtyard's four roofs. The lower one. A head appeared from above the roof-beam into the glare of noon. It bobbed along with a distinct air of investigation. Cossy burbled nonsense syllables of joy that sounded like *Leorix*! Rain clapped her own hands to her mouth. But the figure turned out to be a rather large and ungainly monkey, who swung to the tree and feasted upon its fruits without giving the prisoners so much as a bare-toothed grimace.

"Maybe we could train him and make him a friend?" suggested Cossy weakly, without much conviction.

"Oh you, you'll befriend anyone," replied Rain. Cossy turned upon her such a look of hurt and contempt that Rain felt appalled at her own haphazard cruelty. The monkey jeered at them both and pitched a half-eaten fig, and then went on his way.

"Wait!" Rain called to it.

Talking to a monkey, how deranged she was becoming.

The whistle of a fig through the air, splatting in a purple-yellow splash at her feet. Another twinge, a clue, a correspondence of memory to be identified. Something pitching through space below her, something lost forever.

5

The day before he was to return to the Magistrate's chamber, Lucikles was again summoned to an audience with the Bvasil. The writ from Porox didn't mention Leorix, so this time Lucikles denied his son's request to come along. "You've had more liberties and experiences than most boys your age. Stop acting huffy. Stay home and mind the house."

"I'm capable of minding the house," intoned Mia Zephana.

"Mind your own affairs, too," replied Lucikles, who had become tired of his mother-in-law already. His city house, though as large as her farmhouse, felt closer, tighter. He wished she would go back upland, but someone would have to offer to accompany her, and he couldn't spare the time yet.

This time Kerr Porox met Lucikles not at the House of Balances but at a side door of the palace itself. The establishment had been opened for something like normal business, and various administrative types were scurrying about the polished floors, their slippers making the sound of a shallow tide upon rounded stones. "The Great Mara has a backache today and isn't interested in posing upon his throne," said Porox. "Even with cushions it's a punishment, he says. He will see you in a consulting salon."

Lucikles felt faint.

He sallied with a comment near to heresy. "Bvasils with spinal tension, Magistrates with wonky legs. Governing is a grueling career, isn't it."

"Mind your tongue while you still have one."

"Do you know what this is about?"

"Nothing is ever about what it seems, at least in a palace. It keeps us on our toes, guessing. There you go. Remember to exit the room by backing up. They say this practice is in deference to the Great Mara, but I've always guessed the convention was invented by suppliants who didn't want to be stabbed in the back by the Bvasil as they were leaving his divine presence."

The room was bright and rosy. Carved cedarwood screens slotted against high windows let in floats of light like goose down feathers upon the marble marquetry.

On its clatter of poles the apricot-colored banner, a royal standard of sorts, was bunched up and leaning upright in a corner like a huddle of like-colored flags.

Leaning on a divan, his bare feet propped up on the back of an indignant-looking poodle, the Bvasil was consulting a codex of holy scripture. He tossed it aside. "What is this, who are you, the next irritation, hello," he said.

"Kerr Lucikles of the House of Korayus. Minor Adjutant with responsibilities in the Ephrarxis Isles and the Hyperastrich Archipelago, specifically the matter of Maracoor Spot."

"Oh, yes indeed, the main event of the morning if not the whole month. I remember you. Excuse my deportment. The spine is seditious today. I should have it taken out behind the palace and flogged." He laughed silkily at his wit.

"How may I serve?"

The Great Mara touched a hand upon his sportive plume of hair as if it were a tame mouse, petting it softly without causing disarray. "No one knows much about the matters of this unregenerate season, my friend."

The Great Mara called me *my friend*, thought Lucikles. He felt giddy as a boy the age of Leorix, recalled back to when he was currying favor with the hot sparks in the lyceum. Then he thought, oh no, is the Bvasil's term of affection a prelude to my execution?

"Let me rehearse what I know," continued the Bvasil. "We'll see if you have learned anything to contradict or to confirm our understandings."

"Your Magnificence."

"To begin. We need to hear if anyone you've communicated with on your tour of duty was aware that the Skedian fleet intended to surprise us in our beds. I myself was in the country don't you know and I didn't hear about it for several days, so I was out of the fray. Still, apparently it was an appalling inconvenience. And terrifying."

"You know who the attackers are?" Lucikles was startled that word of this hadn't gotten around.

"We think so. Skedia, or Skedeland, if I have that right. A people known primarily to ethnographers of history. In actual fact I've been told they were considered extinct if not downright mythical. Their warrior prowess, their cunning, blah blah blah. But apparently they still inhabit a cold stretch of coast so far to the south of us that commerce between us has scarcely been feasible. Let alone comity. The distance between their land and ours too vast for them to contemplate crossing. But something changed last month, and they took advantage of it."

"Something changed."

"The great storm. The storm that blew in from the south, that reportedly tossed that green foreigner into the very mouth of Maracoor Spot, where the kingdom's greatest treasure has been hidden for several centuries. We now know that the Skedes maintain an active navy, perhaps as a defense against their more local enemies. We're only guessing here, mind. The supposition holds that with the shift of unseasonable winds, and with high seas favoring a quick run to the north, they may have felt their own gods were inciting them to launch an attack on us. It's bruited about in some quarters, quietly of course because all this is hush-hush, that they were hunting for the Fist of Mara, so cunningly tucked away on Maracoor Spot all these generations. The Skedian fleet came to the capital city first. Its military ransacked the armory and the treasury. They took so little of consequence—a few shiny cornets and ceremonial collars, some maces of archival interest but nothing of significance—that it begs the question of what they were actually seeking to accomplish here. Certainly not a trade deal.

"In any case, it can't yet be determined who the Skedes may have captured, kidnapped, threatened. The court is still in too much disarray for anyone around here even to take attendance. *So* shoddy. But there is a chance that the admirals of the Skedian fleet learned of Maracoor Spot, and its centrality in our religious customs. This would cause even the dullest of them to suspect that the holiest item of our treasury was held in secrecy there. So it seems only a matter of time before the Skedes descend on Maracoor Spot. That's why the court had you remove the amulet. You have done well."

Lucikles bowed his head. "May I be permitted a question?"

"Probably not, but I'd have to check the protocols, and we're in too much of a hurry. So go ahead."

Lucikles tried to think of how to express his enquiry. "The Fist of Mara. The holy amulet. What people know of it is largely from fanciful legends told to children. Why is it kept so far away from the country? What use has it, other than as an object of reverence? I mean no disrespect in posing my thoughts like this—"

"It has no *use* that we know of," said the Great Mara. "Rather, it's a bloody inconvenience and a weight for the nation to own. It is dangerous. That is why it's been kept far away, and locked forever in an ironstone strongbox that helps shield its force."

"What force does it have?"

"A force of nullity, not of agency."

"I don't pretend to understand what you mean."

"If you must know, it would make the women of Maracoor barren, if it could. Is that blunt enough for you? Centuries ago when it was uncovered from a scorched pit in the northern badlands, it was housed in a town up there called, appropriately enough, Wreckling Hill. Every woman and girl child in the whole town became barren within the decade and the population died out in sixty years. It took quite a while for ministers of the period to wonder if that object disinterred from the soil outside the town might be the cause. The case was proven when the totem was removed and people from other villages rushed in to squat in the abandoned homes. The newcomers had no problem sweating and begetting and their children came out whole and ferociously childlike."

"The Fist of Mara—couldn't it be destroyed?"

"How do you destroy a vengeful object? If you pulverize it, you merely atomize the danger—aerate it—perhaps that would be worse. If you sink it beneath the waves, perhaps you poison the bounty of the sea that feeds your nation. If you bury it, it might cause crop failure and whatnot. Earthquakes. I don't know. Nobody does. Thus, and I see in your expression that you are taking this in, was the holy island of Maracoor Spot selected as a repository. And so evolved the ritual of the Brides of Maracoor. Reaping a safe daily life for their fellow citizens, those women who serve as brides to the nation. I mean, that's what I'm told anyway. By reliable historians who would have their tongues torn out and stuffed in their bums if they were found out to be lying."

Lucikles felt the gorge in his belly tilt sideways and burn. "All those brides over the centuries—on assignment from the crown for . . . for what?"

"To guard the Fist of Mara. To keep it away from us. Each bride to give her span of years for the safety and prosperity of the land that gave them birth."

Lucikles hoped his belly wasn't broadcasting its upset. "Each of those brides over the years—subjected to the infinity of barrenness—without knowing it?"

"There were to be no men, that was the point," said the Great Mara. "So what did it matter? You sound offended. But you know where the brides came from. You secured them yourself."

Lucikles said icily, "I was never informed of the cost to them, Your Grace, only of the honor of being chosen to serve their homeland."

"I don't understand the issue. The poor brides—yes, I see you know how I am going to finish my sentence."

It was true. The brides were all abandoned girl infants, found on the steps of temples. Sometimes in gutters. None of them old enough to carry a memory of the mother—or nursemaid—or father inconveniently married otherwise. Or of anyone who might have left the unwanted creature someplace where she might be found and helped to survive. It had been part of Lucikles's brief to select the new brides when an older one had passed away. In the decades of his tenure he had brought to Maracoor Spot, each in her time, infants he had named Kliompte, Scyrilla, and Acaciana. With the impending death of Helia, he'd have been expected soon to forage for the next mewling bride to consign to a life of exile on Maracoor Spot.

"I am sorry I asked Your Grace this question," he said.

"I sort of thought you understood. I mean, you've been at this for quite a while, no?"

"The custody of information in the court, bizarre. Capricious even. I never gained the confidence of my superiors."

"Pity. I suppose I've broken the rules in talking about this. Still, what're they going to do, turf me out? I'm the Bvasil, the divine Great Mara in human form. And the times are very erratic indeed. Pass me a biscuit, and spread some of that orange curd upon it first."

Lucikles felt he had to leave the audience within minutes or he would risk soiling himself, such were the protests of his bowels. "I don't know if there is anything you need from me now."

"I thought if you wouldn't tell anyone else, you

might tell me if you thought that this Rain creature was in league with the Skedes. This would help us decide if she is to be executed as an enemy of the people or merely, oh, banished."

Lucikles nodded his head and made the most deferential clasp of his hands—his knuckles pointed at the Great Mara and his own fingernails turned to his chest—to imply he would rather claw his own heart out than to give offense to the deity. But his words belied the gesture. "I couldn't answer in any case, if it meant I were to put another person in danger."

"Oh, I think you could," said the Great Mara with a sweet blandness, smacking his lips upon the cracker. "For instance, if I were to decide that your own youngest child—a girl, my henchfolk tell me, is her name Star?—were to be selected for the honor of being the next bride of Maracoor, and you relieved of your duties as Minor Adjutant in charge of the colonies? I think you'd see through to reason. Am I wrong? I mean, we have preferred infant girl children as new brides, but times are out of whack; I could command otherwise. Your Star is still young enough not to mind. Much. So tell me: is Rain implicated in the attack upon our nation? Your happiness hangs on your telling the truth."

Lucikles was blind as stone but he spoke as a longtime civil servant. "Your Magnificence, to propose a correspondence between a stranger's arrival in Maracoor Spot and the assault by an enemy navy is to see meaning where none may obtain. The world is built on coincidence."

"So would it be merely coincidence if I were to choose your Star as the next bride?" But the Great Mara didn't even sound vicious, just curious. "It seems to me the nature of the world is all one thing or all the other. Either there is nothing but coincidence or there is nothing but established fate. The brides braid our times to our lives on a daily basis. I have a headache. You have brought me nothing. I conclude that you're telling me you know of no relationship between the appearance of Rain and the incursion of the Skedian navy. Correct me or there we leave it. In time you will enjoy the benefits or suffer the consequences of your assertion."

"What about the ghost world?" asked the Minor Adjutant, for this might be his last professional moment. "How can it be that rumors of minotaurs abound, and the sightings of creatures from myth are rampant? Dryads and mermaids and minor gods, the known creatures and the impossibilities, swarms of midget witches, a cadre of flying monkeys?"

"You should get your eyes checked. I see nothing but the tired and tiresome human adherents of this holy court."

"Where did the Fist of Mara come from, dug up in a pit?" He was now scrambling for every last thing he could know, in case it might be of use at protecting Star from being abducted. "And where is it, now I have brought it home?"

"The legends have it that the amulet appeared in a trough of burning sand and scorched fields. Heaved up from some fiery furnace below the ground. Or as if in anger the Great Mara in the heavens had pitched it from the highest skies above us, to wound our nation. Or perhaps the Snouted Moon spit it at us. In any case, to care for the amulet properly has been our burden ever since. Where it is now is a state secret. You're a good man, Lucikles; you have been central to this effort—"

"Begging your pardon, Your Magnificence." His nether regions having issued a warning blat, no further explanation was needed. He raced from the room with his head to the door and his rear befouling the salon of the supine deity.

6

On the morning of their appearance in the court of the Magistrate, Rain managed to persuade the matron to let her pace in the courtyard alone. Without Cossy for once.

Oh, Rain cared for the girl, she did. She allowed Cossy the youthful shiver of her attachment to Leorix, imagined or otherwise. But Cossy was getting on her nerves. The younger girl had gone delusional. Such repeated fixing of her hair, constantly asking for advice. She was building up her slight friendship with Leorix into a faux-romance. Something out of nothing.

Rain wanted to examine why this should so bother her. The shell was cracking. That Tip, that memory of someone called Tip, someone important in her life. She needed to conduct a biopsy upon everything that she was learning with focus, without flinching, without distraction. So Rain paced the courtyard, as if to build up momentum for a jump. For a great leap over the rooftops, for an escape, an escape by air . . .

On one side of the House of Detention she heard a chittering. The same monkey who had filched the figs had climbed high in a sentinel pine that rose beyond the lower of the buildings framing the courtyard. The tree was twice as high as that building's roof. All its bottom branches had long since died off, but the upper half of the tree was well supplied with needled limbs. Here the monkey was swinging about and tossing down pinecones, as if to get her attention.

With the smack of a bit of dried tree upon the dust of the courtyard, Rain grasped the first claw-hold of true memory that she could see clearly. She'd been high up in the cold and glassy dawn air, high above rolling coils of thick cloud. Iskinaary flying behind her and to the right. The clouds below parted; she saw that she was lower in the air than she'd realized. With her left hand grasping the pole of her broom, she'd dug her other hand in a satchel. She had brought something heavy and unwieldy out. She had clutched it to her breast like a book. It was a book, in fact. She had flung out her arm. The book had opened its old leather covers and begun to wing out of sight through the closed clouds, plunging toward its watery grave, a plummeting masterpiece to be lost, lost forever.

The Grimmerie.

She had jettisoned the great tome, of whatever provenance, she couldn't remember. She had consigned it to history, breaking its hold over her, over whomever had come or could come across its pages and read it to abuse the world.

Remembering, her hands went to cover her face. Being born didn't involve running and jumping, or flying or falling. It involved being as still as possible, not breathing, learning to wait.

The monkey leapt upon the fig tree again, and began to throw figs at her, as if in celebration of her recovery. She ate the inside of one and then threw a handful of sloppy skin back at him. He ducked and scolded her and darted away, across the roof and up the trunk of the sentinel pine. Screaming a commentary, he disappeared into the screen of the branches at the top of the tree.

7

Lucikles and his son were recognized by the court officials, sworn to full and honest disclosure, and seated on a bench to one side of the room. Oena had given them small fans made of woven palmetto, which they plied before their faces. Already they wished they'd thought of bringing a flask of water with them. This waiting, a half a bell already, was it designed to make everyone more anxious? It was working toward that end. Rain and Cossy had yet to appear. Presumably they'd be brought forward through a low door beside the bench.

A small commotion sounded in the vestibule outside the main doors of the courtroom. The Minor Adjutant turned his head. Borr Apoxiades wouldn't enter from that direction; he had his own suite of rooms for resting and negotiation behind the bench. The fracas subsided, lowered muttering took its place, and after a few moments the doors were opened to admit Iskinaary. He entered with his head held at an awkward angle. Perhaps he meant to seem proud, even haughty, but he looked as if he had swallowed a cricket two sizes too big for his throat.

Behind the Goose, in their proper dark veils and eyes trained to the floor, entered the brides of Maracoor. Those who were left, that is. All except Helia. Scyrilla and Kliompte walked abreast, and Bray and Tirr followed.

Lucikles rose to his feet, and after a moment, Leorix did too. Gossiping on a bench in the corner, the court officers didn't know what they were seeing, but they sensed the gravity of the occasion and they fell silent. One of them—a woman—waited a moment and then she stood, too, and bowed her head.

Without asking permission, Lucikles left his place and approached the cordoned area where the brides were being offered a seat. Iskinaary remained on the floor and did not sit down.

"Oh, don't look so surprised," said the Goose before the Minor Adjutant could speak. "I returned to that island with a small fishing boat, as I told Rain I would do. I had scared up a capable crew. Emphasis on *scared*.

I had to threaten them with spectral damage to their families if they didn't help out. As none of them had met a talking Goose before, they weren't all that hard persuaded. They'd all been made jittery by other phantasms and sightings and nasty dreams."

"It sounds so like you," said Lucikles.

"So we must have passed right by the *Pious Undergarment* or whatever she is called. On the high seas, perhaps at night or in one of those fogs. Ours was a cozier concern, rather saucily called the *Little Fish Wish*. We made good time. In the right conditions, a lighter boat skims faster than a ponderous big thumper, I learned from our Captain. Sits higher on the water; less drag. Upon arrival at Maracoor Spot, I found that you'd already returned to haul Rain away. Not to mention the youngest bride, who is, what, suspected of some kind of mischief? You can't imagine the discord that had broken out among the peaceable brides who remained—"

"Perhaps I can, just," said Lucikles.

"It wasn't my fault," said Scyrilla, and stuck out her tongue at the Minor Adjutant.

"—and in the end," continued Iskinaary, "they insisted upon returning with me so they could rescue their youngest member if possible, or be held in community prison with her if not. And lo, we made it on time for some kind of theatrical entertainment, is it? Curtain about to go up?" The Goose was tired and more cross than usual. Lucikles suspected he had had enough of the brides, who sat in shock at the unending spectacle of urban life in the capital city they had never expected to visit.

"This is a court of moral adjustments," he told the Goose, "not a playhouse."

"I'm not an idiot," snapped Iskinaary. "I was making a joke."

Lucikles looked at Scyrilla and Kliompte, the two brides nearer him. They returned his gaze with frank hatred. He deserved it more than they knew, but there was no mending that error now. "I don't know what you can do here," he said to the four of them. "But it's brave of you to come."

"We can witness," said Tirr. She was probably the senior bride now, given that Helia was absent. "That's all we've ever done, is witness. That's our calling. We're doing it in a new way today."

"And Helia? She didn't join you?"

"She insisted someone was needed to bleed and to wrap the cords of history lest the whole world come undone. She wouldn't leave Maracoor Spot. She thought our arguing to go made a mockery of a lifetime's worth of foot scarring. Four lifetimes' worth, I suppose."

"From what I've picked up, Dame Helia might have been implicated in the murder of Mirka had she made it this far," intoned the Goose. "She was smart to stay put."

"Everything is unraveling anyway," said Kliompte. "It's such a mess."

"But it's *nicer* without the scarring," said Scyrilla. Lucikles glanced down. Each of the brides was wearing a pair of simple tooled sandals. Scyrilla's were a pale pink. "A merchant just gave them to us in exchange for a blessing."

"A kind word," said Bray.

"Right," agreed Tirr. "Not a blessing, really. We don't have the power to bless a mosquito. Nor does a mosquito need such from us. But the sandals are welcome."

"I think they're pretty," said Scyrilla. "Mine are the prettiest. But there was a blue pair I wanted more. They would have matched my veil."

The host of the chamber struck a note upon the bronze disc. The bell tone silenced all the talk. Lucikles made his way back to his seat just as Borr Apoxiades was entering the room. The Magistrate took his time adjusting a bevy of small cushions around his back and hips—it was amazing there was room in the chair for him and the pillows both. The bad knee required special obeisance. Only when he'd bolstered himself comfortably enough did he look across the rim of his spectacles to survey the room. He conferred briefly with an aide and signaled the host, who in a bored, formal voice directed all present to rise and pledge honesty and honor. All stood, except for Iskinaary, who was already standing. Whether Iskinaary's quawking was the oath or a mask of pretense wasn't questioned. Lucikles and Leorix pledged a second time.

When silence obtained again, Borr Apoxiades looked over at Lucikles and raised his eyebrows, as if to say, A regular circus in here, today, what? To the veiled women he offered a veiled welcome of sorts. He must have been told who they were or they wouldn't have been allowed in, but he seemed not to want to extend them the rights of speech.

"Those under suspicion have been pledged to honor and honesty already," he said, "so they may now be enjoined to enter." The host unlocked the low door. Cossy entered, ducking and then straightening up, and she looked around. She spied Leorix first, and her face bloomed spring camellia. But then she saw the other brides of Maracoor, and she burst into crying.

She was unveiled, and her unpinned hair fell loose as corn silk. To the brides she looked unnatural and alien, those glossy tresses on public view. The brides all hid their faces except Scyrilla, who waved a low palm at Cossy and grinned as if to say, Look at us!

Iskinaary got up and waddled across the room to peer closely at Rain, who had followed the girl. The host of the court tried to shoo him away, but the Goose hissed and arched his neck and made as if to beat his wings. Rain's eyes grew wet. Both host and the Borr remained still until the Goose had inspected Rain for damage. When he was satisfied, he marched stiffly back to his post by the brides, looking regal and a little miffed.

"Let me clarify the metes and bounds of this session," said Borr Apoxiades. "The stranger to our land, known as Rain, is here in service to the question of the death of the bride called Mirka. There are separate questions about this stranger's agency in the recent visitation to our shores of the invading Skedian fleet from the south. For now, this is an investigation around the uncomely matter of an accusation of murder. Let us try to concentrate. My knee is killing me today. I fell coming up the steps—likely I should shed a little poundage."

Many in the court bowed their heads in deference to the reality of pain.

Lucikles petitioned to approach the bench, but Borr Apoxiades told him to state his concerns for all to hear.

"I am not a prosecutor or a defender," Lucikles said. "In fact, I'm not familiar with proceedings like this. So I'm not even sure why I'm here."

"The host of the court has brought charges. You're a witness neither for nor against. You're under oath merely to speak up if you find that anyone makes a statement that contradicts what you are certain to be true. That's easy enough, isn't it?"

"I'm not certain of anything—all I know is what I heard."

"Well, if what is said today contradicts what you heard before, you let us know, shall you? You've already made your deposition so we have it on record, but you are a loyal party to this Bvasilry and this court, Kerr Lucikles. We should be grateful for your keen ear on the matter. Now, let's to it."

8

The proceedings ran about half the afternoon. Lucikles noted how the amulet itself wasn't described or even identified—the focus of attention was the casket in general and its apparent capacity to render common and healthy ingestibles fatal to the human being.

Several of the brides wept to hear the accusations of murder pressed against their youngest sister.

The court asserted that the child Acaciana, working by herself or with Rain, had manipulated the key to the strongbox in question. Through a study of the accused's fingertips made the previous day, the alchemical augurer had ascertained beyond doubt that traces of the child's idiosyncratic essential oils remained upon the head of the key. Regardless of whether or not the senior bride had imparted knowledge of the key's whereabouts, the child had secured the key somehow. She must at the very least have been a collaborator in this exercise.

Lucikles spoke up at one point. "Without offering an opinion about guilt or innocence, may I point out that the presence of shreds of herb in the Vessel, by evidence of freshness recently placed there, doesn't prove that the herbs were used in the death of the bride known as Mirka. A crime may have been intended and a death still could have occurred naturally before the crime could be carried out. There is a vexing reality called coincidence."

"That's a bit rich," said Borr Apoxiades. "Though we have with us the good brides responsible for making things happen, no? So let me question them. Which one wants to speak for the lot of you?"

Scyrilla raised her hand and the other three batted it down. Tirr stood up at her chair.

Borr Apoxiades raised the matter to Tirr and the other brides in general as to the strapping good health of that harridan, Mirka. Tirr didn't volunteer a single word in response but she nodded assent or shook her head at his supposals. No, Mirka had never had so much as an ingrown toenail in her life. Yes, she had a healthy appetite, and she always ate every scrap and drank every drop put before her. No, she wasn't the jolly sort who made everyone feel better about themselves. No no no.

"Still, even the most perfectly healthy of us die," Lucikles pushed.

"Enough out of you," said Borr Apoxiades. "Circumstantial evidence it may be, but the circumstances are considerable. In this room we don't need to hazard a guess as to the motivation of the child. As to this so-called Rain Creature, while she's only here under observation today, her alleged infractions will be dealt with by those more practiced in international concerns. It will be up to another court to determine if the stranger conspired with the child to get the key to the ironstone box in order, perhaps, to abscond with it, or its contents. Ours today is a simple enquiry of murder, not of treason. Is there anything else anyone has to offer on the matter?"

Rain stood to speak. Cossy clutched her hand. They were linked as if by chains.

"I don't understand the justice system of this place," Rain said. "But can it be correct to level an accusation of murder against a child who isn't more than ten?" Lucikles felt a surge of relief. This was the point he'd wanted to raise, but in fear it might rebound upon his own family in some unforeseen way, he'd held his tongue.

"You may be an agent of some primitive foreign concern," replied the Borr, "but you're also a guest of our civilized nation for the moment. We accord you some rights formally. So I will answer you. Yes. The House of Balances is correct in prosecuting this case. Murder is murder. If a child is deemed culpable of killing Mirka of Maracoor Spot, said child will be treated accordingly as any murderer would be. Well, she won't be put to death herself, I don't mean that. We do show mercy. But she will be imprisoned with other felons, and in less hospitable circumstances than the House of Detention, I can tell you *that* much. She may be young but she's old enough to have learned right and wrong."

"If what I'm told is accurate," said Rain, "the child has spent her whole life imprisoned on that island. In cruel circumstances, in a kind of slavery. It's an unnatural existence. Twisted, depraved even. How can she have learned right from wrong as applied in a free society? How can those notions possibly have been taught her by her companions, who've never known any more than she does about liberty or—or the responsibility of choice? They are each of them compromised. Choice has been denied them their whole lives."

The brides collectively bristled.

"It's unfair, it's cruel," continued Rain. "I won't have it."

"You!" said Borr Apoxiades.

Leorix sat up and Lucikles sank back, appalled. Stop, he willed Rain. *Stop.*

"I'm not a lecturer in social ethics but I do realize this much," said the Borr. "Every one of us makes a contract with the world as we know it. In the limited society of Maracoor Spot, murder is still murder. And this girl knows it, and so do her sister brides. I will retire to judge the matter and to confer with the host of the court and one or two legal advisors backstairs, and return momentarily. Do not leave the chamber unless you need to use the facilities, and in that case a guardian will accompany you."

"I'm fine where I am," said Iskinaary, and let loose on the floor, a kind of critical commentary to which there was no clear reply.

The brides remained paralyzed where they were. Lucikles leaned over to mutter something to Leorix only to discover that the boy had slipped out of his bench, and was already beetling across the room to where Cossy and Rain sat behind a braided silver rope held in place by brass stanchions. To follow him would be to intrude, but Lucikles had Cossy's interest at heart even if there was little he could do to intervene. He hurried along to where his son was huddled with the two prisoners and the Goose.

Rain looked with steel eyes at Lucikles and said, "You. You brought us here. Are you going to get us out?"

"I have no leverage in this room," he said. "I'm wielding what influence I have behind the scenes."

This was untrue. Lucikles would never forgive himself for having implied this. He had promised honesty and honor, and betrayed both.

Rain was flashing angry. "No child can be held accountable for an adult crime. Especially a child who has been denied access to education. A child denied the full sloppy round of social mishaps and experiments. Her life has been tricked away from her—and now she's to be held accountable for a debt as if she were a full-fledged member of her tribe?"

"If you did what it seems you did," said Lucikles, addressing Cossy instead of Rain, "which is a crime of adult proportion, the court says you must pay the adult price for your deed. If you're old enough to kill, you're old enough to be suppressed from killing again."

"Papa," said Leorix softly, "don't. Don't."

But Lucikles couldn't help himself. "You netted your own fate, child."

Cossy seemed to have lost track of the room. She held Rain's hand in one of hers, and Leorix's in the other. The boy was looking tenderly at her, as if he would save her himself, since his father couldn't do it. Of course, thought Lucikles, Leorix had had just the training in life that, according to Rain, Cossy had needed and not received. Leorix had been taught by his parents how to regard other people, and he'd had practice in caring for his own two sisters. Living in communities where new young always arrived to be tended was how mercy was taught. What bad luck of timing, that Acaciana had not yet had a pet child of her own upon whom to practice love.

But it was Helia and the others who braided time and cozened fate, not Lucikles. He had to shrug his way out of this. "Here comes the court host, we must return to our seats," he told Leorix.

"*Do* something, Papa," whispered Leorix as the gong was struck again.

And risk consigning Star to an island where she would never see her family again, nor any men but some new overseer, nor bear her own children?

Lucikles thought: no. There is a limit to what any father can do.

When Borr Apoxiades returned, he didn't bother to plump up the pillows. He didn't even sit down. "I've just heard some worrying reports," he said. "Our army is being called up. We've had bulletins about a militia said to be approaching from the south, along the coast. Skedelandia again most likely. It could be mere hours or days away but adult citizens who qualify are required to report to the registry of defense. We will conclude these proceedings forthwith and make our own arrangements."

You're making an arrangement to take the first phaeton heading north, guessed Lucikles.

"As the presiding Magistrate in this matter, I state the following conclusions. The bride of Maracoor known as Acaciana is determined guilty in the charge of murder of her fellow bride, Mirka. She is sentenced to twenty-five years of prison in Odigos Holding or such establishment of similar virtue. She will be transferred there in the morning. What will happen to the investigation of her possible accomplice—yes, you, Rain from who-knows-where—this is beyond my jurisdiction. Especially now. Rain, your own culpability as a potential enemy of the state will be reviewed. Tomorrow. I'm afraid it will be quick. I can't say that this is a propitious time for you to come up against such a charge, what with the nation in turmoil over an imminent assault upon its walls."

"This can't be just," sputtered Lucikles, getting one sentence out at least, to save his soul. "To punish a child as if she were an adult, for a mistake made due to an unformed conscience? What will the gods say to us if you carry this sentence out?"

"If the gods have a say in this, it will go all the harder," said Borr Apoxiades, irritated at having his judgment questioned. "Whose justice would you rather have lowered upon your own brow, Kerr Lucikles? The justice of the gods or that of men?"

"Is there no mercy in any justice?" whispered Lucikles, almost hoping he wouldn't be heard.

But Borr Apoxiades heard him just fine. "Institutional justice is an operation built to bend to law. Whenever justice serves mercy, it is only a coincidence."

The brides were beginning to sob, but with strangled, bitten-back moans. Lucikles could mutter nothing more. He put his face in his hands. He sensed his son rising to his feet. Above the fray Lucikles heard Leorix lift his voice to say, "Your Dignity, I will take her place."

"What rogue behavior is this, now?" said Borr Apoxiades. Had he not stopped to favor his knee—it had been seizing up—he'd have been out the door.

"Hush, you're not allowed to speak!" said Lucikles, and clapped his hand upon his son's mouth. Leorix pushed it aside.

"I volunteer to exchange places with Cossy, and to trade my freedom for hers," shouted Leorix over his father's fingers.

"Oh, the drama of it all, please!" snapped Borr Apoxiades. "It's not to be thought of. We don't make such transactions except in the case of spouses and siblings, once in a while. And you're too young, for one thing."

"How can I be too young?"

"Stop it!" shouted Lucikles, trying to box his son's brains out, but the boy ducked away.

"I'm three years older than her! She's old enough to be convicted of a crime like a grown-up and, and, you say I'm too young for my offer of substitution to count? How can she know what she was doing as an adult, but I can be said to be out of my depth?"

"You had other advantages—you know better—" cried Lucikles.

"I know well enough to know what I'm saying!" He turned to his father. "You told my mother I had crossed the line to adulthood. Were you lying to her, and to me?" He slipped his tunic off his shoulder and rotated his back so his father and the entire courtroom could see the tracks of wolf claw across his shoulder blade and down his side. "This is my mark of initiation."

"Ewww, gross," said Borr Apoxiades, and departed.

9

The room descended into mayhem. Lucikles wept with relief that his son's noble gesture had been rebuffed. He had to get Leorix home, he had to get his family out of town again, back to the plateau, maybe even farther. He could do that much. For Cossy and Rain he could do nothing more.

Leorix was weeping and reaching out for Cossy's hand, but Lucikles bullied the boy along before him toward the exit. Above the fray of quawking and bridal grieving, he heard Porox answering a question posed by the court host. "Apparently that clot of creepy flying monkeys, some people have claimed to see it, it's landed at the palace of the Bvasil. They had flown so far south they spied the Skedian marching army. They are on some weird monkey mission of their own, but having brought their enquiry to Maracoor Crown, they also sounded the alarm for us."

No one else heard what Porox said, as the uproar continued. Rain and Cossy were led away through the little door. The Goose threw himself upon the door, beating it with his wings, to no avail.

10

Cossy had wept all her clothes damp, and so when it started to sprinkle and then intensified, she hardly noticed. Around the child's shoulders the green girl wrapped herself. The guardians of the law hurried a carriage forward so the prisoners could be returned to the House of Detention.

After all the commotion in court, the silence but for the child's heavy breathing helped Rain to begin to sort out the present from the past. In the welter of her thinking she retrieved the sound of that sentence spoken on the margin of the room. Flying monkeys. Looking for someone.

The Grimmerie.

A great volume of magicks.

Flying monkeys.

Tip. Tip, a boy she had loved, and who had been taken from her. Or from whom, perhaps, she had fled.

Flying monkeys.

"All is not lost," she murmured into Cossy's hair. "The egg is cracking at last, and some good may come of it even now. I hope."

"I'm sorry, Mirka," sobbed the child, to the wild uncaring world outside the carriage windows.

They spent a sleepless night. Cossy couldn't speak what phantom fears plagued her, but kept curled up near Rain's hip. Rain sat with her back against the wall. Neither of them ate the curl of bread thrust at them through the food flap at the bottom of the door.

11

Dawn broke with a paradiddle of distant thunder. At least one hoped it was thunder and not the artillery of armies already clashing to the south of the city. The matron and her officers, eager to evacuate the buildings, entered the cell to secure the shutters into their locked position. Before they continued their progress through the corridors, they rushed Rain and Cossy toward the courtyard as a kind of holding pen. The matron slung the plate of bread after them. "You're being evacuated this morning. Eat while you have a chance. Who knows what happens next in this life," she said. "I'd let you loose like a pair of bad goats was it up to me, but it's not, and when all this is over I would like this position again. Look, Greenie, when they come to get you, take this filthy broom with you.

I have no use for the mangy item. You're not coming back here by the sounds of it."

The winds were high. Spatters of moisture clattered like hail on the roof tiles. "We have to keep strong," said Rain. "In all this upheaval there are chances for us. More now than when you were trapped on Maracoor Spot."

"Trapped. But it was my home," said the girl.

"Leave it behind. There's always more world to the world."

No lightning, but the thunder seemed nearer. It was coming from the north. The winds took up a circulating wildness, as if dancing a hornpipe fueled with brandy sparkshot. Then Rain herself whirled about as something caught the edge of her vision. Iskinaary had flown to the lowest roof, and behind him, landing two three four, a ragged corps of winged monkeys. The indigenous monkey, wingless but unafraid, came down from the tall pine tree to knuckle his way along the tiles and to guard his fig tree from poachers, or maybe to make friends.

"We can't airlift you out," called Iskinaary. "I can't hoist you, let alone both of you. Afraid to say these ambassadors can't manage it either. But we will shadow you wherever they take you, Rain. We'll keep you in our sights, and we'll devise a rescue."

"It was the Grimmerie, wasn't it," called Rain into the wind. "I drowned it in the ocean, and all the world's locked magicks have come unsprung."

"I can't take you *anywhere*," said the Goose. "Listen, you're not in charge of the world. That's a common error that humans make. But can we talk about this later? We're detailing ourselves to you for your own protection. So clam up."

"If you can't lift me, can you get Cossy?" called Rain. "She's lighter than I am. We're not leaving this child behind."

"The murderer? Figures. You never do things the easy way," said the Goose. "Look out, fellow travelers— the force of it—!"

The Goose and the winged monkeys, and the native monkey too, were all swept off the roof by a menace of wind. Rain could hear her advocates scrabbling across tiles and hurtling to the ground. She looked up, expecting to see lightning—the commotion was that fierce—but of lightning there was none. Still, the crown of the pine, the top half of that mighty tree beyond the courtyard, torqued forward with a shriek of splitting timber. A wet whoosh, a terrific crack against the roofbeam of the lower building.

Rain pulled Cossy back as the green missile rushed

along the inward sloping tiles, point down. It landed in the courtyard with a crash, taking out the fig tree for good measure.

With the girl's hand gripped tightly in her own, and the broom tucked under her arm, Rain scrabbled through the pine boughs until she'd reached the trunk. "Let's go," she said. They climbed the inverted treetop by using branches as they would the rungs of a ladder. They kept hold of each other almost to the top. There, Rain had to let go of Cossy's hand so they could step off the tree onto the tiles, grip the roof-ridge, and brace against the winds of whatever was coming next.

In the street below, Iskinaary and the monkeys were recovering from their tumble. Four or five streets to the north, the neighborhood was already dense with downpour; it hadn't reached them yet. It would provide cover. "We're going to slide, and they're going to catch us. Sort of. I hope," said Rain, and hollered to attract the attention of the monkeys.

"But where are we going?" asked Cossy.

"I don't know where you're going," answered Rain, "and I don't know how long it will take to get to where I'm going. Sooner or later, one way or the other, I'm going to Oz."

Cossy didn't understand what Rain was saying, didn't know that syllable, Oz. What she heard was the severing of their future. The collapse of possibility, a groan like the sound of the unseen beasts groping underground in Maracoor Spot. It flushed her ears till she thought they would pour blood like twin fountains. The green girl had a different life ahead of her than Cossy did. It would lope off and go its way.

Other apprehensions broke free of their moorings and rushed at the girl with the same unbalancing force as the winds.

Because—like almost all of Maracoor Crown—the House of Detention was situated upon a slope, and because the low brace of buildings faced the distant sea, Cossy could spy the ocean horizon and the rain clouds approaching from the north. She was suddenly, and for the first time in her days, free—free of Maracoor Spot, free from the grasp of men who would hold her captive.

She felt this rather than saw it, but what she now knew, in a more clinical way, was a sudden possibility. The death about which she'd been so curious—if it happened to Mirka or to Helia had hardly mattered—it was hers to examine now. Her own death, her own choice, hers to learn whether death was any different from the sharp crack of other separations. Like that of hers from Leorix, who'd been ripped away from her by his father. Like that of Rain with other agendas in her eyes.

There was a vote to be taken here, and she was the only one voting.

If Rain had flown out of her other life and into Maracoor Spot, there to begin the crisis that had broken everything in the world, so Cossy could fly, too, and end it.

She came up with a makeshift magick.

A spell that I
Might try to fly—
Or else to—

With the wind under her skinny arms, snapping her skirts like a ship's rigging, Cossy kicked one commissary-issued sandal off and then the other. She lifted her arms and spread her unyoked ankles. She freed her scarred feet from the scarred world and flew toward yet another world, wherever it might be.

12

Helia worked the nets alone that day. On Maracoor Spot, no sign of weather. It had been trouble indeed these days to get down the slope and back again. Whether she had suffered a genuine spell against language she didn't really know, but she didn't need to find out—there was no one to talk to. She did the work that, eight decades ago, she had been brought to Maracoor Spot to do.

Queen Bride.

About midmorning, Helia's oakthorn staff slipped and fell in the water. It floated three feet out. She doubted she could raise herself to her feet without it. It would either float away or it would float back. She just kept on, twisting the nets of time to allow the day to bring to her and to the nation all that it would choose to bring.

Some short moments later, a wave hit her ankles and the stone step with unlikely force, and in such a way that it back-splashed itself erect, a fountain spray. For a moment the sea hung suspended, liberated from gravity, not unlike a dyani in a hearth. Looking at Helia, looking at the staff. It didn't kick the oakthorn staff nearer the shore and back within Helia's reach. Its feet were bound.

13

Leorix and Lucikles hustled back to Piney Quarter without speaking. Perhaps not ever speaking again, for all Lucikles could guess. His son had been saved from immolating himself in his own goodness. If the cost of that rescue was a severance of filial feeling, well, that was the fate that Helia had netted for them out there, all alone on Maracoor Spot.

Leorix's eyes streamed with rage and frustration, maybe hatred.

Lucikles hardly cared. His son was still alive.

The flying monkeys couldn't have scooped down to hoist Rain out of the courtyard of the prisoners' holding pen, but they managed to rally enough to rush to Cossy. She had lifted in the wind with an expression of brilliant belief in her face, and plummeted. Three monkeys broke her fall upon the paving stones. She thrashed in a nest of wings, but she too, was still alive.

Rain dropped from a gutter on her own accord.

"I wanted to die and see what it was like!" complained Cossy.

"Now you have to live and see what that is like," said Rain. "Every day you die a little and get a new chance to find out how next to live. Let's get out of here." Iskinaary was waggling a wing toward a covered passage blocked with stacks of compost and a cart with a broken wheel. Beyond it they could see a drop and the headstones of some sort of cemetery. "That way. We'll figure it out as we go."

Cossy was cross as hell, but she knew that, however short or long her life might be, she never would forget what it felt like to tumble into wings.

14

The four brides of Maracoor had done what they had come for. They had witnessed the fate that was happening to Cossy, who was lost to them forever. Now, in the novelty of this huge city, they were only overwhelmed. Turfed out of the House of Balances, they convened on a street corner to plot history on their own. The ladies from the bordello took pity and offered some lemonade, which the brides accepted. They had only one idea, maybe to kidnap Leorix for revenge, or to take him as a hostage.

But they had to discard this as impractical. They wouldn't know how to start. They didn't know where he was. They didn't even know what to do with the empty glasses from the lemonade ladies. The brides weren't made for anything more specific than minding the world.

So they put the glasses down on a doorstep and eventually found themselves huddling upon the corniche fronting the harbor of Maracoor Crown. A strong wind tore down from the north, wrenching at their veils. Perhaps it was the last, violent afterbreath of the summer storm that had blown upheaval in upon them all. The brides looked dumpy, exotic, and out-of-place. Street urchins and merchants alike eyed them, pointing fingers and snorting.

Among the brides, only Scyrilla retained some enthusiasm for the novelty of travel. She was eyeing a peddler's cart rumbling by. It offered salted pretzels and some sort of boiled sweet item on a stick, a garishly tinted monstrosity tortured into a near pornographic shape. Kliompte, Bray, and Tirr were immune to such temptation.

The rain that had felled the sentinel pine beside the House of Detention was suddenly softer. The brides didn't notice it one way or the other. Their minds were on other weathers. The brides were perched on the margin of the birthplace that they had spent their lives protecting. Their sandaled and scarred feet were planted upon the great blocks of stone that fronted the water. Their eyes trained upon the siege of sea in the harbor, and beyond that, sea, always sea, all the way to the horizon. As if by need alone they could unspool the invisible miles between themselves and Maracoor Spot.

They could not. Somewhere out there, beyond sight, moored in its own time, waited their own prison. There was no home for the brides of Maracoor upon their homeland. The only home for an exile is exile.

FINI

Volume II of Another Day will be called
The Oracle of Maracoor.

Author's Note

Well into the third or fourth draft of this novel, I came upon a review of a terrific volume called *Drawing Down the Moon: Magic in the Greco-Roman World* (Princeton University Press, 2019). The author is Radcliffe G. Edmonds III. The book didn't so much inspire me as confirm some of my instincts about the more domestic magics implied in odes and epics from our shared classical past.